John Reinhard Dizon

Hezbollah

Editions Dedicaces

HEZBOLLAH

Published by:
    Editions Dedicaces LLC
    12759 NE Whitaker Way, Suite D833
    Portland, Oregon, 97230
    www.dedicaces.us

Library of Congress Cataloging-in-Publication Data
    Reinhard Dizon, John
    Hezbollah /
      by John Reinhard Dizon.
    p. cm.
    ISBN-13: 978-1-77076-457-6 (alk. paper)
    ISBN-10: 1-77076-457-7 (alk. paper)

John Reinhard Dizon

Hezbollah

Part One
Tina

Chapter One

Stu Carlucci made his way through the crowds of bankers and brokers as he turned the corner on John Street onto Water Street that morning. It was ten minutes past noon and he was greatly worried that his lunch companion had already left. He got caught up in his musical composition, as usual, and had lost track of time. He only lived a block up from Rosie O'Grady's and figured it would not take much to hurry down. Only he couldn't find anything to wear and had misplaced his keys the night before. He threw a raggedy black blazer over a torn Pink Floyd T-shirt and black jeans, grimacing at the thought of the derision he would face at the popular yuppie luncheon place.

"Didn't think you were going to make it," the gaunt figure at the table grinned malevolently. "You've never been much for follow-throughs."

Stu's world had been turned upside down over the last two weeks. The call from Arista Records had first convoluted his world, informing him that Crack Jam Productions wanted his services to compose a background score for their latest diva, Velveeta. He was told that the previous arranger had left over a dispute and Stu was heading into a major clean-up job. He was able to hook solidly into his predecessor's motif and get the piano arrangement in smooth working order. The brass and string parts had to be overhauled, and these were not Stu's areas of expertise. Fortunately one of his jazz connections was able to step in and help solve some major challenges. Still, he had a three-week deadline to meet and it was forcing him into unwanted twelve-hour work days. Despite the $25K paycheck, it was proving a grueling and unhappy task.

The second call, a week ago, was from his agent informing him that Arista had made a two-recording offer on his demo, *Out Of The Ether*. Stu had been taken completely unawares, largely due to the fact that the rap craze had persuaded most record labels to make serious budget cuts on their rock music projects. He headed directly to the agency, heart pounding in realizing a lifelong dream. Only it sank as a stone when his agent related the terms and conditions of the deal.

"Good morning, Mr. Carlucci," the perky young waitress beamed, trying to remain cordial in the presence of his guest. "What'll you be having?"

"A screwdriver, thanks," Stu smiled brightly as he thanked her again for a menu.

"And…you, sir?" she managed tautly.

"Well, if you won't take a seat, then I'll settle for another pitcher."

Stu had spent the last four years behind the scenes in the mercurial music industry as one of the most capable session musicians in New York City. His earnings had exceeded $50K, yet it was barely enough to pay his astronomical rent expenses and cover the constant upgrade costs of his digital studio equipment. He only kept the studio open to make ends meet between jobs, but more than once it helped him stay afloat throughout the spare times. He played gigs now and again to keep his name alive on the club scene, but in his mid-forties it had grown ever more strenuous.

"So," Stu resolved to keep this on an upbeat scale. "What've you been doing with yourself lately?"

"Well, hopefully publishing my third book of poetry. They say the third time's a charm, let's keep our fingers crossed."

Stu could only see his old friend David Diamond as a total car wreck. He had lost about fifty pounds since the old days, his body resembling a rack for his beaten motorcycle jacket. His bleached blond hair was as a moldy haystack on his skull, its skin appearing as yellowed parchment. His eyes were hollowed and bloodshot and his teeth were stained from chain smoking. His hands shook slightly and Stu was sure he was still being ravaged by alcoholism.

"Say a prayer for both of us," Stu nodded. "Arista finally offered me a deal, they're looking to record *Ether*. Even better, they want to bring our old demo in for a listen."

"Now isn't that a hoot," David chuckled, lighting up a Camel. "Four years later, isn't it somewhat antiquated?"

"They see it as a retrospective into hardcore," Stu tapped his fingers idly on the tabletop. "Hardcore's not selling, but there's a new sound they're calling thrash that's starting to happen on the West Coast. They're figuring that if we can tap into the Metallica market it might make money."

8

"So which way would you go, Stu?" David blew a stream of smoke. "Would you grow your hair down to your ass and spin your head around, or shave it and slam it into somebody else?"

The waitress returned with their drinks, and Stu ordered a large platter of fried mushrooms.

"What was your name again?"

"Rose," she said pointedly, probably for the umpteenth time.

"Well, I'll make it a point not to forget," David produced a magic marker and wrote 'Rose N David' on his wrist before she left in a fit of pique.

"Isn't that odd," he smirked. "She looks like she'd have Guns and Roses tattooed over her twat."

"David," Stu managed to control himself, "I think I can get you ten grand for your share of the demo, no questions asked."

"That'd be a nice settlement for the work product," David swigged down a half mug of beer. "What about the pain and suffering? I'd want to see something along the lines of, say, a small tour."

"Those days are over. For all of us. Everyone's gone their separate ways, they've gone on with their lives. Debbie's got her own business, Johnny's got a title fight coming up, Duke's in the service and, well, you can forget Tina."

"It's the whole thing about unfinished business. The psychological thing, y'know. They won't be able to get it out of their systems otherwise. Do you think they're any different than we are?"

"C'mon, David, let's face it," Stu reasoned. "Here we are, a couple of washed-out old rockers trying to rub a couple of quarters together. Neither one of us even have a band. Look, you make the deal on the demo and I'll get some studio guys together, we'll do something. I'll make it worth your while."

"Here's my offer," David leaned forward confidentially. "You go back to your little world and wait for my call. I'll get in touch with our playmates and tell them what a treat we have in store for them. I'll make them an offer they can't refuse, just like I'm giving you."

"What do you mean?"

"If you don't go back to your pencil pushers and tell them what I want, I'll drop the demo into the nearest incinerator," he grinned evilly.

"You're not that crazy," Stu leaned back with a smirk.

"That demo's not worth anything to anyone but you right now," David chortled. "It's not worth a dime to me, if it was they'd be calling me with a record contract. And it's dated material. If this deal doesn't happen for you now, it never will. As a matter of fact, I think it's worth so much to you that I'll let you call our playmates. And if this doesn't happen, you can call your bean counters and tell them that the demo's resting somewhere in record heaven."

"Your poetry books don't sell, man," Stu was uncharacteristically blunt. "You look like you haven't had a decent meal in days, and haven't bought new clothes for years. You need this ten grand desperately, yet you'd toss it just to screw me over."

"I guess we're kinda like Siamese twins, Stu," David slouched back in his chair. "Not much future for me either if this doesn't happen for you. I'm counting on you, old buddy."

"Don't hold your breath," Stu retorted before tossing a twenty on his napkin and storming off. David waited for Rose to come back and swept the change off the table after drinking both their drinks, leaving no tip as he walked out.

"Is that the way you remember it, Ms. Rivera?"

"It's pretty accurate, from what I remember. I read it a long time ago. I found it disturbing at first. I'd read about a half chapter then I'd put it down for days. Maybe it was a sort of catharsis for everyone. I think we all spoke to each other at one time or another over the phone about it. It was a healing process, it brought a lot of closure to a lot of things that weren't better left unsaid. Of course, there was probably so much we all would have wanted to say to David, to discuss with him."

The interviewer sat with her at her apartment overlooking Central Park. She had just returned from her doctor's appointment where she had gotten some very unwelcome news. It was a mild shock that the interview was helping her overcome. Still, the thought of David caused her to wipe a tear from her eye.

"Did you get to spend much time with Diamond during the tour?"

"Not really," she took a sip of water to clear her throat. "There was a lot of pressure from Lincoln's people throughout the tour. They were trying to get me to work with them and I just couldn't deal with it. The rehearsals with Hezbollah were all I could take. The record people were constantly badgering Stu, but he couldn't do anything without David and Debbie, who were constantly at each other's throats. Duke was always in and out, and we didn't find out until later it was all that CIA stuff he was involved in. He and Stu had a bad relationship in the first place, and this was not helping. Johnny was also under major stress and we still don't know what all that was about. He was like a caged lion and everybody was worried he would lose it and beat somebody up."

"There must have been some quiet time," *Ebony* star reporter Sapphire Starr probed gently.

"Not really, just with Debbie," she reminisced. "She was always playing the big sister. She just got used to protecting me back in the old days, and she couldn't break the habit. It wasn't that way anymore, though. I had Lincoln's people up my nose, and she had Mel Dalton. Neither one of us wanted to admit it, but we had just grown away from each other."

Tina could remember how Debbie was her role model back in the day. She had a temper of her own but could never be as violent as Debbie. Yet she realized how Debbie could play mind games with people and was not always as willing to commit violence as she appeared. She realized why David and Debbie never could develop a romantic relationship: he was a control freak, and she was completely uncontrollable. Despite any physical attraction, they were as fire and water and could never find common ground.

She began to realize how her relationship with Zeke mirrored that between David and Debbie. Zeke was a manipulator just like David, and had the same look and build though Zeke was more the Mediterranean type. Zeke tried to dominate her, which made her go further into her Debbie mode. Was it a mistake? Was there something deep inside that yearned to have a man protect and defend her?

"The *Party Of God* album was completely different than what anyone expected, especially James Lincoln," Sapphire observed.

"I think Stu was more surprised than anyone," Tina smiled softly.

Tina remembered their first day at Television Records where everything had come undone in a matter of hours. She had showed up in a black jumpsuit, ready to work, and was somewhat bemused by the indifferent attitude of everyone in the band. She figured out much later that everyone was just concealing their nervousness, and had no clue as to what they were expected to do next. Spider Larson, the executive producer at Television who reported directly to Novarich Records' chief exec Jerry Blackstone, was in and out of the booth trying to get things going to no avail. Eventually he saw no option other than to place a call to Blackstone, who in turn phoned James Lincoln.

By the time Lincoln arrived, Debbie was swearing and yelling at Tina and pointing angrily at the others. In one corner, David was smoking a joint with Johnny and Roth, while Stu and Duke stood on the other side of the room smoking cigarettes. Once in a while the two groups would converge for a short exchange before going back to their corners.

"Diamond," Lincoln called David over to the glass enclosed guest area. David handed a spliff back to Roth and dutifully followed JC inside.

"What in the hell is going on?" he demanded. "Do you know this is costing me a grand an hour?"

"Well, we haven't been here that long," David ventured.

"Three hours. Three thousand dollars. Larson tells us you haven't done a damn thing since you've been here."

"Great projects do require careful planning," David nodded. "Tell you what, let me do some brainstorming and give Larson something to occupy himself with besides calling you."

"I paid each and every one of you fifty grand for this project, and you have a bonded guarantee for the rest at the end of the tour," Lincoln huffed. "That comes to over a half million dollars, and that's not counting the extra expenses like this. I expect to see some results around here. You gave me your word that you could make this happen, remember?"

"Once you let me go back in there, I can get started," David replied. "Say, uh, we're running short on beverages. Do you think…?"

"Have Larson send out for whatever you need," Lincoln started out the door. "Get it done." He nearly lost it when David smirked back at him, but thought better of it and stalked out of the studio. The others caught the exchange and waited expectantly as David returned.

"Okay, let's get busy," he walked over to an open mic and

tested it, Larson obliging with one of the overhead monitors. David took the mic to the restroom, the others chortling as they could hear him turning on a faucet. He regulated it so that he got a steady drip which echoed softly around the room.

"Go ahead and roll it," David instructed Larson. He next walked over to one of the amps where a studio guitar was plugged in. He turned up the volume and turned towards an open mic, the feedback from the amp humming through the room.

"You guys ready?" he murmured.

"Don't tell me he's gonna play guitar," Duke whispered to Stu as they strapped on their axes.

"One two three four!" he yelled, launching the guitar at the far wall. Debbie and Tina responded with a wall of sound as Duke and Stu ripped into their own lead solos. David rushed over to the keyboards and added his own solo as the five instruments collided in mid-air, eventually finding each others' ranges and building towards a synchronized assault that threatened to blow Larson's soundboard apart. Larson worked feverishly to adjust his levels, and once his work was done the whirlwind subsided.

"Okay, that was the beginning and the end of the album," David told them. "All we have to do now is fill in the gap. I wanted to have Johnny work some spots with some prose I've written. I was thinking about some stuff like the conversation between music and lyrics, how instrumentals and spoken word are fighting for dominance in the industry, like jazz versus hip hop. We can have Debbie sing the first song, kinda like a medley against Johnny's prose. From there we nail down three pop tunes, then do a transition into some punk, then grunge, then thrash, and bring it home with a real tribal rhythmic theme, Johnny doing the prose thing again. We then finish it off with this thing, letting it segue into Stu's next big song. It'll give him just what he needs for his next project as the rest of us ride off into the sunset."

Stu and David met each others' gaze, and the others appreciated the significance as Stu felt the weight of the world lifted from his shoulders.

"What about the stuff from the...demo?" Stu asked quietly.

"Well, it's kinda dated, I think," David shrugged.

"What were you planning...?"

"Have your agent call this number, and I'll have one of the kids drop it off," David handed Stu a business card.

"Just like that," Stu mumbled, staring at the card in his hands.

"Well, you're the career musician, I'm just picking up some chump change. I don't need it anymore, I've got my money," David chortled.

"They call Lincoln the King of Soul," Debbie shook her head, setting her bass aside. "There's the King of Bullshit. C'mon, scoot over, I've gotta see this."

"Debbie, we both can't..." Tina protested as Debbie sidled next to her on her throne.

"Stu, I'll bet you twenty bucks that those two lardasses..." David produced his wallet. At once there was a loud muffled thump before a large Zildjian cymbal crashed to the floor as Tina squealed.

"Ms. Rivera," Larson rushed out from the mixing room. There was a long silence before a tumultuous roar of laughter sent him scurrying back into his booth.

"That record was considered the most important work in the post-punk era, even though it failed to break the Top 100," Sapphire commented as Tina snapped out of her reverie. "If David Diamond hadn't given his life out in that desert, many critics believe that your next project might have brought on the Grunge Era five years earlier."

"I'm...sorry," Tina felt a rush of remorse filling her eyes and throat. "We'll have to stop for today."

"I didn't mean..."

"No, it's not your fault, it's been a long day. We can meet for lunch tomorrow."

"That'll be fantastic, Ms. Rivera."

Tina walked over to the window overlooking SoHo along the East River where she stared out contemplatively for a long while. She knew everything was coming to an end, and she wanted to leave everything tidy, in order, for whoever came in to pick up behind her.

The doctors' prognosis had finally confirmed what she had long suspected. She had a case of muscular dystrophy which was slowly weakening the muscles in her limbs. She was able to play the drums for shortening lengths of time and was being forced to rely on electronic drum pads as her striking power grew weaker. She had to take shorter walks in the park as her legs began to tire quicker. She began to fatigue late in the day and was rising from bed later and later in the morning.

She knew she would have to tell Zeke about it eventually, then her family, her friends, and eventually her fans and the world. It was the thing she feared most, more than winding up an invalid, more than death itself. It was the loss of her privacy, the one thing she cherished above all else. Each person she told would be one more person who would be closing in on her, demanding to know how she was, insisting that they stay by her side to help. Every single one of them would be a bar that would come together to build her cage, in which she would die.

Her life had always been an open book, from the time she left the Party, left Hezbollah, and discovered her untapped brilliance as a percussionist. She became a legend in contemporary music, then as an alternative rock icon. She thought she could find peace in her nest of laurels but there was always someone, somewhere, who wanted a piece of her memories and a chunk of her time. Time was now the most valuable commodity she had left to her.

She would tell Zeke as best she could, then deal with that shitstorm before calling Isabel, then Debbie. Her family didn't need to know until she couldn't hide it anymore. She was their rock, their salvation in their turbulent lives and she could not destroy that illusion. She would stay strong until there was no strength left.

Now there was this rumor of J.C. Lincoln wanting to set up a second Peace in the Middle East Concert, the reunion. He was dying of AIDS and wanted to go out in a blaze of glory. She would have laughed it off, only the voicemail was coming in: from Stu, Debbie, Isabel. There was an avalanche of e-mails and voicemail behind it, and from now on there would be no rest. If she agreed to play she would be locked into the center ring of the circus, and if she didn't they would hound her to the grave.

They could take her time, and the disease might take her life, but what they could never take away were her memories. Those, she resolved, she would share so very carefully and selectively. And there were some she would never share at all.

She thought of her sister Carmen and her son and daughter. They had been her pets, her plants, the center of her universe over the past few years. What was going to happen to them once she was gone (GONE GONE)? Carmen just couldn't get it together, with her stunning face and her swimsuit body, unable to keep her New York Yankee husband or the salsa rock star. She sent Carmen more money than she would have paid Zeke on reverse alimony, to no avail. What did people do with money these days, wipe their ass with it? If Carmen was on crack, it would have been easier to accept, or her kids, for that matter. Alternately, they were the quintessential American family. Both kids were into music, trying to follow in their *Titi* Tina's footsteps. She really didn't give a shit about the money. It just made her paranoid to think what would happen if she was no longer there to give it to them.

Death was something she never really considered, even though they flirted with it every chance they had as kids in Brooklyn. She remembered driving safety pins through her pierced ears, playing chicken with David as they watched cigarettes burn through their joined forearms until either of them had endured enough burnt flesh. They walked into traffic as if they were made of soap bubbles, one time David pulling her out from in front of a speeding bus. She searched her heart, and still found no fear of death. It was all about what she was going to leave behind, and if it would be enough.

She was worth over a million dollars, but what was that after the vultures came in and took the taxes? She really didn't know how much money she had, or where it was. She knew she always had money on her plastic card, and she hated the fact that she never got a handle on how it worked. All she knew was there was a Certified Public Asshole who made sure she had whatever she needed on the card to buy whatever she needed. She needed a man, someone like Zeke to check it all out and make sure it was getting done right, and she hated that he was not there to get that done unless it was on his terms.

This would have been David Diamond's victory, watching any one of them make that big score and not knowing how to handle it. He would have rejoiced to see her floundering in her sea of money, not knowing where it came from or where it would stop. He would have rejoiced in watching her drowning in her money, yet she knew that he would have been the first to embrace her, try and help her deal with her incompetence. He would have fought Zeke for the chance to do so, and that's what she hated most of all.

16

For all it was worth, and being at this stage of her life, why couldn't it have all come together for once? Why couldn't she have the man who would help her protect the privacy of the end of her life, without grabbing what he could take for himself?

She always considered the option of becoming a bag lady, just taking all this shit away and heading under a bridge somewhere. If she knew for certain they'd never find her, she'd be gone in a New York minute.

Only her New York minute had become frozen in time.

Chapter Two

"You know, that shit sounds like a sack of pots and pans being slammed against the wall," David cackled as they listened to the previous night's practice tape. "Say, Tina, suppose we tied one cymbal to the back of your head and another to the wall? It couldn't sound much worse."

"I said leave her alone, motherfucker," Debbie snapped at him as Tina's face dropped woefully. "She's trying her best, just like the rest of us."

"She's right, David," Stu grew angry. "We've got everyone else telling us we suck, we don't need to be tearing each other down."

Tina Rivera could remember back when it all began, back in the Eighties, when she was a pothead out of high school who made friends with a punk rocker named Debbie Munson. Debbie's father had an apartment for rent in his Cobble Hill apartment building and gave her a great deal. Debbie knew a poet named David Diamond and a guitarist named Stu Carlucci who wanted to start a rock band. They all sacrificed their party money to buy equipment and decided to give it a shot. After a couple of practices, they all knew one thing: no matter what happened, it could never, ever sound worse than this.

David got them a gig at a watering hole called the Verdict, and they got kicked out after one three-song set and a second five-song attempt. The family and friends who showed up wished the ground opened up and swallowed them whole to spare them the embarrassment. David had been most relentless at the show, demanding to do one more song even as their equipment was being carted off. Once they returned to Debbie's, his venom was of unlimited supply.

"Yeah, well," David grabbed his jacket and headed out the door. "You rattle those pots and pans, I'm gonna go see if there's a place left for us to hang our hats."

"Okay," Stu sat down on his Ampeg facing the girls after

David left. "Let's try this. Mother Nature created rhythm. Your heart has a beat. Your pulse has a beat. We measure time by beats. We measure beats by time. You just need to focus on that."

"Don't jerk us around, Stu," Debbie sounded bored.

"Look," he insisted. "Check this out. One-two, one-two, one-two. And this – one-two-three, one-two-three, one-two-three. These are the beat patterns for every song we do. Speed them up, slow them, down, it's the same beat, one or the other. Look, I'll show you."

Stu went over to Debbie's turntable and put on a Velvet Underground album. He started and stopped seven songs and showed them the beat. He then got a Ramones album and had them figure out the beats. After a time, they could figure out the beats on a number of albums, from Black Flag to the Sex Pistols.

"Now what you two have to do is keep the beat," Stu instructed them as he took up his jacket and guitar case. "Decide what the beat is, then stay together and play it together. One-two, one-two, one-two. One-two-three, one-two-three, one-two-three. You two have to get it together, I can't do it for you. You're the rhythm section. Show Mr. Big Mouth what you got, okay? See you Friday."

Debbie and Tina spent the rest of the week listening to records, smoking dope, swigging beer and playing along together. They spent more time cursing themselves than each other, and after a time it was almost as if they were crocheting, barely communicating outside of their work unless someone made a mistake. They did not say a word to Stu or David, and the quartet went through the first set that Friday without a hitch.

"Somebody's been practicing," Stu said in a singsong voice as he breezed past Debbie on the way to the refrigerator for beer.

"So how did this come about?" David taunted Tina in the living room where the equipment was set up. "Did Debbie stick a cattle prod up your ass or did she pull your toenails out?"

"Is there something wrong with your thought processes?" Debbie stormed into the room as Stu looked on apprehensively. "Did I not tell you to get off her ass?"

"Relax, Deborah," David smirked. "You've been participating in a social experiment."

"How so, smart guy?"

"Subject A and Subject B, namely you and Thunderfists, have

been consistently proving to the researchers, namely Stu and I, that you cannot play mainstream rock and roll," David explained smugly. "Using negative reinforcement, you've both been conditioned to improve your skills. Yet you still cannot play mainstream rock and roll. The researchers see this but continue on with the project. This demonstrates the fact that this is no longer a mainstream rock and roll project. That would imply that we are no longer complying with music industry standards, or those which society imposes on us as part of their cultural mores. We are therefore making a social statement."

"All great rock and roll makes a social statement," Stu contributed. "Lots of times it comes from the underground, like a wellspring that the music industry taps into."

"Right," David went on. "Since we agree this is social commentary, our whole presentation has to focus on that objective. We have to encourage as much audience participation as possible to make us more acceptable. The more they become part of the show, the harder it is for them to dislike the show. They start losing their identity, and they become us and we become them."

"Clear as mud," Debbie scowled. "How are you going to make this go down?"

"There's a bar my parents used to go to called El Bolero over on Court Street," David explained. "I talked to the owner and he said he'd let us play their Christmas party. It's a pretty mixed crowd, yuppies from Brooklyn Heights and Puerto Ricans from Smith Street go there after work. I think if we do a bunch of Fifties songs and slip in some originals here and there we can go over."

Tina closed her plastic-covered copy of the old novel and sighed deeply, closing her eyes and rocking back in her overstuffed leather recliner. God, she thought to herself, they were so young back then, so naïve. So young.

David was certain that they would be able to pull the wool over everyone's eyes by opening with three oldies songs. He was sure that, by following the formula of Sha-Na-Na, they could get over by playing the classics in double time and create a segue into their own material. What he did not expect was for the off-duty cops, making up the majority of the audience, to see the Party's renditions of their faves as sacrilege. When the band launched into "Welcome To The Party", their theme song, the audience had their fill. They started by tossing wadded-up dollar bills at the band. Eventually they gave way to wet napkins. Debbie went into a screaming tirade just before the owner pulled the plug on the show.

Stu was very unhappy with tapes of the show and announced that he would no longer do vocals with David. He felt that he had more than enough work to do in smoothing out the band's rough musical edges. David, in the meantime, booked them a gig at a birthday party for one of Tina's childhood friends. The crowd was much more receptive and it did a world of good in lifting their spirits. The highlight of the night came when a drunken David pirouetted, slipped and fell into the birthday cake on a nearby table in the apartment owner's jam-packed living room.

He became a Pied Piper after that, creating a call list of friends, family and associates who he phoned before every gig for support. At first there were enormous turnouts that were as great reunions of old friends who had not seen one another for ages. After the novelty wore off, however, the owners of the Puerto Rican bars where David was getting them shows along Court Street and Smith Street were growing impatient with the raucous music that repelled their regular customers. David was forced upriver across the Brooklyn Bridge into lower Manhattan where people were more receptive to alternative music.

Eventually it was a friend of a friend who brought Duke in. Duke and Stu did not hit it off personally and focused their energies on repairing the melodies of their burgeoning repertoire. When David brought Johnny in, Duke sought the kindred spirit and created his own little faction with Johnny, Roth and the Cabales sisters. Tina remained under Debbie's wing as the other half of their rhythm section. David relinquished his spot as front man to Johnny and took up the keyboards on the side of the stage. He became as one of the roadies, one foot on the stage and one foot in the audience.

They were so divided yet so united, it was a paradox she never fully understood. They were truly a family, with all the internecine squabbling and petty bickering, they would fight for one another at the drop of a hat.

In David's case, even die for one another.

They always said that Stu was the brains of the band, David was its soul, and Debbie was its heart. When Stu left it became a Frankenstein monster that succeeded in killing itself. Yet it resurrected in Palestine and realized its destiny though at grievous loss. Now it was trying to return from the grave one more time.

One more time.

There were rumors on the Internet though no one had called for weeks until finally she got a message from Johnny Carmona. She wanted to call him back but was not sure what she wanted to say. It was not clear as to who was sponsoring the show. She knew that James Lincoln had contracted AIDS, and his would be his last show ever if he was even physically able to appear. Some entertainment megafirm thought this would be an excellent salute to the troops leaving Iraq, but who would foot the bill? There was no indication as to whether this would be a USO event or a public performance. Nothing but rumors.

Next there was a voicemail from Stu, then one from Debbie. She almost felt as if she was going to opening a Pandora's Box by calling them back. Yet there was no way she could conveniently ignore them, nor could she even think of doing so. It had just been so long since she had spoken to them, she didn't even know what to say. She knew Johnny was down in Florida with his boxing gym training fighters, and Roth Almontaser had moved down with him. Johnny and Isabel had a grown son who had gotten into music. It had been so long that she wondered what they looked like. They had been the Bonnie and Clyde of the Party, the Sexy Things, and it would be hard to imagine them looking any other way.

She knew that Stu was still playing jazz rock, and they had even done some studio work together though the project went nowhere. Stu had won a couple of Grammys for production work, but recognition for his own albums continued to elude him. He was one of the most popular session musicians in NYC and had grown financially secure, but Tina knew that he would want to make this one big score with Lincoln to finance a last-ditch effort for commercial success. She knew that's why he was calling, why all of them were calling. Only she had made no efforts to call them over the years and she now reproached herself for it.

She knew that Debbie had immersed herself in her private investigation business and had also done well, but she was still single because there was no man who could keep up with her.

Debbie was still a force of nature, and those who sowed the wind with her would forever reap the whirlwind. She had taken her hurricane force with her into the business world, and her blessing and her curse was that she outdid almost every man she competed against. As a result, there was no man who could stand alongside her. She could be wined and dined, cuddled and even romanced, but no one could ever have her to hold, to love or to cherish. How could a man wrap his arms around a cyclone, a tornado, a cosmic storm?

Everyone had always assumed that David and Debbie had an affair, but it was back at the beginning of time, back before the creation of the Party and the dawn of its history. It was something no one ever discussed, like talking about your parents having sex. As far as anyone else could remember, they were like an evil set of Siamese twins, their minds and spirits almost as one. When David was killed in Palestine after the concert, everyone doubted whether Debbie would survive the outcome. She nearly had a nervous breakdown, and went into silent mourning until long after his ashes had been cast into the wind across the Valley of Megiddo. They said she would never find that spiritual kinship ever again, and so far they were right.

Some had thought it was the same with Zeke and Tina, though it manifested itself differently. Tina was the first to violently disagree. Zeke wanted her all to himself, there was no sense of mutual consent or consideration. She still wasn't sure why she married him in the first place, or why it was so hard to divorce him. He was like a demon Gemini who would fight her tooth and nail over everything under the sun. Once she finally gave in on a moot point, he would suddenly formulate a second opinion and end up diametrically opposed to her once more. He hated the band, hated her friends, hated the way she dressed and the way she carried herself. Over and over she would rail at him, "What do you want with me? What do you keep after me for? What do you want with someone you like nothing about?"

"Because I don't love what you're about," he would always say. "I love you."

She felt as if when she began taking percussion classes and people discovered her talent, she had become a Helen Keller whose savant-like ability seemed to personify her. She was no longer Tina Rivera. That was just the name of this percussionist who crazy

23

music types started to worship. She thought they were weird, like people who came out of nowhere and started kissing her ass because she knew how to fly a kite or knit blankets. Eventually there were so many of them that she started feeling sorry for them, started being nice to them. Only there were so many, so damned many. Her private time became sacred to her, and that was what Zeke Cohen tried most desperately to steal from her.

Somehow she knew that this would be the key. Once word got out of her gradual demise, more and more people would be closing in to get a piece of her time remaining. If she could use his jealousy to protect her time from others, then at least he would be the only one she would be forced to share that time with.

It seemed to be her best option, especially with time so quickly slipping away.

Chapter Three

"I can't do it, *Titi*," the girl flailed her arms about in frustration. "I'm just no good."

"Of course you can," Tina gently stroked Angie's hair as she stood behind the forlorn girl. "You're just trying to do too much at one time. You have to walk before you can run, you have to remember that."

"Yeah, but *you* fly through the air," Angie grumbled, turning in her swivel chair. "*You're* Tina Rivera."

"So can you. You're my niece, aren't you? It's got to be in your blood somewhere. It's in your heart, right?"

"Not for long," Angie grumbled.

Angie was her sister Carmen's daughter, and like the rest of the family, she was delighted that Tina had begun calling more often and trying to make herself a part of their lives again. Angie took the opportunity to try her hand at music at her high school, but soon became frustrated by her lack of aptitude. She cried out in distress to Carmen, who turned to her older sister. Tina began calling Angie, and soon they made plans to schedule some studio time.

"No, listen," she took Angie's hand and placed it between her breasts. "One-two, one-two, one-two. A very smart young man taught me that a long time ago."

"Was that David Diamond?"

"No, that was Stu Carlucci. David taught me to never surrender, never give up, always keep fighting, no matter what the odds. He also taught me to never stop dreaming. When your dreams die, you die."

"That's good stuff," Angie smiled. "I think they just taught me something too."

"And they would want you to teach that to someone else," she hugged her niece's head to her bosom.

"Okay, dammit, fight fight fight fight fight!" Angie returned to her percussion set with renewed fervor.

"Don't just flail," Tina placed her hand lightly on Angie's shoulder. "Make you hits count. Another smart young man taught me that."

"Who was that?" Angie looked back quizzically.

"Johnny Carmona."

"The boxer?"

"Yep."

"Wow. You know everybody."

She remembered the last time she visited Johnny, Issy and Roth in Florida. They had gotten him one more fight after the band had returned from the Middle East. The rematch with Ruben Ortiz was not the storyline. Rather, it was all about the sordid career of Johnny Carmona, the topic of a documentary HBO entitled "Heartbreak to Heartbreak". They depicted Johnny's rise from the fight clubs of Brooklyn to the unlikely spot as lead singer from Hezbollah. They narrated the band's Cinderella tale of being discovered by James Lincoln and sacrificed on the altar of fame in the Valley of Megiddo. They told of the trio's anguish over the death of David Diamond, and how it would become a segue to a travesty against fellow palooka Ortiz.

Tina told them she would be able to spend the weekend, and they had set up a jam session at a local studio that was attended by most of the people connected with the Carmona Boxing Club. She realized how deeply they had become immersed in their microcosm. They didn't know anyone who wasn't connected with boxing. They were reliving their Brooklyn past, wallowing in it. It was largely Cubans instead of Puerto Ricans, but there the difference ended. There were cases and cases of beer, people gossiping and boasting while the music played, clapping only when they saw the threesome looking at them. Roth was in his glory, playing his axe like a musical chainsaw. He had actually gotten better since Armageddon. He was battle tested and would never again question his own talents after having played before over one hundred thousand people.

She enjoyed the session, dazzling the gathering with her percussion skills. She remembered Isabel coming over after the session with tears in her eyes.

"If only they could have known how great you were going to be one day," Isabel wept.

26

"I just wish I could've improved a lot quicker than I did," Tina smiled wistfully.

They went to the gym Saturday evening so Johnny could show off for her before they hit the town. Right away she could detect the aura of desperation in the air. Johnny had partied too hard in the Middle East, and crossed the invisible line when he returned to the States. There comes a time in every fighter's career when they are going through the motions, depending on their knowledge and instincts to get them through the next battle. It was like coming across a strange dog and knowing at once whether it is going to bite if approached, attack, or tear you apart. The other fighter senses it, and reacts accordingly. If he knows you plan to go the distance, he knows this is a chance to score that priceless knockout. This is the time to give it all you got, because there is the possibility that this fellow will not fight desperately enough to keep from getting knocked out, or having the fight stopped. Roth knew he was no longer that desperate. Isabel knew it. The only one who didn't was Johnny.

It filled Tina with a deep sense of melancholy though she did her best to hide it. She ended up getting drunk to get into the party mood, and by the end of the night she got all weepy and teary as they started on about the Good Old Days. She heard that Remember When was the lowest form of conversation, and whoever said it was probably right. You always ended up talking about things you couldn't change, or people who were no longer who they once were. They fell into the trap, but it was a lot better than carrying on about where Johnny was going now.

The saddest memory was saying goodbye to Frankie, the little boy so exhilarated by his 'Titi Tina' and disconsolate over her leaving. Every time she visited, he had flash-forwarded to a different moment in time, and she felt awful that she had let his lifeline slip through her fingers. He had gone from the infant she had held in her arms at his baptism to this little boy who spent a half hour showing her all the toys in his room. The next time she saw him he was an emotionally confused young man who showed her his poetry as if revealing his naked body. A couple of years later she knew he was gay, could tell by the friends he hung out with, but dared not say a word to Johnny or Isabel. She knew it would eat at Johnny like a tumor, but there was nothing she would be able to say that would have made a bit of difference.

It made her realize how dysfunctionality was a part of a family history. They always said that those who did not learn from history were condemned to repeat it. None of them learned a damned thing from their history, no, not one. She remembered when she went to visit her mother just before she died. Her Mom had stopped by the apartment one afternoon when she was screwing David, and they froze in place despite the fact that they were as cats at heat before they heard the knock. It took a long while before her Mom left, and when Tina went to visit a couple of days later she was on the business end of a fire and brimstone sermon. It devolved into a shouting match which ended with her Mom smacking her across the face.

"You wish you could have him, don't you!" Tina screamed at her before leaving in tears. They were words she would have given her life to take back, but fate did not give her near enough time to do so. She had gone so fast that Tina's question to David seemed not in the least bit absurd.

"Would you ever do my Mom?"

"Well, she's not a bad-looking woman," David answered with characteristic bluntness. "I wouldn't kick her out of bed, put it that way."

Even the thought of that made her nauseous, and she would have gotten together with David to have returned to that moment in time to take it back. Only David was dead and the spoken words were as a rotted carcass in her memory. She wished she had been closer to her mother, wished she could have seen her oldest child become something more than a misfit and an emotional cripple. It was probably why she gladly accepted the mantle as family matriarch, why she threw open her arms and embraced everyone in this generation of Riveras. Now here she was, in the same position as her Mom, about to abandon them far, far too early. All she could do was think of what she would have said to her Mom, what she would have shared with her. She needed to share all those things with the family while there was still time.

Far worse was her relationship with David. She could have wanted to travel back through time with him and start over again, back before the Middle East, back before he realized his writing career was dead in the water, before the band broke up, before they had their first fling. She would have never put him on that pedestal because it had mortified him. He had never come to terms with his transition from sports hero to shock rocker, and somewhere deep inside he hated what he had become. The more she idolized him, the more disdain he felt towards her because he could not respect anyone who loved what he was. She turned into his whipping girl, and even when she rocketed past everything he had ever accomplished, he could not respect her because she continued to treat him like he was something special.

It was why Duke Gallegos hated him and Stu Carlucci grew to despise him. They understood him as well as anyone, and it became harder and harder for them to deal with his need to spite anyone who wanted to get close to him. His relation with Johnny and Roth was what cemented the barrier once and forever. He was closest to those two because they knew who David was and didn't really care. They knew better than to try and get too close, and David respected them above all others because of it.

She remembered the one night she had accompanied David and his creepy crawlers on a walk through Tel Aviv. They were surrounded by wrestler-size bodyguards, and the Crawlers were as a pack of dogs running ahead, sniffing every lamppost and running back to David intermittently for his approval. Both she and David could not help but think of how much it reminded them of the old days, back when they would stroll along the Promenade in Brooklyn Heights, smoking a joint and daydreaming about making it big one day.

"Can you imagine?" he chortled as he watched the faces of passersby, astonished that such aberrations could be walking the streets with no concern. They had seen Russian Mob *vors* swagger through the bazaars, but none so obstreperous or with the public approval of this bunch. They were morbidly fascinated by the walking scarecrow with his skull face and straw hair, wearing a leather jacket in the desert city because his natural insulation had wasted away. "If someone would've told us we'd be here doing this ten years ago, we'd have thought they were on a bad acid trip."

It was probably then and there that she should have realized he was dying. David Diamond would have never rested on his laurels, it was anathemic to his nature. The David of old would have been talking about breaking loose from James Lincoln and going off on a tour of his own. He would have announced the next day---if there had been a next day---that they had cut a deal with the Israelis to play a benefit for their armed forces. He would have focused his being on blowing the doors off Lincoln's tour. She knew him far too well to believe that he would have recognized anything as his crowning achievement. He had never once believed or realized he had ever gone too far.

He had been the best thing and the worst thing that ever happened to her. He had pushed her far beyond her limits, threw her through a door she would never have dreamed was even there. Yet now she carried his ghost as an albatross around her neck, an unresolved issue that she would carry to the grave. That day was obviously not so far away, but she would bring him with her nonetheless. Maybe this interview with Sapphire Starr would help her find closure at last. Maybe it would be a diuretic that would purge him from her system once and for all.

The trick would be to replace him with Zeke, as it should have been from the beginning. Only Zeke was the same kind of animal while being the exact opposite, an apple compared to an orange. The harder she tried to love him the harder he struggled against her. Yet the more she pushed him away, the more fiercely he fought to stay alongside her.

The final chapter was coming soon, and she would deal with it as it arrived. She would have to tell him of her illness, and they would collapse into each other's arms. It would be like her Mom and David all over again, only this time there would be more time to make everything right. They would be able to face it together, enjoy the time they had left to them.

Time was of the essence, and time was her greatest enemy. She would have given anything to be able to never tell him what would tear his heart asunder.

The one show that stuck out in her memory was the Party's show at CBGB's, the gig she never played. It was before Hezbollah, before Johnny Carmona, back when they first came out from Debbie's apartment and across the Brooklyn Bridge to play with the big boys. David knew this was going to be a major opportunity here, and he would pull out all the stops to make this happen. What Tina did not expect was for David to put her on the sidelines in favor of another drummer.

"Look, you know Tina's not ready for something like this," David was edgy as he confronted Tina and Debbie with his decision a week before the show. Tina was even more indignant as he spoke to Debbie as if Tina was not even there. "We can put her on a mic, she can do backup vocals. If we put her up there with that boom-boom-boom routine, they're gonna pull the plug on us, I guarantee it. Look, there is nothing but heavy hitters over there. They got the Ramones, the Dead Boys, the Heartbreakers, those are all high-powered bands with a monster backbeat. Let Eddie get us through this audition and we'll put Tina in for the gig."

Eddie Patino was a bespectacled Italian kid from Bensonhurst with a $2,000 Pearl drum set and a heavy-handed power style. David had not even heard him play, but was desperate for every advantage that would help them pass the audition at NYC's punk rock mecca. He put out an ad in a Manhattan tabloid and Patino gave them a call. David and Stu went out to meet him, and soon the deal was done and Patino would be on the throne for the CBGB gig.

"This is a crock of shit!" Debbie vented. "So how does this work, if you find someone better than one of the people in the band, you're just gonna replace them? You suck, how come Stu didn't replace you?"

"Look, nobody's being replaced," he insisted. "She's going up front with me, that's all. Once this guy gets us in the door, that's it, he's gone. Look, the show's gonna make us or break us, we live and die with the show. If we can get our show on that stage for a regular gig with one of the regular bands, that'll be our big break. Monday night's amateur hour, everybody knows that. We got to pass this audition. After that, it's sink or swim. We just need our chance, we need our name on that CBGB ad in the Village Voice. That ad is the key to opening doors all over Manhattan. Nobody has a clue how well you played or how you did at the door. All they see is proof that you played CBGB's."

"Yeah, if we weren't practicing here in my place, you would've thrown me out, you motherfucker!" Debbie retorted.

"Look, we got Max's Kansas City and Rockbottom ahead of us. We go in with the regular team, even if I gotta pay for drum lessons before the show."

"That's all right, I'll pay for my own lessons," Tina wiped a tear from her eye.

"Hey, c'mon, guys, we're a team, we're all going to the top together," David assured them. "Nobody's going anywhere but up. We all said we would do anything it took to make this happen for us. This is just something we need right now, the one time. We're going to Max's Kansas City next month, and it'll be the five of us like always. It'll give Tina time to get her act together, plus we'll have the CBGB gig ahead of us. Everything's gonna work, trust me on this."

"Yeah, well, maybe you should use that drum money on singing lessons," Debbie grumbled. "C'mon, T, let's go get a beer. You gonna lock up?"

"Nah, I'm gonna go pick up some smoke."

"Okay, see you in an hour." They had practice tonight, and Tina would be given a mic that would be turned down lower and lower as the night progressed. She would try to act like it didn't matter, but it did. The Party was her life, just like everyone else's. She just hadn't expected David to have given her the shaft like that, and it took a long time before the pain went away.

David's entire scheme backfired that next Monday. There was a big difference between the Party hanging out in the crowd at the legendary club as opposed to trying to crack the lineup. The regulars grew clannish and somewhat defensive as David's roadie crew shoved their equipment down the narrow aisle to the side of the stage. Fortunately, the sizable number of motorcycle jackets suddenly appearing in the midst of the crowd caught the audience unawares. They gave place to the newcomers and waited patiently for their time to pass.

The Party was at the top of its game, with David strutting his stuff up front as a muscle-bound Mick Jagger, making up for his limited vocal skills with a spastic stage routine. Stu was the magic man on guitar, while Duke and Debbie let the hammer down on rhythm upon which Eddie Petito rolled like thunder. The heartbreaker came when they were in the middle of "Barbarella Queen of Pain", as David was charming the snakes with his Doors-like freeform vocals during the extended instrumental. Petito's brand-new drum throne broke, and he walked off-stage to find himself a vacant barstool. David watched in shock as the audience tittered, everyone waiting until Eddie returned to bring their highlight song to a close.

Stu read Eddie a condensed version of the riot act after the gig, but after they got back to Debbie's and put the equipment away, David told Stu that Eddie was history. Stu and David had not told the others that they had made Eddie an offer for a permanent spot, but this solved the problem of dealing with Tina and Debbie. Everyone went their separate ways after the show, and Debbie and Tina headed up to Grace Episcopal Church on Hicks Street with a couple of six-packs. They slipped down the side alley alongside the church and sat down on the steps leading to the side entrance. Debbie knew she was going to work with a hangover tomorrow but was too wired to go to bed so soon.

"You know," Debbie practiced blowing smoke rings, "just because we got tits instead of balls doesn't mean we can't get over on men in this world. There's very few things that separate them from us. Once you clear them off the table, the best person wins, regardless of what you got between your legs."

"Yeah? And how do you figure all that?"

"Fighting's the big thing. The big tough guy's always in charge, from rock bands to neighborhood stores to the corporate offices. In that shithole insurance company I work at, all the top executives are like six feet tall. Take a look around up on Court Street, all the stores are run by the biggest guy in the family. If they hire anyone, it's never anyone bigger than they are. Thye always back away from the guy who can kick the most ass."

"Yeah, so?" Tina swigged her beer.

"So there's ways to beat guys. Look, you grab a guy's wrist with both hands, his knuckles facing you. You fall back and wrap a leg around his arm. That's it, he's gone, I don't give a shit how big he is. Same thing if you can grab the edge of his hand with both of yours and turn it upward. You get it locked tight with all your weight behind it, you can make him cry."

"Well, maybe. But guys fight with their fists."

"That gets tricky, but you can sucker them in. See, you hold your hands outward, like a dog begging for a bone. Keep your hands cupped, like when you're making shadow figures of a duck. From there, you wait until they throw, and you kinda hook it. You shove their punch down and away. It leaves them wide open, but then you have to throw something back. I'd go with elbows and knees. Plus, if you get in close, you can kinda slide down and stomp their kneecap as hard as you can. They won't be able to do shit after that."

"Did you ever try any of that stuff?"

"Nah," Debbie popped a top on a Bud Light, "but I probably could."

"On David?"

"No, that bastard's too tough, he'd pull out of the wristlocks. He'd probably take your best sucker punch too. I bet I could take out Stu or Duke, though."

"Oh my gosh, Duke?" Tina squealed. "If he heard you say that he'd want to kill you!"

"Well, he could try," Debbie sipped her beer.

"You're crazy. I don't think I'd ever take on a guy."

"That's because you're stupid."

"What? Fuck you."

"Hey, you let that fat four-eyed Guido walk in and take your fuckin' job. You didn't even talk to Stu or Duke about it. Even worse, you're not doing anything about it. You really ought to take some lessons. Learn your instrument so you can tell David to shove it up his ass."

"I don't see you taking any lessons."

"My tits are bigger than yours. They're not gonna throw me out unless some stripper bitch comes along. Plus they're using my apartment. If they kick me out they'll be paying twenty an hour for studio time in the Village."

"You're probably right," Tina conceded.

"I'm always right, shithead," Debbie handed her a joint and a book of matches. "C'mon, we need to get to work on these sixes, I've got work tomorrow."

Tina woke up when she heard Debbie leaving for work the next morning. She was collecting unemployment and had six months to go. She decided to check out New York University and find out about their music program. She took the F Train to West 4th Street and walked over, signing up for a consultation with one of their advisors. After about a half hour wait, she was sent on her way for not having any music background to speak of.

She stopped by the cafeteria on the way out and began mingling with some of the kids carrying guitar cases around with them. It wasn't long before a couple of them helped her make a connection.

"Go check out Night Flight over there," they pointed to a grungy-looking young man with long, thick and greasy braided blond hair and a beard. He wore raggedy, faded denim jeans and jacket, and didn't look like college life was treating him too kindly. Tina walked over and sat down alongside him.

"Hey, sister, can I bum a quarter for bus fare? I need to get downtown by three," he spoke with a smoker's rasp.

"I was gonna ask you the same thing. Say, you know anybody who's giving drum lessons?"

"I can give you drum lessons. You probably don't need 'em. Did they tell you I jammed with Ginger Baker in LA?"

"Really? Well, my name's Tina. I play drums for the Party, it's a punk band in Brooklyn."

"Man, punk ain't shit. Now I know you don't need lessons."

"Yes I do. They play too fast and I can't keep up."

"They play too fast because they *can't fuckin' play*, girl," he peered over his granny sunglasses into her eyes. "It's easy to play as fast as you can. When you're going brrrrrr," he blew through his pursed lips, "everything sounds the same. Stick a playing card in an electric fan and see if you can count the beats per minute."

"That's not true," she insisted. "It's one-two-three, one-two-three, and I can't keep the bass drum up with everything else."

"Because you're doing it backwards. The bass drum parenthesizes the snare and the other shit. It's one-*boom*-two-three, one-*boom*-two-three, like this," he began playing an imaginary set.

"How do you do those rolls on the different pieces without losing the beat?"

"Girl, they're like little gremlins trying to bite you," he made snapping motions with his hands for emphasis. "You gotta keep 'em down. You pop the snare, you pop the cymbal, hit the high-hat, hit the crash, they let you know when they get hit. But you got to do them in order or they make fun outta you. They'll make you sound like shit if you let 'em. You gotta listen carefully, because if you let them get over on you, they'll drown you out. A bad hit is twice as loud as a good hit. You get 'em doing what you want, though, you don't need a band. Gene Krupa, Ginger Baker, they don't need a band. They can play a set all by themselves. *Boom*-shh-shh, *boom*-shh-shh-*boom*. There's dudes up on Times Square, they sit out on the street all night just playin' drum solos, and their coffee can's stuffed with cash. *Boom*-shh-shh-*boom*, all night."

"Can you show me?"

"What do you think I'm doing? It's all up here, girl, right here," he tapped his head. "You ever do karate?"

"No, not really."

"Your drum sticks are like them nunchucks that Bruce Lee uses," he got up from his spot on the ledge surrounding the grassy area upon which sat a verdigris-coated monument. He broke into a horse stance and held out an invisible set of sticks. "You don't need a throne. You need to practice without one sometimes so you tighten up your stomach muscles. Budda-budda-budda-boom. Budda-budda-budda-boom. You get your rhythm down with the sticks on everything, your mattress, your bedpost, your lap, eyerywhere, all the time. You work on your speed and timing, and once you got that, then you break into your stance and go far right, far left, as far as you can stretch. Budda-budda-budda-boom. Budda-budda-budda-boom. You beat them little buggers, don't let them make you look bad. Back and forth, smack them down. You don't need a drumset. It's all up here."

"I think I get what you're talking about," she got up and pulled a dollar out of her pocket. "Well, I don't want you to miss your appointment."

"Is that all it's worth, girlfriend?" he seemed disappointed.

"No, I'm sorry," she took it back and pulled a five out of her purse. "Here, I wish I had more."

"So do I," he chuckled. "Now don't forget. You don't need a drumset until you need to go somewhere and play. It's all up here."

She thought about what he said all the way back home, tapping her hands on her thighs along with the ball of her foot on the floor of the subway car, imagining that the roar of the train speeding through the tunnel was Stu and Duke's guitars. *Ra-rumm ra-rumm, ra-rumm ra-rumm.* Little by little she was making a connection to what Night Flight was talking about, and by the time she got to the Bergen Street station she wanted to try it out. She would take Night Flight's advice, however, and keep practicing like Bruce Lee until Wednesday night rehearsal.

Just as she hit the corner of Warren and Smith, she looked in the window of Javier's Variety Store and spotted a plastic hockey mask. It was the Halloween type, a little *Jason* set with the fake dagger. She decided on a lark to go in and pick it up. She remembered David always saying about how the drummer was like the goalie on a hockey team. The drummer was the one who kept things even, the last line of defense. She was going to make it hard as hell for them to sit her down again.

She showed up for practice with her big black purse, and no one thought anything of it as she set up with beer in hand behind her set that evening. Duke picked up some Acapulco Gold and passed it around as they tuned up their guitars (Stu was always sure to tune Debbie's for her). Eventually they went at it, and David did not see what was going on as he stood in the dining room to minimize feedback. He noticed them complimenting her more than usual, but also noticed how her bass drum and floor tom were markedly more coordinated.

They finished their first set and David walked into the living room, marveling at Tina's hockey mask.

"Holy shit!" he chortled as he stared at her. "Holy shit! This is it, Stu, this is it!"

"Yeah, sounds like she's been working on that floor tom," Stu muttered as he walked past David on the way to the fridge for a beer.

"No, that mask," he followed Stu as Debbie cranked up Black Flag on her stereo. "She's nailed it. She's our goalie. We've got a permanent lineup at last."

"Whoa, hold on," Stu said tautly. "I thought you said we were still looking."

"Look, we can get all the hot shots in Brooklyn, but none of them are gonna play in a hockey mask. If she wants it that bad, we gotta let her have it."

"You're gonna let her keep the spot, screw-ups and all, just because she's wearing a hockey mask?" Stu said incredulously.

"Look, it's the show, that's the main thing. They see that hockey mask and find out we got a female drummer, they gotta love her no matter what she does."

"We gotta play with her. Don't forget that part."

"You can make it work, Stu. Help me with this. We're making a monster, I'm telling you."

"It's pretty monstrous, all right. You even listen to the practice tapes?"

"The tapes'll work themselves out. This show is ready to go. We can take this to Max's tomorrow night, though I'd just as soon wait until next month."

"You would, wouldn't you? You don't give a shit what it

sounds like."

"Of course I do. It's just that we're not sending them a tape, we're giving them a show. I think this is turning into the best show in town."

"We're showing our asses out there," Stu retorted as he pulled a Bud out of the fridge. "We're getting a bad reputation that's not gonna go away. These club owners talk, word gets around. I'm warning you, it does way more harm than good going out when you're not ready."

Tina was eavesdropping in the doorway, and was resolved to make good for herself and David. Only she had a gut feeling that Stu might have been right. She would stick it out and give it everything she had.

It wasn't until five years later that Tina came into her own, and shortly after that, it would become a gamble upon which David would stake his very life.

Chapter Four

Tina Rivera walked down Clinton Street, looking around furtively before lighting a joint on the way to Miguel's that Saturday afternoon. She figured she'd get feeling nice before heading over there. Debbie wasn't home, she had taken off early that morning, so Tina went off on her own. She stopped by her Mom's house and had toast and coffee before the family started rolling in. Her Mom went into her housewife (housemaid?) mode after that, and there was no point in trying to talk to her after that.

There was no point in talking to her before that either. Her Mom was from the Old Country, from Playa Ponce in Puerto Rico. She spent her teen years in their house along the beach helping her own mom take care of her four brothers and three sisters. Men in Puerto Rico had a bad habit of either running off and leaving their family or dying before their time. Her *abuelo* took the easy way out, dropping dead of a heart attack and leaving his wife and eldest daughter to clean up the mess. Her Mom was brainwashed by *Abuela* against the evil company of men, so of course Mom took up with the first man that came along to rescue her from her misery. She then fled to New York to escape the son of a bitch, and started life anew with her baby daughter. Tina never had it easy afterward.

Their dysfunctional little group was what kept her going. Debbie was like the sister she never had, and David was an ex-boyfriend, a big brother and a father confessor. The craziest thing about it was that David always had the most logical and conservative advice when she came to him with her problems. He was always encouraging her to get laid and thoroughly enjoyed hearing all the details, the fucking lecher. As far as anything else went, David always had the best advice, and when she listened to him nothing ever went wrong.

She turned up Warren Street, putting out the joint after smoking half of it, getting lots of dirty looks from old ladies out doing their shopping. She didn't give a shit because people were lighting up joints everywhere these days. You almost never went into the Cobble Hill Theatre without smelling someone lighting up. There wasn't a place anywhere in the City you didn't smell a joint burning somewhere. She was pretty sure that one day the City would be putting up No Pot Smoking signs in public buildings, but that was a long, long way off.

The beauty parlor was open for business and it looked like there were a few customers waiting their turn. Tina smiled with satisfaction as she saw the gig flyer taped inside the front window. David had The Party flyer looking more like a haunted house promo than a rock show, but he assured them that it got more attention and was probably right. She walked through the door and saw Miguel fastening an apron around a girl's neck as one guy was putting his jacket back on.

"Hey, Miguel," Tina waved. "Looks like you're busy. I'll come back later."

"Hey, Tina," Miguel smiled. "Say, this is Zeke, he was asking about you."

"You with that band?" the guy turned to her, adjusting his biker jacket.

"Yeah, The Party," she said proudly.

"With those...creepy crawlers?"

"Who the hell do you think you are?" Tina flared.

"I"m Zeke Cohen," the man said coolly. Suddenly she became aware of the dark, dancing eyes beneath the thick lock of hair dipping over his forehead, and the mischievous smile playing on his Cupid-bow lips. "I'm a jazz musician."

"Fucking poser," she exhaled, pushing past him as she left Miguel's Hair Salon, the other customers looking on in amusement.

Miguel's storefront was on the same block as St. Paul's Church on Court Street in Cobble Hill. News of the Carnevale Street Fair had galvanized the community, promising the merchants along the mile-long strip from Amity Street to Carroll Street a windfall profit as people all over Brooklyn and Lower Manhattan were expected to attend. Zeke was a regular customer of Miguel's and had often inquired about the raven-haired Puerto Rican girl who frequented the shop. Miguel was well aware of Tina's explosive temper and took his time before making the introduction. Had she been with Debbie Munson, it never would have happened.

"Hey, wait a second," Zeke hurried to catch up with her. "Why am I posing?"

"Look at how you're dressed," she grumbled uncertainly.

"I've been dressing like this for a long time," he smiled again. "I'm sorry about the creepy crawler thing, it's the term the kids use on the LA scene. So you're in Hezbollah. Cool name. My band calls itself Zeke Cohen and the High Notes. We're playing at Dem Bums tonight, why don't you stop by?"

"Man, I don't listen to that shit," Tina smirked, feeling kind of Debbyish at the moment.

"And what's so shitty about it?" he insisted.

"Well, I'm into my own music," she slowed down enough for him to fall into step with her. The marijuana fog lifted enough for her to see this guy wasn't bad-looking at all.

"I'm sure you heard the old saying about rock and rollers wanting to become jazz musicians when they grow up."

"Yeah, well, our lead guitarist fools around with jazz once in a while," Tina was still defensive.

"Well, why don't you bring him with you? Maybe he'd be interested in some of the stuff we're doing."

"I don't know. What time you guys go on? We've got band practice tonight."

"We're there until midnight. C'mon by when you get done, I'll buy you a beer."

"Okay, we'll see."

Strangely enough, David was the one who made it all work out for her that evening. He showed up so drunk he was singing the wrong lyrics to the wrong songs. Stu was so pissed off that he gave Debbie a lecture on why he was planning to leave the band. Debbie turned around and read David the riot act. David jumped in Stu's shit as a result, and he left the apartment in a huff which caused Debbie to run out after him. Tina took the opportunity to suggest they stop somewhere for a beer to cool off.

Neither Debbie nor Stu were in a mood to complain, and Tina sprung for a pitcher after they found a table by the stage. Zeke was fronting his four-man band, and his eyes lit up when he spotted Tina at the table. They turned up the heat, and Stu was greatly impressed as they launched into a couple of jazz-rock numbers before finishing their set. Zeke came over with his sax player, a muscular blond who clearly had his eye on Debbie.

"What're you, fucking lost?" Debbie blew a stream of cigarette smoke at him, peering up over her shades as he tapped the back of the seat she had her boots propped up on.

"I once was lost, but now I'm found, I hope," he tilted the seat so her boots slid off. She put her boots back up on his lap as he sat down, testing him for a minute before putting her feet down. He pulled over alongside her and began pitching hard, and after a while it looked like she enjoyed what she was hearing.

Eventually the other guys from the band came over to join them, and Stu got into a big discussion about jazz fusion with them as Zeke got to learn more about Tina.

"Say, listen," Zeke proposed as Stu decided to call it a night around 2 AM. "Why don't you come over my place after this? I've got some smoke and some wine over there. It's a little noisy in here."

"Well, I don't know, let me see what Debbie's gonna do," Tina decided.

"I think she's going home with Steve," Zeke grinned knowingly.

"Let me check with her," Tina said, then sidled her chair over next to Debbie.

"Hell no," Debbie's voice was slurred when Tina inquired. Debbie had hit the point where she was knocking out a mug in three swallows, and Zeke's friends kept the pitchers coming. "I got to throw Dickhead off my couch when I get home. If I go home with this son of a bitch, he'll want to get married tomorrow morning. He's already telling me about his grandfather's mansion in California."

"Well, maybe you should think about it," Tina suggested. "He's a good-looking guy."

"Fuck that. Why don't you take the both of them on? I always wanted to see if you could go two-on-one."

Tina proceeded to curse Debbie out before she rose wobbling to her feet.

"I'm outta here, shitface," Debbie slapped her on the back.

"All right, hold on, I'll walk you," Tina grabbed her purse.

"What the heck?" Zeke was flustered.

"I've got to walk her home, she's messed up. I'll call you," Tina replied, and as an afterthought she bent over and gave him a peck on the cheek.

42

"Hey, whuzzup, where you going?" Steve was just as surprised.

"I'm going home, I've had enough," Debbie adjusted her jacket woozily.

"Let me walk you home," Steve started to get up.

"No way. My father'll kill you," Debbie replied, then leaned over and snaked her tongue into his mouth. Her friends watched enviously as he exchanged a long kiss with the beautiful redhead before she pushed him away. "I'll give you a call tomorrow."

"Hey," Steve called as the girls headed out the door. "You don't have my number."

"I'll figure it out," Debbie replied as she closed the door behind her.

"So you're not thinking this is a good of a deal as Lincoln's making it look?"

"Lincoln's a sleazebag piece of shit, Zeke. You need to look this deal up and down and see if it's right for you."

"Hold on, just a second," Tina interrupted them. She and Zeke had met with Duke and Lucy Gallegos at El Faro, Manhattan's oldest Spanish restaurant in NYC. They were seated at a table facing one of the place's famous flamenco murals, and had polished off two bottles of the Faro's renowned *sangria* by the time they finished dinner. Lucy had flown into town from Virginia, taking a break from a corporate case long enough to spend the weekend with Duke at her father Paco's home on the Jersey Shore. She had passed the bar a couple of years ago and was out-earning Duke as a civil attorney. "Who's playing this gig, me or Zeke?"

"Hey, it's your deal," Zeke relented. "I'm sure Duke's just looking after your best interests."

"I don't see Duke walking away from a hundred grand," Tina scoffed at him.

"I already told you, I got this gig whether Lincoln pays a hundred grand or a hundred bucks," Duke held up a hand.

"So why don't you give it to charity?" Lucy teased him.

"Don't you start," Duke snapped at her. "This is chump change compared to what that Jew boss of yours is gonna score off that case of yours. All he ever gives you is scraps off his table anyway."

"Well, that's it," Lucy started reaching for her purse. "I'm not gonna listen to this. I'm locked in an office six days a week with a bunch of walking hard-ons, I didn't fly out here for the weekend for more of it."

"Whoa, whoa, hold on," Duke reached out and held her forearm gently. "C'mon, baby, I didn't mean it. I'm only kidding."

"That goes for you too, buster," Tina chided Zeke, both of them impressed that Lucy still had Duke wrapped that tight.

"All right, I guess I can take it if you can," Lucy relented, pulling her cigarette case out of her purse.

"I was just talking, that's all," Duke tried a different approach. "I didn't know if you needed the money, that's all. I know David and Debbie would run across Lebanon in their birthday suits for that kind of money, not to mention Stu."

"Stu's not doing that bad right now," Tina was defensive. "Neither is Debbie."

"What can I say," Duke twiddled a straw wrapper on the tablecloth. "I'm just thinking about your best interests, like Zeke said. The fewer backs I have to watch, the easier my job is. I mean, David's friggin' nuts. He could've easily changed the name of the band back to the Party. Going in there as Hezbollah is like waving a red flag in front of a bull. The State Department started hearing noise from Day One. The real Hezbollah is saying they won't tolerate any disrespect, and the Palestinian Government is already calling the gig a blasphemy against the Holy Land. What did that idiot Lincoln think, calling this the Crusader Concert Tour?"

"I already told you, it's not just the money," Tina insisted. "It's about you guys, it's about my friends, it's about the band. We spent seven years together trying to make our dreams come true and we failed. Now we get this once in a lifetime opportunity to make history together. How do you think I could possibly pass this up?"

"You haven't listened to a word I said," Duke was exasperated. "A guy walks into a bar and blows himself up. They don't even give you the courtesy of a punch line. This is all about suicide bombers now. These people don't take prisoners, and they don't plan on coming out alive. Those sick bastards on the Dome of the Rock tell them if they die for Allah they go straight upstairs without passing 'Go'. They're lining up for a chance to drive a truck bomb into an Israeli roadblock. The only reason the Israelis are letting this happen is because they're giving the terrorists enough rope to hang themselves. If they stage an attack against the concert crew, the whole world'll turn against them. Israel will be able to end the peace talks once and for all. They'll be justified in keeping things the way they are, New World Order or not."

"You're making it sound like the Government's setting Lincoln and the entire tour up as sitting ducks for the terrorists," Zeke frowned.

"No, that's why I'm being inserted," Duke assured him. "We've got a crack CIA team working aside a handpicked team of Mossad agents. The President wants to go down in history as not only having put a muzzle and leash on Saddam Hussein, but sealed the deal on the Peace Agreement in the Middle East. Everyone wants this thing to work. I'm just telling you as a friend that someone can get hurt out there. I'm telling you that if you don't need to go, maybe you shouldn't go."

"So did you run this stuff by Stu, or Johnny, or Debbie?" Tina asked.

"Stu's the one who gave David the hots for this gig. Debbie still thinks she's joined at the hip with the son of a bitch. Johnny's got something else going here. We think it has something to do with the Mob. He's in up to his ass with them, and we think they're calling in a marker on him. Basically we don't give a shit. If we can take down the Mafia along with Hezbollah, so much the better. If Johnny brings them to the table, we don't care either way."

"And you're good with your sister going along on this?" Tina turned to Lucy.

"Hey, she's married to the guy, what am I supposed to do?" Lucy ran her fingers through her hair. "Everybody knows the Mob's deeper into boxing than ever before. He made a deal with the devil when he signed on with Matrix Promotions. There's nothing I can do about that."

"Besides, if Johnny's acting as a front man for a Mob deal with the terrorists, he's probably the safest guy on the tour," Duke tapped his fingers on the table. "Odds are if they do anything, it'll be before or after the gig. If you stay locked up in your hotel room throughout the entire tour you'll be okay. Unless, of course, they put you in a room next door to David."

"I'm going, and I'm taking Zeke with me," she decided.

"Why, gee, thanks," Zeke rolled his eyes. "I always wanted

to travel halfway around the world to get my head blown up along with my ex-wife. It'll be the honeymoon we never had."

"It's not like I'll be twisting your arm," Tina shot back.

"I wouldn't miss it for the world," Zeke stretched his arms behind his neck

"Okay, so we're all in," Duke sighed. "Unfortunately Lucy will be tied up with her court case, so that's one less for me to worry about."

"Lucky you," Lucy raised a glass to him before taking a sip of wine.

"You oughtta send that one to law school," Duke jerked a thumb at Tina. "She'll make more money than you and she'll never be around when you need her."

"Yeah, forget you," Lucy smirked at him.

"Why send her to law school? I've already got all that now," Zeke sniggered.

Looking back, Tina would never forget that night as the night when she realized she was going and there was no turning back. Yet she knew that it was her destiny, just as much as meeting David Diamond, joining the band and becoming a drummer.

If she was able to do it all over again, even knowing how it was going to end up…

…she wouldn't have changed a damn thing.

Chapter Five

The Israeli government was being boxed into a corner by the nations of the world. The new spin on their containment of the Palestinians was that, if you play the game long enough, the time will come when you find yourself as the villain. The Israelis were facing an implacable enemy who would not rest until one or the other was evicted from their own homeland. To counter this, they had adopted tactics so extreme that they were being accused of being just like the Nazis who they had survived in returning to this land. Eventually they would become a pariah among the nations who even the United States of America could no longer support.

The Israelis decided to take the biggest gamble in its modern history. They would permit the Palestinians to set up their own provisional government in its own clearly delineated sectors where their autonomy would be guaranteed. The theory was that, with the American military in the region after Desert Storm, it would not take much for them to help the Israelis regain control if the Palestinians made a move to take control over the entire Holy Land. Plus, a major attack by any one of the extremist groups supporting the PLO would make it clear that an independent Palestine would never be more than a terrorist nation.

There had been a top-level meeting between the Prime Minister, the military and the Mossad as to how to engineer the destruction of the Palestinian state. It was decided that they would allow the decadency of modern-day society to be the vortex that would draw the extremists to their doom. If the Princess of the Realm were allowed to bring Palestine into present-day society and culture, it would create a schism between the reactionary Muslims and the younger generation who had waited a lifetime for prosperity and luxury to come their way. When they found out that Princess Sabrina had arranged for J.C. Lincoln, a known drug user, to play a concert in the Holy Land along with a grunge band called Hezbollah, it seemed as a dream come true.

They were talking about the event being bigger than Woodstock, which had been the most decadent event in modern history. If the Muslims were faced with having the valley of their ancestors turned into a plain of depravity, covered with sex, liquor and drugs as far as the eye could see, it would most likely be more than they could bear. It would be just as much of a blasphemy to their own people, but if it meant the collapse of the Muslim state, he was certain the people of Israel could endure it.

The more they researched, the better it looked. The leader of the band, David Diamond, was a failed poet whose published work *The Excommunicant* was a collection of rambling heresies and anti-social dissonance. The female bassist, Deborah Munson, was a she-devil who spoke and acted like a man. The opening act, Decentralization, was led by a man named Solomon Grundy, a Jewish anarchist who was a rebuke and a disgrace to his people.

The strategy was simple. They would give the concert entourage the red carpet throughout Israel, providing them a commanding platform from which they could bait and enrage the Muslims. They would encourage the nations of the world to converge on Israel, allowing them to attend Lincoln's carnival and provide a tremendous boost to the local economy. Only when the show itself came to pass, they would withdraw entirely and allow the extremists to exact their revenge and cut their own throats in the process.

Mossad Director Aaron Mandel met with the Prime Minister of Israel shortly before the concert tour was announced. It was agreed that they would give the Palestinians and the Crusaders enough rope to hang themselves. The titular head of state, proclaiming himself King Daoud I, was already under enormous pressure from the Palestine Liberation Organization. They had every reason to believe he and his Christian Liberation Army had ordered the car bombing of four of the PLO's Cabinet members to sabotage the election. When they convened to appoint a head of the fledgling Palestinian State, Abdullah Daoud was a shoo-in. It was only when Daoud revealed to the Israelis that he had reformed the democratic republic into a monarchy did they react.

"You can call yourself the Emperor of Palestine for all we care," a senior Mossad agent told him. "You pull any shit on us and we'll drop you and your gang right into the Dead Sea."

The American President was exultant in having played a key role in bringing peace to the Middle East and establishing an independent Palestinian state. The Israelis were pleased to oblige though they made it clear to the CIA and the State Department that the Daoud monarchy was to be a puppet regime at best. They would brook no subversive efforts by the PLO, Hezbollah or Hamas, and any militant actions would be blamed entirely on the Palestinian Authority as an act of war against Israel. The Americans agreed, deciding that the future of their independent State would be completely in their hands. Now, more than ever, they would be held accountable for the peace and stability of Palestine.

Sabrina Daoud was a jet-setter whose education in the University of Paris had been paid for by blood money earned with the CLA by her father Abdullah over the years. She met all the right people and made the right connections, and when Daoud's ship finally came in she was in the right place at the right time. The French media tabbed her as the Princess of Peace, and soon she was the darling of the press as she extolled the virtues of her father's monarchy.

All she needed was J.C. Lincoln, and she was everything he could have asked for. They had a few long-distance conversations before he flew to Paris to meet her. It was not long before they sealed the deal, and once the Israelis gave their approval, the Crusader Concert Tour became a reality.

No one on earth, not even David Diamond himself, could have ever dreamed of the success---or the tragic consequences---that lay ahead.

"Holy smoke! Your Aunt Tina!"

"How are you guys doing?" she said pleasantly, going around the room to shake hands. They were no more aghast than the producer, who stood in the recording booth with his jaw dropped open.

"Well, it's a long story," Carlos tried to explain.

"Bah," she waved a hand at him. "I'd been spending a lot of time with his cousin Angie trying to help her with her percussion lessons, and some people thought I wasn't spending enough time with Carlos. So here I am."

"It's a pleasure and an honor, Ms. Rivera," the producer nearly tripped himself up stumbling through to introduce himself.

"Anything you want, we'll do. Is there any equipment you need, can I have anything brought in?"

"No, this should do," Tina assured him. "We don't want the boys getting used to things they won't have onstage."

"Anything you want us to do, it's done," Tito, a husky young man in a tank top, came up to her. "Tell us what you want us to do."

"Okay, let's sit down and discuss the project," she pulled up a chair. The quintet rushed for chairs and surrounded her in short order. "What kind of background sound are you looking for?"

"Basically we don't have a background sound," Willie, a bespectacled fellow, spoke up. "We just develop a beat and improvise."

"I'm thinking that my input might be more useful if I can take the tapes home and get a feel for the songs, then find a rhythm pattern that helps develop the moods. Does that sound good?"

"Why, sure," they looked at one another.

"Now, I'm not giving you the run-around," she insisted as they gave her a CD. "In fact, let's shoot for Friday. I'll be back with some tapes of my own and we'll see what we can put together."

"Sure thing!" they happily agreed.

During the cab ride home, she decided that she was going to develop a Brazilian samba beat for their songs. She would select the best of the songs and turn it into a bossa nova number. She figured she might even work a reggae beat in somewhere and see if that would float their boat. She didn't like rap music because of its violent macho overtones, but she decided that if she could help one ship sail in a different direction, others might be persuaded to follow its course if it seemed good.

It just sickened her to think how late in the game this was happening for her. She started hitting her stride and realizing her potential right after Hezbollah broke up. She became an overnight celebrity as a female percussionist appearing with Zeke's jazz band, then began hiring out to salsa bands to improve her circulation. Suddenly the offer to tour Africa came along, and after a whirlwind run through Europe, she became an Internet star. It made the New York scene take notice, and she was a name in the news by the time J.C. Lincoln plucked Hezbollah out of the air for his Crusader tour.

It had been one tour after another for her, and she never had time to watch her nieces and nephews grow up. Hell, all she could do was sit and watch her relationship with Zeke fall apart. Now here they were, all grown up and trying to fit Tina back into their lives. She wanted desperately to accommodate them, but now here they were again. James Lincoln, Debbie Munson, Stu Carlucci, Duke, Johnny, the whole gang...everyone but David.

There was no way in hell she could pass this up, but it was just as certain that she had to include her family in the time she had left on the clock. The doctors said they couldn't guarantee anything. It worked differently on everyone. Some victims took years to go down, others went in a matter of months. All she could do was make the best of what she had, as she'd been doing all her life.

Only this time all she had was the rest of her life...

...and the clock was winding down.

J.C. Lincoln needed something new to put him back on top of the heap. He could feel his deity slipping away, partly due to the fact he had not been in the studio for five years. It was also because the nations of the world had put away their mirrored balls and coke spoons, turning to rap music as the wave of the future. He had successfully blended his rhythm and blues with the disco beat to make his triple platinum album happen, but now the sound was obsolete and he needed something else. He could still rely on his horns and trombones to put his blockbuster R&B hits over the top, but he would have to include some rap songs to sell to this new Generation Y.

He was thinking of laying some of those smooth Marvin Gaye or Al Green overtones on top of a funky beat, but he'd have to see. He wasn't about to compromise his musical identity, because the media would see right through it and he would truly be finished.

The idea of invading the Middle East originated as a thought of going Back to the Motherland. He had been smoking crack with Melvin E. Williams, a childhood buddy who he had blessed as his designated coke supplier over the last couple of years. Melvin's Mafia connections had been forced to open the spigot to meet Lincoln's demands, and Williams had gone from a gram bagger to a weight lifter in a short time. Melvin was using his share of the profits to bribe his way into some of the Village's top comedy clubs, and eventually talent found its way to the top. Williams had become a top comedian, and he and Lincoln were news whenever J.C. ventured from his North Bronx fortress of solitude.

The reality was that Lincoln needed a new album and a tour to promote it on. As his creative juice began secreting, he sent out his research team to create a crash course on rap for him while assigning his musicians to start putting together a twelve-song set. He wanted four R&B songs as good or better as any of his past work, along with four powerhouse funk-rock jams and four sensual beats that would lay the foundation for his new Gaye Green raps. The venue, however, changed as he began channel-surfing on cable to get reconnected to the world.

He realized that the Middle East was where it was at, with Desert Storm having barely settled and the new Palestinian peace negotiations in progress. The leader of the new coalition government had recently been assassinated, and amidst the chaos emerged a new leader who proposed that he be proclaimed the new monarch of a Palestinian kingdom. It was a ludicrous notion were it not for the guerilla leader's daughter, a European-educated beauty who rushed to her father's side in a shameless grab for power and glory. She became the self-proclaimed Princess of Peace, and she swore that she would be the mediatrix who would bring the Palestinians and the Israelis together in an unheralded era of peace and prosperity.

Neither Lincoln nor the Princess' ambitions knew any bounds. He contacted her with a proposal for a Peace in the Middle East outdoor concert in the biggest venue in the history of mankind. Napoleon Bonaparte once stood on the plains of Jezreel overlooking the Valley of Megiddo, stating that he could easily field a million-man army across its vastness. J.C. Lincoln would bring a musical Armageddon to the ancient land, broadcasting the event via satellite on closed-circuit TV to the nations of the world.

What he needed was a second band that would draw the white audiences. He knew that this new grunge sound would probably be the ticket. It was the bastard son of punk and new wave born ten years too late. There would be no competition between the bands, no chance of being upstaged. He wanted the supporting bands to be objects of attraction and wonder as much as the sounds of tomorrow that heralded Lincoln's music for the next generation. The next step would be to research the soon-to-bes, the also-rans, and the never-weres who would play the show of a lifetime for their chance to become the *Rocky* of the grunge music scene.

James Lincoln would fondly recall the days when Toby was working for him, his 6'7", 350-pound manservant who dressed up every day in black suit and tie to take care of J.C.'s every need. The man retired by mutual consent after the Concert, having saved up a million dollars of salary and bonuses. It was shortly after that when Lincoln was thought to have contracted AIDS. If Toby had still been around, the skank who gave him the disease probably wouldn't have got near the inner circle.

Toby made sure the musicians got him his musical scores, the lyricists got his rap songs, and his demographers had mathematical calculations and statistics as to what the sociocultural market looked like. When he was finished, he had four R&B songs that were strong enough to feature in a Broadway musical, four funk-rock tunes that were going to put him back on top of the charts, and four rap songs that were going to put him front and center of the music video scene. "Burning Up Broadway" was about his music symbolized the integrity of the black community resurging amidst gang violence and economic discrimination; "Can't Stop Funkin' Around" was a long-awaited, overdue anthem for the funk-rock genre, and "Talkin' the Walk" was a didactic yet addictive rhyme about how players like Lincoln whose been there done that rap could keep kids strong without going wrong. They were three crossover blockbusters that Lincoln would unveil at the Concert as 'Dynamite in the Desert'.

His researchers finally found the band that he thought was going to put him over the top. There was a punk band called the Party who crossed over into the burgeoning hardcore sound in the mid-80's, renaming themselves Hezbollah (the Party of God) and setting off on a guerilla campaign throughout NYC before the band self-destructed on the verge of commercial success. Their lead guitarist, Stu Carlucci, went on to industrial acclaim as a studio musician but was in a bitter custody battle over Hezbollah's demo tapes. Co-founder David Diamond copyrighted all the material and would not release it unless Stu agreed to a re-recording and promo tour. Without the tapes, Stu's B-side material was not enough to get him the record contract he so desperately wanted. Insiders agreed that if the band reformed, they had the potential to catapult the NYC grunge scene past Seattle in the battle for grunge rock supremacy.

Whoever this guy was, he was a raving visionary who was willing to lose everything before relinquishing his dream to anyone, no matter what the price. Carlucci had offered him money and Stu's backers even offered to put him back in the studio to record his own new material, but no dice. David Diamond never give up those tapes regardless of what they offered, and if he didn't get his deal he would take them to the grave right with him. They could put his tapes in a box six feet under alongside him, and he would want to be buried upside down so the world could kiss his ass goodbye.

"Toby, get me David Diamond," J.C. Lincoln remembered making the fateful decision. "Get our best people on it, spend what you have to, but I want him here in forty-eight hours."

And so the game was on.

"Palestine! What am I going to wear?"

"What do you mean, what are you going to wear? Are you doing drugs again?"

"You know, this is why I don't go down and visit you like I used to," Tina flared. "You are the most negative person I know."

"The most realistic," Zeke corrected her. "Look, you've got a world tour coming up at the beginning of the year. You're going to be playing with percussion groups from sixteen African nations, some of whose music has never been distributed outside of the continent. How are you going to refocus on that after David Diamond's three-chord flea market soundtrack?"

"So now you're supporting the tour," she shot back. "Why can't you get your story straight?"

"I'd support anything before I see you go back in with David Diamond," he stalked away from her glass-encased balcony overlooking Central Park in midtown Manhattan, pacing the white-carpeted floor fretfully. "You don't seem to recall all the abuse he put you through."

"I wouldn't be here if it wasn't for David," she was adamant. "Try to remember that."

"Stu Carlucci put you on that road, if I remember correctly."

54

"Stu taught me to drive," she retorted. "David showed me the highway."

"Listen to yourself. What kind of twisted logic is that?"

"Why don't you get the hell out of here?"

"No problem," he threw on his motorcycle jacket. "You know, you've got to be the biggest enabler I've ever met. Diamond's just bringing you in because the whole rotten show would collapse without your support. James Lincoln is old news, he can't sing anymore, his ensemble gets bigger and bigger right along with his coke habit. This whole damn thing is a publicity stunt, anyone can see that. That Palestine government will fall apart any day now, and Lincoln's running right in there with a milk bucket. Stu Carlucci thinks he got the break of his life, but he'll have more luck putting Humpty Dumpty back together than with that band."

"Fuck you!" she yelled as he walked out the door, slamming it shut with a kick behind him.

She could never forget the hurt and sense of betrayal she felt when Zeke had treated her dream so spitefully, and doubted he was going to act any differently now. She knew that playing a punk rock show was going to require a superhuman effort. If she didn't happen any time soon, it might well become physically impossible. It was turning into another race against time, and if Zeke was not for her, he would be against her. Only this time, his rejection might be more than she could endure.

There was no way of telling how it was going to go down, whether his rage over her considering another go with Lincoln or his shock over learning about her condition would have the greater effect. Both would be traumatic for the two of them, and she wasn't sure which she wanted to deal with first. If they came from her lips at the same time, perhaps she could help him deal with it just a little bit better.

Tick-tock. Tick-tock. Tick-tock.

Chapter Six

She hadn't heard much of anything from Stu since the rumors began. He was one of the first ones to call her, as he had back when word about the Crusader Concert Tour began spreading in 1992. Only back then it was a chess game between him and David. This time it was Stu playing against James Lincoln...and Stu playing against himself.

Stu, like David, had sold his soul to rock and roll. Only Stu had placed his enormous talent on the altar, which turned the man behind the talent into a non-entity, a faceless musician lost in the orchestra pit of time. David had gambled everything he had on a cult of personality, and his David Diamond character lived on despite the fact most of Hezbollah's songs were fading into history. Stu had won a Grammy and an Emmy for his studio work, but his name was appearing as illegible as his fine print credits. David had sacrificed his life for his notoriety, while leaving Stu behind to suffer in the obscurity David had predicted for him.

They were headed in opposite directions from the very beginning, fighting to tear loose from one another like a two-headed dog. Stu insisted that the music was going to be the cream that caused them to rise to the top of the punk rock cauldron, while David was certain that the stage show would make the band stand apart from the crowd. They were both right in their own way. David's refusal to sell the co-rights to Hezbollah's material created the mystique that sold James Lincoln hook, line and sinker. Yet once the band finally took the stage at Armageddon, it was the stage show that made rock and roll history.

Stu had long since made his mark as a near-legendary studio musician, working behind the scenes with some of the biggest hip-hop, TV and movie producers in the business. Only he still had his sights set on scoring big with his own music, a project that seemed destined for failure. Stu, like Zeke, had matriculated from rock to jazz long ago as part of his evolution as a musician. Unlike Zeke, he was convinced that jazz rock still flourished, though it seemed to have even less of a place in 21st century culture than the rock and roll genre that spawned it.

He had a major scoring opportunity with his *Kaleidoscope* project, but Television Records would not gamble on a release in the sagging economy without a previous work that would provide the ballast for the highly-experimental endeavor. The president of Television, Jerry Blackstone, wanted to release *Hezbollah* first to draw in the punk/new wave audience for the *Kaleidoscope* follow-up. Only David would not sign over his share until he got a deal for a promo tour for the Hezbollah album. Once again, the two-headed dog was tearing itself in half before James Lincoln came into the picture.

Tina had tried to collaborate with Stu before and after the Crusader tour, and both times the project went belly up. Tina just couldn't sink her teeth into Stu's material. It was magnificent work on a technical basis, but did not have the spiritual resonance she was looking for. When Stu went into his spiraling guitar riffs ascending into the heavens alongside the astral saxophone and piano melodies, she found herself unable to latch onto it all. Her roots were too firmly entrenched into the ground attack of the punk rock blitzkrieg. When she was finally able to move beyond that, it was towards the earthy pulsations of the Third World tribal beat. Whereas Stu and David had gone off into different worlds, Tina and Stu were in different dimensions.

It was hard for her to conceive of how even Stu and Zeke could not see things eye-to-eye. They had a short fling before the Crusader tour, mostly out of spite for David. Yet their jazz philosophies were as disparate as Stu and David's rock and roll vision. Zeke was more of a jazz purist, and could not abide by Stu's constant forays into rock structures despite what the overall theme dictated. They recorded about three sessions before allowing the project to die in utero, leaving their disagreements behind as they went their separate ways.

She was almost as concerned about breaking the news to Stu as she was in telling Zeke. She knew Stu would beat himself up over not having kept in closer touch with her over the years. He would probably start tearing himself away from his current projects to squeeze some time with her, and that would leave her feeling guilty. This whole thing was turning into a cluster fuck. Not only was she dying, but it was like she was having to make her own arrangements.

Tina had been thinking so much about him that she wasn't overly surprised when Stu gave her a call that very next day. It seemed as if her spirituality was being enhanced by her failing health. She remembered hearing something about the metaphysical law of compensation, how a person's body and mind tend to make up in one area for the loss of ability or power in another. It made lots of sense when she thought of blind people she met who could almost hear a pin drop, or those who could not walk having enormous arm strength. Maybe not being able to squeeze a grape would make her able to see through walls one day.

"Hey, Stewy. Find my phone number on some toilet wall?"

"Nah, not really," she could imagine him licking his lips. "I just had some pretty good news from Lincoln's people. I got to turn the tables on them this time around. You remember how they held the Hezbollah album against my throat when I was trying to get them to sign me? Well, now it's working the other way around. I told them I wouldn't go in on the Crusader reunion project unless they released *Kaleidoscope*. Well, guess what? It's a go."

"That's fantastic!" Tina was delighted. "I'm so happy for you, congratulations!"

"Well, I'll tell you, you're on my short list for people I can call up to go out and party with. Wanna get together for some beers?"

"Why, uh, sure," Tina was caught entirely off-guard. "Where and what time?"

"Well, I was thinking I could stop by in about an hour. Maybe we could swing by Manitoba's over by Alphabet City."

"Sure," she replied softly. "I'll see you in a bit."

A wave of nostalgia flooded her as she remembered the old days, back when David thought of Handsome Dick Manitoba's band, the Dictators, as the competition back in the punk days. She also recalled Alphabet City as the home of A7, a pioneer hardcore club where Hezbollah met their waterloo in bringing their punk onslaught up against an unforgiving crowd of speedcore rockers. It was a turning point in David's rock evolution, one which caused Stu to finally leave the band. David considered it a betrayal over which he would harbor a grudge for half a decade afterwards. David began incorporating hardcore songs into the repertoire, while Stu began the next leg of his journey on the path to jazz rock. They never dreamed their paths would meet again along the road to Armageddon.

She dressed in her punk attire replete with her biker jacket and boots, black T-shirt and jeans. Stu was waiting in a cab outside her Central Park condominium, and they hugged and kissed before the cabbie continued back towards lower Manhattan. They exchanged small talk as they cruised into Alphabet City, and Tina looked wistfully up at the street sign at East Seventh Street. It was the turning point from which David and Stu's relationship would never recover.

By the Eighties, punk rock had undergone a major evolution as the Music Industry sought to water down the anti-establishment message by synthesizing its New Wave product. To hedge its bets, the Industry tried to recoup its glam rock losses by fabricating a 'hair band' genre of heavy metal. Both these new brands of rock were designed specifically for the fledgling video market spearheaded by the phenomenal emergence of MTV. It reestablished the smoke-and-mirrors promotional tactics of the Industry that marginalized the fading heavy metal bands and punk groups steadily losing ground to the new rap craze growing in popularity.

Both David and Stu had nothing but disdain for bands like the Plasmatics and the Dead Kennedys. Stu derided their lack of musical proficiency, while David contended that the songs were played so quickly that the vocals became incoherent. Yet David held a grudging admiration for bands like Black Flag, whose sheer aggression was palpable at times, and Slayer, who had taken the next step in the Velvet Underground's white noise direction. Moreover, it was the manic following of the hardcore bands and the thrash metal groups that gave him the most inspiration. He had to create mosh pits in front of the Party stage, and fill them with pit-slammers at all costs.

The clannish A7 crowd was teeming with hangers-on of the performing bands, all of whom were friendly with one another in uniting for the common cause. David would later refer to them as 'an incestuous branch of the CBGB tribe'. Realizing he had no hope of being offered a return booking, he decided to create as much chaos on the scene as possible. Though stacking their set with their hardest-rocking songs, they would close the show with his parody of the Kennedys' hit song, which he renamed "The Party Uber Alles". Instead of indicting the Reagan Administration as warmongers, David glorified a nightmare zombie world ruled by the Party as a genocidal totalitarian regime. He topped it off by doing the gig wearing a 9th Cavalry Western-style hat, which he correctly assumed the speedpunks would mistake as a cowboy hat. Stu was greatly concerned at what David was doing here, and he warned both Debbie and Duke that he was thinking of leaving the band if this went much further.

"Does he really think anybody gives a shit if he takes off?" Duke scoffed as he stood at the bar with Lucy, watching the roadies setting up their equipment for their set. Duke had bought into David's rock and roll mercenary theme heavier than anyone else. He wore a black beret, T-shirt, fatigue pants and boots onstage along with Cuban Army dog tags, and would apply camouflage face paint before the set. "David's already made arrangements if he goes south on us. We won't lose a step."

"What arrangements?" Debbie and Tina wondered. They had a feeling something was cooking but had grown tired of all the bickering. It was almost as if the band had split into three factions, and it was destroying their morale. David and Stu had evolved into the two-headed dog, and Duke gloatingly stood by watching them tear themselves asunder.

"He's actually talking about picking up an instrument and hiring a vocalist. The sound would improve a hundred percent with a singer, that's for sure."

Tina and Debbie had long tired of defending David's vocals against backbiters, and busied themselves up on stage as Stu and Duke did a last-minute sound check. The crowd tittered as Duke put on his paint and Tina slipped on her goalie mask. Only when David put on his Cavalry hat and took center stage, the show started slipping out of control despite Stu's awesome guitar display in trying to save the gig.

David was as Jim Morrison doing his best Iggy Stooge impersonation. He danced and pranced through his routine, only collapsing into a convulsion on stage right as Stu went into his solo. He palmed an Alka-Seltzer tab, and soon he could be seen foaming at the mouth. He crawled back to the mic and recovered in order to sing the next song, only to stagger to stage left at the onset of the lead break. This time he palmed a blood capsule, and after falling behind the drum set, he rose with a curtain of gore spilling down his face.

Tina recalled that David could have easily broke even, but he never took the easy way out. He continued baiting and taunting the crowd, giving them peace signs, making off-mic remarks about all the hippies in the audience, and announcing that this show was the next best thing to Woodstock II. There were murmurs of violence throughout the building, but somehow the creepy crawlers discouraged the audience long enough to pack up their gear and get everyone safely back to their rental van. David did not even bother to check with the manager for their cut of the proceeds or a return engagement.

There was almost an unwritten rule that nobody talked about the old days. It was crazy that no one even mentioned it. She knew it was probably because it opened up too many old wounds. Too many people got crapped on back then, and it was far too dangerous to insult someone anew and burn a bridge forever. Goodness knows it was beyond belief that the Crusader Tour ever hit the road, especially with David walking in acting like it all just happened yesterday. Tina still couldn't believe Debbie didn't punch David out on Day One.

"So what've you been up to?" Stu would always provide a segue to discuss his latest project.

"Well, I was planning to go down to the MOMA[1] and throw acid in Vincent Van Gogh's face, you know, that self-portrait of his?"

"Yeah," Stu grinned. "I was trying to figure out how to saw the locks off the tiger cages at the Central Park Zoo the other day. Anything new with the music?"

"Nah. I've been getting calls from some of these Third World ensembles. I think I opened up a can of worms with that stuff. They start wanting you to play all these benefits for this and that charity. They forget that some of us are trying to make a living at this."

"Are you?" he grinned.

"I don't know. How about you?"

"I'm doing okay."

She chuckled at his same-old-Stu look. He wore a frumpy black blazer, a black Beatles T-shirt, jeans and black moccasins, looking like just about every other yuppie in Soho. She knew he was probably set for life after those movie and TV deals he scored those awards on. Plus his only vice was being a cannabis

---

[1] Metropolitan Museum of Modern Art

connoisseur. He even did an interview in *High Times* a few years ago, the most radical statement of his life outside of Hezbollah.

"Well, good. You can buy this starving artist a beer," she teased.

The had the taxi drop them off at the corner of Avenue B and Sixth Street, and Stu produced a spliff of blue-tinged Hawaiian weed. They looked around furtively before lighting up, and a couple of tokes were all they needed. They could not remember the last time they lit up in the street, but neither would be the first to admit it. Stu finally snuffed it and put it in a matchbox before going inside the bar.

Manitoba's was a dimly-lit lounge with framed rock and roll pictures adorning the walls, and neon lighting around the main bar. They ordered a couple of Bud Lights, and soon Stu was telling her all about the *Kaleidoscope* project. It had been over ten years in the making, interrupted sporadically by big-money recording deals. When he had time to spare, the right musicians were never around.

"You know, you should come in with me on this," Stu always asked her. "It'd be great, we'd have a blast, just like the old days."

"You know I can't wrap my head around jazz," Tina insisted. "I'd screw everything up. How come you think me and Zeke never did anything together? I start getting into it and all of a sudden I'm playing too fast. You wouldn't believe how much shit I put up with on that African tour."

After a while Stu had one too many, especially after they ordered a few tequila shots, and he went into his own Iggy Pop routine. He started talking loud and flirting with girls at nearby tables, and finally Tina got him to sit at the bar when it looked like a college kid was getting ready to punch him out. He finally got the bartender to come over for a chat, and it was all downhill after that.

- Hey, where's Dick?
- Not here tonight. I think he had something going in Jersey tonight.

He told me he'd buy me a beer the next time I came in.
- Well, I'm sure he'll take care of you when he's here.
- We're with Hezbollah, we've been all over the Internet. You got online service?

- Yeah, I check my e-mail. I don't keep up with that stuff.

- You must've heard about James Lincoln planning that tour in the Middle East. It's a reunion tour, a follow-up to the one from back in '92.

- Yeah, well, good luck with that.

- How about a round for me and my friend? This is Tina Rivera.

- Right, when the boss gets in tomorrow, check with him.

- Fuck you.

- What was that?

For once Tina wouldn't have minded someone playing the celebrity card for her, saying 'Hey! There's Tina Rivera!" to keep them from getting thrown out. Instead they made their way back up to 2nd Avenue and got a couple of quarts of Bud at a deli before making their way back up towards St. Mark's Place.

"So you're going back out there? To Palestine?"

"Nobody's going, you know that," Stu took a big swig of beer after looking around for the cops. "We're all in our fifties, we can't go through all that shit again. Especially the way things are now. Besides, you know there's rumors about JC Lincoln having AIDS. That means it's never gonna happen."

"I'm sorry to hear it," Tina said as they walked up the store-lined street filled with tourists and college kids. "We're really gonna miss you up there. We were expecting you to be the leader of the band this time around."

"Wow, what an honor," Stu was sarcastic. "It wasn't anything David Diamond was any good at then, and he sure as hell can't do anything for anyone now."

"The one thing the dead can do is remind us of things," Tina waxed philosophically. "Where we were and what we've done to get to where we are."

"That's pretty deep for someone whose biggest concern was where the next party was going down," Stu patted her on the back. "I'm not goofing on you. I mean it as a compliment. You've changed more than any of us."

"But you're wrong. Everyone's changed. You learn more and more every day you go through this life."

"If that was true, why are we even discussing going back? It was the most traumatic experience of our lives. How could any of us ever think of it? I was kidnapped by those fanatics over there. I saw David Diamond killed right before my eyes. We accomplished more than any garage band in the history of music. Why in God's name would anyone want to attempt it again? I think you may want to check with Duke Gallegos and ask him if he would ever want to go back to boot camp. He'd tell you just how crazy you are."

"I've been going to the doctor lately. I don't know if I'm gonna be able to go. I'm gonna do everything I can to make it. I just want to make sure we're going as a group."

"Why, what's wrong?"

"They don't know yet," she lied. "They're taking tests, you know how it is."

"It's not anything serious, is it?"

"Who knows? Who cares? Look, I know there's people who could use the money. Johnny's not exactly rolling in money in Florida. I don't think Duke's expecting a golden parachute when he retires from the military, either."

"That schmuck," Stu smirked. "He was David's last hope before Hezbollah broke up. That sure backfired in his face. He thought he was gonna play weekend warrior and go double-dipping for the rest of his life. He sure never planned on 9/11."

"Well, Lucy's doing okay at the law firm. They'll be fine."

"So what's this about money? Everybody can use a little extra. I'm not rolling in it either, but it's not bad enough for me to want to go back into the desert for a couple of months and have those fanatics putting a target on my back again."

"I know Debbie wants it. I'm getting a bad feeling that it's all she's got."

"What?" Stu stared at her as he stopped in front of Mondo Kim's record shop, swigging his beer. "I thought she was all set with that private eye company of hers. Besides, she was seeing that other guy, that executive up in Canada. Don't tell me she blew that deal too."

"Maybe it's a woman thing, I don't know," Tina stared vacantly into the store window.

"Like mid-life crisis?" Stu seemed almost mournful. "Geez, time flies, huh?"

"Hey, you can't stand out here and drink, guys," the clerk came out from the store.

"Fuck off," they said in unison before heading back up the street.

"You know, I don't want to be the one to ruin anyone's hopes," Stu said finally. "I already regret having done that when I left Hezbollah. One thing I've always considered, though. If I hadn't come back and we hadn't gone to Palestine, the Tour might never have happened and David would still be alive. Sometimes things happen for a reason, and when you go back and try and change things, it doesn't go the way you thought they would. I think that's something we really need to think about."

"Maybe you're right," Tina exhaled. They stood at the corner of Third Avenue and finished off their quarts, immersed in thought.

The truth about her medical condition was on the tip of her tongue. She just thought that this wasn't the time.

They ended up breaking night together, talking about life until finally catching a cab by daylight. They would not see each other again until the funeral in Florida a couple of months later.

Chapter Seven

It was the next evening when Tina invited her nephew Carlos up to her apartment. It was a big treat for him as Tina rarely invited anyone to come up and visit. Tina had passed along strict rules about coming up uninvited over the years, and it was all about her privacy. She knew what a big thing it was for family members to be able to visit a Central Park apartment, but was determined to never allow her sanctuary to become anyone's hangout. Carlos was overjoyed to come by, but the mood was dampened when he learned the reason for the invitation.

"We live in different worlds, Carlos. I can never be part of yours, and I don't know if you'll ever want to be part of mine."

"What are you talking about, *Titi*?" Carlos stared wide-eyed at her. "You're my aunt, I love you, how could you ever say I'm not part of your world?"

"I'm not talking about you as my nephew, you know that," she came over and stroked his chin. "I'm talking about music. I'm not a hip hop person, I can't give your music what it deserves. And I'm not really in the music business, God is taking me other places at this time in my life."

"How could you ever leave the business, *Titi*?" he scoffed. "You're one of the greatest percussionists alive!"

"I can't play anymore, Carlos," her voice grew husky.

"What? What do you mean?"

"I can't hold the sticks anymore," she managed. "My hands are getting weak, I can't keep my grip like I used to. Maybe I overdid it with the band."

"C'mon, *Titi*, you're strong as a horse," he chuckled uneasily.

She came over to him and took him by his right wrist. She raised his forearm parallel and gripped it with both hands.

"This is all my strength."

"Geez," Carlos swallowed hard. "Does Mom know about this?"

"This is between you and I. I've got a lot of things going on with this right now and I can't afford distractions. I'll tell the family when the time is right, but not now. I just don't want you to think I don't want to help you. Besides, you've got the talent, and so does your group. You don't want anyone to say that your family helped you get to where you are one day. You can't even imagine how this journey is going to affect you and everyone else involved. You always want to look back and say it belonged to you and no one else."

"Oh, *Titi*," he moaned, tears streaming from his eyes as he took her in his arms for a long time. "I love you so much, you have no idea how much you mean to this family, and to me."

"Well, you mean a whole lot to me," she hugged him. "You're my only nephew. If I had a son, I'd want him to be just like you."

"I feel like you're a second mother, you're just like a mother to me."

"Your Mom's my little sister, and after your Grandma died sometimes I felt like Carmen was my daughter," Tina revealed. "I know I wasn't there for her as much as I could've been, but I've tried to make it up over the years, especially after your Dad left."

"So what is it you got?" he insisted, his eyes having that same mischievous spark and the cute little nose like his mother. Only that spark was being dampened by tears.

"Well," she said hesitantly, "it's muscular dystrophy. I don't think they can fix it."

"*Titi*, people die from that."

"Now, listen, baby, this is our secret, I haven't told anyone, not even my ex."

He fell into her arms and began sobbing as if his heart would break. She slapped him playfully on the ribs and gently worked him loose.

"Now look, I'm just fine right now. Let's have a good time together and enjoy ourselves. Why are we going to act like in some box six feet under while we've got some music to make?"

"I thought you just said we come from different worlds," he wiped his eyes on his shirt sleeve.

"Well, I can keep coming to yours like some kind of space invader," she replied, wiggling her fingers in his face and crossing her eyes, making him laugh.

"I love you, Titi."

"Hey, I'm hungry," she announced. "Let's go get *pasteles*."

She remembered the nightmare sequence after the show at the Valley of Megiddo, after the incredible victory, after the Israeli Army got them back safe to their hotel. The security forces decided it was best to get everyone back under lock and key, and have the press interviews at noon the next day. She had gotten used to the lockdown procedures and thought nothing of it. Most of the girls on the tour spent time either hanging out in each other's rooms or chatting on the phone with one another, so it wasn't like being in solitary confinement or anything.

It was well after midnight before the phone calls were lighting up the switchboard in the lobby, and Tina was among the last to know. Stu had snuck up to Princess Sabrina's penthouse and somehow or other they disappeared sometime thereafter. There were armed guards swarming the building, and it was announced that the band would be meeting in Billy Sixkiller's suite in a short time. When they came for Tina, she felt as if she was under arrest with a pair of riflemen before and after her on the way to the elevator.

The hallway outside Sixkiller's suite was clogged with IDF (*Israeli Defense Force) riflemen, and they made way as Tina was brought to the spacious chamber. There were a dozen plainclothes agents inside, along with the whole band, Billy Sixkiller, and Mossad assistant director Ben Mandel.

"Okay, guys," Tina was mildly surprised to see Duke Gallegos open the meeting. "I guess it's time to lay our cards on the table. The reason why I was able to play in the show was because the CIA assigned me to keep an eye on the rest of you. Everybody knows I'm with Special Forces anyway. They just gave me an upgrade and asked me to run with the pack."

"It looks like you're as lousy on watch as you are on guitar," David smirked, slouched in an armchair in a far corner. He got cursed and swore at by everyone before Duke continued.

"I know everyone was wondering about Billy," Duke continued. "Well, most of you were right. He doesn't work for Lincoln, he's also a CIA agent. We did a pretty good job until tonight. Somehow Stu slipped out of his room, and we think the

Princess had a lot to do with it. We're not clear on how it went down, but apparently one of the CLA (*Christian Liberation Army) guards were compromised. We found a body outside her suite and another man missing. It's possible the missing man was working with Hezbollah."

"So what the hell happens now? We leave here without Stu?" Johnny Carmona demanded.

"We've got a slim---very slim---chance of rescuing them," Ben Mandel spoke up. "We've got satellite coverage all over the area as well as aerial reconnaissance and ground patrols. Right now our biggest concern is stirring up armed confrontations with Hamas or the PLO, which would work to Hezbollah's advantage. It'll give them the diversion they'd need to move the hostages deeper into the desert where we won't be able to find them."

"We're figuring there's about two or three spots they may try to exfiltrate. They're either going to cross the border into Syria or move north into Lebanon," Billy explained. "We've alerted President al-Assad's forces, so Syria could be a bad move unless they've already crossed over. Lebanon's their best move, but again, if we stir up the hornet's nest we could be going up against one of the other militant groups and further endangering the hostages."

"Our gambit would be to send in a unit that resembles a haphazard interception," Mandel interjected. "If we could make it look like a half-assed rescue team got picked off and turned in by militants, it could get us inside the enemy stronghold and pinpoint its location."

"There's one thing I don't follow," David retorted. "You Jews have all the money in the world, and there's this Princess of Palestine on the line. Why don't you just buy her back?"

"As ignorant and misinformed as your statement is, it is the policy of both your government and ours that we don't deal with terrorists. Besides, we're in the middle of the oil well oasis of the world. *They* have all the money in *this* world."

"Point taken," David grinned. "Okay, me and three of my creepy crawlers'll go with you. You can have some raghead impersonators pretend they caught us and bring us in. Put a transponder on the vehicle and I'll have saved Stu Carlucci's ass once again."

"Negative," Duke replied. "You're crazy enough to give us a half-assed chance. Those zombies of yours are walking dead already. We don't need to be bringing casualties with us. I'll take you, not them."

"Well, one of me is worth three of them," Debbie decided. "Count me in."

"No fuckin' way, Munson. Request denied," David yawned.

"Hey, I can kick your ass right here and now," she challenged him. "If he goes I go."

"We were actually thinking of using a Debbie Munson lookalike," Mandel shrugged. "I'm good with it considering the time element."

"So that leaves me and Roth," Johnny spoke up. "We're the tough guys, no way we don't go, right, Roth?"

"Sounds good to me," Roth spread his palms. Everyone knew he would follow Johnny through the gates of hell when all was said and done.

"Okay, we've got our team," Billy exhaled tautly. "Mossad and the IDF suggests we get this show on the road ASAP. You'll be briefed on the way to the command center. We'll give you directions to the rendezvous point where you'll be intercepted by our agents and brought in as prisoners. No matter what happens, you are not to engage in any physical altercations whatsoever. These people are extremely dangerous, and there is an outside chance our rescue attempt may be compromised. If you're not good with this, you can stand down at any time. We're not going to bullshit you, your lives are at high risk here."

"If any of us were in Stu's place, he'd be the first one to volunteer," Debbie insisted. "We're all friends to the end. This whole tour wouldn't mean a damn thing if we leave one of our people behind. Let's go get Stu back and get the hell outta here."

"You go, Munson," David chuckled wryly.

"Hey, wait a second," Tina insisted. "The whole band's going except me? You better make room in that ride of yours. You're not leaving me behind."

"Sorry, there's no way I'm putting more than four people in a car," Mandel replied. "Besides, you're too well known. There's no way in hell the terrorists will believe you got out of this hotel without anybody noticing. They'll know it's some kind of trap."

"You're not going anywhere, you dumb shit," David walked

over to her, pulling her off the couch and hugging her tight. "You're so clumsy, you'd trip over your own feet. You just take my calls, tell them I'll be back in the morning."

"Damn you, David, you be careful," tears began spilling down Tina's cheeks. "All of you be careful."

It was almost as if the whole world collapsed in the next six hours. The rescue team returned and remained incommunicado, snippets of information coming back to her and Susie and the creepy crawlers as time dragged on. Their hearts were in their throats when one of Mandel's agents came to inform them that Stu had been rescued and everyone returned safely except for David. Both Tina and Susie collapsed into sobs, the creepy crawlers devastated by the news. They were also informed that the team had been taken in for debriefing and would not return to the hotel for another hour at best.

It would be years before everything got sorted out, and for some of them it never did. It was a 9/11 scenario in the USA, critics everywhere prepared to accuse James Lincoln of profiting from the disaster if he made an attempt to release films or recordings of the concert event. He nearly went bankrupt until a year later when Princess Sabrina finally convinced French promoters to underwrite the screen debut of the Crusader Concert Tour. The focus was on Lincoln's performances, marginalizing the grunge shows out of respect for David. It was only when live recordings of the grunge sets were released did Hezbollah get the recognition they had so long awaited.

Whenever she dwelled on those dark days it made her sick, made her want to drink and get polluted enough to forget. She had trained her mind to dig deeper, back to the happier times. She remembered Stu again, the one who could always put a smile on her face. He was always encouraging her, challenging her to dig a little deeper, push herself a little further. Somehow he was able to bring her sunshine even on his own cloudy days.

That was certainly the case when they played their Up Against The Wall show at Memorial Park over twenty years ago. David had somehow gotten a City permit to play at the park, and he had invited both the Speedies and the Beastie Boys to appear at the event. The local icons never responded, and so it was that David was left to his own devices. He plastered South Brooklyn and Alphabet City with flyers announcing the show on the lawn facing the Memorial Wall. It was a place where David had played pickup football as a boy, and there was no doubt that it would be one of the biggest spots for a mosh pit anyone could hope for.

Tina remembered having her drumming pads set up on the opposite side of the wall where the roadies were unloading the equipment from their rented trucks. She was living on cheese and crackers as was most of them, having sacrificed her welfare checks for a $1,000 Pearl drum set. She was practicing her rolls on the pads as Stu ambled over, having tuned his guitar for the umpteenth time.

"Ready to crash and burn?" Stu stood by where she sat on the ground, her drum pads beneath her knees as she sat on the marble ledge behind the wall.

"Screw you, Stewie. I'm gonna *slash* and burn, you wait and see."

"You're starting to sound just like him," Stu shook his head. "Have you seen the song list? We're not playing a gig here, this is a hardcore punk rally."

"I don't see what difference it makes," Tina insisted. "We might get a couple hundred people out here. That's more than fits in that A7 dump."

"I just don't fit here anymore," Stu was wistful. "You guys are all just going in a different direction. Even Duke, of all people. He's twice as good as he was when we first started. For that matter, so are you and Debbie. I'd think you two would want something better."

"One show doesn't mean that this is all we're ever gonna do," Tina was adamant. "David's just trying to get us some recognition. The Beastie Boys are headlining at CBGB's and the Speedies are regulars at Max's Kansas City. He can't get us in either one of those places. Look at all we've invested in the band. How can we accept playing in Puerto Rican bars here in Brooklyn forever? Our equipment doesn't even fit in these places."

"I've said it before and I'll say it again, and I know it really doesn't make any difference," Stu sat down alongside her. "It's all about nailing an agent or a record contract. If we get an agent he can get us paying gigs out on the Island and New Jersey. We can get exposure in the newspapers and put together enough money to make our own demo. If we can get a contract with some small label somewhere, it's better than a demo. We'll have vinyl we can send to the big labels and get the deal we deserve. He's trying to take a shortcut, and there are no shortcuts in this business. And I'm not sticking around to beat my head against the wall with this guy any longer."

"You built this band, Stu," Tina put down her sticks, wiping her brow in the summer heat. "Debbie and I wouldn't have gotten anywhere this quick if it wasn't for you. How are you gonna walk away now when we're so close?"

"I'm a musician, Tee," Stu looked out at Cadman Plaza and the Brooklyn Bridge beyond it. The trickle of black-clad headbangers began to thicken as they made their way across from Lower Manhattan to the open-air concert. "I'm a songwriter. I'm here to make music, not to create a spectacle. I just can't believe that none of you can tell the difference."

"I don't believe you're gonna walk, Stu," Tina picked up her goalie mask.

"Seeing is believing," Stu walked away.

It would turn into one of those events they would forever regret as horribly-blurred videos of the show would be sold on EBay for over a thousand dollars a quarter century later. The thrashers went into motion from the opening tune, and Duke and Debbie were happy to indulge them in turning up their amps full-blast. David followed suit as did Johnny, and soon the sound devolved into a white-noise howl of waterfall feedback. Stu was content to turn up all the way and practice his new leads, barely concerned as to whether they fit the song they were playing. It was never detected as the roar made almost all the harmonies from the vocals to the lead riffs indecipherable. Just as David predicted, over two hundred creepy crawlers showed up for the event. Just as Stu told them, he called David and told him he was leaving the band.

The band floundered for a year until Duke announced he had joined the Army. That was the end of Hezbollah, even though Tina always wondered why they didn't try to keep it going as a noisecore band. Still, everything happened for a reason. Debbie would have never started her private investigation agency, Johnny would have never fought in Madison Square Garden, and Tina would have never dedicated herself to her percussion studies. Stu may have found his own path of enlightenment, but so did they all.

History would record that they would reunite at the behest

of James Lincoln and play in the Valley of Megiddo. They would survive to become an underground legend. Only now it was a question of whether they could---or would---do it one more time.

One mo' time.

She only hoped she would live long enough to be there if they needed her.

Tick-tock.

Tick-tock.

Chapter Eight

The roar from the audience was deafening, even before she made it to stage level. It had a palpable presence that combined with the humidity making it almost unbearable.

"Tina! Tina! Tina!"

David and Johnny had gone out first to a tumultuous response from the fans. David stood with arms akimbo, smirking at the hordes from alongside his keyboard while Johnny pranced and bounded across the stage as if prepping for a ten-round fight. Stu followed them out and got a standing ovation from knowledgeable music fans who knew the story of his journey to this pinnacle.

The thunderous response to Tina's appearance seemed to have caused to stage to bend in its ferocity. She swallowed hard and wiped a tear from her eye, taking a quick bow before rushing up to her throne at the platform at the rear of the stage. She did a quick succession of rolls to warm up and was nearly embarrassed by the reaction of the fans to the innocuous exercise.

It seemed as if heaven and hell reserved their thunder for Debbie Munson, who jogged briskly onstage pumping her fist somewhat tentatively, as if embarrassed as Tina by the adulation. She ran into Johnny's arms, then gave high fives to Stu and David before strapping on her bass and sprinting up the platform steps to where Tina sat.

"Can you fucking believe this?" Debbie yelled to Tina.

"No," Tina managed through a tear-choked haze.

Debbie let loose a torrent of bass notes that was as mortar fire throughout the valley, raising the decibel level of the masses to ever greater thresholds. Tina thumped her bass pedal in response and the valley became as a volcano.

"How many times do I have to ask you girls to keep it down?" David's voice echoed through the valley as the crowd broke out in a cacophony of exuberant cheers and catcalls.

"You asked for it, you got it!" Johnny screamed into the

microphone. "The roughest, toughest group on earth, the Band of Steel... Hezbollah!"

David's keyboard riffs screamed across the plain, the girls quick to hammer down the foundation against which Stu and Duke's guitar riffs screamed and soared. They broke into "Welcome To The Party", "Play Unitl You're Dead" and "Overnight Celebrities" before Stu challenged Duke and David to a blues/jazz jam. The girls laughed at each other as they missed riff after riff while the audience and the other musicians remained transfixed by the magic of Stu's fretboard wizardry.

The Israelis had dealt themselves heavily into the marketing deal on the project and had secured the satellite broadcasting rights for Radio Hebron which would transmit the show across the globe on closed-circuit networks. They had suggested the idea of setting up colossal TV screens around the field which would give spectators in the furthermost areas a clear view of the proceedings. The countless multitude exploded into tumultuous applause which turned to joyous laughter and cheering as close-up shots of Debbie and Tina caught them making cross-eyes and pigfaces at each other.

"*Tina! Tina!*" came the chants. "*Debbie! Debbie!*"

"Well, I guess if you live long enough you'll see everything," David shook his head.

"You got that right," Stu retorted over the mic, getting a big pop from the crowd for ribbing David's newfound keyboard skills.

"Okay, if you insist," David shrugged, and at once the band toned down and brought Tina into the strains of "Dream A Little Dream Of Me." The valley became eerily quiet save for occasional screams for Tina, and the darkness was lit by thousands of cigarette lighters saluting her torch song.

"Well, let's hear it for Tina," David was nearly drowned out by the hordes at song's end, "and for El Kabong". Stu gave him the finger as he set aside the acoustic guitar he used for the song.

"Okay," Debbie stepped up to the mic, "here's a song by a crazy Irish bitch about another crazy Irish bitch. This song's called 'Gloria'."

The throng went wild as David winked, bringing his new game to the next level as he led the band into Laura Brannigan's chart-topping song. The plains reverberated as Debbie cajoled the fans into singing along with the chorus. She was as a banshee screaming like a meteor with the band erupting behind her over the crowded valley.

"We don't want to keep you soul music fans waiting," David smirked as he swaggered to the mic. "We've got one more, it's our theme song, as well as that of one of the sponsors of our show."

The crescendo was deafening as Stu, Duke and Debbie gathered around Johnny, breaking into their new song, "Hezbollah". Flashing cameras turned the field into an explosion of tiny lights as thousands captured the end of the phenomenal event on film. Johnny ran back and forth along the edge of the stage like a madman, nearly falling off a few times as he screamed the lyrics across the valley.

> *You're not restricted by time or space*
> *You got your pieces all over the place*
> *And you don't care who or what is in your way*
> *It's all about how many you kill today*

Stu and Duke shared a mic as they caterwauled the chorus, stepping back intermittently as Duke hammered down the chords, Stu ripping the night with his blazing leads. David was as a demon in a Goethe play, fiendishly hammering the keyboards with a devilish grin on his bony face. Debbie shrieked the chorus lines into her mic, tresses billowing as a crimson witch as the desert wind whipped across the stage.

> *Hezbollah…you know you're gonna get it*
> *Hezbollah…you know you'll regret it*
> *Hezbollah…Armageddon is waiting for you…*

At song's end, it seemed as if the valley would explode, virtually shaking from the roar as the band members tossed their instruments aside and rushed to one another in jubilation. The emotion rose to ever greater proportions as the throng watched longtime rivals Stu and Duke holding each other in a mighty embrace, Johnny pulling Roth and Isabel onstage to join him and

Tina in a victory dance, and Debbie rushing into David's arms though shocked that she nearly bowled him over in his cadaverous state.

There had been bootleg tape and home recordings of the gig, but as everyone learns, tapes and CD's are magnetic and become depolarized in time. J.C. Lincoln's videos were now worth a ton of money but Tina, along with everyone else, was seriously doubting he was going to get $150 million for them. It was labeled the greatest underground rock show of all time, but in a world dominated by Lady Gaga and Justin Bieber, J.C.'s reach may have finally exceeded his grasp.

The reality was that if J.C. was as sick as they said he was, there was no way in hell he was ever going to go on stage and perform in a show of this magnitude. There were no more Woodstocks. This was going to be the last show of its kind, and it was doubtful that the Israelis were ever going to sanction it. The Palestinian free state ended up in disaster, and the next time it ever came to pass, there would be military troops filling the Valley of Megiddo instead of rock fans. There might be another Peace in the Middle East Concert, but a dying J.C. Lincoln was not going to be the one to pull it off.

Yet Tina could not help but consider the fact that it was a dying David Diamond who fought against all odds to make the Nineties concert a reality. David was nearly wasted by cancer, and when they did the autopsy after he was killed, they found enough in his stomach to declare it a miracle that he was able to stand erect on stage that night. Maybe he had forestalled his death long enough to create a miracle, but she doubted Lincoln was as tough as David.

She realized it was time for her to call Debbie Munson.

Her heart went out to Debbie the minute they saw each other in the front area of Keene's Steak House on West 36th Street. She was still drop-dead gorgeous, but it was not hard to see that she had blossomed from a glamorous young girl to a beautiful mature woman. Tina was considered by everyone to be a sexy, attractive lady but was thankful that her looks had never defined her as they had Debbie and Isabel Cabales. It was hard enough getting older without having to worry about one's looks adding insult to injury.

78

"Hey, bitch," Debbie wore a $500 white business skirt suit, Gucci purse and shades, squeezing Tina hard enough to take her breath away. Tina exchanged hugs and kisses before the maître d' escorted them to their table. She could not help but notice that half the men in the place were watching Debbie's butt.

"Well, you look great," Tina chuckled. "How's life treating you?"

"Like shit. I've got these new kids whining about the surveillance jobs and I'm getting burned out on the insurance claims. I never thought after twenty-five years I'd still be busting my ass doing this stuff," Debbie stirred her margarita.

"It'll get better. It always does."

"So what's this thing about going back to Palestine? Are you coming in on it?"

"I don't know," Tina frowned, sipping her blush wine. "I was hanging out with Stu the other day. I don't think he wants to go."

"You mean that son of a bitch answered the phone?"

"No, he called me."

"Ooh. Wait until I get my hands on him."

"He says you call and hang up before he can get to the phone."

"I can't stand that fucked-up answering machine of his."

"Well, there you go. Two people calling each other who don't leave messages."

"So why doesn't he want to go? Are you going?"

"He doesn't think he can go through all that again. I'm having trouble with my hands. I'm not sure I can do it, not like that, not the way we play."

"You got money up the ass. Why don't you hire a backup to play offstage, like Elvis did? You can even have somebody run a drum machine. All you'd have to do is sit there."

"Hmm," Tina mused. "Now there's an idea."

"I got some crazy kid calling the office for about two weeks now," Debbie leaned back in her seat. "I made the mistake of calling about some ad on Craigslist for a start-up punk band. I don't want to blow him off, because I know I need to get some stage time if we go through with this. I haven't picked up that bass in about five years, at least."

"Well, I kept inviting you to come out and jam, and you just kept blowing me off."

"C'mon, what are we gonna do, sit around and play along with tapes? It'd be shit if we got together by ourselves. If you brought that husband of yours, it'd be worse than shit."

"We're divorced, smarty," Tina chided her. "He wouldn't come anyway. Besides, what's wrong with playing along with tapes? That's how we learned to play in the first place, remember? It'd be just like the old days, it'd be fun."

"Hey, we played at Armageddon, and you expect to go back and play with tapes?" Debbie squinted at her. "We could get a couple dozen kids to come to any studio in New York to come out and jam with us."

"There you go," Tina smiled as the waiter brought their shrimp cocktails.

"So you're not gonna do it."

"I don't know if I can," Tina insisted. "I won't be the holdout, though, I'll tell you that. If everyone else goes I'll go. You know Dukie's still in Iraq, and Johnny's training those boxers down in Florida. We might be able to talk Stu into it, but who knows if Dukie and Johnny can go. I haven't heard anything from either one of them. I spoke to Johnny and Roth and Issy last year around the holidays, but I haven't heard from Dukie for years."

"If we get Stu we don't need Duke," Debbie said flatly.

"That might be a big if. I told you, he's got lots of stuff in his head from last time."

"Well, damn, if you didn't want to do it you should've just said so," Debbie seemed upset.

"Aw, come on!" Tina was disappointed. "Are you telling me that's the only reason you came out?"

"You know better than that," Debbie stared at her.

"Well, good. You almost hurt my feelings. Now, listen, tell me the truth. You're my best friend, you know that. Is it about the money? You said it yourself, I'm doing okay. And besides, I'm sick. I don't want to leave behind anything that someone else can use, especially you. You know what I'm saying?"

"What the fuck are you saying?" Debbie demanded. "What's wrong? You need to tell me the truth. What's going on? I know you're lying to me."

"I'm not gonna lie," Tina was adamant. "I'm not gonna tell you a bunch of stuff and get you upset over nothing. They're doing tests, there might be some kind of nerve damage. They're telling me I shouldn't be playing. You know doctors, they're full of shit most of the time. They find out you got money and all of a sudden they have all these expensive tests you got to take."

"Yeah, yeah," Debbie exhaled, taking a bite of jumbo shrimp. "I'm in the business, I know the deal. We took down one doctor who ripped some rich old lady off for almost nine mil for what amounted to $500k of treatment at most. It makes you sick. If we walked away from this next show with some decent money, I'd go ahead and retire, I swear."

"A hundred grand?" Tina lowered her voice. "Suppose I gave you a hundred grand?"

"Stop it!" Debbie slapped her hand on his table before wiping her eyes. "You're scaring me, shut the hell up. You're gonna make me cry. I don't want your money. It's me. I need to do this. I'm gonna be fifty years old. I need to prove to myself I can do this. If I don't do this I'll spend the rest of my life wishing I did, I know it."

"But you don't have anything to prove, none of us do," Tina was emphatic. "We played the show, we stuck it out even though those Arabs were threatening our lives on TV. You go on the Internet and people say it was the greatest live show of all time. People say Debbie Munson is the greatest female bassist of all time. Plus you went in there with the guys and rescued Stu and the Princess, you saved their lives. You can't do it again, it's impossible. God forbid you would have to do it again."

"Okay, forget the rescue stuff, I know that's not happening," Tina saw the emerald fire in her eyes. "I'm talking about just playing, and enjoying the experience this time. The last time we were a bunch of stupid loudmouthed kids. We didn't see or do anything, we didn't even go see where Jesus died. I was walking around the whole time hooked up to Mel Dalton. We had the Mossad, the IDF and the CLA following us everywhere we went. I don't even think they have a Hezbollah anymore. If they do, they'd probably pay us for the publicity."

"Yeah, sure."

"Who cares anyway? There'll be no pressure whatsoever. Who's gonna give a shit about a bunch of forty-somethings wandering around in the desert playing punk rock? The biggest problem we'll have is getting a permit to play in the Valley of Megiddo from the Israelis."

"They say James Lincoln has AIDS. That's worse than

having muscular dystrophy. Your immune system starts shutting down. I don't know a whole lot about that stuff, but suppose he got some kind of regional virus? It could kill him before we got close to showtime."

"Nah, bullshit," Debbie washed down a piece of shrimp with a sip of margarita. "Those Arabs over there got all the money in the world. They can load him up full of super-drugs and make him good as new. Matter of fact, this could be the best thing for him. You know how it is in this country. It takes them ten years and millions of dead people before they approve the use of any new drugs. Over there, if it works, they use it. If he goes over there, he can buy his way into one of their hospitals and it could save his life. Besides, you know they see him like some kind of folk hero over there. He's the black guy who played the Peace in the Middle East Concert. He's like the Barack Obama of R&B. They might even treat him for free."

"Listen to what you're saying," Tina managed a smile. "He's gonna go over there and check into a hospital to get treated for AIDS. How's he gonna play a concert?"

"Hey, dumbo. Who gives a shit?" Debbie made a face at her. "Once we sign the papers and we show up over there, it's game on. We become the main event, he can get a brain transplant for all we care, right?"

"Okay, so nobody's gonna care if the Barack Obama of R&B plays or not. Everybody'll be glad to watch a bunch of fifty year old punk rockers instead, right?"

"Hey, whose DVD's are being watched all over the planet?" Debbie arched her eyebrows. "I heard people are getting $100 for shitty bootlegs of our show on EBay. You might get to see his part of the show on some MTV nostalgia feature or some black network segment. Nobody gives a shit about R&B. Everybody still gets off on punk. They play Ramones songs at football and hockey games all the time. We're forever."

Tina finally changed the subject and Debbie had little problem with it. This had become Debbie's crusade, and sitting here arguing was not going to change it. Tina was not about to tell her how sick she was. It would be a double whammy she wouldn't be able to deal with.

She would find out in time---just like everyone else.

Chapter Nine

Tina remembered inviting Zeke out to Paco Cabales' beachfront home on the Jersey Shore shortly before the Crusader Concert Tour began. Paco had been David Diamond's best friend in the old days, and two of his daughters married members of the band. Paco was a neighborhood legend back in South Brooklyn before Hezbollah. He fought in WWII, Korea and Vietnam, was in the Rangers and Green Berets, and had five Silver Stars and five Bronze Stars. After Hezbollah he became part of the underground cult legend.

Paco was one of the thousands of Vietnam vets who got sprayed with Agent Orange during the war. He was dragged into the class action lawsuit, and when his ship came in he bought the beach home for himself and his daughters. He decided to hold a housewarming party for the old gang, and it coincided with the bombshell announcement that Hezbollah was being invited the Palestine by James "Continental" Lincoln. It was a momentous occasion for one and all, and Tina decided she was not going to leave Zeke out of it.

He tugged at her heart strings from the moment he walked through the door. She had arrived early in great anticipation of seeing the old gang after almost a half decade, and wanted to be right there with Paco greeting the arrivals. She shared his pride and joy in seeing each and every one of them come through the door, from his daughters to the band members to David's creepy crawlers. She didn't feel so bad about Zeke being somewhat of an outsider after David brought those guys. It was almost as if someone's hick town uncle had thought nothing of bringing his dogs to a birthday party.

She shared Paco's joy in greeting his daughters Isabel and Lucy, and was just as exhilarated to see David, Stu, Duke, Johnny, Roth and Debbie again. Zeke was very diplomatic with everyone, even knocking down a beer with David as they discussed the Lower Manhattan music scene. She always knew that they respected each other as men though they had no time for one another as musicians. Zeke remained very much the gentleman, and it wasn't until Debbie and David nearly knocked over one of Paco's lampstands did they decide to take a walk outside along the beach by themselves.

"So you're going to Palestine with these people," Zeke asked, cutting a sexy figure in his black clothing, his dark hair fluttering in the river breeze. "Do you ever read the papers or watch TV? They stone women over there for going around without veils. How do you think they're gonna take Debbie Munson and the Guttermouth Gang?"

"We're talking a hundred grand per person," Tina replied, causing Zeke's eyes to widen. "I mentioned it to my sister Carmen, she's got a secretary job on Wall Street. Her friends told her that I'd be smart to put half of it in stocks. I could live on the rest and go on tour without having to worry about paying bills for a year, see where it takes me."

"Did he put that in writing?" Zeke cleared his throat.

"C'mon, this is James Lincoln."

"What, you don't think these music industry douchebags don't renege on their promises? Don't you remember what happened with me and Columbia? We laid the basic tracks for fourteen songs before they yanked the rug out from under us. It's all about the bean counters. The minute their economists predict a possible loss, they pull the plug with no questions asked."

"Yeah, but Carmen's friends say that the Arabs're bankrolling the whole deal through Princess Sabrina," Tina insisted. "You know, why is it that you're never happy for me? Why do I have to defend everything I do?"

"I don't want to see you get hurt, that's all. Those friends of yours, they probably want this so bad they'd do it for ten grand. You get a lawyer to work for a percentage, and tell Lincoln to send him a copy of the contract before you start making plans. At least do that."

"Well, I don't know any lawyers."

"You can use mine. Barney Ross, he's an entertainment attorney, specializes in contracts. He'll probably charge you a grand but he'll assure you the deal is iron-clad. Matter of fact, he doesn't step away from the table until it is. He'll send it back twice for alterations, the third time he's talking fraudulent business practices. People don't mess with this guy."

84

"I appreciate it. Sometimes it seems like you care."

"See? This is how it starts," Zeke was exasperated. "I only came out here to be with you for the holidays. It's hard for me to be in the same room with David, and Debbie's no better. You know, I actually picked up a copy of that book of his, *The Excommunicant*. I found it in this rathole book store in the Village. I don't know how he could possibly be making any money off it. The best he'll do is the sales he *might* make off the Tour, if there ever is one. I'll tell you, I never read such blasphemous, obscene, rambling scribble in my whole life."

"Well, it's paying his bills. He's doing as well as either of us are."

"Yeah, well it looks to me like they're gonna be riding your skirt tails on this deal."

"Everybody in there's doing okay. You don't need to be putting down my friends all the time. What makes you better than them anyway?"

"I don't know, you tell me. You married me."

"Yeah, and I divorced you, too," she couldn't help herself.

"You're my wife, and you always will be," he growled, pulling her into his arms and lowering her to the sand before crushing his lips against hers. She had gone so long without a man that her heart raced with anticipation. She felt him undoing her jeans and pulling them down. She had always had a fantasy of sex on the beach, and she would always remember thinking that it was going to be as good a time as any.

She hoped beyond hope that things would start improving between them, but as the next week progressed, the chest-thumping grew louder and louder until she couldn't hear his words any longer. He went on and on about David and Debbie as if to test her loyalties, to see how much she would take before she began defending them. She had been caught in the trap too many times. She knew the next part was about how her loyalties were with them instead of him, like a child trying to get his mother to take sides in a sibling rivalry. That was the opening bell for the next fight, and she no longer had it in her.

Her visit to her sister Carmen that next week was no more or less edifying. Carmen was getting close to a second marriage and seemed no happier than she was during her first. The new guy was a minor-league baseball player who was flying back and forth from Puerto Rico trying to keep their relationship alive. There were dozens of calls, most of which ended in bitter recriminations and shouting matches which Carmen won by hanging up the phone and pulling the plug out of the wall.

Tina caught a cab to Carmen's high-rise apartment building, which drew lots of attention outside as it usually indicated someone was arriving from out of town or the hospital. Fortunately at this time of the morning, there weren't enough people who could afford squandering minutes of travel time to work to inquire. Carmen would be preparing for work as well, but had no problem setting out an extra cup of coffee and toast for her beloved sister.

"Tina, you got to be kidding me. Are you sure?"

"You must really think I've got a sick sense of humor."

Zeke Cohen dropped his forehead against his clenched hands and remained there for a long while. He finally looked up at her with tears streaming from his eyes.

"You don't lay down a ton of money at the first garage you go to," he managed. "You get a couple of other estimates and then you decide."

"They already have their second opinions, and thirds. This is final."

"What…what are we gonna do?"

"We'll just go back to doing whatever we always do," she walked back to her kitchenette. "You want coffee?"

"It's time for you to come home," his voice broke to a near-whisper. "Let this place go, sub-let it, whatever. Your terms, whatever you want, I don't care. I want you to come home."

"Listen to you!" she marveled at him. "You think you can shovel shit over anything, don't you!"

"This isn't shit, Tina."

"Oh, no?" she confronted him. "Just like you trying to screw anything that moved during five years of marriage, and pulling that control freak act on me like I was the one messing up? You're a user, Zeke, and I don't think I have anything left you can use."

"Okay," he wiped his eyes, "maybe I wasn't the kind of man I wanted to be. Maybe I had some kind of psychological thing. Maybe I was trying to prove that women found me attractive. That had nothing to do with how I felt about you."

86

"It had everything to do with me! You didn't think my love was enough for you!"

"Yes it was. But it wasn't all your love. You loved music."

"So did you!"

"Not more than you. Never more than you."

"Don't you think it's a little late for all this?"

"No. Please. Come back to me."

Tina stared out the window for a long time, the image of Zeke in the glass looming over the shoulder of her own. Somehow he had always been there, an angel on her shoulder, someone who was always there during good times and bad. She did not always abide by what he had to say, but he was always there nonetheless.

"I don't know if I want to close it down here," she said without facing him, "but I'll come by tomorrow and we'll talk. Okay?"

"Okay." With that he turned and left.

She decided to stop by Carmen's apartment the next morning, wrestling with the idea of telling her what was going on. It was the whole idea of having to put up with the caterwauling that bothered her. She fell apart at their mother's funeral, and Tina was pretty sure this was going to be a repeat performance along an extended run. There would be daily phone calls, blubbering and howling, and the kids. Oh, God forbid, the kids.

"Why do you have to come by so early? You know I have to be at work," Carmen griped as she flittered from room to room, pulling off articles of clothing and replacing them with others, putting on makeup and combing her hair while making them both toast and coffee. Tina had a soft spot in her heart for toast and coffee. She remembered how Debbie's mother always gave her toast and coffee when she went up to visit in the mornings. Those were some of the best breakfasts she ever had.

"What, do you want me to leave?"

"You know better than that. Those kids are gonna be all over my case when they find out you were here while they were out. All you had to do was call and I could have you over for dinner."

"You're my sister, can't I come by and see you if I feel like it?" Tina remembered how their Mom used to fuss when they came by unannounced. She wanted time to get the house straightened up and have a meal ready. She never seemed to understand that they didn't give a damn if the house was hit by a tornado and there wasn't a bite to eat.

"I'm glad you came, you silly nut," Carmen grabbed her from behind and squeezed her neck as she flew past en route to the bathroom. "I just want everything to be right when you come by, and I want the kids to see you. They worship the ground you walk on, you know that."

"Well, I love them, and I love you," Tina managed. "I---I just wanted to talk to you."

"Yeah, what's wrong now?" she said as she began running the shower, running back out long enough to bring Tina's toast and coffee over.

"Did you get anything back from the doctor's office?"

"Yeah," Carmen replied, filling her mouth with toothpaste. "What about you?"

"You first," Tina draped her hands over the back of the dining room chair, resting her chin as she watched Carmen.

"I've been thinking about it. I don't think it's gonna happen."

"What do you mean, not gonna happen?"

"You heard. I've got enough to deal with raising two kids."

"Are you talking about getting an abortion?"

"No, I'm gonna close my eyes and wish it away, stupid."

"You can't take a life just like that. That's a brother or sister to your kids. That's my niece or nephew. That's family."

"Yeah? Well, why don't you squeeze one out for a change? It's easy for you to say, sitting up there on Central Park with all that money. Maybe if you gave Zeke a kid, your attitude would change. You get your belly stretched for a year and change diapers for the next two, see what you think then."

"How can you say that? Look at those kids you have."

"Yeah, well, I'm over forty years old. I can't take time off work, people are gonna look at me like an idiot. Plus, Luis is gonna bail on me when he finds out. He can't even take care of himself, much less a kid. I can't even get him to commit to moving in with me. He doesn't deserve being the father of my kid."

"How do you know? Maybe it'll straighten him up. Why don't you tell him first?"

"Bullshit," she said after brushing her teeth and spitting the paste into the toilet. "He's gonna pull that Latino male routine and tell me how he wants a kid in his life. He thinks it'll be like some pet he gets to come over to play with whenever he feels like it. He thinks he gets to have a grandkid without having a kid first. Once he realizes he has responsibilities, see how fast he starts moving towards the door."

"You can't do it, Carmen. Suppose we lose another member of the family? There'll be one less, then another, then another. Soon there'll be no one left."

"What do you mean?" Carmen stopped short after pulling her dress over her head, staring at Tina.

"Just what I said."

"What did the doctor tell you? What's going on?"

"Don't change the subject. You need to think about what you're doing."

"No you don't. You're using this as an excuse to keep a secret from me. I want to know what the doctor said."

"We'll discuss it after we finish talking about you."

"Uh-uh, no, ma'am," Carmen came over and stood before Tina. "My daughter came in here a few weeks ago after visiting you and she was all messed up. I thought you two had an argument but she swore it was something else. She's been locking herself in her room, she hasn't been herself ever since. You told her, didn't you?"

"Told her what?"

"Don't you give me your double-talk! I'll get it out of her, I'll go to your doctor's office! I'll call Zeke right now and make him tell me!"

"Okay, I'll just leave if you're gonna have an attitude."

"No, you finish your toast," Carmen grunted, storming off to finish brushing her hair. Tina could see her watching from the next room as she ate one piece and washed it down with coffee.

"Look, why don't you put it up for adoption?" Tina asked. "Did you ever think of that?"

"You're not getting away with this," Carmen came back into the living room, her waist-length hair growing thicker as she groomed it. "I'm coming over your place after work and you're gonna tell me everything. And don't even think about going out drinking because I'll call Zeke and we'll go find you."

"It's not good," Tina exhaled tautly.

"What's not good?" Carmen's voice trembled.

"The tests. Look, you come by tonight, I'll show you the papers. Come by yourself, okay?"

"Dammit, why don't you tell me now?"

"I don't want you to get all worked up. I'm gonna get a second opinion."

"See, I'm gonna be messed up all day," Carmen began crying.

"Look, why don't we just forget it?"

"No, I'll be there by myself. We'll talk then, okay?"

"Fine," Tina stared at her. "You better not kill that kid. You either have it or give it to someone."

"We'll talk about it tonight."

The sisters both realized this was going to be one of the longest days of their lives together.

Chapter Ten

"Ms. Rivera, we are going to have to request that you do not leave this room under any circumstances."

"Why?" she jumped from her bed as Dr. Sardaq strode into the room along with two of his blackguards.

"There was a terrorist operation conducted earlier this evening against certain members of your troupe," Sardaq peered out the window at the twinkling city lights below. "Mr. Carlucci was abducted shortly after having been a guest at the suite of the Princess Sabrina. The Mossad felt that involvement by elements of the IDF might have led to the murder of the hostage by the extremists. They engineered a high-risk commando maneuver that resulted in the rescue of the hostage at the cost of the life of one of your companions. Our concern now is to avoid further exposure of your entourage to minimize the possibility of retaliation by the subversives."

"One of my…companions," Tina managed.

"I regret to inform you that Mr. David Diamond is dead."

Tina threw the lamp on her night table across the room where it shattered the large mirror over the dresser. As she bounded off her bed she was intercepted by Sardaq's men and held until her hysteria subsided.

"If it is of any consolation," Sardaq explained, "we were told that you were excluded from the arrangement due to the fact that your fame would have compromised the rescue attempt they were planning. As it turned out, the Mossad was able to take advantage of your friends' life experience to set a trap for the kidnappers. Someone as well known as you would have placed the operation at risk."

"They couldn't have even told me?" she raged. "Not even Debbie?"

"The time element was unstable," Sardaq motioned to his men to clean up the mess. "The Mossad summoned key members of the group to Sgt. Gallegos' room. Mr. Diamond apparently sensed something was transpiring and joined the group. The Mossad was against both he and Mr. Almontaser participating but they were voted down."

"Participating in *what*?"

"The CIA was able to locate the abductors via satellite tracking. The victim was taken to a heavily-guarded property along the West Bank. If the IDF would have intervened the victim would have been murdered immediately. The Mossad decided that a small group disguised as Bedouins would have the best chance of infiltrating the camp. The decision was to have Ms. Munson and Mr. Diamond brought in as captives. The rescue group was successful but there was an exchange of gunfire and Mr. Diamond was killed."

She waited until they left before dialing Johnny's suite.

"Isabel!"

"Tina! Are you okay?"

"What…what happened to David?"

"He…he's gone," Isabel was crying.

"Why didn't somebody tell me what was going on?" Tina began weeping.

"It was the Mossad. They told Johnny that I had to stay in the room. They tried to keep Debbie out but you can imagine how that went down."

They laughed and cried together for a long moment.

"Come over here when the coast is clear," Tina insisted. "I don't care what time it is, you knock until I open up. I'm not going anywhere until you get here. If Debbie comes, I'll make sure we come for you."

There was no way in hell those guys were going to keep those girls apart at a time like that. It wasn't long before Isabel, Tina and Susie converged in Johnny's suite, and the rest of the group mustered there in short order. James Lincoln's entire entourage had been petrified by the news and remained locked in their hotel suites. It was learned later that Lincoln locked himself in his bedroom, posting Toby at the door with an AK-47. His doctors were faced with the dilemma of sedating a man who already had more narcotics in his system than a human body could bear.

What was really weird about the whole thing was that Isabel, Susie and even Debbie had been almost rivals when it came to David. Tina knew that she and Susie had sex with him, though she only suspected Isabel and Debbie. Now here it was, at the hour of his death, and everybody was coming together and bonding because of it. Life was weird. Death was even weirder. Was it going to be what would draw the girls together one more time?

It made her sick to think of telling them, yet she would not be able to deal with the guilt of telling them too late. This son of a bitch could sneak up on her at any time, take her down so she couldn't walk. They would never forgive her for that, for not sharing her last party times with them. She would have to plan it carefully, work it out so that one announcement didn't overlap the other. Or else it would turn into some psychedelic Irish wake where she was attending her own funeral.

She had a couple of drinks, which was rare for her in the middle of the day, and it made her drowsy so that she finally dozed off. She knew the day was slipping by but she didn't give a shit. They said dying people got all hyper as they ran out to experience life for the last time. She was getting tired, and was starting to feel like she had come to the end of the race and was damned if she was going to run it again,

At once she heard a knock at the door and was startled to see it was five-thirty. She answered the door and Carmen stood there for a long moment before she fell weeping into Tina's arms.

"What's wrong?" Tina pulled her inside and closed the door.

"I called Zeke and made him meet me for lunch. He told me everything," Carmen sobbed.

"Oh shit," Tina rolled her eyes, ushering Carmen to the couch in the living room.

"How could you not tell me? How could you be so mean?"

"Because I knew you were gonna get like this! You remember when Mom died, you were like a vegetable for a month. You've got kids now, you can't afford to be like that. Plus, I got things I have to do. I can't have you hanging onto me twenty-four/seven. Besides, I told Zeke that we don't know if it's all that bad. I'm going to see another doctor next week. We don't know whether the first guy is just trying to rack up some insurance claims."

"Zeke told *you* that. You told Zeke this was the doctor's confirmed diagnosis."

"Listen," Tina grabbed her hands and gazed into her eyes. "I just don't want this to turn into a circus. If it's my time, I want to go out peacefully, with just my friends and family around me. No fans, no media, no outsiders. You know we never got to share as much time together as we wanted to. Let's take advantage of this time. We'll start spending more time together, you and me and the kids, okay?"

"Okay," Carmen grabbed her and held her tight. "Okay."

"I'm thinking I'm gonna move back with Zeke," she gently pulled free from her sister's embrace. "I'm thinking there's no point in being here by myself. It'd be too easy to hide from everyone."

"Did you tell him?" Carmen wiped her eyes.

"Nah, I think I'm gonna just drop in on him. If he throws me out I'll just come back here."

"Don't be stupid," Carmen's tears began flowing again. "He's gonna be the happiest man alive, you know that."

"So will Luis, if you tell him you're gonna keep the baby. Please. For my sake. Name it after me. Let me leave something behind."

"Oh my god, oh my god," Carmen dropped forward, leaning over her knees. "This can't be happening, it can't, it can't!"

"Don't you see, this is it, this is the beauty of it," Tina encouraged her. "This is how it's gonna go down. That baby was destined for this. That baby was sent to take my place in this family."

"Okay, I'll do it," Carmen sat up and held her hands. "I miss Jose. I miss the kids' father. He's with someone else, he's got a new life, but I still love him and I miss him so much."

"We gotta move on, *nina*," Tina smiled at her. "Life goes on. Sometimes you can't look back or you get stuck and you can't move ahead. You can't get to where you got to go."

Tina remembered the pain and sorrow of carrying a torch for David Diamond longer than she cared to remember. She knew him from the neighborhood shortly after his parents moved back to LA after his graduation. He refused to leave NYC and they left without him, and Tina remembered him being like a stray cat she found on the street. He slept on her couch and eventually joined her in bed, and when he began sleeping with a barmaid on Delancey Street she did everything she could to keep him around. She thought she would lose him until he appeared one day with Stu Carlucci and was talking about starting a band. She clutched at

94

the opportunity like a drowning girl at a straw, and when they discussed the need for a practice space she thought of Debbie Munson.

She knew Debbie from the neighborhood and they had met at a couple of parties over the years. Debbie was a beautiful girl though she dressed like a rocker and had a very short temper. She was very jealous at first but eventually realized that David and Debbie had found kindred spirits in each other that they dared not risk beyond a platonic relationship. Her dreams of rekindling her relationship with David, however, were dashed anew when the Cabales sisters joined the clique. It was at that point that she realized that David was a hopeless Casanova with an inability to commit.

Now she thought back and couldn't remember. She thought she might even have to get her copy of *Hezbollah* to remember how it all happened. Did she sleep with David before Debbie did, or had it all been a teenage fantasy? When did she leave her apartment to move into the Munsons' building? Where was her apartment in the first place? Was she losing her mind with this disease? She should have known whether or not David was circumcised. She enjoyed fellatio, liked getting a man to where he couldn't stand himself, and she should have remembered things like that about David. All she had left of their relationship was her memories, and she wasn't certain if any of that was left. If she was not sure if she had ever slept with him, then she could not be sure if she ever really had that real intimacy with him at all, or if Debbie herself had.

At once she started thinking about Zeke, and tried to remember when they had their close encounter of the best kind. She remembered it was a rainy night, and they came into his apartment like kids just out of the shower, with that wide-eyed freshness like no other. Human beings hardly ever see each other like that, except at swimming pools, or Baptist ceremonies...or when it rains. They saw the innocence that neither of them still had, yet leapt at the illusion as cats pouncing on mice. They devoured each other that night, and he got hooked on the taste like a Bengal tiger having eaten human flesh. She loved the taste of him like no other, but when his price continued to escalate, she decided it was time to kick the habit and move on.

The worst part about it all was that she really did want to belong to someone. Not as a plaything or a sex toy for David Diamond. She knew that his was an insatiable spirit, that he always needed other worlds to explore, that he could never be locked into a relationship, a situation or a tie that binds. He could never have been the one, but it would have been different if he could have gone out and come back with the same devotion with which he left. She could not have dealt with him coming back to her as if kicking tires, thinking that he could always find someone as good as her or better. She wasn't Debbie Munson, she wasn't Isabel Carmona, but she was Tina Rivera and that should well have been good enough.

Now it was all about making it happen with Zeke.

She sat in the cab outside Zeke's condominium for a long while before paying the cabbie and exiting. She carried an overnight bag just in case they struck a deal. She felt intimidated somehow and was having trouble negotiating any dependency on Zeke. The thought of an argument, a misunderstanding, any miscommunication made her feel queasy. The thought of having to run home and readjust her frame of mind to being alone again was unbearable.

She felt as if she was standing on the edge of a cliff, looking down into an abyss. When she looked up at the stately building its prestigious veneer gave her a sense of warmth and welcome. She realized that this is how it would be. If she looked down, that would be the direction in which it would go. If she looked up...then so would everything else.

She lifted her bag from the sidewalk upon which she had laid it and cheerily greeted the doorman. He gave her a big smile and opened the door to the home where she would spend the rest of her days.

Part Two
Isabel

Chapter Eleven

"So what do you think, Mom?"

"It's really good, Frank," Isabel smiled, walking behind her son and softly caressing him under the chin.

They sat in the kitchen that morning, Isabel having served him toast and coffee before he announced that he had written some new hip-hop lyrics he wanted her to hear. She was somewhat taken aback by the clarity and focus of his work. She sensed an anger somewhere beneath the surface, yet the rhymes and the urgency of his message flowed over it like a river. Somehow it reminded her of Hezbollah. She considered the fact that every generation found its own level of discomfort in the world their parents made for them. Try as they might, though, there was little they could change.

"Did Dad write his own songs back then?' Frank wondered. "He never talks about it."

"You know how he is," Isabel walked back over by the stove where she stood whenever anyone visited her kitchen. "Boxing's his life now. He left a lot of pain behind in Palestine, and I think he wants to leave it there."

"I saw a bootleg tape of them last week," he revealed. "The quality is terrible, you can't copy it. Even so, you'd get hundreds for it on EBay. The guy who owned it never even plays it, he only put it on because I was Dad's son. I just couldn't believe it. Dad was unbelievable. He was like a spirit creature, something from the netherworld. I've seen dozens of his boxing tapes but they're nothing like this. My friends would give anything to meet him but they know he hates them."

"He comes from a different time," Isabel insisted. "He can't even work a cell phone."

"It's not that," Frank was morose. "You know it."

"It *is* that," she came over and patted his shoulder. "Believe me, we know everything about being different. He snatched me out of the cradle, you know. I was only sixteen. If it was in this day and age, he would've done time."

"It's hard to blame him," Frank looked up at her. "You were so beautiful. You still are."

"So why don't you find someone like me?" she teased. He grabbed onto her arm with his fingers as if to pinch her and she playfully slapped his hand away.

"My gosh, then there was the boxing," she continued to reminisce. "Then the music. Everybody hated what we were doing. David would pay people to come see us. We even fought with each other. The band broke up after Stu and Duke quit. We didn't see each other for years until that get-together at your Grandpa's. Then, all of a sudden, there was Palestine."

"You've seen so much, Mom," he admired her. "And you were so young."

So young.

"What are you planning to do with it?" she tried to change the subject.

"I don't know. I know some guys who have a hip-hop group, I was thinking of letting them check it out but I wanted to get some feedback first. You know how people are. If they think it's crap they won't take time for any more of your stuff."

"You shouldn't put all your eggs in one basket. So what if they don't like it, it's not the end of the world. There's other bands."

"Yeah, I know. It's just that I'm not a social animal like you and Dad and your friends back then. Plus, you know how it is for gays. You can never really trust everyone. Some people are accepting just to be cool. You can never tell what's going on behind your back."

"Hey, guy, you don't know what it was like back then," she chided him. "Lots of people thought punk rockers were the barbarians at the gate. It was us against the world most of the time. Well, your Dad, of course, but since I was his girlfriend most people saw me as one of the enemy. Talk about for better or worse, I knew the drill long before we got married."

"Well, you guys had connections, you lived in New York. It was a different time."

"I don't know where you get this idea it was a walk in the park," she was bemused. "People just started getting their own PC's back then, and nobody had camcorders or all the stuff you have these days. If we had half of the stuff that's out now, we might have gotten a different deal than the one we got from James Lincoln."

"James Lincoln made you famous," Frank reminded her.

"Yeah, but that Crusader Concert Tour made David Diamond dead."

"Did you love Diamond?" he asked softly. "I've heard the rumors, read that novel."

"No, not like your father," she stared out the window into the sunshine beaming down over Miami Beach. "We went out once or twice. We were all kids back then. He went out with your Aunt Lucy, he dated everybody. Like I said, I was just a teenager. David captured my imagination, but your father stole my heart."

"Did you have any of your own dreams? Wasn't there something you wanted to do of your own?"

"I don't know, not really. I don't think I was much different than anyone else. I've got things I'd like to try, but it wasn't like I had this ambition to get rich and famous."

"Like Dad?" he grinned.

"That's what I love most about him, his spirit. He said he got it from your grandmother. Never say die, fight, fight, fight until the last bell. He always said that maybe he got too much of that from her. He always said he sometimes regretted he didn't know when to quit."

"Did you really get to know my grandparents --- his parents?"

"Not really, they lived here in Florida and we only came to visit a couple of times. They were elderly and in poor health. I told you we brought you here when you were a baby."

"Are you sorry he didn't know when to quit?"

"No, because we would've never came here and bought this gym. It got him away from New York and all the partying, it gave him something to live for. I'm glad we didn't have to bring you up in New York. You could've easily ended up getting caught in a rut."

"The biggest city in the world?" he munched his toast. "I kinda feel like I got shortchanged."

"Well, as your mother, I can assure you I don't think you did. Things aren't exactly perfect here in Miami, but at least breaking bad isn't expected of people here."

"It's like they say, you can't pick your parents and you can't choose your beginnings."

"Why, do you wish you had different parents?" she turned to look at him.

"Of course not. I love you and I love Dad. I just --- sometimes I wish --- he could be more understanding."

"It's that whole macho thing of his, you know that," she insisted. "He got that from his father, he's been like that all his life. He just doesn't know any other way. It hasn't been a cakewalk for me, let me tell you. It's pretty hard being a female around guys who view female sentiment as weakness. I think that was one of the things that kept this marriage healthy, having a child. He finally started seeing things differently as a father instead of a fighter."

"Oh, really? When did this start happening?" Frank grew testy.

"When he started seeing that you weren't a carbon copy of him, when he realized you were your own person. I'll admit he was disappointed at first. You know how it works: denial, anger, sorrow, then acceptance. Just don't forget that he loves you no matter what. He's a proud man and he's stubborn but he'd give his life for you. You have no idea how many times I defended you and argued with him, and all I was doing was making myself his punching bag. If I had just kept my mouth shut, he would've gotten to the acceptance stage a lot quicker."

"There's a lot of lost time he owes me," Frank exhaled tautly. "All that time he spent in the gym with other people's kids while I was out playing by myself. He was teaching other kids to fight back while I was running from bullies."

"That's not fair. You never wanted to have anything to do with boxing."

"Yeah? Well, who was it who said they didn't want me to follow my father's footsteps and get my brains knocked out."

"That was when you were a little boy. I didn't want you to be one of those kids being thrown into the ring like a fighting rooster. Of course I wanted you to be able to defend yourself."

"See, that's the whole problem. Here we are like ten years later. You explain it to me now, but how was I supposed to know that? You see, I think that's where it all started. He thought you were driving a wedge between us. That probably helped everything fall conveniently into his little pigeonhole. The reason why his son turned gay was because he was mollycoddled by his mother. That explained everything, didn't it?"

"Don't even go there," Isabel was adamant. "I wasn't going to have you pre-programmed to go get your head knocked off. When you started school I stood back and let you find your own way. Nobody can ever say I tied you to my apron strings, ever."

"But don't you see?" Frank said quietly. "The line was already drawn. He *perceived* that you didn't want him getting me involved in that part of his life. I *perceived* you didn't want me to have anything to do with boxing."

"So now it's my fault. I drove a wedge between you and your father because I didn't want to see you get hurt."

"No. That's not that I'm saying. Mom, I've been thinking about this for years. I've been trying to figure out how it all went sideways between me and Dad. It wasn't about me coming out, that was just the straw that broke the camel's back. It was all the little things. Me coming between the two of you…"

"That's crazy."

"That's natural. You two were madly in love and then all of a sudden there's a child compromising your attention. That's not you, that's not him. That's nature. Animals eat their young over it. He started using the gym as a crutch, didn't he? Spending more time at the gym while you spent time with the baby. You figured at least he wasn't at the bar, so you blew it off."

"So where are you going with all this?"

"Nowhere," Frank shrugged. "Right here. Neither one of you had a frame of reference. You had Dr. Spock, not Dr. Phil. You guys were thinking, what would our parents have done? How can I blame you for what you didn't know? I'm just trying to understand it, that's all."

"I was a bad mother, is that what it is?"

"No, you were the best mother in the world," he got up and embraced her gently. "Dad might not have been the best Dad, but he's *my* Dad. That's all that counts."

They stood there in each other's arms and had a good cry together.

She would go into the bedroom and inspect her image in the gloom when she was home alone. Her hair had a slight frizziness to it that undoubtedly came from years of overheating with blow dryers, and her skin moisturizers had become a daily requirement. She had faint crow's feet and frown lines, her breasts had sagged and her pooch demanded that she exist on a coffee and salad diet. She and Johnny still enjoyed their sexual attraction but there seemed to be more work and less passion involved as the years passed by.

It was boxing that became her rival over the years. In retrospect, it had always been the false god he adored. Hezbollah had given place to it; it got him involved with the Mob and nearly got them killed. All the money they made in Palestine went into it, and now all that was left was their modest home and an aging gym. She had been wise enough to talk him into squirreling some away in mutual funds, and there had been enough to weather the famines though the feasts grew fewer and farther between. Still, he was as a gambler steadfastly investing in his horses, and all she could do was stand by and pray that he didn't lose everything in one bad deal.

"That Fleming kid called this morning," Isabel confronted him the previous afternoon. "He wants you to call him back. You know he's trying to borrow money, that's what he does every time he calls you."

"Aah, the kid's having a hard time. He just got a construction job and they withhold the first week, plus they pay every two weeks, so he's three weeks in the hole," Johnny waved his hand. "He's a helluva fighter, he's got a good jab and he hooks to kill. If I can get him on that card in Tampa next month, Roth and I'll work his corner and make a nice score."

"What about Ferguson?" she retorted. "He'll never get back in that ring."

"Geez, Issy, the man's practically homeless. What do I do, leave him in the gutter?"

"It won't be long before we're out there with him," she stalked off.

Roth was as the lightning rod in their relationship, their cornerstone. No matter how stormy things became, they could hold onto him for dear life and he would not break. He was like the legendary Rock of Indian legend to which the natives turned with their innermost thoughts. Though the Rock never spoke, they turned their souls inside out and usually worked through their problems, accrediting the Rock and its legendary powers for their epiphanies. So it was with Johnny and Isabel.

She also had her sister Lucy, who she kept in close contact though they rarely saw each other over the years. Lucy had graduated medical school and was a doctor at Richmond General Hospital. Her son and daughter loved their Aunt Issy and sent her cards and letters on the holidays, which Issy saved in a scrapbook. They had sent a fair share of photos of their Dad preparing for action, and they were rightfully proud though, like their Mom, they missed having him home though there was nothing they could do.

"Well, I'm as proud of you as the kids are of their Dad," Issy reassured her as they chatted long-distance one rainy night while Johnny was at the gym and Duke was out to war. "If only Dad was alive to see how his daughter turned out. Sometimes I wish it had gone that way for me. I should've started going to school instead of hanging around the gym all that time."

"It's never too late," Lucy was encouraging. "Besides, I'm sure Frank got the best of it. You don't know how many sleepless nights I spent worrying about leaving the kids with the babysitter so often. You did the best thing for your son. Now he's older, maybe you can take some classes if you feel like it."

"Sometimes I just don't feel like I've done anything with my life like you have," Issy was disconsolate.

"I haven't done anything special. I've just helped sick people feel better. You and Johnny have touched lots of young people's lives too, don't forget that."

She thought of the Flemings, the Fergusons, all the young fighters who came and went. Most of them lost their vision after endless, grueling hours of freezing in the cold, sweltering in the heat, urged on by Johnny as they honed their skills in knocking other men senseless. Those who endured paid tribute to Johnny out of their paltry checks but it was never enough. There was the small handful who went on to greener pastures, forever mentioning Johnny in their interviews though never earning him a cent.

There was always the Christian aspect of it, seeming so distant now though it was actually Part Two of their life story. You were supposed to get recompensed for the good things you did in life, because God owes no man...or woman. How many of those guys sat here in her kitchen over the years, greedily sopping up the gravy from the meal with morsels of bread, thanking her profusely for the best meal they had in days, months, years? How many of them swore they would never forget her kindness, that she was the mother they never had? After they got the big break, the big fight, they forgot all about Johnny. And they damn sure forgot about her.

Of course, there was Roth, who was always there with her and Johnny, the mast that always made sure their ship got back to shore. He was the crazy man back then, the one who was always in friendly competition with David, seeing who was the biggest Joker in the deck. He swallowed Valiums like candy along with David as they swigged their beer, though his slender frame caused his collapse hours earlier than David. They stood out in traffic like mindless zombies, both bragging of the number of times they had gotten hit by vehicles when the drivers did not see the figures walking down the center stripe in the middle of the night. They fell down stairs, slipped and fell in their own vomit, carved symbols and signs into their flesh with shards of glass. Yet somehow Roth endured, and David was dead.

Roth was here, and God forgive her, he reminded her of Fiddler in *Roots*. He was here on Johnny's plantation, enduring year after year, waiting for a crop that they would never harvest. He told them that he would only be there until he got his own thing together, and they set up his room on the bottom floor of their two-story beachfront home. He felt comfortable there, comfortable with Johnny, and had the same dream that they would discover a fighter that would win the title. He stuck it out with Johnny, year after year, long after Isabel gave up hope. It was more than likely he had given up hope as well, but he stayed because the Carmonas had become his family. He still went out on weekends on Saturday nights and bedded his whores, but he crawled back on Sunday to rest himself to return to the gym Monday morning.

Sometimes she found it hard to feel sorry for them. Sometimes she thought about the panic attacks she felt as she watched Frank leave the house on the way to school, thinking selfishly about her youth was slipping away like slush down a NYC sewer. Suddenly she was somebody's mother, sitting in her living room all day, getting older, watching soap operas, waiting for her son to come back from school and her husband to come back from the gym. What was she waiting for? Was there anything beyond what she was expected to wait for?

And suddenly, out of nowhere, came the phone call. Out of nowhere, Hezbollah rose from the dead, rose from her memories, and threatened to turn her world upside down again. She could only wonder that if what she had built over the last two decades was strong enough to withstand the impact.

Chapter Twelve

Roth Almontaser tossed the plastic bag onto the table, where David Diamond retrieved it and eagerly dug into its contents like a sack of candy. He rolled a joint quick as a flash, and soon the three guys were pleasantly stoned from the effects of the high-grade cannabis.

"So I hear you're a boxer," David smiled.

"I'm working on it," Johnny Carmona replied. He was a middleweight, 5'9' and 160 pounds, hard as wood. He had a close-cropped head of dark hair, shadowy eyes and a two-day stubble that made him look like a fighter from a 40's penitentiary movie. "You look like you work out."

"Mostly lifting pints and quarts these days," David chuckled. "I quit playing hockey last year to focus on the band."

"Man, that must be so cool," Johnny rhapsodized. "I always thought about how much rock and roll was like boxing. I mean, you get up there, under them lights, all them people out there sharing that adrenaline, it's like a ritual. You gotta know what I mean. That's the only thing that keeps you going up there."

"It's not all that hard to do, not like boxing. You should try it sometime," David's mind was working.

"Try it," Johnny scoffed. "I can't sing for shit."

"Neither can I," David chuckled. "As a matter of fact, it might even be holding us back. I've been thinking about focusing on the keys and having someone else do some of the heavy lifting. You should come by and check it out."

"So what do I do if I can't sing? Just dance around?"

"I'm thinking you and I probably sing on the same pitch," David mused. "If we sing together we'll kinda be covering up for each other. Plus, we've got that wall of sound working. My keys and Debbie's bass are like the Iron Curtain. We drown out Tina and give Stu and Duke all the buffers they need to bounce their guitars off. Look, if you get up there and bounce around like in the ring, it'll give the stage show a big boost. Think about it."

"Sure, let me talk it over with my trainer," he nodded at Roth. "We'll letcha know."

Johnny and Roth showed up at the next practice at Debbie's apartment on Friday night, and Roth brought spliffs of Panama Red for everyone. Stu seemed skeptical until they went through their traditional jam song, "Louie Louie". He was mildly surprised to find that David and Johnny's voices blended together well enough to hide their deficiencies, and Johnny's enthusiasm gave his vocals a quality lacking in David's careless monotone.

"He handles the music and I handle the business," David pulled Johnny aside after practice. "He's good with the sound. You're in."

Johnny noticed divisions within the ranks on Day One, and decided that perhaps David might have seen purpose in the newcomers acting as good-will intermediaries. Debbie and Tina tended to hang out by the drum set, while Stu and Duke commiserated by the guitar amps. David spent his time with the roadies, and there was always kibitzing between the factions though they seemed conciliatory at best.

As it turned out, the end of the nightly session became the most important moment of his life.

Johnny watched amusedly as Duke rushed to the door to greet the latest arrivals. His girlfriend, Lucy, was a petite girl with cherubic features and an hourglass figure. Duke's macho attitude melted like ice and he was as a puppy by her side.

At once Johnny was thunderstruck as her sister came into the room. Isabel was as tall as Lucy, about five feet, with the same voluptuous figure. Only Isabel's doe-eyed, full-lipped, tawny-skinned presence lashed out at his senses.

"Don't make it so obvious," Roth sidled over to him. "If your jaw hits the floor everyone's gonna see it."

"Hey," he mustered up his ring bravado as he strolled over to where Isabel stood. "I'm Johnny Carmona."

"I'm Isabel," she said softly. "Nice to meet you."

"Too bad you weren't here earlier," he grinned. "We weren't so bad tonight."

"What do you do?"

"I'm a boxer. They're talking about letting me get beat up on TV."

"Wow, that's cool. I meant with the band."

"I'm the announcer. Say, can I get you a drink?"

"Sure."

Johnny walked over to Debbie's makeshift bar, where everyone contributed bottles and six-packs regularly. He poured Isabel a rum and coke as David sidled over to him.

"You know, I stopped making it with her when I found out she was just seventeen, like in the song," David muttered. "Her Dad's a big war hero, he's liable to cut your nuts off."

"You know, I'd be a fuckin' nut myself if I was to take your word for it."

"You pay the price, you take your chances," David sniggered, walking off.

Isabel remembered it like it was yesterday, how suave and sophisticated he seemed with his debonair Latin charm. She had told everyone she was a year older than she was and made Lucy swear to it. She had been intoxicated by the band from the moment that she accompanied her dad Paco and her sisters Lucy and Shanna to a rehearsal a couple of months ago. Her Dad met the group in a Puerto Rican bar on Smith Street one night after practice, and they hit it off splendidly. He invited them to his home where they met his daughters, and David took it to a personal level by having a fling with Shanna. It didn't last long, and then he started messing around with Lucy but she wasn't the type to be messed with. She was looking for a serious relationship and so was Duke Gallegos. From there he moved on to Isabel, and they made out a couple of times but did not want to take a chance with a 'seventeen-year-old'. Johnny Carmona did not have that problem.

The band was bigger than life in a working-class neighborhood riddled with broken homes, substance abuse and borderline poverty. Most people saw them as eccentrics, a bunch of good kids gone wrong in hitching their wagons to a bizarre new fad. When they first started out they sounded like a bad garage band, but when they found their niche in punk rock it wasn't anything anyone in the neighborhood was ready to listen to. Going hardcore closed the door to any possibility of local acceptance, but you had to see this band in order to believe it. And, as David Diamond kept pointing out, once you saw them chances are you might get hooked.

Watching Tina at the time was almost comical, like a Dutch girl working frantically to keep the dike from collapsing

110

around her. Debbie was almost a parody of a bassist, hammering at it until she broke a string, swinging it violently as if trying to clear a space around her. David was like a broken marionette, rocking and reeling to and fro until he dropped in a heap, then getting back up to find another place to collapse in, singing in sync throughout. All the while, Stu found his own comfort zone where he remained as the Wizard of Oz, playing the strings wonderfully in keeping the songs from exploding into disaster. Duke was relentless in playing right alongside him, determined not to be upstaged or left in the dust despite whatever guitar tricks Stu pulled out of his sleeve.

David suspected that Stu was not long for the band, the personal animosity with Duke and the directional disagreements with David having him looking towards an exit. He decided to take up keyboards to compensate, and thought that someone like Johnny would not only fit the bill as a front man, but might draw some boxing fans as his ring notoriety grew. Having Roth Almontaser tagging along as his sidekick only sweetened the deal. Roth's over-the-top personality was a perfect match for David's outrageousness.

Johnny, Roth and Isabel were the Three Musketeers, and their inclusion into the Party circle never changed that. She and Johnny double-dated with Duke and Lucy a number of times, but outside of that, Roth was always included whenever they went anywhere. Their private time came when she visited Johnny's apartment, and when his phone was off the hook, no one came by unless they were called. She remembered when they first started making love, how responsive her body was to his touch, and how wonderful his sleek muscles felt against her. It was still like that after nearly thirty years, and they never lost that magic even though they seemed to be losing so many other things.

The biggest mistake they made was getting involved with the Mob. Johnny was determined to succeed at any cost, and when he was told that he could not make it without Mob support, he went along despite Roth and Isabel's apprehensions. She didn't like the connected guys they constantly had to deal with, even though they got Johnny on ESPN after his fourth fight for them. The money started getting better and better, and soon Johnny was making more everyone in the band combined. He started missing shows and practices, but everyone understood the situation and never complained. Eventually Stu left, and Duke managed to build a new wall of sound without David's support when Johnny wasn't there. Still, it wasn't the same old Party anymore, and when David renamed the band Hezbollah, everyone realized they were going off in a radical new direction.

Johnny was in a constant state of anxiety, partly due to his strict training regimen and also over the guerilla campaign that David was conducting on the streets of New York. He was taking them out wherever and whenever he could: at private parties, street festivals, barrooms, restaurants, bowling alleys, even rest homes and asylums. It was almost embarrassing to show up to some of the gigs, and humiliating when they got bad receptions at places they had no business playing. He would lie his way into shows, claiming they played a specific genre, then showing up and playing three songs as advertised before launching into Hezbollah's sonic blitzkrieg. He had great fun making home movies of some of the shows, and he would play them back at band practice to everyone's grand amusement. Only everybody, including Johnny, realized that this was degenerating into public spectacle which was becoming more important to David than the music.

She remembered how conscious she was of her looks back in the day, and it was like an obsession as she realized over the years. They called her the Supermodel, and she spent almost an hour a day in the mirror to make sure she lived up to it. She watched her weight to the point of anorexia, and everything she earned at part-time jobs went towards her wardrobe until Johnny started taking her shopping on a regular basis. David invited her onstage to dance with them when a show went exceptionally well, and she and Johnny would come up with dance routines that would bring the house down. She lost count of how many times guys from the audience came up and tried to hit on her, only to get boxed in by band members or the entourage letting them know their presence was unwelcome. Johnny was always cool with it, knowing that his Supermodel was just too much to resist for many a man.

The biggest problem she had was with the Mob guys, and she would never dare mention anything to Johnny for fear of a confrontation. They always invited him out to Sheepshead Bay or Bensonhurst, and they spent big money for expensive drinks and exquisite meals as they regaled their new prodigy with anecdotes about Mob life or the moneymaking rackets they scored on. They were overly respectful when Johnny was within earshot, but if they cornered her alone they would promise her the moon and stars for a chance to win her heart. She was truly frightened when such overtures were made, mostly over dread that one of the psychopaths might try to take Johnny out of the picture to get to her. Fortunately he was too valuable a commodity, and she told no tales so that they never had a problem.

She remembered when they first learned that the band was about to collapse once and for all when Duke began verbalizing his fantasies about joining the military. Ronald Reagan had crushed the Cuban-led troops in Grenada, Roth's homeland, and there was large talk about Noriega's Panama being next on the hit list. Duke dreamed of being a Green Beret and jumping out of planes on top secret missions to destroy Communism. David's fatal error was in feeding his fantasies with the guerilla theatre analogies, pumping the band up with notions of being supercommandos on a campaign to overthrow the Music Industry. Duke was ready to go out and do it for real, and David never suspected it until it was too late.

As she found out later, he had told Lucy about visiting an Army recruiter and receiving tons of literature through the mail. After he took the tests and was accepted, he waited until the last minute before telling David of his decision. It was the end of the band and everyone knew it, and the group slowly disintegrated afterwards. Debbie started hanging out around David's Uncle Fred, learning the ropes and finally getting her own private investigators' license. David began concentrating on his poetry and finally had his collection published. Tina started taking percussion lessons and soon discovered prodigious talent that took her into the stratosphere. Johnny rededicated himself to the ring, and soon his Mob buddies had him on the road to the world middleweight championship.

It was the internecine feuds that were so destructive over time. They were always stuck in the middle between best friends or in-laws, and it was a vicious circle that seemed inescapable. Duke had nothing but contempt for what he saw as Stu's condescending patronization, and eventually grew to dislike David for his Machiavellian agendas. When the lightning hit the bottle in the early Nineties, Duke had been assigned to rejoin the band as part of a covert operation, but he was as much against the idea as David and Stu. Johnny was expected to be the peacemaker, but no one had any idea the kind of backstage problems he was having of his own.

His Mob connections came back to bite him in the ass, and Johnny was sickened when he found out that two of their top torpedos were being assigned to his boxing entourage. The boxers were being sent along as a sideshow to J.C. Lincoln's main event, and everyone was titillated except for Johnny himself. He knew that Jack 'the Rat' Raccuglia and Vic 'the Maniac' Maniacci had not been sent to the Middle East just to carry his gym bags, and when Johnny and Isabel found what they were there for, they were horrified.

She would harbor a grudge against the American military, the CIA and Mossad for the rest of her days, and it made it exceedingly difficult over the years in her relationship with Lucy. If it had been planned and handled differently, David Diamond would have never gotten killed. As everybody found out later, he would have died of cancer shortly afterward, but it didn't have to end up the way it did. Duke was deeply affected by David's death, but still had the gung-ho attitude over the years that she could not abide by.

"Hey. You see the news?"

"Yeah, I did. Have you heard from anyone? Isabel asked Johnny as he came home for lunch that afternoon.

"Nah, you know I never keep my cell phone on. One of the kids at the gym mentioned it, and I went by Chico's where they had *Al Jazeera* on. I can't believe it, after all these years. You think it could be true?"

"Lincoln may *think* he's going to put together a reunion tour. If he's got AIDS, it's never gonna happen. You remember that boxer of yours who caught it from a needle a few years back. Those people just fall apart all of a sudden. Their system breaks down, and all of a sudden they're dead. If JC's doctor lets him go through with this, he's going to end up just like Michael Jackson's doctor, with lawsuits all over his ass."

"Yeah, like my hands are all over *your* ass," Johnny came over and fondled him.

"Cut it out if you want me to fix lunch," she swatted him away.

114

"So what do you think?" he asked, slouching into a chair at the kitchen table. "We scored a hundred grand last time. In this economy, what do you think he'd pay us? A quarter mil? A half mil? That's nothing to sneeze at."

"Johnny, get real," she insisted as she chopped an onion. "That was over twenty years ago. We were kids back then. You've got a business now, you've got responsibilities. You haven't been on a microphone for who knows how long. You just can't jump up and fly back to Palestine and play a gig, especially with all the trouble going down over there."

"What's different now than it was then?"

"Yeah, ask yourself that question," she shoveled the onions into an oily pan. "David got killed out there last time. Who gets killed this time?

We're too old for this shit, Johnny, forget it."

"Hey, you know another way I can pick up that kind of money for a month's work?"

"What do you mean, a month's work?" she palmed a couple of eggs as she stood with fists on hips facing him. "You'd have to put a set together, rehearse for at least a month before you could even think about it. Plus you'd have about a month of promo to build interest in the show, at the very least. What makes you think you could fill the Valley of Armageddon again with an AIDS patient and a band of over-the-hill punk rockers?"

"What, you don't think I still got it?" he got up and thrust his pelvis at her. "C'mon, baby, let me show you what I still got."

"Asshole," she chuckled, turning away to break the eggs into the pan. Damn, the son of a botch still turned her on. "Look, why don't you call Tina from the gym later on? I'll call Lucy and see if Duke's heard anything."

"Duke's in Iraq. What makes you think he can even get to a phone?"

"Yeah, that's right, Duke's in Iraq. What makes you think they're gonna give him time off to go play a punk concert? Get real, mister."

"He's already over there. He can jump on a heli-copter and show up at the gig like Elvis."

"Keep dreaming, mister," she warmed a tortilla on another burner.

"Didn't he win a Silver Star over there last year?"

"Yeah, and he doesn't like to talk about it."

"He'll talk to me," Johnny smirked.

The thought of the violence and the horror of the Middle East made her tummy churn. It was something she never expected to have to deal with again. Now, all of a sudden, it was a ghost of the past looking right through her kitchen window.

And the sight was making her sick. All over again.

Chapter Thirteen

"Don't do anything unless they start some shit. If they do, Isabel, you start walking, catch a cab, head to the airport, go to your sister's, don't look back."

"I'm not gonna leave you, are you out of your mind?" she retorted.

"Look," Johnny grabbed her by the shoulders and gazed into her eyes. "You're the most important thing in my life. If anything ever happened to you I'd blow this whole hotel to kingdom come. I don't know what's gonna go down up there. I got sent for by Angelo Vacirca. He's one of the biggest scumbags in the New York Mob. He shits on everyone he comes in contact with, and if he does it to me I'm gonna throw him out a window. And then I'm a dead man."

"Leave her out of this, Johnny," Roth advised him.

"No!" she was adamant. "You're not leaving me out of anything. I'm going with you!"

"You cannot handle this guy," Johnny said hoarsely.

"I've handled David fucking Diamond," she insisted, "and I'm going."

"Okay," he looked at Roth intently, "let's do this."

When they arrived at the suite, they came into a semi-darkened room where a tall, angular man with a blond, oval skull and a boxer's build stood wearing a white shirt with rolled up sleeves and olive green silk pants. His arms were folded arrogantly as he faced his visitors, Johnny could see six thugs lounging casually in the shadows around the room.

"Angie Vee," Johnny addressed him hoarsely.

"Johnny Cee," the man replied. "I'm having trouble balancing my books this month. My accountant tells me it's going red on my Ten Count investment. I got a hundred grand that should have gone back to black a few months ago."

"Your people made me go in for all those tests and treatments when I sprained my wrist last month. I told them it was just a sprain."

"We got that back through the insurance. I'm talking about the party money. That was front money that was supposed to be paid back after the fight. Now there's no fight."

"There'll be a fight, Ang."

"Hey, Sweetheart," Angelo leered at Isabel. "Haven't seen you around before."

"She's *my* sweetheart, Ang," Johnny said tautly.

The room fell into a deathly silence for a long moment, punctuated only by the heavy clang of a metallic object thudding on the parquet floor. Angelo's small, Asiatic eyes were almost invisible in the dim light, standing motionless as if they stood before a mannequin.

"You better get my fuckin' money."

Johnny, Roth and Isabel silently made their way out the door and down the hall, not speaking until long after they had left the building.

The trio had no inkling of how dangerous Vacirca truly was until long after his bullet-riddled corpse was found in a body bag underneath a wharf along the East River. Vacirca saw the turmoil convulsing the Gambino Mob as a power vacuum that could portend the ascent of the Colombo Mob as the new leader of the Five Families in New York. In turn, he perceived the chance to monopolize the drug market on the East Coast as a highway to power and perhaps becoming the next Don of the Colombo Family.

He had long heard of the legend of the Golden Triangle heroin that had been marooned in the Middle East after the Vietnam War. It was considered fool's gold, far too risky in navigating through the storms of the Middle East and dealing with Hizbullah in bringing it across the Mediterranean into the crafty hands of the Sicilian Mob. Yet, with over $200 million as the jackpot, Vacirca saw it as an all-or-nothing power drive to the top. The Crusader Tour was providing him with a once-in-a-lifetime opportunity he was certain not to squander.

His next move was to contact Vic 'the Maniac' Maniacci and Jack 'the Rat' Raccuglia, two of his top torpedoes. He met with them in Red Hook and briefed them on his plan to extort the upcoming new comic sensation, Melvin E. Williams. Williams was known for his personal connections with James Lincoln, and had developed strong ties with the Colombos in opening a pipeline for Lincoln in

118

supporting his outrageous coke expenditures. It would be Williams who would provide the inside conduits in establishing the Mafia circuits within the tour group infrastructure, ensuring the subterfuge in smuggling the contraband through customs where it could be rerouted to the seacoast.

By the time Maniacci and Raccuglia had contacted Williams, Melvin had already bought into Lincoln's megalomaniacal scheme to implement his Peace in the Middle East Tour and reestablish himself as the King of R&B. Williams was traumatized by the extortionists' demands but saw no choice other than to comply. They had given him three options: work with them, take a chance on being fed to the corrupt NYC Vice Squad for drug trafficking, or end up at the bottom of the East River.

Vic and Jack's work became simpler as the negotiations on both sides of the planet streamlined. Mahmud Sirhan had already been selected by the Imperial security forces under Sardaq at the official photography group for the Crusader Tour. Once the boxing tour group was set up, it would facilitate their direct connection with the CLA and, ultimately, Hizbullah.

It was nearly a week after their meeting with Vacirca that Johnny was summoned to Little Italy to meet with Vic and Jack at Umberto's Clam House. Once again he brought Roth and Isabel with him, and they were taut with apprehension as their hosts did their best to lighten the mood. When Vacirca realized his serpentine charm was having no positive effect, he finally got down to business.

"Okay, here's how it's gonna go down," Vacirca grew deadly serious. "I'm putting together a phony company, Lights Out Promotions. That coke addict Melvin E. Williams owes me big time. He's gonna put the bug in Lincoln's ear to let us tag along on the Concert Tour. You'll have a whole entourage coming with you, and Vic and Jack are going to be the boxing managers. You'll be sparring with the ragheads' top guys, it'll be all over *Al Jazeera*. That's all you got to do, cover for Vic and Jack, and I'll consider us squared away for all the money you owe me."

"So what are they gonna do over there, kill somebody?"

"What the fuck did you just say?" Vic stared murderously at Johnny.

"Look, why don't you just give these two guys their own plane ticket?" Johnny ignored Vic as Isabel insistently nudged his foot with her shoe.

"You people are going to Israel. These guys got priors. They're not stepping foot in Palestine without a cover. They have something they need to pick up for me, and once they bring it back, you and me are even."

"Hold on. You mean they're smuggling shit for you?"

"Like I said, they're picking something up. Either that or you put my hundred grand on the table, right now."

"Okay, you still got to run this by Williams to get it cleared with Lincoln, right?"

"I already said that."

"If it's good with Lincoln, it's good by me. It's his show, he's running things."

"Good. Then we got a deal."

She would never forget the feelings of fear and loathing she harbored throughout the whole time they were on tour. There was never a time when she was not terrified that the Israelis would discover the gangsters in the entourage and blame Johnny for having brought them in. She knew how these people operated, she had been exposed to them since she was a little girl growing up in Red Hook. Everything they did was backed up by violence and murder. She warned Johnny not to get involved with them, but it was always the same argument.

"The Mafia *controls* boxing, Issy, now more than ever," Johnny was adamant. He said it back in the Eighties, again before the Concert Tour in the Nineties, and once more when they agreed to leave New York and start anew in Miami. "It's just like those *Godfather* movies. They've gone corporate, they went in and *bought* Las Vegas. When you visit Vegas, you stay in Mob hotels and play in Mob casinos. How do you think you get in a boxing ring that doesn't belong to the Mob? It's a fact of life, baby, you can't get around it."

"So why are we staying in it? Why don't we just get out?" she entreated him.

"And do what? Give singing lessons? Go back to high school and get my diploma? This is who I am, Issy. Boxing is my life. Maybe I can't do it myself, but I can teach some kid to do it for me, for us."

That was how her life turned into a *Rocky* movie. Roth stood at his left shoulder, Isabel on his right, forever standing by him as he pursued his dreams down the eternal rabbit hole. The

120

endless stream of hopefuls coming to the gym, hoping to put their lives on the line in pursuit of their own dreams. They came in all shapes and sizes, kids from the wrong side of the tracks trying to find out if they were tough enough. Most of them weren't, and the ones who lasted either went back to the gangs and went to jail, or got hooked on drugs. She wished there was a crystal ball that she could have used to spare Johnny the disappointments. Only he wouldn't have listened to her anyway.

The birth of their son should have been the most rewarding time of her life. Instead it began the most grueling struggle of her lifetime. In retrospect, she might have blamed it on the soy milk kick that Johnny got on, insisting that the baby be given a diet of soy milk once he was weaned. She did her homework and agreed it might be a good idea. Only now, two decades later, researchers were claiming that soy is loaded with estrogen and is a probable cause of boys becoming sexually confused. She wondered when *that* class action suit would get filed.

It started with the boxing thing, when she was resolute that Frank would not be raised as Johnny's pit bull puppy. She would not see her son thrown into the ring before he got out of grade school, getting his brains scrambled before he got through algebra. Johnny was affronted by her decision, but she never regretted it. What she rued was the distance it placed between them, and eventually it turned into a textbook psych problem. Frank began to seek father figures elsewhere, and she had no doubt that his habit of hanging out at the local rectory created the trauma that changed her son's life.

His friends were less athletic and more artistically inclined as time went by, and soon he was hanging out exclusively with what Johnny would refer to as 'sissies' when he was in a benevolent mood. There was a wall built between them, and eventually Frank stopped bringing his friends around altogether. The two had less and less to say to each other, and it got to be as if they were taking turns skipping the evening meals. She would have to read them the riot act to get them to have dinner together, and those nights were bereft of dialogue as they seemed as if they couldn't wait to get away from the table. For the better part of eighteen years.

It was even harder when the family flew to New Jersey to visit her Dad before he passed away a couple of years ago. Paco Cabales was a neighborhood legend long before anyone ever heard of Johnny Carmona or Hezbollah. Paco began realizing the subtle changes in Frank's personality, and whatever he could not say to Frank or Johnny, he saved up for Isabel.

"You had better start keeping a closer eye on that boy," he would lecture her whenever Johnny stepped out to have a couple of beers with one of the old gang and Frank's Aunt Lucy would take him shopping. "He's getting involved with the wrong kind of people, I can tell you that just by watching him. Have you ever had any reason to think he might be doing drugs?"

"Listen, Dad, you have no right to make those kind of accusations," Isabel would grow irritable. "I've never told you Frank was using drugs, and I never told Lucy any such thing."

"His entire attitude's changes, and it gets worse from year to year. He doesn't have any motivation, he has no fire in him. I'm his grandfather, there has to be some part of me somewhere inside him. His father is Johnny Carmona. You can't tell me that this boy comes from those two bloodlines with no trace of either one? There's something wrong, I tell you. I was a drill instructor after the war, I was one of the ones who developed the Green Beret program."

"Yeah, yeah, I know, I know," Isabel shook her head as they sat in Paco's spacious living room at the family beach house. "And I told you over and over, every child is different. Look at Lucy and I. She was always a ball of energy when we were kids, and I was the shy one. Now here she is with a law degree, and I'm the one helping to run a boxing gym."

"I'm not talking about that extrovert/introvert bullshit. I'm talking about manly qualities, having normal interests like every boy his age. He's not interested in girls or sports. Every time I try and talk to him, he never tells me anything, same as you. Are you trying to tell me that his whole world revolves around nothing?"

"He listens to music, he watches TV, he goes to the movies, he goes to the mall, he hangs out with his friends. He's not in a gang, thank God for that. He's already got problems communicating with his Dad. He doesn't need anything between him and his grandfather."

"Why don't you send him out her during his summer vacation?"

"I'll ask him, we'll see."

"Why are you going to ask him? Just send him."

"What do you think's gonna happen? You gonna put him through boot camp?"

"Something like that."

"Like I told you, he doesn't need to build another wall in his life."

"Wall? I'll teach him to go right through the wall."

"Yeah, or put his head through it," she scoffed.

Frank began to come out of the closet in his sophomore year in high school. He told her one night when they were having one of their mother-son discussions. She knew it was coming, like a knife in her gut, and it was like a nightmare in which she was absolutely powerless to stop it. It wasn't that she was homophobic or couldn't accept what he was. It was the effect she knew it would have on his relationship with his father his grandfather, and the world around him. Even though this Administration was making great strides towards gay rights, the battle wasn't even halfway over. She told Frank that, and his answer was entirely uncharacteristic.

"Well, I got the genes for it, don't I?" his voice was almost sarcastic. "My Dad is Johnny Carmona, my grandpa is Paco Cabales. If I've got to fight for my rights, then bring it on."

It wasn't long after that when Frank moved in with his boyfriend, and a door was closed behind him when Johnny found out. Isabel never really discussed it with Johnny, but she could tell by the look in his eye that he had suffered an injury that would be with him for a lifetime. People would see Frank on Miami Beach, at the clubs and at the malls. By then there was no doubt about who he was with or who he was. The rumors spread, but the closest it ever came was to Roth, who would commiserate with Isabel when Johnny wasn't around. Even so, no one would ever dream of mentioning it to Johnny. Nothing was worth taking that kind of chance.

It was after his graduation when Frank and his boyfriend Blade invited her to dinner for the first time. She asked Johnny to come but he came up some lame excuse and Isabel ended up going alone. She met them at Olive Garden, her stomach twisted in knots. Only the both of them looked like a couple of yuppie schoolteachers, dressed in semi-formal wear replete with neckties and open collars. Blade was a perfect gentleman, and it was only the deep respect and affection she could discern between them that would have made anyone think twice about them. She had a wonderful evening with them, but when she got home it was the first time that she and Johnny had nothing to talk about.

It gnawed at Johnny's heart until a couple of weeks later when he and Roth went out on a bender. He came home three sheets to the wind, and when he came into the bedroom, he was ready to lance the boil.

"He's gonna end up with one of those faggot diseases!" Johnny raged. "He lets them suck his dick, he fucks them in the ass, he's gonna get that faggot plague, and there's no cure for it! You remember Dale Brannigan, he got that shit from a needle and it killed him! I'm gonna bury my son because you couldn't put your foot down and stop this shit when it first got started!"

She hadn't seen him like that since they left New York. She refused to come out of the bathroom until he finally went to sleep on the couch. That was another first she would never forget. They made up the next day, and that evening in the bedroom turned out to be another night to remember. He acted as if they had been apart for a month. Nevertheless, not another word was spoken about Frank again.

It was a month later when Frank got a Dear John letter from Blade. He revealed to Frank that he had gotten an unfavorable medical report from his doctor and did not want to be a burden. Frank's heart was broken but Isabel was even more distressed. She was greatly worried about the nature of whatever it was that drove Blade away. Johnny's drunken tirade echoed in her heart, and she knew her husband enough to realize that he was releasing a poison that had festered for a long, long time. He was merely venting the pain that Isabel was feeling now.

Months later, Frank was complaining about a lack of energy, feeling as if he was catching the flu. Only the cold season had not arrived yet, and she encouraged him to go see a doctor. He was like his father in that way, he relied on his natural strength to overcome his maladies. Only his cough got worse and worse, and was beginning to interfere with his job as a substitute teacher. Finally he went in to see the doctor, who opted to put is through a series of tests. Frank hesitantly obliged, and was called in a week later for some follow-ups. The results of the first tests were confirmed, and Frank was given the news that would shatter the Carmonas' world.

"Hey. Mom," his voice was hoarse from all the coughing,

124

but there was something else. She would never forget hoping that it was news of Blade's death, rather than what she feared was coming next.

"What---what did they say?"

"It's not good, Mom. I'll be over for breakfast tomorrow."

She told Johnny she was having cramps and was going to bed early. He had a rough night at the gym with one of his best guys getting stitches, so he would have a couple of drinks before bedtime. She had no problem with that. She would take three Nyquils to knock her on her ass before the most terrible day of her life just ahead.

Chapter Fourteen

"So what's wrong now?" Johnny grunted as he cut into his sirloin steak that evening.

"Frank has AIDS."

Johnny set his fork and knife sown softly on his plate and stared down at it for a long time. Isabel watched tearfully as he dealt with the impact.

"When did you find out?" he asked tersely.

"This afternoon."

Johnny clenched his fists, then suddenly grabbed the plate on both sides.

"Please. Don't."

He eventually released the plate and returned his fists to either side of the plate, staring at a spot somewhere between his water glass and infinity.

"So what happens now?" he managed.

"We have an appointment with a specialist Monday," Isabel managed. "There's some different therapies they want to discuss with us. They want us to consider our options before we decide what's best for him."

"What's best?" Johnny demanded, tears welling in his eyes. "Best for who? There's no cure for that shit. They're gonna take all your money so you don't got a dime for the funeral."

"So what now?" she flared. "Are you going to give up on our son? Again?"

"Don't you try and dump that shit on me, Issy!" he yelled as she dissolved into tears.

"Okay," he came up behind her, wrapping his arms gently around her waist before turning her so she could bury her face against his chest. "Okay. We got to clear the table, put everything aside and take care of this. I'll tell Roth, he can mind the gym while I deal with this."

"You don't have to do that," she hugged him back. "All I want you to do is make peace with your son. Don't end up

126

thinking there was something left said one day."

"What should I do? Take him on a trip? Hang out with him? After all these years, where do I start?" Johnny gently released her and wandered towards the window.

"Why don't you buy him a beer?"

Johnny took the short drive down to Tampa Beach where he met Frank at a small lounge overlooking the shore. He made sure that it was a college hangout that would be less discerning of their clientele. He did not want to wind up in a bar brawl and expose Frank to any more danger.

"Frank," Johnny spotted him at the end of the bar. He walked over to him and hugged him for a long moment. "How you feeling?"

"Okay."

"What're you drinking?"

"Whatever you're having."

Johnny ordered two Crown Royals on the rocks. He felt like Frank was testing him to see if he remembered Frank's drink. It began to irritate him but he checked himself. At once he began to realize how testy he got around the kid, and it loosened him up somewhat. He liked to sit at the bar by the jukebox but decided it would be best if they got a booth.

"Want anything to eat?"

"Nah, I'm okay."

He searched the kid's face as he had not for a long time. He could see his own rugged jawline, his piercing eyes and his pouting lips. He had more of Isabel's smooth tawny skin and her thick mane. He also had the slight Cabalcs build that precluded him from indulging in contact sports. Not that it mattered now. Not that anything mattered now.

"So what do you got going?"

"What, with the doctor?"

"Yeah, you know," Johnny shrugged.

"They're doing tests, you know how that goes. Kinda like curing a cold. Once you got it, you got it."

"You need anything?"

"Yeah," Frank leaned forward slightly. "I need you to know something."

"What's that, Frank?"

"Suppose like, before I was born, you went into a fight and did the *Million Dollar Baby* thing," Frank narrowed his eyes. "Suppose you took a cheap shot and fell and bumped your head, and you wound up in a wheelchair. Suppose you and Mom weren't able to have kids. Do you think she would've blamed you for the path you chose instead of being a rock star?"

"Rock star? Hah!" Johnny snorted, looking away scornfully. "Rock star. David Diamond got me in the band to cover his ass. Neither one of us could carry a tune in a bucket. I'm a fighter, kid, that's all I'm good for. *Was* good for. Did your Mom ever tell you how we ended up in Palestine?"

"Not everything," Frank tapped his fingers on his glass. "She has problems talking about it, just like you."

"Smart kid," Johnny sniggered. "Well, then. I had problems with the Mob. They controlled the game then, always have, always will. I owed them money, and when James Lincoln and Stu put the project together, they made me an offer I couldn't refuse. They tied a boxing promo on my tail and stuck a couple of wiseguys in the entourage. I got my career back together and a good friend got killed."

"Why are you telling me all this?"

"I don't know," Johnny cleared his throat. "So, what's your point with the alternate ending? I crack my head, I can't have kids, stuff happens. It didn't happen like that."

"Suppose it did," Frank probed.

"What's your point?" Johnny snapped.

"You chose your path through life," Frank stared at him. "You knew there were risks, but you followed your heart. You did what you had to do."

"Yeah, so?"

"Well, then," Frank stirred his drink, then dropped the straw. "So did I."

There was a deathly silence as Johnny struggled to control his emotions.

"Okay," he relented. "No use in crying over spilled milk."

"Do you think you would've been happier? Not to have wound up crippled, but..." his voice trailed off.

"That's stupid," Johnny scowled at him. "You're my son. I don't care what you've done. It doesn't change that."

"It's not what I've done, Dad. It's who I am."

128

"Okay," Johnny said huskily. "Fuck that. You're my son. That's all that matters."

"I know this has been hard for you. It wasn't about hurting you. It was about being who I am," Frank said quietly. He always resented his father not being able to accept that part of him. Yet at the same time he knew what a dagger in the heart it was for this man.

"Yeah, well. It is what it is. So what's the story with this thing? How are you feeling? What are we gonna be looking at?"

"I think Mom's probably got literature on it. It knocks out your immune system so your body can't fight infections and diseases. You end up dealing with everything that comes your way, basically. A common cold can turn into pneumonia."

"But they're working on cures, aren't they?" Johnny insisted. "How much does it cost?"

"There is nothing right now. People around the world are contributing to research. Movie stars have put up millions. Elton John's put up millions."

"Yeah, that…" Johnny began, then checked himself as his voice trailed off. "I'm sorry."

"It's who you are," Frank grew bitter, his emotions surging. "You'll never change."

"Look, no more bullshit. No more gay, anti-gay, political, philosophy, whatever kind of bullshit," Johnny wiped a tear from his eye. "It's you and me and your mother. We can't change the past but we can face this thing together, as a family. We can't let any differences steal what time we have to change this thing, to turn this thing around."

"I don't believe in miracles. But I love my mother, and I love you. I agree, we'll spend a lot more time together, we'll share what's left. I want you two to have a lot of happy memories."

At once Johnny's head dropped and his shoulders began shaking. Frank watched with a small sense of satisfaction before his heart went out to his grieving father.

He got up from his seat and slid into the booth alongside him, putting his arm around him and hugging him close. He considered the irony of being able to do what he wished his father had done for him throughout the course of his soon-to-be-shortened life.

It was two in the morning by the time Johnny returned along with Roth and a half case of beer. She saw the headlights of Roth's Camaro go out in the driveway and pulled on her robe to go out and confront them.

"What kind of shit are you guys up to?" Isabel railed at them. "Who's gonna open your damned gym in a few hours? Those kids are gonna be calling over here and I'm gonna have to lie for you? Uh uh. Roth, you go on home and *you*, mister, get your ass inside right now!"

"Hold on, darling," Johnny was already tipsy. "Back up. I went down and had a couple of drinks with your son. I called Roth and asked him to meet me. I told him what was going down. He's just here to help me keep my head on straight."

"With a half case of beer? You're not using Frank as an excuse to go out and get messed up. Don't you think I wanted to go out and get smashed? We need to hold it together. This business is just getting started. We got a long journey ahead of us, and you're not going to start it off like this."

"I told you, you should've stayed over at my place. You could've got up and gone straight to the gym," Roth shrugged.

"No, that's not gonna get it either," she walked out on the lawn towards them. "He's a married man, he comes home at the end of the night."

"You're right," Roth admitted, always the voice of reason. "I just thought he might've avoided all this."

"He doesn't avoid coming home to his wife."

"I agree. The problem is that most of the damage was already done by the time he called me. I was just trying to avoid seeing it get much worse."

"Well, having him stay over at your place was not cool."

"Yep, that's true."

"C'mon, Issy, cut me some slack," Johnny came over and began reaching for her.

"Get in the damn house," she slapped his hands away.

"Hey, I'm in a lot of pain here," Johnny started his grandstanding, which was going to make her go ballistic if she didn't put herself in check. "My son has AIDS. I just found out my son has AIDS today. I went down to have a drink with him, and it was the first man-to-man talk we've had in twenty-one years.

130

Twenty-one *years*, Issy. That's a long time. And what are we talking about? All the years we lost, all the tie we never spent together, all the conversations we never had? No, we're beating around the bush about how thinks are gonna go down now we know he's gonna die."

"This is not the time or place for this, Johnny. Not on the front lawn with you drunk at two o'clock in the morning."

"She's right, John," Roth stepped up beside him. "Go on in and get some sleep. I'll open up tomorrow. You take a time out, get your head together. You and Issy have a lot of stuff to talk over."

"My *son*, Roth," Johnny dropped his head on his friend's shoulder. "My fucking son." He broke down and began weeping as Roth turned to Issy with a look of helplessness.

"Come on," Issy did everything she could to keep from collapsing on Roth's left shoulder. She came over and put her arms around her husband's waist. "Don't do this out here. C'mon inside, we'll deal with this tomorrow. Together."

Johnny hugged his old friend and kissed his cheek before heading back to the house, carrying the weight of the world on his shoulders. Only he was unable to appreciate the fact Isabel was bearing it right alongside him.

"Oh my god, Issy. This can't be right. Did you get a second opinion?"

"I think I'm gonna be hearing that question a lot from now on."

"You call me up out of nowhere to tell me my nephew's dying. Don't you think that's the first thing I'm gonna ask you?"

Isabel called her older sister the next morning while Johnny was still asleep. She knew that Lucy was probably getting ready to face a busy day at her law office in Virginia, but she wanted to get that call out of the way first. She had no idea as to how Paco would react, and at least if he called Lucy she would be ready. Isabel knew she needed to get these calls out of the way first. She knew she would have to call the old crowd. Frank still had emotional ties to them, not due in small part to the Hezbollah legendry. It was something Frank took pride in, being connected to that, and most of the old gang saw him as family. Aunt Tina, Aunt Debbie, Aunt Susie, Uncle Stu...the whole bunch would have to be told. There were a lot of tough calls ahead.

"I know. Say, I know you have lots of big-time connections. If you come across any…"

"Hey, little sister, why would you even ask me?" Lucy's voice got husky. It said a lot as Lucy was one of the most emotionless people she knew. "I'm all over this. Is Johnny's insurance gonna be able to cover this? You know there's a lot of experimental stuff out there, and with private research it can get pricey."

"I have no idea," Isabel resented having to deal on Lucy's level. She was a housewife, like it or not, and she was hardly prepared for the shitstorm of bureaucratic red tape ahead. "I'm just gonna take it as it comes."

"You're my sister, Issy, and you can call me any time at all. Don't sign anything or agree to anything you're not sure of. I'm just a phone call away, you know that."

"I appreciate it."

"I know you've told Johnny. Has he spoken to Frank yet?"

"They got together last night," Isabel couldn't keep from crying. "You know, this really sucks. Why does it take shit like this to bring people together?"

"Listen, I can fly down there tonight. I'll have my staff---"

"No, no, that's okay. I'm fine. I need some quiet time with Johnny. He's gonna be going through some really tough times ahead. I just pulled him off the sidewalk in front of the house at two in the morning. He was out there with Roth and a couple of six packs. I don't want him to start coming apart. I'm not gonna be able to deal with it."

"You need to tell him, Issy. He needs to be the man. He can't be pulling this Peter Pan act on you forever."

"I know, I know," Isabel tried to check her anger. She hated it when Lucy tried to analyze their marriage. "Are you gonna tell Duke? You know they always had a good relationship. Maybe if Duke calls him it'll help him get into a different frame of mind."

"Yeah, I'll do that."

"Where's Duke now, still in Iraq?"

"What, you don't read the papers? We pulled out of Iraq in 2011. He's over in Afghanistan now."

"Geez, isn't he over coming home? He's done his time, especially at his age."

132

"It's that Special Forces stuff he's involved in. They say they still need him over there. I think it has a lot to do with him, too. He keeps talking about 'his kids'. I think he's too emotionally involved. I don't know what's gonna happen"

"Well, just remind him he's got my niece and nephew who come first. You don't want them growing up like Frank, without their father being there for them."

"What a life, huh?" Lucy sighed. "Well, let me go, I'll call Duke. I can make some calls for you if you want, if it's okay."

"No, that'd be fine. I know I'm gonna have messages on my cell phone up the wazoo, but what the heck. I'll call Dad myself."

"Okay, honey. You stay strong. Give Johnny my best. I'll call Frank as soon as I get off work."

"All right. Love you."

As soon as she hung up, she had a panic attack in realizing they were practically preparing for Frank's funeral before he was even gone. It was as if they were giving him no chance whatsoever. She cursed herself for not having gotten into all that computer and Internet stuff when it first came out. Now she would have this huge ton of crap to deal with, going onto all these websites and making all these connections in a race against time. She was not going to give up, not as long as there was a glimmer of hope. Still, she could have been better prepared for what was already here, and had to be even more prepared for what was to come.

She didn't know where to turn next. Frank was the one who was dying, he was the most important. She had to keep in as close contact as possible without making him think she was crowding him. She also had to keep watch on Johnny to make sure he didn't go into meltdown. There was also all this research bullshit to make sure they would exhaust all possible resources before even contemplating worst case scenarios. All this before she could even think of calling the gang and letting them in.

This was one hell of a mess that no woman should ever have to deal with. Yet it was on her plate, and she had to take that first big bite.

One thing was for damned sure. No daughter of Paco Cabales was going to give up without one helluva fight.

Chapter Fifteen

Johnny, Roth and Isabel involuntarily tensed as the elevator door sighed to a close behind them. They made their way along the hallway to Room 1413, where they were permitted entry by a small, wiry Palestinian.

"Right this way."

The trio followed him down a narrow hallway into a spacious lounge area where they were astonished by the sight of Vic Maniacci and Jack Raccuglia seated on either side of Melvin E. Williams, who sat petrified at the center of the long leather sofa.

"Long way from home," Johnny managed as Vic motioned for them to have a seat.

"Angie Vee thought it'd be best for us to stay close to the money," Vic explained. "Plus, in order to keep our ears to the ground, we got you with the band and this guy with the ringmaster."

"Okay," Melvin exhaled tautly. "You got to realize that I cannot go against James Lincoln. He's got serious weight on me that I can't get out from under. If anything goes sideways and he realizes I betrayed him, he can destroy my career."

"You motherfucker!" Vic slapped at his face as Jack nonchalantly took an ice pick out of the ice bucket on the mirrored brass table before them. "You think we don't know you've been dealing dope to that jig for the last ten years? Where do you think the dope comes from? You get the authority to deal kilos in Harlem, who do you think turns on the spigot to fill the ki? You been working for us all along and you don't even know it!"

"Okay, look," Johnny scowled, "not in front of my girl. What do you want done?"

"I told this ape that me and Jack are going to join your training entourage as assistant trainers," Vic turned towards them. "We're gonna get on top of the set-up crew so we have access to the transport vehicles. From there, the ragheads are gonna deliver the shipment and we handle it from there. Your hands don't get dirty, you just cover for us and we do the heavy lifting."

"So why do you need me!" Melvin wailed. "What is it, do you want money!"

"Yeah, gimme fifty million and we're even, you fuckin' *melanzane*!" Jack snarled, lashing out and stabbing Melvin in the face with the icepick. Melvin screamed and fell off his chair, curling into a fetal position while sobbing in terror. Isabel buried her face in Johnny's shoulder as he glared malevolently at Vic.

"Big number, Johnny Boy," Vic scowled. "What you owe ain't a drop off the duck's ass. We just need the favor and we can't afford for you to say no. You and him and us, working together to make this thing happen. If it don't, we might as well all get shovels, go out to the desert and dig some six foot holes for each other, because that's where we'll all end up if this thing goes sideways."

Isabel remembered the incidents leading to the Mossad sting operation as if it were yesterday. According to various source compilations, the North Vietnamese Army had contracted the Viet Cong to smuggle seven hundred pounds of brown heroin across the Golden Triangle into Laos just before the end of the Vietnam War. With the fall of Saigon, American naval operations made it impossible for smuggling operations to continue. Sources agreed that the smugglers transported the shipment across Laos into Burma, where it was placed on a vessel and taken across the Bay of Bengal to Maldives. From there it was crated and transported on a fishing boat to Pakistan. Insurgent groups were contracted to move the shipment to the Iranian border where it remained for almost ten years.

Authorities and informants alike agreed that problems arose when the insurgents came into the deal. Upon learning that the shipment had a street value of $200 million, they insisted on a 10% commission to be paid in advance. The drug cartel in Europe was furious but had no option other than to contract a mercenary force to recover the shipment. Negotiations came to a standstill until the Mafia was able to reach an agreement with Hizbullah in Iran.

Hizbullah was able to convince the Pakistanis that street values were inflated figures and that they, in fact, were the actual negotiators of the deal. They invoked *sharia* (*Islamic law) in persuading their Muslim brothers to turn over the shipment for a handsome reward. The next step was to move the product out of Iran across the Mediterranean to Europe or, preferably, directly to

America. The Israeli military presence throughout the region made it a daunting task.

The militants' ace in the hole was King Daoud's top enforcer, Dr. Sardaq. Sardaq was a chief executive in the security service in Iraq and had vital connections with both the State and the clergy. It made him one of the most powerful men in Tehran, and when he defected to the CLA it was rumored that all his connections in Iran remained intact. When Hizbullah was contacted by Angelo Vacirca through the Sicilian Mafia, they immediately reached out to Sardaq, who became their broker by default.

The Sicilian Mafia turned to their connections with the Corsican Mob in Morocco. The Corsicans would provide the most expedient options in transporting the contraband from Palestine to Morocco, from where it would be moved to Europe. They immediately reached out to their black-market connections in Palestine and made positive contact with the JLP.

It was at this point, Isabel would later find out, that Sirhan and Abdul Mehdidoud were compromised and forced into the Mafia scheme. Sirhan's family in Beirut was targeted by Hizbullah, who located relatives in Tehran that provided the necessary leverage. Mehdidoud, who had also been extorted by the JLP, had no choice but to make a deal with Sirhan to become part of his photography crew in order to infiltrate the tour entourage.

Isabel could not believe the bizarre nightmare world they had been drawn into. Here they were in the Waldorf-Astoria with Melvin E. Williams, one of the fastest-rising comedians in NYC, and they were treating him like a whipping boy. Not to mention that Johnny should have been able to walk into any police station the New York and have these bastards taken down. Chances were the police would give them an apology before setting them free.

Vic tossed a handkerchief into Melvin's face before Jack got up and dragged him back to the sofa.

"C'mon, ya fuckin' mook, don't act like you're mortally wounded. Man up, dude."

"Please, man, not the face. Don't mess up my face," Melvin whimpered.

"Just trying to make a *point*," Jack chuckled, looking around for appreciation for his pun.

"That's a good one, Jack," Vic obliged him. "Okay,

Melvin, no hard feeling. I think we all know where we stand. You go back and tell that nigger that he stands to rake in a ton of money on the cable deal when we start videotaping the boxing sessions and sending them back to the States. I'll cut him in fifty-fifty, I don't give a shit. Of course, anything that gets kicked back to our friend Johnny here comes out of his cut."

"I don't want nothing," Johnny spoke up. "I just want outta this fuckin' mess."

"Good. So if I was you, I'd make it a point to go to Lincoln yourself and tell him what a good thing this is. Right away you get the sports fans in on it. Lots of people who don't give a shit about music will turn in just to see a boxer up onstage. Most of them'll watch just to see if you make a jerk outta yourself."

"Yeah, right," Johnny continued to hold his temper.

"Now don't forget, I'm not taking no for an answer," Vic gave them a final warning. "I don't give a shit if you gotta threaten to pull outta the gig. You tell them you got obligations to your promoter, and that's how it's gotta be. As for you, Melvin, I don't care if you gotta suck the guy's dick. All I know is, there better be lots of room on those planes for our gear when those flights to Palestine are ready to roll."

Johnny and Melvin agreed to make plans to meet with James Lincoln at the earliest opportunity the next morning. Melvin was just about ready to fall apart, while Johnny was fighting to keep his own cool. She knew it took everything he had to keep from declaring war on the hoods, but it was a war that he couldn't win and was sure to get Isabel and Roth hurt. Roth was supercool as usual, but she knew he was having just as much trouble in putting up with the Mafiosi's attitude.

"Why don't you let me talk to my Dad, or Duke?" she insisted when they returned to their apartment in Bay Ridge that night. "Everybody's acting like these Mafia guys are God or something. They can't be more powerful than the military, that's ridiculous."

"What are you gonna do, have your Dad send his Green Beret buddies in here?" Johnny was derisive. "This is the Mafia, they pay off the police department. We owe them money we don't have, and they're not gonna wait until we get paid for the gig, you know that. Look, we'll be okay, there's no reason why Lincoln shouldn't go for it. If we have to, we'll get in touch with Princess

Sabrina. The sports angle is genuine, she'll have to see how much more publicity it'll get for her father's regime. Everybody wins with this thing."

"You know those bastards are up to no good. They're going to get caught smuggling those drugs of theirs, and we'll all get locked up."

"Baby, you got nothing to do with it. You and Roth are free and clear. If they make a deal and hang me out to dry, I'll take my medicine, but nothing can happen to you or Roth."

"What are you talking about? How am I going to go on without you in my life?"

"I said don't worry. We'll come out fine, you'll see."

Melvin sent a car out for them the next morning, and they took the long ride to the North Bronx to Lincoln's multimillion-dollar mansion. She would look back on those days, a girl in her mid-twenties being invited to the home of one of the greatest R&B stars of all time. It never really dawned on her, not until a long time afterward. She remembered wearing a cute red and black zebra-striped blouse and black slacks. She recalled the mansion looking like a museum with its thick marble walls, fountains and plate glass windows. Everywhere they walked she had to be careful that her spiked heels didn't slip on the marbled floors.

They were met in the enormous circular lobby by the monstrous Toby, who led them down the cavernous hall to Lincoln's study. She wondered why Toby didn't go into boxing. He was big enough to kill two men. She also wondered if he carried weapons in that suit of his. He could probably fit six guns inside one breast of his jacket. She always wondered what his voice sounded like. People would ask him questions and he pretended he didn't hear them.

"Well, well, my rock stars. My man Melvin tells me you trying to be sports stars now."

Lincoln was dressed in a suit as usual in an office that looked like some of the smaller planetariums she had visited when she was in school. It had a huge glass dome for a roof and there were no walls, just shaded windows separated by huge granite columns that rose to the top of the dome. He sat behind a desk that looked like an oak platform, and Melvin was seated in an armchair beside Lincoln's golden throne. Lincoln came around to shake hands before they all took seats before the desk.

"Yeah, my promoters are pretty hot to make this deal with you, they asked me to come up and put in a good word with you," Johnny said airily. "You know how it is, with King Daoud trying to get this kingdom of his up and running. The music's gonna be a great thing for him, but the boxing might make it better. We were thinking maybe I could spar with some of the Olympic fighters in the region, you know, stir up some publicity. We're gonna be there for a couple of weeks anyway. It'd be a good thing for the promotion, good publicity for the tour, good for you. They talked to Melvin, they said they could spread some cash your way."

"Oh, there'll be more than enough money to go around," Lincoln eased back in his throne. "What I'm worried about is distractions. I don't want people to start taking their eyes off the ball. Do you know why I picked the Valley of Megiddo for the show?"

"Yeah," Johnny shrugged. "Something about you could seat a million people there."

"Right. Napoleon Bonaparte said that. He never got to see a million soldiers on that field. We---all of us---can see that if we do this right. A million people, that's a lot of people. Can you imagine what it'd be like to have to get to the bathroom?"

They all shared a laugh.

"We have to have everyone in the Middle East wanting to witness this event. We can't have people thinking, 'I'll come see it next time'. There will never, ever be a next time. We can't let people think there'll be another one, or anything close to it. We can't have people think, well, maybe I can skip seeing Johnny Carmona on stage, I'll go see him in the ring instead."

"I don't see it that way," Johnny was adamant. "They come out to the sessions, they're just seeing guys moving around. They go to the concert, that's a once in a lifetime event. Hey, we're gonna put it all on the line for you up there. You will never see a rock band give you what we will give you up there. On a stage like that, I'll climb to the top of the light tower, to the top of the speaker towers, and dive off into the mosh pit. That's gonna be the biggest mosh pit in the history of the world."

"Well, I don't know about that," Lincoln speculated. "You know to those hundred thousand at the rear of the field, you may look like a flea jumping off a camel's ass."

There was a pregnant pause before everyone broke into laughter again

"Look, in my mind, if happy musicians make better musicians, I'm all for it," Lincoln folded his hands atop the highly-polished desk. "I just will not tolerate distractions. My doctor's gonna keep an eye on you. If you suffer any heat-related problems, I'm pulling you out of the exhibition. Now, one thing you need to let your people know: no drugs. The Israelis, with that Mossad, the IDF and the rest of them, they gonna be up the ass. If they catch any drugs coming into the country, we all gonna pay the price. And I can assure you, if I can make any kind of deal, the offending party will spend the rest of their life out there before I spend one day. I already told Diamond and Carlucci, and you need to let your people know."

"Drugs?" Johnny looked back and forth between Roth and Isabel. "What do I look, punchy to you? Like Muhammed Ali? Those people make their women walk around in the desert with tablecloths over their heads, a hundred degrees. They get down on their knees and pray to the fuckin' wind three times a day. They get pissed off at somebody, they go into their store with a stick of dynamite up their ass. You think I'm gonna bring drugs into their country? Fuck no. Not me."

"Besides, you know our deal," Roth spoke up. "We take offers anyplace, anytime. We come back here and get a call from Atlantic City for good money, and we gotta turn it down because we can't pass the piss test? No way."

"You know, you're right about that," Lincoln nodded. "So, how's Diamond doing? You speak to him lately?"

"He's okay, you know," Johnny was nonchalant.

"Last time I saw him he looked like he was ready to hang in somebody's window for Halloween," Lincoln grunted. "I'm not planning to do that gig without having Lurch on the keyboard, know what I'm saying? I'm paying for the whole crew, not Hezbollah minus one."

"Hey, David's okay," Johnny assured him. "I seen him crawl out of bed with the flu to play a gig, more than once. This band is his life. You brought him back from the dead to do this show. You think he's finally made it, reached the top of the mountain, and he's gonna blow it? No way, man. You can count on him more than anybody, maybe except me and Roth."

"How about Munson? I'm starting to wonder about her. From the reports I got, she had her life straightened out. She's going with that hockey player, she's got that private eye business running smooth, she's settling down. Only I'm getting a little concerned about her stepping back into the role. See, there's a difference between playing a character and becoming the character. I'm starting to worry that she's going over the top."

"Nah, fuck that," Johnny disagreed. "My ace is with Debbie. She's the toughest bitch I ever met, but she's crazy like a fox. How do you think she kept ahead of David Diamond all these years? That's what you need to focus on. Debbie's helping David get psyched. She's leading him by example. She's leading him over the wall, but you can be sure she'll drag him over if she has to. You get Debbie, you got David, and vice versa. It's not about letting you down, it's about letting each other down. It'll never happen, bet on it."

"I am betting on it. Fifty million."

"*What?*"

"That's between the three of you, and Melvin the Fly on the wall. King Daoud and the Kingdom of Palestine is putting up half. I'm pretty sure Princess Sabrina has gotten half of that from her European connections. I'm putting my ass on the line. Of course, I got my investors in Hollywood, but they ain't gonna like getting burned on this. The State of Israel is brokering the deal, but they're not guaranteeing anything. We're putting in fifty mil, we got to come out way over fifty mil. Way over."

"I'm sure you know what you're doing," Johnny exhaled.

"We've got it figured out. We just need to make sure there are no unforeseen circumstances. You know, in show business, one hand washes the other. That's how I made it, that's how Melvin made it, that's the way you're gonna make it."

"He's telling you like it is, brothers," Melvin E. Williams agreed. The puncture mark from the ice pick looked like a popped zit this morning.

"Hey, one hand washes the other, I dig it," Johnny grinned at Roth and Isabel.

"You want your boxing show, you keep your eyes on Diamond and Munson, and the rest of them crazy mofos," Lincoln instructed him. "But especially those two. Deal?"

"Okay, Boss. You got it."

"You and Debbie, are you two close, like friends?" Lincoln asked Isabel.

"Well, we've used each other's makeup kit, if that's what you mean."

"I mean, you'd be willing to help John out, talk her outta doing crazy shit, right?"

"You mean like keeping the bull out of the china shop?"

"Whatever you can do, girlfriend."

They all shook hands before Toby led them back to the garden entrance. Johnny and Roth were exuberant, but Isabel was really starting to think about what keeping an eye on Debbie Munson entailed.

Chapter Sixteen

"You'll never guess who called here yesterday," Roth called over as Johnny switched on the fluorescent lights upon entering the darkened gym that morning.

"Klitschko?" Johnny smirked.

"*Rolling Stone.*"

"For who, the kid?" Johnny asked incredulously.

"They called for us," Roth guffawed. "About that rumor on the Internet that we were putting the band together for a reunion gig in Iraq."

"Johnny," Isabel appeared almost as if on cue from the shadows at the doorway. "I was calling you before you got in the car, I followed you up here. *Rolling Stone* just called the house."

"What in hell?" Johnny stared back and forth at her and Roth. "What rumor?"

"Millennium Productions announced a 20th anniversary show commemorating the Crusader Concert in Palestine," Roth explained. "That's what I'm hearing."

"This is crazy," Johnny shook his head. "Who do we got? David's dead, I'm running this place, Tina's too big for this shit. I haven't spoken to Stu since Palestine, or Debbie, for that matter. Besides, I'll look like a fucking jerk up there. It'd be like me getting back in the ring. I got a kid who wants to do that shit, let him go instead."

"Why don't you give them a call and see what this is about?" Isabel asked.

"Who, Millennium? For what?" Johnny stared at her.

"How much money are they talking about?" she asked.

"Did you not hear what I just said?" he pointed at the full-length mirrors on the nearby wall. "Do you see that? I'm forty nine years old. My hair is turning gray. I can't even spar with the grade school kids anymore. I strain my voice when I yell these days, and I couldn't sing in the first place. They take one look and it's over. Forget about it, Issy. We had our time."

"Our son needs his," she said huskily. "We need the money."

Johnny and Roth looked at each other before Isabel rushed out of the room.

"I don't know where to start," Johnny sat down on a bench. "Dye my hair, start working out again, maybe do some karaoke, get my voice back. It'll take a while, it's not going to happen overnight."

"Forget it," Roth came over and patted Johnny's shoulder. "She's just venting. It's like her telling you to go up and fix the roof."

"You think so?"

"I know so."

"It's a lot of money on the table. Maybe I could wing it."

"You could go back in the ring and try to wing it too."

"Yeah, but this isn't like fighting."

"It's more like the roof. You could do more harm than good."

"Maybe you're right," Johnny looked at the middle-aged man in the mirror. "You could be right."

Isabel went back to the office area, staring sightlessly out the window as she assimilated the firestorm of emotions welling in her bosom. Her thoughts kept turning to David, how everyone thought it would have been impossible for him to survive the tour, much less get onstage to do the show itself. Yet he passed the test with flying colors, and it was only a twist of fate that caused his demise. Johnny was in far better shape, even at this age, than David was over ten years ago. Plus her son's very life was at stake.

"You know, I'm having trouble with this," Johnny came into the room after a few minutes. "When we first heard this on the news, I was hot for it and you were saying we were past our time for this. Now I've talked myself out of it and you're upset. Are you just being argumentative, or are you trying some kind of reverse psychology? Tell me what's going on here."

"We didn't know about Frank," she wiped her eyes. "We didn't have this situation to deal with. We don't have the kind of money we may need to deal with this. Maybe I was wrong. They have reunion gigs all the time. All those Seventies bands are still out there making money, and they're old enough to be our parents. Maybe just one time, for this one show. I don't know, Johnny, it's up to you. If you don't think you can pull it off, then forget it."

144

"So what, you think I still got it?" he walked over to where she stood by the window and stroked her hair. "Maybe if I dye my hair, get back in shape, I can pull it off?"

"I don't know, John. You have to ask yourself that. You have to ask Roth."

"Hey, Roth!" Johnny yelled out the door. "C'mon in here for a minute!"

"You know, it's not like we have to make a decision right here and now."

""Don't worry about it. Hey, Rothie! C'mere!"

Now all of a sudden they were seeing each other in different lights, through different eyes, looking at each other as if they had not been inseparable for the last two decades. Johnny assessed Roth's lanky build, not as slender and wiry as he had been twenty years ago. There was a slight paunch, just enough to get him up to a size thirty pants size. Johnny was going to have to bust his ass to get down from a thirty-four to a thirty-two. Roth hair was graying as well, but nothing a bottle of Grecian Formula couldn't handle for either one of them.

"So what, you think you're ready to go back onstage?"

"It's not just the two of us," Roth was characteristic-ally noncommittal. "You got a few other people you need to talk to. I could pull my guitar out of the closet and make some noise. I don't know how it's gonna go down in front of a roomful of people, much less at an outdoor concert."

"Outdoor concert," Johnny chuckled. "You believe this guy?"

"That's what I'm asking myself. What're you gonna do, tell everyone you're going on vacation? Who'll mind the store? Reggie Fleming is gonna disappear, and as far as I can see, he's the only one who can keep us from ending up back on square one. It's an either-or situation. If I were you, I'd get some front money from Lincoln to at least cover your ass back here. Get caught up, get some new equipment, try to attract some new talent. This way if everything falls apart, you can consider it a business loan from Lincoln. That's my advice."

"You don't think we can get anyone to fill in for us while we're gone?"

"Name me someone you'd feel comfortable giving the keys to for a month."

"Shit," Johnny and Isabel looked at each other.

"So if I got Lincoln to give us some front money, maybe I could hire somebody to watch the place," Johnny mused. "I know a couple of old pros who could use the cash. And if we scored big, maybe we could afford to keep them around, especially if they brought some kids in with them."

"It's the money, John," Isabel said softly. "I wasn't thinking that far ahead when I first heard about it. We didn't have the issue with Frank, and I wasn't thinking about what the money could do for the gym."

"My advice for both of you is not to get your hopes too high," Roth suggested. "We haven't heard from any of the others yet. Issy, have you called anyone about Frank?"

"No, not yet," she exhaled. "It was hard enough calling my sister and my Dad. I'm still trying to get it together with Frank as it is. You know how independent he is, and what a private person he is. I can't just barge into his life and be an overbearing mother all of a sudden. I can't afford for him to start pushing against me."

Her voice trailed off and she turned away from them. Roth and Johnny exchanged knowing looks before walking back out into the gym. Once they got busy setting out workout gear for the day, she was making a beeline towards the exit.

"See you at lunch?" Johnny called after her.

"No, I'm going to go by Frank's."

"Tell him I said hi. Tell him to call me."

Frank had an apartment on Northwest 27th Avenue, not far from River Cities Community Charter School. It wasn't far from where the gym was located on Grand Avenue. He spent most of his time at Blade's apartment before they split up, and had rarely been home since. She had kept a respectful distance since he left home in deference to his lifestyle. At this stage of the game, she was tying him back onto her apron strings regardless of whether he or anybody else liked it or not.

She trotted up the stairs to the second floor apartment, as if getting there a couple of minutes quicker would guarantee she would find him home. She stopped outside the door to catch her breath before knocking, then checked herself before tapping calmly. She waited before tapping again, then started back down the hall.

"Hold on. Be right there."

146

He opened the door and had a frowzy look which indicated he didn't have any assignments today. If he wasn't gone by now, he would already be up and about preparing for an afternoon class.

"Hey, whuzup? Chilling out today?"

"Hi, Mom. Want coffee?" he asked, kissing her on the cheek before leading the way inside. It was a small bachelor's apartment, three rooms along with a kitchenette and bathroom.

"Sure."

She went into the living room, always proud of Frank for keeping the place as neat as he did. If it wasn't for her at the house and Roth at the gym, Johnny was like following a small dust storm around.

"So what're you up to today?"

"I was gonna ask you the same question."

"Well, I was thinking about going to the clinic and getting something for this cough. I want to keep it under control as long as possible, hopefully until the end of school this summer."

"Why, has anyone said anything?"

"No, well, you know kids. They notice everything. You get a persistent cough and they'll spread rumors you've got TB."

"They don't know that you're... I mean, you haven't said anything about..."

"No, it's not like being black, Ma," Frank chided her as he brought two mugs of coffee into the living room. "I don't feel like my sexual orientation is a matter of public record, though I wouldn't deny it. It works both ways, though. If word got around and they noticed afterward I had a persistent cough, I'm pretty sure there wouldn't be too many spots available on the schedule from that point."

"Yeah, you're right, it's none of their business."

"Enough sugar?"

"Yes, it's fine," she sipped her coffee, setting it down on a coaster on the coffee table.

"So what, you were just here in the neighborhood?"

"No, I decided to come by," she was brusque. "Now, listen, Frank, I'm not going to make excuses to anyone for coming by to check on you. If it was any of my family or friends who contracted an illness, I'd be coming by regularly. That's all there is to it. If you're not home or you're on your way out, that's fine. But I'm not going to be making up with reasons for coming by to see you."

"Well, why don't you give me a call before you come by? This way you're not coming all the way over here for nothing."

"You won't answer the phone, you know how you are."

"All right, now I will. I promise."

"I don't want you shutting me out, Frank. I want to be with you while we're dealing with this. I want you to reach out to your father. At least meet him halfway, I know he's going to be reaching to you. We have to face this as a family."

"Okay, okay."

There was an uncomfortable silence.

"You know," Frank cleared his throat, "the thing about family. I'm sorry you're not gonna get any grandkids out of this deal."

"Don't talk like that. This fight hasn't even started yet."

"Not just that. You know what I mean. Well... yeah, who knows. If I find another partner, maybe we'd adopt or something, who knows."

"Well, if it wasn't something that bothered you before, why worry about it now? We've got enough on our plate as it is."

"I don't know," he rubbed his scalp thoughtfully. "It's something gay people kinda joke about. They call straight people 'breeders'. You know, like there's already too many people in the world. Only we don't think so much about the family thing, you know, leaving grandchildren for someone. Would you have a problem with an adopted kid, it not being your own blood?"

"Why would I? If the child called me its grand-mother, would I call them a liar?"

"No, I know you wouldn't," he said assuringly. "You know, out of the whole band, you and Uncle Duke were the only ones who had kids. I wonder why that was."

"That's a good question," she mused. "I guess Tina and Zeke couldn't keep it together long enough to have kids. Debbie and David and Roth never got married. I guess me and Duke and Lucy were the lucky ones."

"You call this lucky?"

"Now come on. You're my son, I love you. Whether you ever get married or not, that's your decision. You've blessed my life, and that's all that counts."

"I just feel like...maybe I haven't lived up to your expectations."

"You live up to your own expectations, that's all anyone can ask another person to do."

"You don't know how much it means to me to hear you say that," his eyes got misty.

"Look, why don't you let me go with you to the clinic?"

"No, I'll be okay. You go on home."

"You could use some company."

"Okay, look, if you go home, I'll catch up with you at dinnertime, how's that?"

"That's be great," her eyes glowed. "Dinner at six."

* * * * *

"Look, Jerry, you're the man of the hour," Johnny insisted as he and Roth stood near the ring at the gym with the stocky black man. "Fleming may be the future of this club, but you're the one who's been carrying the flag for us. You know how it is, it takes time for a fighter to get established. You've paid your dues, you're ready to step up. You've been fighting in the clubs for five years, you've been to Atlantic City. This is your time, you can get to the next level if you want it. You give me three months – ninety days – and I can get you to Las Vegas in confidence, no questions about whether we're ready or not. We will be ready."

"Well, who you got in mind?"

"I don't know, it's a funny market right now. You got all that MMA shit going on right now, guys are going back and forth. That mixed martial art bullshit, that's a meat market. It's like going to watch dog fights. They just go to watch somebody get torn up, they don't give a shit if a guy can fight or not. A guy tries his hand at boxing, he can't cut it, he gets into that shit and gets his ass handed to him. Then he comes back and says he has MMA experience. And the boxing guys are so desperate, they take him right in. I'm not saying there's no talent out there, you just gotta keep your eyes open."

"So why don't you get me a couple of easy fights, let me work my way up?"

"You're five-and-two," Roth interjected. "We get you some bums to fight, pump you up to eight-and-two, the promoters can see what we did. You need a good win right now, put a solid name on your resume. You take out somebody good, somebody like Jimmy Jaxx. If anyone questions our six and two, we say Jimmy Jaxx."

"That Jimmy Jaxx is a tough mofo," Jerry looked away.

"Hey, you could be seven and oh right now, I wouldn't have to make this kind of move," Johnny pointed out. "Look, you know it's all numbers in Vegas and Atlantic City. You go down in flames at seven and oh, the guy who put you down ended a streak. Five and two, the ticket-buyers think the promoter's padding the card. If the main event's not a big draw, you're gonna get a poor house, plain and simple."

"It goes both ways," Roth spoke up. "They get a so-so main event but a competitive undercard, people know it'll be an entertaining night. You try and take the easy way up, the money's gonna be slower. You need a big win to reestablish yourself."

"I just don't know if I'm ready for someone like Jaxx right now."

"Jerry, you're twenty-seven years old," Johnny was emphatic. "That's long in the tooth for just seven fights. If you want to make this thing happen, the time is now. If I get you Jaxx, or maybe Rutherford, you take either one of them out and I got a lot more leverage at the table next time. If we're on call, and somebody pulls out of a mid-card fight, that's your break. You could easily get ten grand for something like that. Plus, if you win, you know I'm going for fifteen, twenty grand next time. That's where you need to be right now in your career."

"It's nice money, and I could use that money. Still, you know I can't afford to lose another fight. If I'm not ready…"

"What are we talking about here? I will get you ready. I will help you win."

"All right, John. I'll give it a shot.

"It has to be your best shot, Jerry," Roth told him.

"Look, you come over for dinner tonight, I'll tell Issy. We'll eat, relax, and talk this over."

"I don't wanna intrude…"

"Hey, don't worry about it. Roth'll be there too, okay?"

Just then the front door opened, and Isabel came into the room.

"Hi, baby. Guess who's coming to dinner?"

"Hey," Johnny said hesitantly. "Same thing I was gonna ask you."

Chapter Seventeen

Johnny Carmona would never forget the sea of humanity swirling in the desert before them that night. It was almost a frightening sight, the image of everything he knew about the Bible but was afraid to ask. The people in the front rows were screaming, yelling, cheering. Beyond them were nothing but bobbing heads and flailing limbs. It was if the earth had split asunder and all of humanity had cascaded down into this place.

He looked down along the platform to his right and saw Isabel with her Crusaders T-shirt, her long streaked hair billowing in the forceful winds emanated by the humongous fans surrounding the stage. She shook her fist overhead with pride, blowing a kiss at him as he bounded up and down, jogging in place as he did before his fights. He knew at that moment that she was heaven sent, that there would never be another person in his lifetime who he could ever love as much. She had been in his corner during the biggest victories and defeats in his life, and there could never be anything greater than this.

"Hey, you people out there!" he was channeling Tony Montana, the main character in *Scarface* who Johnny loved to imitate. "Take your pictures! Take plenty of pictures! You ain't never gonna see a bad guy like this again!"

"You keep running around like that you're gonna fall off the stage," Roth yelled at him above the roar of the amps and the crowd.

"So what?" he leaned over towards Roth. "They'll just pick me back up and put me back up here. They love me, man!"

Stu joined Johnny at the front mic, nudging up against him as Johnny wrapped an arm around his shoulders. They stuck their faces up to the mic and began caterwauling the chorus together:

Overnight celebrities
Every minute one is made
Overnight celebrities
Come on and join the hit parade

It was David's paean to the tidal wave of hardcore bands that were flooding the market, who made it possible for Hezbollah to rise to the top of the river of sludge. They were making their own recordings in their basements, buying their own jewel cases, copying their own CD's and selling their own music. There was a hardcore market halfway around the world that looked at David and his band like a bunch of over-aged has-beens who were merely going through the motions. Only Johnny and the band were here in front of a million people. They had beaten the odds. They had won.

Only they would never believe how quickly the rapture of victory would be obliterated by the trauma of the greatest tragedy of their young lives. The gig ended up around ten PM, and the band was returned by helicopter to their hotel. A helipad had been set up on the roof, and once the Mossad and the Palestinian Guard got everyone back into their rooms, it was mission accomplished. Or so they thought.

Things were happening so fast that no one realized just how chummy Stu Carlucci was getting with Princess Sabrina. It started with Sabrina hobnobbing with the band, and led to her joy in finding out that Stu had partied with the French punk band Plastic Bertrand a few years ago. Having earned her degree at the University of Paris, she had been a big fan. They spent most of the banquet before the Concert together, Sabrina having invited Stu to the King's table. It was still disregarded as Stu was hardly a ladies' man and Sabrina was a notorious celebrity chaser regardless of their flash-in-the-pan status.

Once the band had returned to the hotel, it would be found out later that Princess Sabrina had phoned Stu and invited him up to her room. She invited him to come up to the Presidential suite to hear records. There was no way in hell Stu was not going. Moreover, he was a card-carrying member of Hezbollah and a founding Party member before that. He was not going to ask permission from anyone to go meet a girl, even if it was Princess Sabrina. The last person on earth he would be asking was Duke Gallegos, and the second to last was Billy Sixkiller.

Long after the fact, it would be discovered that Dr. Sardaq, King Daoud's Director of Security, was actually a double agent for Iran. He had monitored the conversation between Stu and Sabrina and did nothing to prevent her from freezing the automatic security code to the elevator so Stu could gain access. He also made it possible for agents of Hizbullah to make their way up to her room and pose as room service to get inside.

After word got out and they had the meeting in Duke's suite, the six of them left in two SUVs (*sport utility vehicle). Duke and Billy led the way, having a transponder inside their truck which was being traced by four Israeli helicopters flying above the clouds. Roth, Johnny, David and Debbie were in the second truck. The plan was to follow the desert road heading towards the Lebanon border, which was the most obvious exit strategy for the kidnappers.

They would be moving through Bedouin territory where the nomads had their tents pitched all over the desert area within viewing distance from the road. Plus there were numerous livestock pens and storehouses in the area. It favored the insurgents as possible hideouts but were off-limits to the Israelis without probable cause. In a situation like this all bets were off, but a miscalculation would not only alert the terrorists but even cause them to make a desperate move. The last thing they needed at the end of this concert tour was to have Stu and the Princess decapitated.

Billy was in continuous communication with Mossad as Duke sped up the highway. They determined that the kidnappers had turned off the highway and would seek refuge until dawn. Aerial surveillance was unable to detect any suspicious vehicles moving north towards the Lebanese border. They were using sonar devices to seek out any sizeable groups of campers or livestock herders. The possibilities were being narrowed down to a half dozen target areas.

Duke's SUV abruptly dropped back as he signaled Roth to pull ahead of him once they had gotten twenty miles out of Tel Aviv. Roth did so, and they proceeded another five miles before Duke began flashing his headlights and emergency lights. Duke then pulled ahead of Roth, cutting in front of him before veering off the road towards a farmhouse about fifty yards to the east. The agents knew the maneuver would have confused anyone who was watching as Roth followed Duke as they rolled to a halt outside the farmhouse.

Duke and Billy exited the SUV with their Uzis hanging

from their necks as six armed men emerged from the farmhouse. Billy, who spoke Arabic, told them there had been rumors of a kidnapping and that his crew had captured two of the Americans who had gone out in search of their friends. He signaled to Roth and Johnny, who opened the truck doors and motioned to David and Debbie to get out. Armed with Uzis, they ushered the two punkers to the farmhouse. Billy continued speaking in Arabic as David and Debbie were led into the building.

The house appeared as a communication base, its tables covered with maps, computers and mobile devices. There were two men inside the room, clad in military fatigues and wearing holsters as were their comrades. In the far corner were two figures appearing to be secured on bunks. Everyone knew it must have been Stu and Sabrina. The two group leaders conversed in Arabic with the militiamen, staring at the newcomers suspiciously.

"Well, what are we gonna do here, swap spit or talk shit," David demanded in a loud voice.

"Shut the fuck up," Debbie hissed at him as Billy screamed at him in Arabic.

"You shut your mouth, you dog!" a burly man yelled in a thick accent.

"Dog?" David scoffed. "You people have been eating nothing but dog food on tortilla bread since I got here, and you're calling *me* a dog?"

"I told you to shut up!" the man stepped menacingly towards David.

With that, David hawked and spat right in the soldier's face. The man was aghast at the glob of green slime as he wiped it away. In response, he pulled out his Glock-17 and shot David right between the eyes.

The room exploded as Debbie dove to David's side as he toppled backward to the floor. According to plan, Roth and Johnny stood back to back, holding their Uzis at the ready. Duke and Billy threw themselves to the ground, rolling and firing at the uniformed men in the room. Within seconds it was over, and they could hear helicopters whirring in the skies above as Billy ran to free Stu and Sabrina.

"Duke, call an ambulance!" Debbie cradled David's torn head in her lap. "He's in bad shape, we need a doctor! Now!"

"Debbie," Duke's Uzi hung limply at his side, his voice hoarse as he was shaken by the sight of his fallen colleague. "He's gone."

At once the entire room was stunned by the feral scream that filled the room as Debbie's heart was pierced by the realization of what had happened. Roth put his Uzi down and fell to his knees alongside Debbie, pulling her away from David and hugging her face against his chest. He filled his hands with her titian tresses, holding his cheek against her head as if she was the most precious possession on earth.

"Johnny," Duke cleared his throat, nearly moved to tears at the sight of Debbie collapsing. "Help me get him up on the table."

"No!" Stu stood in shock behind Duke, holding fistfuls of his own hair on either side of his head, his eyes wide with horror. "No fucking way! No! No!" Duke signaled to Billy, who ushered Stu and Sabrina towards the door where a squad of heavily-armed IDF troops were barging through the entrance.

Johnny would never forget the helicopter ride back to the hotel along with his bandmates, all of whom were numb with shock. They would learn that David's death had come months earlier than the cancer that had filled his intestines would have killed him. It was of little consolation, as they had not even been afforded the chance to celebrate their success with the Concert. They had gone straight into lockdown to preclude any possibility of an attack by Hizbullah. As it turned out, they went out and found Hizbullah themselves.

Isabel collapsed into Johnny's arms when he and Roth got back to their suite. She had gotten the news in Tina's suite along with Susie. The girls were so distraught that they returned to their own rooms until the survivors returned.

"He went out the way he wanted, just as if he planned it," Johnny stroked her hair as Roth poured them all big shots of whiskey at the living room bar. "He gave his life to create a diversion. We took out the terrorists before they got off a shot. He was the only one who got hit. He saved Stu and the Princess' lives."

"I can't believe it," she said over and over, weeping uncontrollably.

"Neither can I. He got what he wanted, though. The world will never forget him."

And so it was over, the event of a lifetime, just like that. James Lincoln grabbed what little spotlight was left, explaining that he was under orders by the Israelis not to discuss the events of the previous evening after the Concert. The incident was conveniently swept under the rug, though rumors swirled that Stu and Sabrina snuck off on a midnight tryst amidst an after-hours joyride with the band. The carousing led to an accident during which David Diamond was killed. Once again he had garnered more notoriety in one single evening than he had achieved in a lifetime.

The plane ride back was terribly subdued as if they were returning from a funeral. The band and its entourage felt as if the plane was a car with a body in the trunk. David had written out a will in felt tip and hotel stationery, bequeathing his $100,000 to Charlene Buchbinder. She was assigned by Novarich Records as his babysitter and had indulged his sexual fantasies throughout the tour. Charlene had suffered a nervous breakdown upon learning of the handwritten will. All of David's NYC belongings were left to Debbie Munson, who also seemed on the verge of collapse.

Parting was not sweet sorrow, it was the final insult on the list of injuries. They were all physically and emotionally drained when they reached JFK Airport. Most of them had trains, planes or automobiles to catch. Debbie came out of her ennui and seemed as if she was saying goodbye to everyone for the last time. Johnny wanted desperately to go for a drink with her but Isabel had a splitting headache and was barely functioning. The last they saw of her was at the airport lounge where she seemed to be having a heated discussion with Mel Dalton. It would be revealed months later that she and Mel broke up, and Debbie nearly committed suicide when she got back to her apartment. She would reveal in an interview that she did not have the guts to pull the trigger.

Isabel would never forget that time. The only other times in her life that surpassed it were the day of their wedding and the birth of their son. She remembered being that punk rock girl, the countless hours she spent in the mirror, making sure her mascara was without a loose grain, her eyeliner as if painted by an artist, her foundation perfectly blended with her skin, her lipstick as if that of a porcelain doll. Her hair was always symmetrically styled, and the more she and Johnny spent on her wardrobe, she looked all the more gorgeous. On that night of the concert, Debbie Munson owned the stage but many could not keep their eyes off the sidelines where Isabel stood. It was her time, it was their time, and somehow they knew that they had reached a peak that they would never see again.

After they left NYC and moved to Miami, she gradually let

go of her supermodel looks, It was a slow process, and she wasn't sure of when it started or where she really turned the corner. Mousse wasn't as important after a while, and the natural look began reclaiming her beauty from the miracles of the makeup kit. She realized she didn't really need the foundation as long as her skin was kept in perfect condition; lipstick was lipstick whether it cost $5 or $50. Johnny loved her regardless of whether she spent five minutes or fifty minutes getting her eyeliner right, and she was still being told how beautiful she was regardless of how much or how little time she spent in the mirror. She was always checking, just to make sure they weren't blowing smoke up her nose. Only after Frank was born, she wasn't checking all that much anymore. She was now somebody's mother, and she knew that mothers were always beautiful even when they were a hundred years old. Still, she wanted to look good for Johnny, and she continued to get more than her share of compliments.

She could never figure out what went on in Debbie Munson's mind. When she read the article about Debbie thinking of committing suicide, she tried to call repeatedly with no luck. She had Johnny make some calls and, just like everyone else in the old gang, she found that she never returned calls. Isabel finally reached her at her business, Munson Investigations Inc. (which she not-so-curiously called MINK). They chatted for a half hour, and Isabel never brought up the article. She didn't feel as if she was talking to the old Debbie. Something was missing, and somehow she felt like it was David. Debbie still hadn't recovered, and possibly never would.

It just didn't make sense to her how Debbie would want to kill herself. There had been a dark rumor back in the day after Stu and Duke left the band that she had swallowed a bottle of pills. Her Dad was the one who found her, and to this day Paco Cabales refused to speak of it. It was well-known that Dad thought of Debbie as a third daughter, and whatever happened that day would remain a secret he would carry to the grave. Still, Debbie was not a coward or a quitter. It was totally unlike her, but no one would ever be able to reach out and prevent it from happening again. No one would ever be able to get close enough to do so.

The feeling of death hovering around her made her sick. She found herself thinking of David more than she had in a long time. It must have been her subconscious correlating what was happening with Frank. He was being stolen from her way, way before his time.

Who knows how much David could have accomplished upon returning from Palestine with a hundred grand in his pocket? Who could imagine what they all would have lost if Debbie had come back from the Concert in one piece, just to pull that trigger? And what will the world have lost when Frank Carmona was dead and gone?

"Hey, baby," Johnny greeted her when he came home from the gym that evening. "Guess we'll be having a quiet evening tonight."

"Yeah," she cleared her throat. "It sure was great having Frank and Reggie over last night. Who would've thought they were gonna hit it off so well?"

"Aah," Johnny exhaled tautly. "Frank's always had a great personality, chip off the old block. Just like both his parents. That's why I always had a problem. He could've done anything he put his mind to."

"I wish you'd…"

"Hey, honey, I'm sorry," Johnny came over and put his arms around her waist from behind, nuzzling her hair. "You shouldn't take it like that. I'm not writing him off. I'm just talking. Who else do I have to talk to? I'm gonna have Roth checking into a depression clinic if he has to listen to any more of my shit."

"I know," she tilted her head back against his. "I was just thinking about David and Debbie, and it made me sad. Why are we having to lose everybody so early? Oh my gosh, what am I saying?"

"Don't worry about it. Don't beat yourself up. We're gonna fight this thing, and we're gonna win. You never seen Johnny Carmona in a fight he didn't win. It don't start now."

"Don't you beat yourself up either. Don't try and turn this into a win or lose thing," she turned around and hugged him. "We just have to stay strong for each other, think positive, and hope for the best. This is what Frank wants, and it's all about Frank. It's not about you or me, but it doesn't mean we're not part of it. Let's just hold on tight, and face this as a family. It's the best we can do."

"Okay, you're right."

"C'mon, let me buy you a beer."

She took his hand and led him to the kitchen where they had a few beers together. A couple of hours later, they went to bed without supper, finally dozing off in ecstasy a half hour later.

They still had each other.

Chapter Eighteen

"C'mon, Tina, you're the toughest one in the gang, don't give me that crap."

"It's not crap, Johnny. How could I make something like that up?"

"Did you tell anyone else?"

"Not yet. Especially Debbie, I know how she is, it'd hurt her too badly. I'll let her know when the time comes."

"I can't handle this shit, Tina, I can't handle it," Johnny pressed the phone receiver against his forehead.

"You've got to be strong. For Issy."

"Yeah, okay. I'll see you soon."

Who was going to be strong for him, he wondered.

Johnny Carmona had finally gotten in touch with Tina, and the Annunciation had just been train-wrecked by what she just told him. What in fuck was muscular dystrophy? He heard that people died from it, and the thought of it made him sick. First his son, now one of his best friends. What kind of world was this? What was happening to his life? How does everybody just start dying, one after another?

He had called her from the gym, and all he could do was stare out at it and contemplate the fact that it was all he had left. It was all he would leave behind. There had been lots of kids who came here with weak or broken spirits, and he helped pick them off the ground and taught them to fly. He made lots of friends in the neighborhood, and it made him laugh to consider himself a pillar of the community. There had been some great prospects who came through his doors, but those who had not moved along to greener pastures had lost their way in scrounging around for sex, liquor and drugs. He had one or two kids who looked like they might do something, go somewhere, but in this business it was very much like winning the lottery. You never won, and no one you knew ever won, but surely someone somewhere did.

"What's wrong?" Roth leaned up against the doorframe as Johnny stared absently at the wall in the office. "Did you tell her about Frank?"

"No, she was telling me about her."

"What's wrong with her?"

"She's got some kind of problem. This muscular dystrophy shit."

"Muscular dystrophy?" Roth squinted. "That doesn't sound right. What did she tell you?"

"I said the same thing you did. That's what she's got. She said she was meaning to call but kept putting it off. She asked for us to keep it to ourselves. The only one she told so far is Zeke."

"Wait a second. You need to look that up on the Internet. That shit's incurable."

"Yeah. I know."

"What do you mean, you know? Has she gotten a second opinion?"

"You know, why is it that everytime somebody gets some bad fuckin' news, right away they're supposed to go out and get a second opinion so they can hear it twice," Johnny vented. "You know, they got medical malpractice lawsuits where you can sue some motherfucker for giving you a bullshit medical report."

"Hey, it's like going to a transmission shop and getting told you need a complete overhaul. People are in business to make money. They're the first ones to tell you to get a second opinion to avoid getting sued."

"She already, got a second fucking opinion. That's it, man. That's all there is to it."

"This is Tina we're talking about here."

"Yeah, I know. That's who told me."

"Fuck," Roth walked in and slumped into the table in front of Johnny's desk. "First Frank, now this? How're you gonna tell Issy?"

"Same way I just told you, with my balls in my throat."

"So much for that concert tour," he exhaled quietly.

"Concert tour? That's what you're thinking of?"

"It's a fucking joke, man. Look, I'm gonna hunt down those lost sheep of yours, Fleming and Ferguson, get my mind off all this shit. We need to find out where they stand and move on. If they're out, someone else needs to step up."

"Yeah? Like who?"

"I've been getting word about this Jamaican kid on the East Side. He's already been thrown out of three gyms around here. The last one was an MMA (*mixed martial arts) place. From what I hear, he's looking for someone he can respect. Crazy kid with a killer punch."

"So what, with all the shit I got going on here, you're gonna bring me some nut case?"

"Hey, turn the clock back thirty years. That's what they used to say about you."

"Go ahead, talk to him, what difference does it make? If he doesn't listen to you he won't listen to anyone anyway," Johnny leaned way back and massaged his face. "The whole fucking world's falling apart. Nothing makes sense anymore. If you can make sense to some crazy kid, who knows. Maybe you can save the planet."

"Yeah, one life at a time, didn't you say that at one time?" Roth got up to leave.

"That was before my kid started dying. I can't even save my own kid."

"Look, give yourself a break. Take the day off. Go home and screw your wife."

"Hey, bend over the desk, I'll screw you."

"Go screw yourself," Roth headed out. "I'll see you later."

"Okay. Later," Johnny waved him off.

Roth squinted to adjust his eyes to the darkness as he walked into Chico's Lounge, a Puerto Rican shithole ten blocks west of the gym. Chico was a fireplug of a man who chewed tobacco and spit juice between his cheroot breaks out back on the patio. Mingo was a tubercular little man who obsessively mopped and cleaned the place from dusk to dawn. Though they both stood five-foot-two, no one on Miami Beach would want to get caught between them in a street fight if one of them had a blade.

"Hey, you ugly sons of bitches. Is that why you keep it dark in here all the time?"

"No, we keep it like this in case you show up," Chico smirked at Roth as he pulled a Heineken from the ice box behind the bar. He showed it to Roth before popping the top.

Roth sauntered down the bar to where a young, lanky mulatto sat drinking a Bud and Seagram's boilermaker.

"You Jose Marcial?"

"You a cop?" the blond kid with the cornrows stared straight ahead at the wall mirror.

"Nope."

"What're you looking for?"

"I heard you like to fight."

"That all depends," he turned and sized Roth up.

"You got a reputation for fucking up. When you're not doing it to other people you're doing it to yourself."

"Maybe the people you're talking to got some big mouths," he turned away again, sipping his beer.

"Could be," Roth sat with one ass cheek on his stool, half standing next to Marcial. "Could be it's common knowledge."

"So what you want, man?"

"I'm from Carmona Boxing Club. Might be able to help you get your shit together."

"You saying my shit ain't together?"

"I just walked in. You tell me."

"Johnny Carmona. You're the Grenadan. You guys train kids at your place."

"We had Fleming. We had Ferguson. I'm looking for fresh."

"Fresh flesh."

"You got that right."

Suddenly the door opened and a massive figure appeared in the doorway. Knobby was an ex-Mob enforcer from New York who got too unreliable and was advised to relocate. He was a hardcore alkie who went on blackout binges and was dangerous as a buffalo at 6'4", 310 pounds.

"Hey, whaddaya got going, all spics and niggers this early in the morning?"

"Don't start your shit," Chico groaned, shoving a Bud in front of him.

"Fuck that piss. Gimme a whiskey."

"Kinda early, don't you think?"

"I said whiskey, you little pissant."

"There you go, why don't you help *him* get *his* shit together?"

"Who the fuck said that!" Knobby bellowed.

162

"Man, it's too early for this shit," Roth never once looked behind him.

"Drink your beer, old man. Give it a rest."

"You fuckin' nigger, I'll knock your dick off," Knobby rose from his barstool.

"Bring it to me, you fucking drunk."

Roth veered to his right as Knobby made a beeline towards Marcial. Suddenly the middleweight was on his feet, hoking a vicious left into Knobby's side before throwing a right cross at his chin. The giant staggered back like a wounded dinosaur as Marcial continued throwing hooks and straight rights. Knobby was driven back step by step until at last he tripped and fell backwards through the front door. He rolled like a brown bear across the sidewalk as Marcial followed him out, just as a police car spotted them and hit the strobe light.

"Hey, can I get him out of this?" Roth produced his wallet as the cops came out of the vehicle to handcuff both men.

"You offering me a bribe, buddy?" a black cop demanded as he frisked Marcial.

"No, I'm just looking to make it right. It was just a misunderstanding, I saw the whole thing. The bartender'll back me up."

"You can straighten it out at Miami County," he and his partner loaded Knobby in the car, calling for backup to transport Marcial separately.

"There's no way I can fix this here?" Roth asked plaintively. "I'm with John Carmona at the gym down the way. He's one of our guys, he's okay."

"Oh, I know you. It's been a while. Well, look, you keep this guy outta these shitholes during the daytime. This ain't the first time. Next time he's gonna get thirty days, even if one of our guys has to sit in the courthouse all day."

"Appreciate it, officer."

"Fuck him," Marcial snarled as the cops removed the handcuffs and drove off.

"It'll be the other way around," Roth ambled off towards his car. "Get straightened out, you come on by the gym, see if we can get something going."

"I'll be around," Marcial shuffled off in the opposite direction.

Johnny made his way up the steps to Frank's apartment shortly before lunch, knocking when he heard commotion inside the apartment. He waited patiently as his son came over to the door and looked through the peephole before letting him in. He fleetingly thought of the movies he had seen where an assassin fires a bullet through the peephole of someone he didn't like.

"Hey, Dad. Whuzup."

"Not much. I decided to take a walk, get away from the gym, stretch my legs. Figured I'd walk down this way and stop in for a minute."

"Glad you came by. C'mon in, sit down. You want coffee?"

"Yeah, sure, why not."

"How's Ma doing? She's been coming by almost every day, I was surprised she hasn't come over."

"We had a rough morning, some bad news from New York," Johnny sat down on Frank's comfortable sofa facing his economy-sized flat-screen TV.

"Go on, turn on the TV if you like. Maybe the fights are on," Frank was setting out coffee cups in the kitchenette.

"Nah, I'm fine. Roth had a run-in with the cops this morning trying to fish one of the fighters out of a bar. I'm in the wrong business. I should've opened up a bar. That's where all the fighters are at."

"So what's up in New York?" Frank brought him a coffee before sitting in the armchair across from him.

"It's your Aunt Tina. She's pretty sick, and this is the first anyone's hearing about it. I'm the only one of the old crew she's told about it. Your mother's gonna call her sometime today."

"Tina? What's wrong with Tina?"

"She has this… muscular dystrophy. I didn't get a whole lot of info from her. Your Mom's gonna get into it with her."

"Muscular dystrophy? Are you sure that's what she said?"

"What do you think, I heard it in passing?"

"That's a…that's an incurable illness."

"Maybe you could…nah, let's let your mother call and go from there."

"Geez," Frank lowered his head. "So, how'd this go down? Did you call to tell her about the reunion thing?"

"Well, no. I called to tell her about this thing you're having. She's known you since you were a baby, she has a right to know. I opened the conversation with the reunion stuff, and then she hit me with that."

"When it rains it pours, huh?" Frank shook his head.

"What, that's all you got to say?"

"Aw, shit. Don't tell me I'm the first one you're unloading this shit on."

"Okay, okay, I'm sorry. You're right. Roth walked right out the door and your mother almost fell apart. That makes you the punching bag."

"I'm real sorry about Tina. I'll call her."

"No, wait until your Mother talks to her, it's better that way."

"Whatever. Let me know."

"Say, you got on real good with Jerry Ferguson the other night, huh?"

"Yeah, he's cool people. He knows a lot about the local hip hop scene. Knows a few of the people I hang with."

"So did you tell him about... the thing of yours?"

"What thing's that?" Frank stared at him.

"You know," Johnny shook his head. "What's it matter? One thing leads to the other."

"That's primitive. You don't know most people with AIDS gets it from needles?"

"You don't look like no junkie."

"Do I look like a queer?"

"Hey, c'mon, gimme a break."

"People shoot between their toes. Guys who shoot up don't all lie around in hallways."

"So what's the deal with Jerry? Is he hitting it?"

"I doubt it. If he's going to the gym, I doubt it."

"Well, he hasn't been going to the gym."

"I don't think he's doing anything. You can never tell, though."

"How about the other thing? Did that come up?"

"What, do you mean if I told him I was gay? Are you worried your fighter might be queer?"

"I'm just asking, that's all."

"So how does all this come together for you?" Frank

narrowed his eyes. "You think the only way someone would wanna hang out with me is if they were using drugs or they were gay?"

"I didn't say that!" Johnny grew angry. "I'm just trying to figure out that jerkoff Ferguson. He don't make too many friends."

"How do you know that? You and Roth hang out with him?"

"Hell no. I don't know, he never spends time with anyone at the gym, he never invites anyone."

"Did you? Far as I could tell, you and Mom and Roth left all your friends behind in New York with the band. You never made any boxing friends."

"It's a different world," Johnny shrugged. "Bunch of gunslingers, everyone looking to go up on someone else. With the band, it was us against the Music Industry."

"What's the difference, you and the boxers against the promoters, the boxing establishment?"

"What boxing establishment? Bunch of fucking idiots? Rich Jews run the music industry. They have hundreds of kids coming out of Juilliard, Harvard, wherever the fuck, working for them. There's no comparison. You gonna compare RCA to the IBC?"

"Who told you all that, David Dianomd?"

"Probably."

They heard the sound of a car pull up outside, then the sound of Issy's footsteps on the stairs. Johnny swallowed down his coffee before getting up and embracing Frank, slapping him on the back.

"Hey, guys, what's up?" she was slightly winded from the stairs.

"I was just on my way out," Johnny hugged and kissed her. "I'll see you back at the house."

"Oh, come on!" she protested. "Let me make lunch!"

"I gotta go find Ferguson," Johnny trotted down the steps. "The son of a bitch may need another free meal."

"Hey," Isabel came over and caressed Frank's face. "You okay?"

"Yeah, I'm good," Frank wiped his eyes.

"What happened?"

"I don't know," he managed. "We just had our deepest conversation in fifteen years."

Chapter Nineteen

"You're damn straight I'm going, Gallegos. Don't even think of screwing me out."

Word of Stu Carlucci's abduction shot through the hotel like lightning. Within minutes they had congregated in James Lincoln's suite, and shortly thereafter suited men from the Mossad had arrived to brief them on the situation.

"I'm with the CIA," Billy Sixkiller dropped the bombshell as the briefing began. "I was assigned here along with Sgt. Gallegos as a protective attachment to your entourage by the Government. Carlucci was taken by extremists we believe are associated with Hezbollah. There was content in the ransom message that indicated they may not be rank and file members."

"We have access to a satellite tracking system that has calculated the whereabouts of the abductors," Capt. Ben Mandel of the Mossad revealed. "There is a desert plain about ten kilometers outside of Tel Aviv bordering the West Bank area inhabited by shepherds suspected of being supporters of Hamas. They own a small ranch that is regularly visited by Bedouins and traders. We've long suspected it as being a way station for smugglers but it's too heavily guarded and we've had nothing solid to go on until now."

"So this is a perfect excuse to raid the place," David smirked.

"This is why I don't want you out there," Duke flared. "You're a loose cannon, you've got no agenda but your own, you do whatever you can to create dissonance for your amusement. You'd endanger lives and have fun doing it."

"Maybe…" Mandel mused. "Now, suppose he and someone close to him who trusted him… like Ms. Munson…"

"No," Johnny spoke out. "No fucking way."

"Hold on," Debbie responded. "Hear him out."

"They decide to go out and see if they can find out where Stu is. They start asking around on the street and are grabbed by Hamas sympathizers. The militants have no place but the way station to take them."

"It sounds like a plan, sir," Lt. Cohn agreed. "Your Dad thinks Hamas may be prepared to smuggle the hostage into the West Bank before daybreak."

General Aaron Mandel was one of the most powerful Mossad operatives in the Palestine theatre of operations. He had the full cooperation of the CIA throughout the Middle East and worked closely with Interpol on the European front. Mandel was grooming his son as his successor and it gave Ben enormous power and resources in combating terrorism in the region.

It was about 3 AM when the ramshackle truck bounced along the rocky trail through the barren desert towards the fenced-in acreage along the outskirts of Tel Aviv. Two jeeps on either side of the gated entrance converged and armed men wearing khalats and robes emerged to confront the truck.

"We found these infidels in the neighborhood asking questions about a kidnapping," Billy Sixkiller wore clothing similar to those of the guards. The guards peered inside as saw Debbie and David seated with arms tied behind their backs, three robed men seated behind them in the triple-rowed vehicle.

"Why do you bring them here?" the leader of the guard demanded.

"They are part of the infidel entourage. If we had them killed it would bring the Jews against the neighborhood. We felt it would be best to bring them here."

The leader motioned to his men, who opened the gates. The guards reentered the jeeps and bracketed the truck as they escorted it towards the main compound about a quarter kilometer inside the perimeter. One of the robed figures stepped towards the two Americans and prodded them towards the compound when they emerged from the truck. When the red-haired girl turned and cursed at him, he grabbed her by the neck and hissed into her ear before shoving her ahead.

"It's gonna be okay," Johnny had placed his lips against her ear, kissing her before thrusting her forward. "I'll die before leaving you here."

"Don't worry," David muttered, the last words he ever spoke to anyone but the man who killed. "I got this."

Johnny remembered them shoving David and Debbie through the door, Billy exchanging words with the Palestinians. All of a sudden, David's brains got blown out and the place exploded. He and Roth went back to back as planned, and they began opening up with their Uzis. He remembered spraying bullets at one of the Arabs, who spurted so much blood and got hit from so many directions that Johnny would never know if he had ever personally shot a man to death. There were lots of sleepless nights after that, but none more so than when Isabel told her story the night before they left New York to move to Miami.

"Abdul Mehdidoud told me everything before we left Israel," she told Johnny on their last night as New York residents. "I never told you because I was afraid you'd say something and it'd get back to those Mafia guys. They had already questioned you and Roth about it. I was afraid that if I told you, you two might talking about it somewhere in public. If someone overheard you and you got called back in, who knows what could happen."

Abdul knew Paco Cabales from the neighborhood, and was a casual visitor to the apartment back when Mom was still alive and she and Lucy were just kids in grade school. Abdul was a native Palestinian and had family on the West Bank. Only he grew up in Brooklyn and had never even visited the Old Country. The only reason why he could speak the language so fluently was because his mother spoke to him in both languages from the time he was born. In this day and age he could have been an interpreter. Back then he was just an Arab who spoke that desert stuff like all the other ragheads that had built a sub-community in Cobble Hill.

He told Isabel how it all started, about the day he got called into the Arab-American Community Center on Court and Wyckoff Street. He was brought to a rear table where Sirhan Farhat presided over neighborhood affairs. He was a *mullah* (*cleric) from the Old Country and held as much sway as a Chief Rabbi in the Jewish community, or a Bishop among the Catholics here in the Diocese. Abdul treated him with the utmost courtesy as the old man told him a fantastic story.

"Our brothers in the Organization contacted me when they heard this thing was going to happen," the old man stared through bifocals from beneath his khalat, slowly twirling his cane in his long-nailed fingers. "They need an insider, someone who can be as a fly on the wall among these infidels. There are other things going on behind the scenes, things that this black musician and his people know nothing about. We have to make sure it stays that way. We need someone who can assure us that it stays that way. We have decided it will be you."

"What is it that you think I can possibly do?"

"You are a professional photographer. The Cabales girls, those two sisters, know you all their lives. Their father Paco served with Special Forces in the military, he has connections. His son-in-law Duke Gallegos is working with the CIA in Latin America. We know this. All of them will vouch for you if you make them understand how valuable it will be to have a family friend, someone who knows the language and has family there, to accompany them."

The mullah went on to explain that Abdul's family had been victimized by the Israelis along the West Bank and were in desperate need of protection from the PLO. If Abdul were to help his brothers in this time of need, his family would not only be protected but possibly relocated to Lebanon if the crisis on the West Bank became untenable. If King Daoud's monarchy were to stabilize the region, his family would be moved into their own home as soon as the opportunity arose. It was an offer that Abdul could not refuse.

When they arrived in Palestine, Abdul was able to feather his nest by taking award-winning pictures of the band that bordered on the fantastic in Palestine. There was Debbie parading around with her 'Mother of Harlots' T-shirt, David being stared at as a modern-day Jonah having been vomited onto the shored of the Holy Land, Tina sitting in with street musicians in the bazaars, and Johnny sparring with teens in hotel lobbies. He got to look up family members he had never met, and things seemed idyllic until the face of evil showed itself.

He had no idea what the conspiracy entailed or how deep it reached. He was escorted by Lar Darab, Dr. Sardaq's giant of a henchman, to a meeting with Jack Racki and Vic Mackey. Jack and Vic, who were the head trainers in Johnny Carmona's boxing entourage, revealed their true identities and told him of their mission. Abdul would be required to accompany them as they met with the PLO squad that would be transporting the seven hundred pounds of heroin from Iran. The narcotics would be substituted for the padding in the ten heavy bags that were brought over for Team Carmona's exhibitions. The entire operation would be conducted while the country was distracted by the Crusader Concert. Though Darab was fluent in all dialects throughout the region, Vic wanted to make sure they had their own interpreter to prevent a possible double-cross.

The speakers for the concert were so loud in order to be heard across the Valley of Megiddo that they drove for a long time of driving before it became inaudible. They were headed towards the Syrian border where the Iranian smugglers had been provided safe passage to bring the drugs into Palestine. They met a team of six PLO riflemen at the border and loaded the heroin, packed in five steamer trunks, into a minivan which they drove to the rendezvous point.

It was a warehouse ten miles from the border that appeared deserted as the gangsters' truck approached. Darab had brought six Iranian commandos with him, all who had posed as CLA (*Christian Liberation Army) soldiers, King Daoud's Praetorian guard. No one knew of Dr. Sardaq's duplicity, and he filled the ranks of the Palestine Security Service with double agents who would do his bidding. With Darab as his right-hand man, he was in virtual control of the Palestine police state though even King Daoud remained entirely unaware of the situation.

"Okay, listen," Vic Maniacci pulled Abdul to the side as Darab led the group into the warehouse. "If anything comes out of anyone beside a burp or a fart, you tell me what they said. You stay right next to me no matter what happens, and you translate every fuckin' word you hear. Got it?"

Darab cautiously switched on the light over the doorway and peered into the shadows within. He was dressed in a beige suit while Abdul and the Italians wore black workout clothes, the CLA gunmen clad in khakis. As they adjusted their eyes to the shadowy darkness, they were startled by the sight of riflemen in fatigues lining the walls.

"The leader told Darab they have the delivery in their trucks waiting outside," Abdul muttered to Vic. "Darab told them to bring it in. There seems to be some payment due for services rendered."

"Jack, you know anything about that?" Vic hissed.

"Who gives a shit? That's between the ragheads. All I know is that Darab needs to get the H in that truck and back to our shipping container so we can get this thing done."

Angelo Vacirca had arranged for the rental of a shipping container at a port in Tel Aviv. It provided the smugglers a place where they could pack the plastic-wrapped kilos into the heavy punching bags and return them to the airport for loading once the concert tour group prepared for departure. Vic and Jack were greatly impressed with how smoothly the operation had been planned and would doubtlessly move towards completion without a hitch.

Darab continued exchanging words with the PLO leader, who then led his men towards the front entrance. Vic, Jack and Abdul stepped aside as the CLA men made way. Just as the PLO leader followed his men through the door, Darab drew his Glock-17 and shot the man through the back of the head. The CLA men charged out behind the PLO militants and gunned them down within a matter of seconds.

"Holy shit!" Vic and Jack were wide-eyed, Abdul nearly puking at the sight of the brains spilling from the PLO leader's torn skull. "What did you just do!"

"The Israelis had their American lackeys monitoring activity along the Iranian border," Darab explained in stilted English. "These fools were sent on a humanitarian mission to transport food supplies for Palestinian refugees. They smuggled the heroin along with the provisions. We had no intention of paying money to the PLO. Besides, these were six of their best operatives. They have lost far more than their smuggling fee."

"I'm glad I'm not gonna be here when they find out what you just did," Vic shook his head, heading out the door past Darab.

"Where do you think you are going?" Darab growled. "The three of you will help us get those trunks into our truck! Time is of the essence!"

Jack and Vic cursed and swore as they followed Abdul out to the PLO van parked in back of the building. Only two of the CLA soldiers came along, yanking open the panel doors to reveal the five steamer trunks. The trunks weighed one hundred and fifty pounds apiece, and the three men were soaked in sweat by the time they unloaded the van.

"No wonder that son of a bitch is wearing a suit," Vic wiped the sweat pouring from his face. "You'd think they'd have had the brains to bring a hand truck."

"What, in the fuckin' sand?" Jack pulled his shirt out of his pants to wipe his face. "Gimme a break."

"Come on, you help us bring trunks inside," a rifleman urged them.

"What are those other guys doing!" Vic demanded.

"They keeping watch, make sure no one else coming."

Vic was beside himself with anger while holding his tongue as he grabbed one end of a trunk, a rifleman grabbing the other. They carried the trunk through the warehouse and out front where the side doors of the van were propped wide open. The CLA soldiers stood with their backs to the warehouse, smoking cigarettes and chatting idly as they looked out at the distant skyline of Tel Aviv. By Vic's second trip, he was nearly exhausted, dripping with sweat and fit to be tied.

"Okay, big shot, you got any more shit we need to do before we get back in the air conditioning?" Vic demanded.

"Hold on," Darab stared towards the highway. "What the hell is that?"

The group stared in apprehension as two SUV's veered off the road, following the same gravel path as had the CLA in arriving at the warehouse. The riflemen switched off their safety catches as the team leader strode forward to meet the vehicles.

"They are saying that they are with Hamas. They were notified of the delivery by the Iranians through the Muslim Brotherhood and they were dispatched to ensure the shipment makes it back to Tel Aviv. They say the recipient has paid extra for this additional coverage."

"What the fuck!" Vic was incredulous. "A.V. didn't say anything about this! He must've set this up to make sure we didn't pull anything, that paranoid fuck."

"You know Angie Vee," Jack shook his head as Darab stepped closer to eavesdrop. "That son of a bitch don't trust his own mother."

"Why are they getting out of the trucks?" Vic looking around, resting his gaze on Darab. "Look, this isn't part of the deal. This truck goes straight to the waterfront. We're not reloading the merchandise onto somebody else's truck."

"Hold on, hold on!" Darab headed out to the black-uniformed men as they marched towards the CLA team.

"He's telling them he will accept their escort but the product is already secured," Abdul explained.

At once the interlopers raised their weapons and began firing at the CLA commandos. They were entirely caught off-guard and were shredded by the crossfire. Vic, Jack and Abdul hit the sand as Lar Darab was riddled with bullets. Dr. Sardaq's peerless killing machine took over a dozen bullets before collapsing face first to the ground.

"This is it," Vic tried to turn his sand-covered face. "It's a set-up. We're fuckin' dead."

"Make a deal," Jack spat sand from his lips. "Offer 'em anything. Have 'em call that nigger Lincoln, anything!"

"Get up, you dogs," the leader of the death squad strode forth. "You've served your purpose, you're not worth killing."

"What did you just do? These guys just took out those PLO mooks over there. They were making sure this was going where the Iranians were paid for it to go."

"We lied to this bastard," the man nodded at Darab's corpse. "We are not Hamas. The Hamas works for us. We are Hizbullah."

"Hizbullah? That's the name of that jerkoff band."

"Shut the fuck up, Jack."

"Hold on," he insisted. "Angie Vee's gonna have us whacked! This was supposed to be a done deal! Look, we know you guys aren't drug dealers. We need to know what to tell our people so we can buy this shit back. Gimme a price and who we can contact."

"What are you talking about?" the leader was puzzled. "You are the ones who called us."

Suddenly the skies overhead erupted as a deafening storm descended upon them. Helicopters began swarming overhead as giant locusts, hovering ominously as loud-speakers blared orders to drop their weapons. Spotlights illuminated the scene as the terrorists saw no choice other than to comply.

"Okay, you dogs, get moving," a rifleman dressed in desert camouflage waved them towards one of the helicopters.

"Where are we going?" Vic asked. "Who are you guys?"

"We are the IDF," the soldier replied. "We are the ones who sent Hizbullah out here. The Mossad knew the CLA was going to double-cross the PLO. We always make sure the playing field remains even."

"What the fuck is this out here, alphabet soup?" Vic was incredulous as he was prodded to the waiting chopper.

Abdul later found out that the Mossad knew all about the Iranian deal with the Mafia. They had only to figure out a way to turn the conspirators against one another and have them kill as many of each other as possible. Vic and Jack were deported immediately, and the heroin sold back to the Iranians for double

174

the price they were paid by the Mafia. The reasoning was that it would do far more damage by going back into circulation than sitting in some military warehouse. Not only would the Mafia have to pay another fortune for the same merchandise, but it gave the Israelis another chance to confiscate it again.

It would be years later when the fictionalized account was published that the world would learn how it all went down. Dr. Sardaq learned that his men had been double-crossed, and he immediately put Plan B into effect. They would arrange to have the Princess kidnapped and exchange her for the heroin from the Israelis. Only the Israeli Air Force had already been deployed and were more than ready for any contingencies. They were quick to react to the abduction and had only to complete the rescue with as minimal a cost as possible.

Johnny would always be thankful that they lost just one man. Only he would always carry the guilt of having accepted David's death in such a way. Yet he knew how easy it would have been for the Arabs to have killed Debbie as well. All he would have had to do was turn the gun on Debbie. One move, one pull of the trigger.

"Johnny, c'mon, get her out of here. Roth, Abdul, let's get the *khalats* around him and carry him out. Real easy, okay?"

"He's gone, Duke," Billy whispered behind him.

"Fuck you," Duke snarled back.

Debbie was as a banshee, screaming and wailing, twisting with demonic fury as three IDF soldiers struggled to pull her away. The Israelis had fallen upon the camp with a vengeance, helicopters dropping commando teams across the site while clearing their paths with automatic fire. Bodies were strewn in puddles of bloody mud as the IDF secured the field in short order. Johnny and Roth gently pried Debbie loose from the soldiers and led her away as the medics came for David.

"Duke," Billy insisted. "It's a miracle no one else was killed. Sometimes you got to count your blessings. The girl could've got hit."

"I could've got hit. Why didn't I get hit? I'm the soldier, it's my job to get hit," Duke stumbled to his feet in a daze.

"You got a girl waiting for you back home. This guy doesn't have anyone. That's why he volunteered. It was him for Stu, and he knew it."

"Duke," Johnny grabbed him by the lapels. "Did you know how this was going down? Did you know David was gonna get it?"

"Don't you ever ask me that again," Duke grabbed his future brother-in-law's wrists and twisted them outwards to break his grip. "Ever."

Johnny never did. Only now, the situation was reversed. Duke and Johnny would meet again, maybe at the hospital, maybe at the funeral. Duke would ask Johnny if he knew how this went down. It would be Johnny's turn to tell him that.

Don't ever ask me that again. Ever.

Chapter Twenty

"Man, I tell you, Johnny, I just ain't got it no more. I ain't got the instinct. If I go in there I'm gonna lose. I just don't have the desire to beat a man to death with my fists no more. If I ain't got that, I ain't got shit."

Jerry Ferguson came by that morning right after Johnny and Roth opened the gym. Johnny knew the chickenshit picked that time because they would be busy, plus they wouldn't want to embarrass themselves by airing their laundry in front of the other boxers.

"So that's it, you're gonna walk away, hang it up," Johnny glanced over at Roth, then cocked his head as he stared at Ferguson.

"Man, I was thinking about it all night after I came to your place for dinner, met your son and all. Did he tell you we got together for beers the next night?"

"No, he didn't say anything."

"He told me all about his hip hop music, how he had been thinking about cutting his own CD. Man, I could've closed my eyes and thought I was listening to you. He's over there talking all about taking your shot in life, making it count, not leaving anything unfinished. That's when I realized you people had a special way about you. I knew I'd be cheating you if I went in and gave it some half assed effort, making weight just to make the fight. I'd be going in there trying to go ten rounds with Jimmy Jaxx, and that ain't right, that ain't the way. I know you two are great trainers, and you can bring out the best in anyone. You need to get someone who wants it, Johnny. I'm not worth your time."

"Can't argue with that," Johnny looked from Roth to Ferguson.

Johnny couldn't get over what Ferguson said about Frank, and it filled his heart with sorrow. Where did the kid get all that stuff from? Was this some kind of exit strategy? He couldn't motivate him to run out and get him the paper, for god's sakes. It was just a string of failures, one after the other. Sure, Frank did

177

good in school, but other than that, there was never any common ground. His artwork, the hip hop music, the homosexuality – they were in two different worlds. Even when he offered to send Frank to an art teacher, he tuned out. Said he had to find his own vision. Head of concrete, just like David Diamond.

"Hey, John," Roth came back inside after having watched Ferguson clean out his locker. "Come get a look at this."

Johnny was irked by having to get up. He just felt like sitting there. Nevertheless, he walked over to the door next to Roth and looked out.

"You gotta be shitting me."

"Go check it out."

Johnny walked over to where the black kid was sitting on the spectators' bench, watching the boxers.

"Hey. You're Jose Marcial."

"So they say."

"You come in to look around?"

"Yeah, I guess."

"You don't strike me as the kind of guy who goes to gyms to look around."

"What's the dues here?"

"Twenty a month."

"I got fifteen."

"I'm good with that."

"You got a ride? You bring your gear?"

"I'm wearing sneakers, I'll take off my shirt. I can move around, show you what I got."

"I know what you got. You wanna go get your gear?"

"I'll be back tomorrow," he dug into his pocket and pulled out a couple of crumpled bills.

"I'll see you then."

Isabel went by to visit Frank around that time, and he was slow to answer the door. She was somewhat concerned by waited patiently until he let her in. He seemed unusually pale, and she insisted that he sit down and relax while she made him breakfast.

"What's wrong?" she insisted. "You look a little under the weather."

"Aah, it's my stomach. I'm not feeling too hot. We'd better skip breakfast."

"No, then, I'll make you some soup," she insisted. "Let me drive you over to the doctor's office or the emergency clinic."

"Mom, you're gonna have to start getting used to this. I can't be running to the clinic every time I'm not feeling good."

"Suppose it's a complication or something? You can't take a chance with not getting it checked out."

"Look, Ma, I don't have a whole lot of money. Blade sent me a couple of thousand after we broke up, and I cashed in my 401k after I found out I got the virus. I'm holding up okay, but I can't go running there every time I turn around, and I'm not gonna let you or Dad pay for it. That's out of the question."

"Do you hear what you're saying? You're my son. This isn't about money. You have a life-threatening illness. I am not going to have something happen just because you were too proud to take money. I'm calling your father right now."

"Whoa, hey, slow down!" Frank insisted. "I've just got an upset stomach. Look, if it gets any worse I'll give you a call. I promise."

"I'm not going anywhere."

"Oh yes you are. Dad's gonna be home for lunch in a couple of hours, and we're not gonna start letting this get in the way. Not happening."

"Tough call, huh?" she managed. "Now that you and your Dad are opening up. I know he's not about to get upset that I'm here with you, but if you're gonna throw me out…"

"Throw you out," he got up gingerly and went over to where she sat, pulling her to her feet and giving her a hug." "You go on and fix Dad's lunch. I'm gonna go take a nap. I'll give you a buzz just as soon as I get up, if it makes you feel any better."

"Promise?"

"Yep, I promise."

She reluctantly drove back to the house after Frank walked her down to the car. Something wasn't right. Her instincts told her that he wasn't feeling nearly as well as he was acting. Yet he was right, she couldn't go around acting like Chicken Little. She didn't even want to think about Johnny getting to where he started blowing things off if she got bent out of shape every time something happened. If something did happen and he wasn't there, it would be unendurable. It would be even worse if Frank started shutting her out. She was just going to have to learn to roll with this a little better.

When she got home, both Johnny and Roth were there on their cell phones, and immediately she knew something was up.

"I just got a call from Casino Miami Jai-Alai," Johnny rushed over, giving her a big hug and kiss. "One of the fighters dropped out from the semi-final tonight. The promoter there gave us a call. We're trying to get in touch with Reggie Fleming but we're getting disconnect messages. I'm thinking we're gonna ask the new guy, we got no choice."

"New guy? What new guy?"

"That guy I told you Roth met with in the bar a couple of days ago, Jose Marcial. He came in this morning, paid me most of the dues for the month. He looks like he's been skipping meals and he's got a mean streak down his back like a skunk. They're gonna get us five grand, that's an easy five big ones on our end."

"I got him," Roth called over, then opened the sliding glass patio door and stepped outside.

"Gee, that's great, honey."

"Great? That's two fifty in my pocket. Not bad for a few hours' work. How's Frank?"

"He says he's got an upset stomach but I'm worried. He looked kind of pale and he was
moving around like he was in pain. He said he was gonna take a nap, he promised to call me when he gets up."

"Okay, good," Johnny headed over towards the patio. "Be sure and call me if anything happens."

"You're gonna be at the fight. How am I gonna reach you?"

"Just leave me a message, I'll call you as soon as I get it."

"All right, I'm gonna start lunch. Tell Roth I'm making him a plate."

Johnny stepped out onto the patio and Roth handed him the cell phone.

"Hey, it's Johnny."

"Yeah, it's Jose. I just stepped on the scale at the neighbor's house. I'm at one sixty-five."

"Shit. Well, look. Can you walk to the gym?"

"Yeah. Why?"

"I want you to buy two packs of gum, chewing gum. Put both packs in your mouth and start chewing. You keep spitting all the way to the gym. It's an old timer's trick. You might be able to spit out the five pounds. Give it a shot, okay?"

"Yeah, I guess it makes a little sense."

"Now look, as soon as you get there, we're gonna drive straight to the casino and get you on the scale. I don't think they're gonna call it off if you're a couple of pounds over, but I don't wanna take any chances. Got it?"

"Yeah, I got it."

"You feeling good? You up for this?"

"Five hundred bucks? I'm gonna kill the mother-fucker."

"Before expenses."

"Yeah, right, I know."

"See you in an hour."

Isabel watched as the partners wolfed down their lunch before taking off. They dutifully made it through their salad before scarfing down their baked chicken sandwiches and washing it all down with iced tea. Johnny used to leave the salad before realizing it continued to turn up in different forms of gradual wilt in succeeding meals. He finally got the message that he was going to eat his veggies and there would be no two ways about it.

"Okay, baby, wish me luck," he came over and hugged and kissed her again. "If they approve the fight, I'm taking you out to dinner tomorrow night."

"Worry about that after the fight's over. Go get 'em, champ."

No sooner did Johnny leave than her cell phone went off. It was Frank.

"Hey. Ma. I'm not feeling all that hot. I think I'll take you up on your offer, just in case."

"Omigosh. Your father just left."

"No, don't worry about it, don't bother him. Like I said, it's just in case. Maybe I'm coming down with something, they'll probably just give me a shot or something."

She felt as if she was about to panic but fought desperately to control it. She had been surfing the Internet (as best she could) and found that the disease disables the immune system. It meant that a common virus could take him down hard. It was like that Tom Cruise movie when the aliens died because of an earthling virus that they had never been exposed to. This was making her feel more helpless than she ever had in her life.

"Okay, I'll be right over."

Johnny and Roth waited patiently for Jose Marcial, and when he arrived they hit the highway and headed for the casino. The promoter was there along with their opponent's manager and entourage and the casino owner and his people. The representatives from the World Boxing Association were also there, and the doctor weighed Marcial in at one sixty-two. The other team was not as concerned with the number as they were with the look in Marcial's eyes.

"Seven fuckin' pounds," the other manager was adamant. "That's almost fighting out of his weight. My guy's coming in at one fifty-five. He was already giving five pounds away to Matos. Seven's too fuckin' much."

"Hey, what the fuck are we gonna do?" the promoter demanded. "The main event's not that strong, if this fight tanks there's gonna be a bunch of refunds, I lose my shirt. You knew that coming in, that's why your guy got extra. Now here we are, I'm gonna be standing here with my balls hanging for an extra two pounds?"

"My guy's a contender, we're 15-0."

"You fuck me on this, I'm calling in markers. You won't get another decent fight before next year when I'm done."

"Hey, come on. What's right is right. You give us another two grand, one for me and one for my guy."

"I give it to you in chips, you do what you like with 'em," the casino owner spoke up.

"Comps," a casino manager told the WBA officials.

"Okay, we'll sanction it if you sign off for it."

"What'd you say his record was?"

Johnny and Roth looked over at Marcial.

"Four and two," he replied.

'Ah, fuck it," the other team relented. They signed the contracts as did Marcial and Johnny. They were given comps for dinner and a show and told to report to the dressing room in three hours.

"I should call Issy," Johnny was chipper. "Say, how'd you lose those two fights?"

"Disqualification."

"Shit," Roth chuckled. "Glad you didn't say anything."

"Mrs. Carmona?"

182

Isabel brought Frank to a nearby clinic, and when he appeared as if he was about to pass out the medics called for an ambulance. They took him to Mercy Hospital on West 41st Street and brought him into the emergency entrance. A series of preliminary tests were done before he was rushed into surgery.

"Were you aware that Frank had a peptic ulcer?"

"Why, no, he never mentioned it."

"Do you know if he had a complete physical after he found out he had AIDS?"

"He just told us a week ago. Everything's been happening so fast."

"So you're not really sure what the timeframes are here."

"Doctor, what is going on?"

"The ulcer's bleeding and there's an infection. With the virus, it's created a critical condition. We're had to send him in for emergency surgery."

"Oh my God."

"Is your husband living with you?"

"Why, yes."

"You may want to contact him."

Johnny looked into the eyes of the devil in the ring that night. It was the devil he saw in the mirror throughout his own 25-5 career, the devil that would fight to the death before it was beaten or broken. Roth saw it too, the devil that caused him to stand behind Johnny against all odds. Roth knew he had found a man who would die rather than quit, the kind of man he had always wanted to be, the kind of man he had never met before or since. It was a man possessed, and that was what Jose Marcial was.

The fight was an incredible event. The skill and experience of Marcial's opponent was what enabled him to survive ten rounds. Most spectators agreed it was like watching a bullfight, and the promoters were quick to schedule a rematch. This was beyond Johnny's wildest expectations. Marcial got a taste of good money and a casino fight and he wanted more. None of them had any doubts about the money. The casino paid them with a voucher which they cashed at a cashier window. Five grand wasn't shit in this place.

Both Johnny and Roth saw the string of messages from Isabel on their cell phones, but waited until they got done with Marcial first. The three of them agreed on that a long time ago, business was business. It was ironclad between Johnny and Roth back when they were selling weed before they joined The Party. When Isabel came in with them, she agreed to the rule. Roth finally stepped out towards a lounge area to call Isabel as Johnny went to cash the voucher and pay Marcial off. The kid had a big smile on his face when he shook hands with Johnny and walked off. When he returned, the look on Roth's face said it all.

"Isabel's at the house. You need to go home."

"Where's Frank?"

"You need to go home, brother," Roth's voice was barely audible.

Johnny looked away and caught a glimpse of the face and the eyes that had finally given up the devil. He saw it in the mirror in the wall a few feet away, a reflection of a man who had finally been beaten. Only that was not the man that Isabel would need tonight.

He turned towards Roth and motioned with his fingers. Roth held his palms out and Johnny threw a couple of combinations as was their ritual throughout the years.

They then hugged each other for a short time before heading for the exit, preparing to do battle with the Devil one more time.

Part Three
Debbie

Chapter Twenty One

Debbie Munson remembered the first time she ever met Vic Maniacci and Jack Raccuglia. It was over a week after she heard of them for the first time. Fred Diamond, David's estranged uncle, gave her the heads up after a mobbed-up guy made the connection. She was on a routine insurance investigation with a Midtown jewelry store and came across something that looked suspicious. The store owner hinted that she would be better off letting the store cut its losses, but Debbie wouldn't hear of it. Her sleuthing skills were being tested and she wanted to solve this case.

"Hey, Debbie."

"Uncle Freddie. Whatcha know?"

"I got a strange phone call the other day. Are you still on that robbery investigation at Shapiro Diamonds?"

"Yeah, it's cooking pretty good. How'd you hear about it?"

"The guy who called me told me he was a friend of a friend. He said the jewelry store was mobbed up and you've gone far enough with the investigation. Sounds to me like you've hit a firewall."

"Well, hell, Fred. Looks a lot to me like an inside job. There's almost no way somebody could've tunneled into that place, beat the alarm and cracked the safe in that timeframe. The tunneling time looks good and so does the alarm kill. They had the safe combination, there's no other way around it."

"You're probably right. That may be why you need to let it go. If it was Mob guys, you know they're not gonna let it go to court."

"Should I be afraid?"

"I'd be."

"Well, that's because you're not a crazy Irish bitch."

"I don't want to see anything happen, Deb. Why don't you talk it over with your Dad? I'm sure he wouldn't steer you wrong."

"Yeah, he'd talk you into taking a ride with him down to Mulberry Street. Don't lose any sleep over it, Uncle Fred. It'll be okay."

It was two weeks later on a Tuesday evening when she saw

a car parked across the street from her office on Times Square and a man loitering in front of the building. She had an excellent view from her third floor office window, her female intuition telling her something was up. She packed her .38 Smith and Wesson in her thigh holster beneath her suit dress and decided to take the fire stairs to the alleyway exit just in case.

Debbie Munson's blessing and curse in life was her overconfidence. In retrospect, it was all about her being absolutely fearless. She had no fear of death and would rather be killed than disfigured, which made her far more dangerous in a jam than anyone might think. In this situation, she could not help but admire these guys for being as professional as they were. The guy in the alley slammed the door behind her as soon as she emerged, having seen the lights go off in her window minutes ago. The guy on the street came running as soon as he heard the door.

"Okay, bitch," the squat, husky guy came forth as he slipped a pair of brass knuckles over his fingers. "We called you and we warned you but you don't listen. Now we're gonna give you a little beauty treatment so you can take some time to think it over."

"Oh, please don't hurt me," she said in her sexiest voice, rubbing her butt against the crotch of the tall guy who was holding her from behind. She had gotten some serious assfuckings with this routine more than a couple of times in her romantic life, and she could tell by this guy's boner that he was no exception. He was more about dry-humping her than holding her, and it gave her enough time to rake her high heel down his shinbone. He lightened his grip long enough for her to shove backwards, dropping into a crouch and drawing her revolver.

"I got my connections too," she said, looking from the husky guy to the fallen guy as she aimed the gun at his face. "Maniac Vic and Jack Racki. I could kill both you greaseballs right here."

"You gonna blow away two guys right here on Times Square?" Vic reasoned. "You wanna do that?"

"You tell your fucking boss it's a wash. I give you a pass and I drop the investigation. You ever come around here again and I'll go down to Mulberry Street and blow your fucking brains out in broad daylight. Then I go into the wind. Got it?"

She got a kick out of Jack on his knee to her side, holding his hand over his face as if desperately hoping he might be able to deflect the bullet.

188

"All right, I'll let 'em know," Vic replied. With that, she turned the gun on Vic and made her way around him, backing out of the alley before disappearing toward the subway. She could see they made no attempt to follow her as she trotted down the steps.

She called Mel Dalton and asked him to meet her at CBGB's afterwards. She was emotionally exhausted by the time he arrived, and they found a table where she told him what had happened. He was greatly upset and wanted to make some calls, but she would have none of it.

"It's a wash," she insisted. "All they wanted was for me to drop the case. It's over. Look, why don't we go back to my place? I just need to relax. I thought I could unwind here, but I'm just too uptight."

"Sure, darling," Mel reached across the table and held her hand before they finished their drinks.

By the time they reached her apartment, she was walking on a high-tension wire. She walked over to the window and stared out until he came over and put his arms around her waist. She turned around and snaked her tongue in his mouth, and it was all he could do to bring her into the bedroom. They yanked their clothes off and ravished one another, until eventually she turned her luscious butt towards him and pretended he was Jack Racki.

"Oh, please don't hurt me," she said in her sexiest voice. He shoved it up her ass and fucked her until finally giving her a reacharound. They exploded together and collapsed into each other's arms. It was an episode that neither of them would ever forget.

Debbie Munson tossed the dog-eared paperback onto the night table alongside her bed and stretched languidly before gazing at the ceiling for a long while. Finally she pulled herself out of bed and trudged over to the mirror for her morning inspection.

She cursed and swore at the white hair that appeared in her left eyebrow, and raked her dresser top for a nail clipper to pluck it out. She frowned at the creases in her brow and the lines along the edge of her mouth. She was still considered one of the hottest women in the neighborhood at the age of fifty, but it gnawed at her like cancer to know that she would never again be the woman in *Hezbollah*, neither in book nor band form.

She inspected her body in the full-length mirror and was somewhat content with its appearance. Her strong Irish legs were still as shapely as ever, as was the rest of her firmly-muscled figure. There was the hint of a pooch over her pantyline but her large melons held their weight as well as ever. She owed an enormous debt to Lady Clairol for her red mane, but remained free of cosmetic repair otherwise.

She thought it so ironic that the fictionalized account had topped the *New York Times'* best-seller list while the non-fiction account had barely covered publishing and advertising costs. Most critics said it was because the historical version spent more time discussing the political and espionage angles than covering the band and the behind-the-scenes scenarios. They were probably right. The only time she re-read the historical book was when she thought about David. She read the fiction book whenever she needed inspiration, and she had re-read it dozens of times over the years.

When they came back from Palestine she cashed her million-dollar check and invested heavily into Munson Investigations. She scored a windfall on her name alone and traveled the world, mostly as an armed guard for fine arts, jewelry, furs and precious metals. Most corporations figured that her high profile would discourage cowboys from coming out of the woodwork and pulling a high-risk heist job on their transports. As her profile waned, so did the demand, and it had been over a year since her last overseas job. She was back to her pre-Palestine days of serving subpoenas and domestic surveillance, and it continued to pay the bills though her 401K was a done deal.

She set her cappuccino maker up and proceeded to check her voicemails from her Midtown office. There were a couple of solicitations…and a call from the kid again.

Jerry Kevlar had called about three times trying to set up an interview at the office for a business proposition. Each time she called she got Voicemail, and more and more of a feeling that this was a musician. Undoubtedly he was going to ask her about joining or starting a band.

She wondered if this was God nudging her towards the arena again. She had pulled the *Hezbollah* novel out of the bookcase a week ago as if she needed to recharge her batteries, remind her who she was and what she had gone through to get here. Menopause was on its way like an invading army, business was slow, and looking in the mirror was like a farmer inspecting his vineyard before the drought. No one could stop the clock, not even Debbie Munson.

She knew she could close MINK (Munson Investigations, Inc.) down tomorrow and probably be the more financially secure for it. It was just that she felt the need for the final act, the last hurrah before the final curtain. Maybe it would be one more business trip to Europe... or one more rock and roll show. She hadn't played for more than a year, and hadn't appeared in public since, well... Palestine. Was she getting the fever back? Why was she reading that old novel again? And why was this kid calling?

"Hello?"

"Finally picking up, eh? This is Debbie Munson."

"Hold on," she could hear him clambering to turn down background music. "Hey, hi, this is Jerry, great to hear from you."

"So what's up?"

"I... was wondering if I might be able to schedule appointment to come up to your office to discuss a business project." He had a sexy bass tone voice and seemed articulate, upping his brownie point total.

"Why not?" she said airily. "I'll be in about 2 PM."

"Great. See you then. Great talking to you."

Jerry Kevlar showed up at her office on the Avenue of the Americas near Rockefeller Center right on time. He was a tall, muscular young man wearing a motorcycle jacket and boots, a white T-shirt and black Levis. His hair was slicked back and he could have easily been pegged as a rockabilly musician.

"So whatcha got?" Debbie asked casually as he took a seat in from of her desk in the mahoganized office. She wore a beige power suit with a white blouse and nylons, looking much like the yuppies they had both sworn to marginalize.

"I've got a three-piece band that practices out of Soho," Jerry said casually. "We're air tight but we just can't get a break. We're a great grunge band, and every one of us considers Hezbollah one of our biggest influences."

"If you told us that thirty years ago we would've laughed our butts off."

"We may not be the only band that thinks that way," Jerry said confidently, "but we're the only ones out there with the attitude to bring it back."

"Hey, man, good for you," Debbie smiled pleasantly.

"We'd like to show you. Why don't you come down and check us out?"

Debbie rolled her eyes, leaned her face against her outstretched finger, then tilted it quizzically as she looked at him.

"You're not thinking you're going to ask me out."

"C'mon, Debbie," Jerry threw his hands up.

"You got a business card?"

"Sure," he produced his wallet and handed her one.

"Demolition," she grinned. "Cute. Write down the address, I'll give you a call."

She arrived at the rehearsal studio in SoHo and was introduced by Jerry to the guitarist and drummer. She fought hard to keep from laughing. They were acting like Joan of Arc had walked into the room.

"I've got the novel and the biography of *Hezbollah*," the drummer was wide-eyed.

"Yeah? Well, so do I."

"Was that what it was really like?"

"Let me ask you something. Do you remember what your first grade teacher's husband's name was?"

"Well, uh… hmm," the young man mused. "That was like twenty years ago."

"The stuff in that book was like twenty-five, okay?"

"Point taken."

"Okay, look," Debbie Munson walked to the middle of the room and faced the trio. "I'm not going to be the president of my own fan club. We're either going to be professional musicians or nothing at all. We come in here and rehearse, leave our private shit at the door. If we go out for beer, which I doubt, we can socialize then. I'm not trying to be a bitch, but this is compromising my time and I can't afford to sit around and shoot the shit when we should be working. I'm good for two nights a week, an hour a night, if we do a gig I'm in for the night. Agreed?"

"Sounds great," Jerry replied.

They began jamming on Hezbollah's instrumental, "Rise of

the Machine", and immediately she noticed that the kids were real tight. The guitarist, Johnny, had a slicing, thrashing rhythm with a mechanical, hypnotic quality that reminded her of David's keyboard style. Jerry's technique was basic power chords that complimented her style. Craig played a big, loud drum that would give them a butt-shaking dance beat every time.

"We were thinking you could do the vocals on the Hezbollah stuff if you want," Jerry handed her a song list with some chord notes. "You can take over any of our stuff you like once you get them down."

"Well, let's hear your stuff," Debbie took a sip of beer. "I've heard the old stuff about a million times."

The band kicked into 'Barbie', a song about the Nazi war criminal known as the Butcher of Lyon. The lyrics were an indictment of Vichy France's duplicity during WWII and comparisons to the modern regime. Debbie found the bass lines simplistic and easy to handle and was soon thundering away in style.

"Man, if that's not classic Debbie Munson," Craig smiled as he did some drum rolls after the tune ended.

"Not bad," she admitted. "What else you got?"

Jerry decided to run the gamut of their original tunes in medley form, barreling from one song into the next with no time to come up for air. Debbie's fingers were sore at the end of the onslaught but she wasn't about to call a timeout in front of these upstarts.

"So what do you think?" Jerry asked when the maelstrom came to an end.

"It's okay," Debbie packed her bass guitar as the others filed out the studio door. "Like I told you, I have a business and the hours are unpredictable. I'll be here when I can make it, if I can't I'll call and we'll reschedule. I don't want you to think I'm committing to anything because I can't."

"Okay," he agreed. "If you can give us enough time to put things together, I think we can get a showcase gig and maybe get some record people to come down and see what we got. If they put money on the table we can go from there."

"You got high hopes, buddy," she chuckled. "If there was such a big market for Debbie Munson music, I don't think I'd be private dicking right about now."

"If it had been five years later, you could've gone right up there with Nirvana and Pearl Jam," Jerry insisted. "The Crusader Concert was like a time warp that didn't reopen until the Grunge Era."

"Yeah, well," she grinned, "we'll see."

She left the studio with a strange feeling of nostalgia, though feeling just as self-conscious in having committed to a bunch of kids old enough to be her own. Yet they were all in their thirties, and it could have been a lot worse. She decided to see where this trail would take her, and if it got her in shape for another Hezbollah reunion, well, so much the better.

It would be the first step on a twisting road she would never forget.

Chapter Twenty Two

Dick Munson trotted down the steps into his three-story brick apartment building on Clinton Street that morning, returning from his routine walk downtown for his paper, cigarettes and Off-Track Betting slips. He let the door slap behind him and listened intently as he stepped into the vestibule adjacent to Debbie's basement apartment. He heard no noise and could not help but feel a thrill of trepidation in his bowels. They were howling it up until the wee hours this morning. She knew the law as far as having male guests overnight was concerned. If she had anyone in there, he would pull the bastard's head off before strangling her to death and putting a gun in his mouth.

He pushed lightly on the door and it gave way. He stepped inside the sweet stench of marijuana smoke lingering in the air. He saw her light on in the next room and slapped the door closed, stepping hard so not to catch her unawares.

"Hi, Daddy."

He looked into the room and saw her lying on her tummy, dressed in a T-shirt and denim shorts, munching on an apple, her ankles crossed as she read a novel.

"Whatcha got there?" he asked, lighting a cigarette to give himself an excuse to ignore the pot smell.

"It's *Fahrenheit 451* by Ray Bradbury," she looked up at him. "It's about society burning all the books they don't like. This way they can force their opinions on other people."

"Well, I'm glad to see you reading for a change."

"What do you think about that?" she sat up on the edge of the bed.

"What, opinions? They're like assholes, everybody's got one," he said airily. "You can't force your opinion on anyone. They may have a different opinion and just keep it to themselves."

"Don't you think people should speak out and say what they think?"

"Sure. You have a Constitutional right. You shouldn't say

things to hurt other people, but you should never be afraid to speak the truth."

"I like hearing your opinion."

'Yeah, well, I'm your father," he reached over and ruffled her hair. "You going upstairs to see your mother?"

"I'm going shopping downtown. I'll pick up cookies at the College Bakery on the way back."

"She'd like that," he said as he walked out. "See you later, champ."

That short discussion between father and daughter would have a lasting effect on Debbie Munson, to her father's consternation. In weeks to come, her world view was going to go through major changes, and her father's words would serve as a moral compass. She would see the American music industry as implementing a Fahrenheit 451 doctrine, blacklisting music that did not conform to their new wave or rap music agenda. She would also accept the responsibility of promoting a message for people, by people and to people who did not represent the general population or its cultural values.

The man who would make the difference in her life was an outsider trying to find his own place in society. David Diamond was an ex-jock who aspired to become a poet, yet was repelled by the street poetry that became the rap music that dominated the airwaves. He came two decades after the coffee house subculture of the Sixties, and was a ship without a harbor until Tina Rivera came along. She met Stu Carlucci at an outdoor festival and found that he was a guitarist looking for a band. He was so desperate that he would take anyone with no experience necessary. Tina saw David as the solution to everyone's problems, the savior for whom they had all been awaiting.

The problem with Tina is that she needed to get a life. Debbie knew her from the neighborhood and told her Dad that she needed an apartment. Dick let her rent the place in the rear of the basement level, and soon she became Debbie's loyal mascot. She was mercurial and emotionally fragile, and Debbie tried to keep a respectable distance between them so as not to become Tina's handler. They hung out together now and again, and when Tina told her about David, it piqued her interest. Tina made the introductions, but Debbie immediately realized David was screwing her. She would have to catch him by himself to find out what he was all about.

David slipped her his phone number, and she arranged to meet him that Saturday morning. They met at Memorial Park so there was little chance of Tina running into them. Debbie was dressed in a black T-shirt and jeans, David similarly clad in blue. She noticed he had dyed his close-cropped hair blond, a style he would wear until the night he died. Most people who didn't know him thought he was queer until they had a word with him. His athletic physique and imposing aura quickly convinced them otherwise. They usually came away thinking there was something wrong with the personable young man that they couldn't put their finger on.

"I'm thinking I can buy an amp, a mic and a stand and go from there," David said as they smoked a joint near the Memorial Wall that would provide a backdrop for one of their most memorable gig years later. "If you could come up with a bass and an amp it'd work. Basses only have four strings, and the riffs aren't that hard. Maybe Tina can pick up a conga drum or some bongos. Maureen Tucker of the Velvet Underground started out beating on an upside-down garbage can."

"Are you kidding?" Debbie scoffed. "Tina'd put her whole welfare check on a drum set, she wants to belong to something so bad."

"Maybe we all do," David looked at her. "Don't you?"

"Depends on what it is. I'm in no hurry."

"That's how I felt until I met Stu. He's like a puppy dog on the way to the gas chamber. He puts everything he has on the line, and he does it with his guitar. He's raw talent, he's a natural phenomenon. He just needs someone to give him a sense of direction, and I want to be that man."

They wandered along the Promenade, back and forth across the Brooklyn Bridge, and throughout the Heights that afternoon talking about music, poetry and life. He discussed Baudelaire, Rimbaud and Poe the way most guys talked about their sports heroes. He seemed to know everything about rock and roll and explained how the blues started it all back in the slavery days. It was all about rebellion, and he agreed with Debbie that the Music Industry was taking that voice away.

"You're right, Ray Bradbury was a visionary. Only they're burning records instead of books. One day people won't even know rock and roll ever existed if we don't do something about it."

They got together the next day, and everyone made a commitment to buy the necessary equipment. Only the next weekend when they had their first practice, it sounded like a recorded train wreck. They continued to jam together, and Stu played with grim desperation as David sang and recited his poetry over the din regardless of how horrible it sounded. Finally Debbie and Tina couldn't bear the shame, and eventually they got better and better.

She always had an odd relationship with David. There was a sexual tension between them, but they both realized that if they ever slept together it would break up the band. David took to chiding the girls on a regular basis, berating Debbie with a high-handed attitude while lacing into Tina until Debbie came to her defense. David's routine was to address her as 'Deborah', lecturing her like a schoolteacher until she responded with a torrent of obscenities. That would be Stu's cue to break out into his latest lead riff that would leave them all mesmerized. David would refer to him as the Snake Charmer for a long time thereafter.

The turning point in their relationship came after a strange sequence of events. Debbie was invited to dinner one night by the boss' son after work. She cancelled practice to do so and was dressed to kill for their date. He heard her talking about her band with her co-workers and had his mind made up about her. They went for drinks after dinner, and he slipped her a mickey before bringing him back to his apartment and screwing her after she passed out. That Monday, he not only spread the word of his conquest but began treating her like shit. She spilled his morning coffee in his lap before walking off the job.

There was a black social club on Butler Street between Smith and Hoyt Street where drinks were cheap and the locals feared to tread. Debbie wound up there and got plastered well before closing time. Once again, the beautiful redhead in her semi-formal wear was too much for the predators to resist. She got mickeyed again and ended up in a drug dealer's apartment at the end of the night.

David had given her a skull-and-crossbone choker that she took to wearing on weekends. She was wearing it as a sign of defiance at work that day, and the drug dealer stole it from her as a souvenir. David could tell that something was wrong when she cut him short after he inquired as to its whereabouts. He coerced Tina into finding out what happened, and when she got the full story, David disappeared.

Nobody knew where he was until he showed up to practice the following Saturday drunk as a skunk. He trashed the practice, singing the wrong lyrics to songs and missing cues left and right. He made fun of Stu for stopping and restarting the songs, and badgered the girls endlessly. Finally he got on one of his Deborah soliloquies, and she had as much as she could take.

"Listen, you son of a bitch, my name is Debbie to you, got it?" she thundered.

"All right, *Munson*," he retorted, pulling an object out of his pocket and tossing it at her. "Nothing personal."

As he stormed out, she looked at the thing he threw at her. It was the little skull-and-crossbones, having been torn loose from the silken choker. She called an end to practice shortly afterward. After everyone left, she went to bed and cried herself to sleep.

From that day on, he called her Munson when he got on her case, and she never seriously bitched him out again. She heard lots of rumors about how he got the pendant back, and she would always think of him as the brother she never had. After he was killed, he left a hole in her heart that could never be refilled.

When the band broke up, Debbie went on to open her private investigations company on a wing and a prayer. There were a lot of hard feelings and she hadn't spoken to any of them for a couple of years afterward. She had given up her rock and roll aspirations and focused her energies on building her new business. It was almost five years later when the past finally caught up with her, and it all came back with a simple phone call. Debbie impatiently punched in the code on her phone to review her voicemail one morning, and the first message came as a shock that nearly caused her to drop the phone.

She punched 'replay' and distinctly heard Stu's voice coming through as casually as if he had just called her yesterday. Son of a bitch. She could count the number of times she had heard from him over the past half-decade on one hand.

He said that they were having a reunion party at Paco's in Jersey next Friday and everyone would be there. Just like that. At least he left a callback number, even though she was sure he would never return the message.

She remembered the day that Stu left the band. It was like the President had been shot. David got a call from Stu asking if they could meet in Manhattan. Tina had just scored a half ounce of

Acapulco Gold and was going to party with the band before practice. David was irked before he left, and smoldering when he got back. He called all the roadies and the creepy crawlers in and gave them a big speech on 'no surrender, no retreat'. They had the World Trade Center gig ahead, and Duke Gallegos was nearly in a state of shock over moving up to lead guitar by default. Yet they pressed on.

Duke quit after the show, and that was the end of Hezbollah. Johnny got his first pro boxing break at Trump Plaza and had to quit partying and staying up late. Debbie, David and Tina were like the Three Musketeers but eventually they put the equipment away. David finally struck a deal with some publish-on-demand company and set out on a publicity campaign with his poetry book, *The Excommunicant*. Tina got a minority student loan and began taking piano lessons with Carlo Menotti in Manhattan. Debbie went to visit David's uncle Fred one day and took a job serving subpoenas at his private eye office. The rest, as they say, was history.

She had nearly paid off the business loan her Dad had co-signed to secure the stake money to get MINK up and running. Fred Diamond had sent her several clients after announcing he was moving back to LA due to health reasons. She was breaking even and had a few days when there was enough for a new power suit and shoes. She had settled into her routine and was becoming used to living the life of a normal person…until this.

It had been four years of soul searching, second-guessing as to why it did not happen for them. The hardcore bands made it, the thrash metal bands made it, why not Hezbollah? They were hard enough, fast enough, better looking and smarter than the competition. She was not overly disappointed by the station in life she had arrived at, yet there were so many unanswered questions. Maybe the reunion would help answer some of them. Stu was still inside, Stu would have some answers.

"So what's up, David said he'd come in?" Debbie asked after finally winning a couple of games of telephone tag with Stu. She marveled at herself at how antsy she still was in talking to people over the phone. Business-wise she was great. She had conducted more than a few lengthy interviews with prospective clients over the phone. On a personal level, she was more inclined to meet the caller somewhere for a chat. She got that from Dick

Munson. Being on the phone with him for five minutes would be setting a personal record.

"Yeah, he wanted a touring deal, so this was right up his alley," Stu replied, conveniently glossing over the fact that David had rejected his offer of buying the Hezbollah demo tapes. "You know he was always looking for that one-timer."

"I'm not following that part about James Lincoln wanting us for his concert tour," Debbie was skeptical. "The guy could've gotten anybody to go out with him. Why us?"

"That's a good question.

I heard he had personally researched the best of the unsigned bands during the Hardcore Era and came across us. There was something about Television Records being a Novarich Records label and Jerry Blackstone got the word about us."

"Hell, I'm so far out of the loop I don't know who Blackstone is. So have you talked to anybody recently?"

"I had lunch with David a couple of weeks ago. He hasn't changed a bit. You mean you haven't talked to him?"

"You know the old crowd. Dumb sons of bitches don't know which side of the receiver to speak into."

"Yeah. Well, I'm looking forward to seeing you again."

"You too, Stu. See you at Paco's."

Looking back at it now, twenty years later, she still wondered if it had been worth it. True, they all walked away a hundred grand richer and earned their place as rock and roll legends. Only David Diamond was dead – not that he wouldn't have died anyway. It was just that they would have had more time with him, they could've prepared for it. Hell, three of the Ramones died of cancer, and they got heroes' farewells from all their constituents. The problem with David was that he would've rejected it. He would've left a goodbye note and flown off into the sunset.

She could understand how these kids from Demolition felt. It would've been like Hezbollah having tracked down Lou Reed and got him to come jam with them. She sure as hell didn't feel like that, even though they did. She just saw herself as having been lucky enough to having gotten her day in the sun. Every once in a while people asked if she was 'that' Debbie Munson, and she usually was able to blow it off and get back to the topic of discussion. She had done interviews from time to time, but people got the message that she wasn't very cooperative and eventually stopped calling.

The jam session with the kids left her feeling as out of sorts as ever. It was a rush, a damned good one, and they were certainly a good band. They were tight as a drum and the energy was great. Jerry was a great vocalist and rhythm guitarist, and Phil was a solid lead guitarist. Jimmy was a kickass drummer who was as good as anyone she could remember. Maybe not as technically proficient as Tina but topnotch nonetheless. It gave her a feeling of déjà vu when they started playing the old Hezbollah songs, and she knew they had devoted a lot of practice time to them. Their originals were just as great. If she had been twenty years younger, who knows. She might have even given Jerry a tumble.

Problem was, she was pushing fifty, and this was no laughing matter. Once this got out, the press would be merciless. Women her age were called cougars these days, cradle-snatchers and worse. They'd probably accuse her of screwing everyone in the band. And how old were these guys' mothers? Probably her age. If one of them showed up for practice, that would be Debbie's last day. And how old were their friends and hangers-on? Was she going to be surrounded by thirty-somethings? Was she going to be the old lady in the room? This shit was definitely not going to work.

If she was going to make this Crusader Reunion Tour work, she would have to get some stage time somewhere. This was probably the best chance she would get. She was so far behind Stu and Tina, it would be embarrassing. She wasn't much for jamming with CDs, she needed the interaction and energy of jamming with others. She would have to resign herself to playing with these kids, maybe going out a couple of times. Sure. Three and out. That would be the best move.

Debbie Munson and Demolition, or Demolition with Debbie Munson? Maybe she wouldn't even let them use her name. Word of mouth always worked for Hezbollah, it should be good enough for these kids.

What a bunch of shit.

Chapter Twenty Three

Paco Cabales felt as if he had reached the end of a long journey. He had no way of knowing it had only just begun.

He had fought the courts for almost fifteen years before his Agent Orange settlement came through over his exposure in Vietnam. It took him from famine to feast overnight, enough to buy a tidy little beach house overlooking the Jersey coast. With his wife deceased and his daughters married, he was alone in his luxury and only wished it had come in time for the band to have enjoyed it. David and the others had played their last gig in '80, right after Stu left. Paco considered the irony of Stu being the one to have called and set the whole thing up.

Even though Duke married his older daughter Lucy and Johnny married Isabel, it was David who his heart yearned to see. David was the brother he never had, the son he always wanted, the kindred spirit he had never known. Lucy took David home to meet Paco one day, but when his wandering eye set on Isabel it was all over. Yet a lifelong friendship had begun, and even though David went through his daughters like grain through a goose, he and Paco would remain friends to the end.

He remembered both of them spending their last dime buying each other drinks at waterfront bars and borrowing money to drink under the Brooklyn Bridge when they ran out. Paco was the band's number one supporter, and his girls were more than slightly embarrassed on numerous occasions when Paco and David went on benders proclaiming themselves the Heroes of the 21st Century. Yet everybody loved Paco as much as they respected David, and he was like an honorary member of the band. He was there when they crashed and burned at their debut at the Verdict before a dozen people, and he watched them crash and burn at their last gig at the WTC before over a thousand people. He lived and died with them, and now they were coming home to roost.

Paco was a decorated war hero with six Silver Stars, Bronze Stars, and a Purple Heart Cluster. He had more holes in his torso than homeless people had in their worst pair of pants. There was a plate in his head and pieces of shrapnel that surfaced once in a blue moon. He was studying law until his wife died, after which his battles with the bottle escalated until the Party came into his life.

They called themselves the Party until David began wielding more and more control over their stage show, the presentation and the publicity campaign. He went from guerrilla theatre to pranksterism to civil disturbance, and renaming the band Hezbollah (the Party of God) was just another step along the way. Stu's efforts to redefine and enhance the band's skills and repertoire were bearing fruit, and he was sickened by David's vision quest for notoriety superceding his own goals of building the band's prestige as a competent musical group. The better they got, the more heat David brought them, and it was tearing Stu apart.

Paco knew it was over the day that the cops surrounded the stage at the WTC gig and moved in to pull the plug on the show amidst the swirling lunchtime mob. David had pushed the envelope off the table and now had nowhere to go. He could not go forward any further, someone somewhere was going to blacklist this act. He could never go backward, not after this. This was their Tet Offensive. This war was unwinnable.

It was hard for him to accept that David had moved on. He spent most of his time on the Greyhound bus lines and fleabag motels, ecstatic over invitations to public readings and University lectures, clinically depressed when there were none. David was coming by once a week, then once a month. By now, they had not seen each other in almost a year. Stu guaranteed that David would be here, and Paco was exuberant.

The first arrivals were the girls, along with Johnny, Roth and Duke. It was a heartwarming scene as the girls fawned all over their Dad until he could pry himself long enough to do tequila shots with the guys. Paco walked them around the house as they congratulated him for his long-overdue windfall. Paco knew that he and Duke would be sharing their war stories in private, and Paco was looking forward to it. Johnny and Roth proceeded to regale him with boxing stories until the other guests started filing in.

Tina and Zeke showed up, and the girls were all over Tina as Zeke, ever the diplomat, seemed genuinely happy to see the guys again. She had become a celebrity of sorts, and everybody wanted to hear all about her latest appearances at Carnegie Hall and the foreign musicians she had jammed with. She was as self-effacing as if she was being asked to talk about her job as a stable hand, and it made it all the more intriguing to those who were still fighting desperately for another day in the sun.

Debbie Munson came in, and Paco's heart nearly skipped a beat. She was a full-grown woman now, as if she ever had not been, but it was if she finally grew up. She was wearing a $200 black power suit with a white satin blouse, white nylons and black heels, and if she did not give you a hard-on then you did not have a dick. She kissed Paco on the lips and he could not get over how incredibly gorgeous she was. She still had a smart mouth and she shattered the illusion within minutes, but that made her even more Debbie and her presence was overwhelming. The guys were all over her, and Isabel and Lucy were self-conscious as usual until Debbie rushed over to them. They fell under Debbie's spell just like everyone else.

Stu Carlucci was next to arrive, and Paco was elated at the sight of his pasty-faced old friend with the eager eyes and rumpled blazer, licking his lips intermittently as he suppressed his nervous energy. Stu lit a joint and he and Paco mellowed out on the veranda overlooking the beach, reminiscing over past times and fond memories. Johnny and Duke joined them intermittently before a great commotion at the door drew the attention of the entire gathering.

David Diamond and his entourage of creepy crawlers entered the door like a black-clad three-ring circus. His four friends broke into animated conversations about nothing in general with everyone within carshot. He walked around the room greeting everyone, giving out high-fives, knocking out a half-bottle of Heineken as soon as one was handed to him. The Star had arrived, and he knew it as well as everyone else. Debbie Munson felt like she was on the outside looking in, watching with amusement as David worked the crowd. They had talked on the phone a few times over the last month, so she would let him wag tails with everyone else before going over and chatting him up.

He was wearing his sunglasses as always and she could not see his eyes, so David was flitting to and fro around the living room before he lunged and grabbed her in a side headlock, lifting her and cushioning her in a pro-style wrestling takedown. The entire room was aghast as Debbie's long legs flew in an arc, and her skirt lifted so everyone could see her thong panties. She twisted onto one elbow and began punching him in the groin as hard as she could before wriggling loose, tossing him over and straddling him. She slapped his face and twisted his nose as he tried to bite her crotch before she let him up.

"What the fuck?" his creepy crawlers stood astonished, certain they were going to get beaten to pulp and thrown out along with David.

"This is Debbie Munson!" he proclaimed as if to a packed auditorium. "This is the toughest bitch in rock and roll! This is my partner and there is none other like her!" He gave Debbie a high-five and walked over to Tina, taking a full bottle of Heineken from her.

"Hey, do I got any shit on my suit?" Debbie walked over to the creepy crawlers, wiping some carpet lint off her suit, arching her backside towards them. They stared speechless, and would not have touched her if her ass was covered by palmetto bugs.

"Debbie, Debbie," she would remember him coming over to her and hugging her for the longest time. When he finally let go there were tears in his eyes. She almost choked up herself. She knew this was the changing of the guard, the passing of the torch. Back in the day, Dick Munson and Paco Cabales were considered two of the bad-asses in the neighborhood along with Fred Diamond. Now her Dad was all about OTB, Fred had retired to Los Angeles, and Paco was calling it a day here in New Jersey.

"Don't sweat it, Paco," Debbie insisted, squeezing his neck with a big hug. "We're gonna do you proud. We're going to Ragland to kick ass and take names."

Both Isabel and Lucy wanted to pay his way out there but he would have none of it. Johnny and Duke were both making a hundred grand on the deal and could have easily afforded it. Paco just wasn't going anywhere. He had been in the trenches with Hezbollah, he helped David carry his cross. He had shared their pain and gave them everything he had to offer. Both his daughters were marrying band members. He was sitting this one out. He would tie a yellow ribbon around the old oak tree, and the party would resume when everybody came back safe and sound.

Everyone except David.

"At ease, Sgt. Gallegos."

Duke took the position but was offered a chair by the three officers in civilian clothes seated around the room. He dropped into the seat across the desk from the senior officer, the other two seated in armchairs to his left.

"How's the weather down there in Medellin? Looks like you're getting a great tan."

"I prefer working at night, sir," Duke was affable. "Much cooler."

"Do you still play guitar, Sergeant?" Major Bellows, behind the desk, flipped through Duke's dossier.

"Occasionally, sir. Kinda like riding a bike, you never completely lose the hang of it."

"You had a band with a David Diamond back in Brooklyn before you joined the service," Bellows peered over his glasses from Duke to the dossier. "There was a police report about an incident in a church in the Wall Street area where you both used to work. Your name was mentioned in the report. Diamond was put on probation, and you joined the service shortly afterward."

"I... quit the band that day," Duke was hesitant. "I told him in a church because I didn't want him to create a scene. Unfortunately it wasn't much of a deterrent."

"He lit up a marijuana cigarette in the church," Bellows stared at him. "The priests called the police, Diamond was arrested and you were brought in for questioning. About a year later he publishes a poetry book called *The Excommunicant*. This friend of yours isn't too big on religion."

"We were never close, sir. More of a business relationship."

"Your band recorded a demo called *Party Time* that never went anywhere. Another one of your old band mates, a Stuart Carlucci, nearly got a deal with Arista Records but they wouldn't put out his album unless the first demo was released. Carlucci turned to Diamond, who had the product in his possession. Diamond wouldn't turn it over unless there was a reunion in the package. Turns out they met to discuss this at Frank Cabales' house."

"Paco," Duke's brow furrowed.

"You were aware of this reunion."

"My wife was invited, along with the family. My father-in-law just got the house, it meant a lot to him. I understood it was to be a housewarming of sorts. I wasn't aware of who was invited."

"They played the gig at the Bottom Line in Greenwich Village a couple of weeks later. One of the attendees was James Lincoln, the rhythm and blues entertainer. Do you know him?"

"I've got a couple of his records, sir."

"Here's where it gets tricky. Lincoln's a convicted drug user who has a number of drug busts on his sheet. Somehow he got the idea of staging a comeback tour in Palestine. He's having lots of issues with his criminal record and catching a lot of flak from the State Department. The unexpected development is that the Mossad wants this to happen."

"The Mossad?"

"The Israelis think that the Palestinian Authority is undergoing a power transition from the PLO (*Palestine Liberation Organization) to a terrorist group called Hamas. Hamas has strong support from Hizbullah in Iran. Unfortunately for the Mossad, they have been unable to penetrate Hamas up to now and need someone to open a window for them."

"I see."

"You'll be joining the tour group in Tel Aviv along with Billy Sixkiller," Colonel Boehm spoke from the far wall. "He's one of the top CIA agents in the Middle East sector. "Sixkiller is going to be hooked in tight with Mossad, they will provide you with full logistical support through Agent Sixkiller."

"Your mission is to provide us with a detailed analytical report on any and all insurgent networking throughout the tour group's area of operations," Major Glass instructed him. "It'll be similar to the work you did in Bogota last year. Work the inroads as best you can and provide detailed reports to Agent Sixkiller, who will be in close contact with the Mossad in this joint CIA operation. Any contact between the Mossad and you will be initiated directly by Sixkiller. You will have no contact with the Mossad outside of this protocol. Understood?"

"Yes sir."

"Needless to say, if you reveal any details of this mission to anyone involved with the tour, you will be brought up on charges of compromising State security."

"Yes sir."

Debbie remembered learning all about the arrange-ment the night David was killed, and she read about it over and over in the non-fiction account and the novel. That son of a bitch. He certainly held all the cards then, just as he had them now. With David gone, they would need him more than ever. They might have gotten away without him at the Crusader Concert, but this time around they would need all the help they could get.

Only now he was in Iraq, part of a Special Forces team sent to advise the Iraqi Army in their life-and-death struggle against the Islamic State. What in hell was the stupid bastard still doing in the service? That was a no-brainer. At this stage of the game, they would never let him out. America was deeper in shit in the Middle East than at any other time in history. It was a coin toss as to whether Duke would be playing in the Valley of Megiddo or fighting there. He was three years younger than most of the other band members, but that still made him about forty-seven. She heard he had been awarded the Silver Star and the Bronze Star over there, on a course to catch up with Paco someday. Not to mention the Purple Heart cluster. He was probably like Christopher Walken in *The Deer Hunter*. He probably wouldn't know what to do when and if he got out. Lucy had her career, she probably gave up on his crazy ass a long time ago.

Besides, Debbie had her own problems to worry about. These crazy kids went out and booked them a gig at a Soho nightclub. Don Hill's was one of the newer clubs struggling to survive on the exorbitantly pricey NYC scene. Just as she expected, Jerry used her name as a marketing angle. The club called bullshit and Jerry had to give them one of her business cards. After getting her answering machine three times, they left her a message confirming their booking at the club in three weeks. Debbie let them know at their next jam session and they were exultant.

"Now look, don't get your drawers twisted," Debbie warned them. "I told you this is a three-gig deal. I just want to get some stage time in case that Crusader Reunion Tour materializes. I don't care how good or bad we do. We do this, then one or two more and I'm done."

"No problem, I just wanna play Don Hill's," Jimmy grinned from ear to ear. He was a hulking guy at 6'4" and 270 pounds who played like a butcher with a meat cleaver. When he took the buffers out of his bass drum it sounded like cannon fire.

"Yeah, well, when you see how much they charge for drinks in those shitholes, you may never want to go back," Debbie chided him as she popped a top on a Bud Lite during their practice break.

"Won't be a problem for me. I always bring my own supply," Phil raised his metal flask to her. He was considered one of the best bassists in Manhattan but gladly switched to lead guitar when Debbie came aboard.

"Yeah, well, don't come crying to me when the bouncers start kicking the shit out of you," she smirked.

"Hell, they're gonna have to get past him," Phil jerked his thumb at Jimmy.

"I think this is gonna be fantastic," Jerry was as optimistic as always. He reminded her a lot of David in that regard. Demolition was going to make it by hook or by crook, and Jerry would stake his life on it. She only hoped he never ended up like David did, and she was getting off this ride long before she would ever have to find out. "This is a major club, and we'll be getting some major press. Whenever you're ready to go another round, Deb, I know we won't have a problem getting to play anywhere we want."

"How about Madison Square Garden?" Debbie teased him. "I always dreamed of playing the Garden."

"Well," Jerry was straight-faced, "I can make some calls."

Both Jimmy and Phil began hooting and chucking empty beer cans at him. Debbie ducked out of the way as Jerry fired back before retreating to the far end of the spacious rehearsal room.

"Okay, you assholes, let's get this over with," Debbie slung her bass around her neck and switched on her amp. "This old girl's gotta go earn a living tomorrow."

"What old girl?" the guys asked, looking up and down the room.

"Face it, Debbie, after the Reunion Tour you'll never have to work another day in your life," Jerry assured her.

She only hoped deep down that his words would prove true.

Chapter Twenty Four

"It's been a wonderful evening, Luc," Debbie exhaled as they emerged from his Lexus outside of her apartment that night.

Jean-Luc Renaud was an ex-teammate of her old beau, Mel Dalton. Luc, as his friends called him, invested his salary in fine arts and had a string of galleries from New York to Montreal to Paris. He had contacted Debbie about providing an armed escort for one of his dealers purchasing the entire collection of an up-and-coming young painter residing in the Montmartre district of Paris. It was not unheard of for thugs to waylay the purchaser in such a scenario and either blackmarket the shipment or hold it for ransom. Luc, of course, was far less interested in hiring Debbie than establishing a relationship, and their gourmet meal at an exclusive Soho restaurant got the ball rolling.

"I am so glad that you enjoyed it," he kissed her hand before departing. "Please consider my proposal carefully and call me if you have any questions. I shall be in town next week and would like to meet you for lunch to discuss your response."

"Not going to take no for an answer, huh?" she laughed.

"Not quite that easily," he smiled back. "*Adieu, ma cherie.*"

Debbie watched him drive off and pranced towards her doorway. She pulled up short as she saw the black-leathered figure sitting on the ledge by the side wall.

"What the hell are you doing here?"

"Well, no call, no show, I was hoping nothing happened," Jerry stood up from the ledge. "You're in a dangerous line of business, you never know."

"Yeah, well," Debbie grumbled. "I just had an important business meeting with a major client and things got scrambled. Sorry."

"I blew almost a whole paycheck to pick up something special for band practice," Jerry said regretfully. "The guys were kinda pissed but I told them it'd have to wait until you showed up."

Jerry opened up a small roll of tin foil and Debbie marveled at its contents.

"I've never seen anything like that before. How cool!"

"If you got a pipe we can try some."

"Not here, you kidding? How far are you from here?"

"Just a few blocks. I can get a cab."

"Go for it."

And so began one of the most convoluted episodes of her life.

She was still contemplating how she ever got from Point A to Point C in such a quantum leap, but she was here regardless. Somehow or other they ended up on the stage at Don Hill's a week later. It seemed as if it was going to turn into a fiasco from the very beginning, and as it unfolded it caused her to bond to these damned kids more than ever. She remembered how David would forget to rent a truck the night before, or the trucker canceled at the last minute. It would leave them playing Beat The Clock as David would run through the truck rental ads in the Village Voice, desperately trying to cut a deal within hours of the scheduled event. The band and the roadies would listen as he ended up in a cursing and shouting match with a trucker over the phone, hanging up angrily before inadvertently calling the same person back ten minutes later, apologizing and renegotiating as best he could.

"Next time why don't you hire a chimpanzee to rent the truck?" Debbie would tease him. "it couldn't do any worse of a job."

"I offered the job to you and Tina, and you lunkheads keep calling the zoo!" David would yell back, breaking the tension as everybody had a good laugh before he would start over again.

Only this was the 2010s and ribbing was considered bullying, which was considered uncool and could land you in court. Plus the fact that these were pretty good-sized fellows who would've beat each other bloody if push came to shove. She sat in her apartment on the evening of the gig, rolling her eyes and toying with objects on her desk as they quibbled with one another on the stream of conference calls that started and ended every five minutes.

"Listen, you buttheads, you better just load your shit into taxicabs and make your own way over there," she finally blew up. "Your truck is not gonna happen. Either that or haul your shit down into the subway, because unless you call me from the club and let me know you're there, I'm not going. And you'd better have an amp for me."

It was less than an hour later when Jerry called and informed her they were awaiting her presence at the club. She called a cab and headed down to the street with mixed emotions. She was understandably nervous, not having played in public since appearing before a half million people in the Valley of Megiddo. What was it, over twenty years ago? Yet she felt a weird maternal instinct towards the guys, hoping that everything worked out for them. She knew that everyone was making this a Debbie Munson event, but to her it was all about the guys.

She arrived at the club and was immediately recognized, being waved through by the doorman as she walked in and got her bearings. She saw the stage tucked in along a side wall and spotted the guys at the far corner of the bar. They came over and greeted her, Phil taking her bass and setting it up for her as Jerry took her order at the bar. She decided on a vodka and tonic, wanting only to wet her whistle before the task at hand.

"Nervous?" Jimmy asked as he swigged his beer.

"Nah. You?"

"Yeah."

"Hey, you're sitting all the way in the back, all you got to worry about is keeping time. Not that I don't know what you're going through, but you get used to it. Tina used to wear that goalie mask of hers, and part of the reason was so people couldn't see her playing with her eyes closed."

"Shit," he laughed, shaking his head. "I keep forget-ting all you've done. You actually played with Tina Rivera."

"Yeah," Debbie rolled her eyes. "I keep forgetting myself."

There was an opening band who kicked up their heels and got the audience moving, though all eyes kept shifting over to where Demolition sat at a corner table. They kept reminding people that Debbie Munson and Demolition was coming up next, causing her to make faces every time to the delight of the guys. They loved the fact that she genuinely did not want to be seen as the star of the show. It made them feel special that she wanted to be seen as one of them.

"Okay, Demo, you're up next," one of the stage hands came over as the opening act finished their set.

"All right, guys, let's go up there and kick some ass," she slugged down her drink. They got up and marched onstage, Jerry placing an order for another drink for Debbie before he joined them.

The fans buzzed with anticipation as the band opened their set. They chose "Pipeline" as a tribute to Johnny Thunders, Phil breaking out his Keith Richards-style licks as Debbie's bass lines were as a mortar barrage. The club had specially miked her amp so the sound man could turn her up to the max. She distracted herself from her nervousness by going back and forth between the band members making wisecracks. They, in turn, were caught off-guard and forgot all about the packed room. When they began going through their repertoire, she began joining each of them on their mics during the choruses. It not only made for photo ops for the fans but picked up the team spirit as each of them awaited their turn to sing with her.

Johnny Carmona always compared playing a gig to a good workout at the gym. She always thought that was a great analogy. You worked up a sweat, and once you got in sync it became a blur that was over before you knew it. They closed the set with Iggy and the Stooges' "Search and Destroy", which Debbie sang to a standing ovation. The chant of "*Deb-bie! Deb-bie!*" went up, and she exchanged fist bumps and high fives with the guys before they headed back to the closet-sized dressing room.

"Un-fuggin-believable!" Jimmy bearhugged first Phil, then Jerry.

"You lay that sweaty shirt on me and I'll give you a fist bump on the nose," Debbie playfully warned him. Jimmy's hair was dripping and his T-shirt was soaked.

"Geez, I hope they got a videotape of that last song," Phil was ecstatic. "That'd go viral on You Tube, I'd bet a million bucks."

"These bastards don't let you tape the performan-ces," Jerry scowled. "Did you see them giving people shit for taking cell phone shots of us?"

"Yeah, I would've loved seeing them pull that shit on us back in the day. David and Johnny would've probably gone out in the audience and taped the shows themselves."

"You guys wouldn't have lasted too long," Jimmy was wiping his face with fistfuls of napkins.

"Why the hell you think we started playing out in the street?"

"We'd better start packing before people start going by the stage for souvenirs," Jerry reminded them. "I can take your bass with me and bring it to next practice."

"Yeah, sure," she agreed. "I'm gonna have one more vodka and tonic, then I'm outta here."

"I got it," both Phil and Jimmy chimed in.

"Whatever," she smiled.

"Uh, Ms. Munson?"

"Sorry, no autographs," she ribbed the tall, well-dressed back man who towered over where they sat.

"Mr. Bull would like to have a word with you, if you please."

"Who?"

"You mean Jack Bull?" Jerry was wide-eyed. "I heard he had a piece of this place."

"Well, Jerry's the leader of the band. I'm just gigging with them."

"Mr. Bull would like to speak with you."

"I guess that settles that," Jerry grinned at her.

"So what, does this guy play rap music or something?"

"Hip hop," Jerry corrected her.

"Oh, a hip hopper."

"A hip hop artist," the black man pointed out.

"Of course," Debbie picked up the fanny pack she had worn onstage instead of toting a purse around. "Well, then, let's go see Bull Jack."

"Jack Bull," the black man reminded her.

"Yeah, right. Take me to your leader."

"If we're not here, I'll give you a call tomorrow," Jerry told her.

There was a passage to the upper floors of the building, and the black man led the way up a dark stairwell to a brick wall office space. It was recently overhauled to include polished wood floors, plate glass windows and 21st century office furniture. Debbie walked up to the mahogany-topped desk behind which sat Jack Bull. He was a tall, well-built black man dressed in a $1,000 silk suit and matching black shirt and tie. His hair was cropped short and his goatee well-trimmed, almost blending with the prison tattoos on his neck.

"Ms. Munson. My pleasure," he stood up and was impressed by her firm handshake. "Please, have a seat. Would you care for anything?"

"Nah. Nice club you have here."

"I'm a silent partner. That was quite a stir you created downstairs."

"Couldn't have done it without the guys."

"And vice versa. Have you spoken to James Lincoln lately?"

"What, about the Crusader Reunion Tour? No, I don't think he's called anyone yet. I personally think it's a bunch of Internet bullshit. First they say he's dying of AIDS, then they got him planning another concert in the Middle East."

"I remember back when Johnny Ramone passed away in 2004," Jack leaned back in his black leather swivel chair. "They had a benefit for him with some of the biggest names in rock and roll coming out. He listened to the whole show on his cell phone. He died shortly afterward."

"So you think that's how J.C.'s got it planned?"

"Who knows? You probably know him better than I do. He lives in an ivory tower. His life is rhythm and blues. For him, experimenting is throwing in some soul music now and again. He looks down at what I do the same way he looked down at what you did back in the Nineties. Only now he sees you as part of his legacy. He sees me as a disgrace to his profession, just like he did you."

"I wouldn't put it quite like that. He was --- is --- a businessman. What he did back then was all about money. Only he ended up getting used by people greedier than he was. I don't think he's got another fight like that in him, but I guess we'll see,"

"You see what I see. He'll never make that trip. The Israelis would never approve him coming back into Israel carrying AIDS. Not to mention that drug deal he nearly went down for. He can try and put something together, but he'll never take part of it. And I don't think his ego will allow him to sponsor a reunion he won't participate in."

"Well, you know how that goes," Debbie smiled wryly. "Everybody's got an opinion."

"Yep. Like assholes," Jack grinned. "Anyway, bottom line, the tour is never gonna happen. I want you to work for me."

"What?" she smirked, "Playing rap music?"

"Hip hop. You sound just like Lincoln," he rested his elbows on the desk as he peered into her eyes. I'm thinking of putting you out on tour to promote a two-record deal. Three months, no heavy lifting. Just you, not those kids. I've got my own

216

songwriters and studio musicians. We'll mix it up, half pop tunes and half alternative. There's a big market for reunion tours and retro concerts. We get that big money cross-current of boomers Xers, Ys and the Millenials."

"Problem is, I got a business to run."

"I did my homework. Your business grosses about a quarter million dollars a year before taxes. The overhead on your Times Square location is killing you even though it brings in good clientele. You do most of your own work, hire out minimally, it probably lets you bring home a hundred, hundred-fifty a year. I'm willing to pay you a half million dollars. After taxes, that'll probably be about what you could make in three years. Plus consider the fact you'd only have to suspend operations for a half year at most."

"Damn, that's a good offer. I'm afraid I'll have to pass."

"That's it?" he squinted at her. "Just like that?"

"I'll think it over but I doubt I'll change my mind."

"So why would you turn something like this down? Is it because of who I am, what I represent?"

"What, being black? Hell no, J.C.'s black, remember?"

"No, I'm talking about hip hop, my so-called gangsta roots."

"Nah. Frankly I could give a shit one way or another."

"So talk to me, Tell me what's up."

"You have any farmers in your background?"

"Not that I'm aware of, but I'm pretty comfortable in saying my ancestors had plenty of experience working on plantations."

"My Dad once compared having your own business to having a farm. You buy the land, the equipment, and make a personal commitment. You bust your ass, give it everything you got, and when you're done all you can do is sit back and pray that it happens for you. When it works, it's kinda like having a kid, or so I hear. You try to bring it up right, help it establish its own reputation, and hope it does something good people can remember you by."

"That's a good analogy. So you don't want to abandon your kid for a half year. What if I hire a staff to keep it running for you? A professional management team with professional investigators."

"What's the deal here?" she scoffed. "Did you wanna fuck me or something?"

"To tell the truth. Ms. Munson…"

"Debbie."

"Debbie…you're a very beautiful woman, but you're not my type. No offense."

"None taken."

"I just hate to see talent and opportunity go to waste. Look, we both know you're probably not gonna want to do this again five years from now. Time waits for no man or woman. Plus, James Lincoln's stirred up a lot of controversy and has created opportunity. It's not strictly business on my end. He held a news conference on the tenth anniversary of the Crusader Tour and had a lot to say about the hip hop scene. He talked a lot of trash about me when I was on the way up. He had a lot of shit to say about people who were helping me. I think that putting you on the charts on my label is gonna be payback."

"Okay, now I get it. Look, let me sleep on it. Obviously I want to see how things pan out with Lincoln. It's not just me, it's getting back together one more time with Hezbollah. If it doesn't happen, maybe then we can talk. Like you said, time waits for no one. James Lincoln doesn't have a whole lot left, from what I hear."

"You give me a call," Jack stood up and gave her a business card, shaking hands again. Debbie thanked him and headed out to the street afterward, graciously slipping through all the well-wishers along the way.

It was definitely a helluva lot to think about.

Chapter Twenty Five

Debbie stared balefully at the thick-shouldered men seated across her desk that evening over twenty years ago. She remembered it like it was yesterday.

"You know, we told you to leave it alone. You could've made a nice score, everybody just walked away, no problem. Now you got the cops involved. How do we clean up this mess?"

"You're the one who made the mess. Your embezzler thought he hired some bimbo who was going to ruffle some paper and sign off on the insurance claim. If he wasn't so damn sloppy he wouldn't have got caught. Now my license is on the line and I can't let go, and neither can you."

"You don't understand. There are people who want to put a rocket up your skirt over this. You tell the cops there's a threat on your life, you got to leave town. We'll send you to Hawaii, expenses paid for a month. They get someone else in, we clean up the mess."

"Yeah? Well, suppose you go back to the guy who hired you and tell him I put a threat on your life, see what he thinks. My business lives and dies on my reputation, just like yours."

"You hear this?" Vic began chuckling to Jack, pointing at her. "She's something, huh?"

"Sure is," he grunted back. "Look, lady, suppose we provide your client sufficient reason to release you from your contract? Like suppose we cut off those big fuckin' tits of yours and ship them to him in a box?"

She remembered that day as if it was yesterday, yet it was a day that she had told no one about. She earned her personal badge of courage that day, but would not speak of it because she did not anyone involved in such things. She tracked it like shit on her shoe all the way to Palestine, and would never want to step in it or anything like it again.

"Hey, fuck you, Jack," she lost her cool, yanking open her desk drawer and pulling out her .357 Magnum. She cocked it before slamming it on the desktop, causing them to involuntarily flinch. "You think you're gonna come into my office and give me shit? You either make your move or get the fuck out!"

It was the next night when she saw the two Mafiosi in the alley downstairs. After that, she didn't see them again until they were watching Team Carmona unloading the boxing equipment at the makeshift training camp in Tel Aviv. Once again, the one who was there for her in that harrowing time was Mel Dalton, who she was more and more realizing was The One Who Got Away.

"Mel! It's those two greaseballs, the ones who I told you jumped me in that alley the night I met you at CBGB's!"

"Are you sure? We'd better tell Billy Sixkiller, he'll be able to deal with it."

"No, wait, we got to think this out," Debbie led him away from the ballroom where the ring was being assembled. "Obviously they got an in with the WBA. This has to be a Mafia set-up. They're here for a reason, and it's not about helping Johnny. They're using the boxing exhibitions as a cover for something bigger. I'll bet it's drugs."

"You know, these Israelis have one of the most sophisticated intelligence networks on the planet. If they suspect one thing being out of line, they can close this whole tour down. Plus the fact we're all foreigners here. We may not be able to get out of here as easy as we got in."

"I don't want to expose you to this shit. Maybe it'd be better if you left and came back when I have everything straightened out."

"Are you out of your mind? I'm not leaving you here. Sixkiller's our best bet in this situation. We can ask him to keep a secret, we can take him into our confidence."

"There's something up with Sixkiller. He and Dukie are as thick as thieves. There's a chess game going on here, and we need to figure out who's playing."

As it turned out, she eventually found out that Maniacci and Raccuglia had cut a deal with Hizbullah to bring a major shipment of narcotics from Iran back to the USA. They were making their move while the band was onstage in the Valley of Megiddo where the world's attentions were distracted. Only they were the victims of an Israeli triple-cross during which they were arrested and the narcotics confiscated.

Both the documentary and the novel agreed that the abduction of Princess Sabrina and Stu Carlucci was a desperate attempt by Hizbullah to recover the narcotics in a trade with the Israelis. Debbie had no doubt that was the case. Only David, in death as in life, was able to turn the whole situation around by sacrificing his life and making himself the focal point, the center of attention. He became the martyr, leaving Stu with a debt he could never repay. The reason for the kidnapping became an asterisk in the history books. Hizbullah lived on, Hezbollah became part of rock and roll history and Maniacci and Raccuglia returned in failure to NYC. They faded into obscurity, a fitting end to two rotten scumbags.

She had no doubt it was why Stu seemed to be distancing himself further and further from the band, and rock and roll in general. He had been trying to get away ever since he left Hizbullah the first time. Only David seemed as Captain Ahab, trying to take down the Great White Whale that got him into the business. He caused Stu to get sucked into the Valley of Megiddo, then left Stu with the Debt after sacrificing his life. Hell, all Stu wanted was to establish himself as a jazz rock musician. His heart wasn't in rock and roll anymore, but no one would let him escape.

She wound up calling him the day after the gig, the second time in a couple of weeks after they had not spoken in over ten years. She wasn't even sure if it was longer than that. The band had gone their separate ways after the tour, and the only time they called each other was when there was a media campaign that dragged them back into the spotlight. First there was the novel, then the documentary to set the record straight. After that there was Lincoln making his big score in selling the film rights to the concert. They picked up some chump change, just as they did when the live album came out. It was mostly the band patting each other on the ass before going back to their private lives.

"Yeah, I saw on the Internet that you guys got over big time. Congratulations."

"Well, you know I'm just doing it to get my chops back. I hadn't been onstage since the Concert."

"It doesn't sound like you lost a step. They were calling you Hurricane Debbie."

"For a Thursday night, we were probably the best deal in town."

"The next time you guys play out, give me a call and I'll come to see you."

"So what are you hearing from Lincoln's people?"

"Man, I'm starting to tune out on that shit. The friggin' guy's dying, give me a break."

"I was hanging out with Bull Jack after the gig."

"Wow, that's cool."

"He's thinking Lincoln might go ahead and bankroll the deal to collect one last score."

"Yeah? Well, I haven't heard anything from anyone."

"Do you think maybe you should check him out?"

"Hey, it's not my band. I just came in for the touring deal, remember? When I walked off, I left David the keys."

"Somebody's gotta step up. Don't forget, you and David were the ones who started the band."

"You know, I'm fighting to save my career right now. I'm trying to sell a demo I've been working on for five years. This isn't a good time for me. Why don't you and Tina get behind it? You know Tina's hot as hell right now. She's the one you need to call."

She met with Tina for lunch after that, and it was a highly unsettling experience. She knew that Tina had some kind of medical issues, though she wouldn't go into details. Debbie wanted the Reunion Tour more than anything else, but there was no way in hell she would risk Tina's health. She and Tina had been friends for about thirty years, and probably felt closer to her than anyone else. Yet she knew that Tina wanted to see the reunion happen. Maybe Stu was right, maybe Tina could put her weight behind the campaign and help bring it about.

"Hey, bitch."

"Hey, Debbie. How are you?" Tina was enthusiastic but her voice sounded tired. Debbie didn't like the fact it was almost noon.

"You okay? You sound like you just got up."

"Nah, I was just taking a nap. I had a long night last night."

"Are you okay? You need me to come over?"

"I'm fine," Tina was emphatic. "What, it's against the law to take a nap?"

"Nah, but it's against the law for me to kick your ass."

"Oh, yeah?" Tina laughed. "So what's up?"

"I just got off the horn with Stu. He hasn't heard anything from Lincoln yet."

"Well, Deb, maybe it was all just a bunch of bullshit. You know how those Internet rumors surface. That's why I don't even like to go out anymore. People come up and start asking me about shows in places I never even heard of."

"Yeah, like New Hampshire?"

"Oh, fuck you."

"You know, Stu made a good point. He was talking about how he's all tied up with his studio work right now. You know, he keeps rehashing that jazz rock bullshit that nobody's ever gonna buy."

"I know, poor Stu. That's what he wants to do, we can't make him give up his dream."

"Yeah, but can't you see how this can work for him? If he does the show he'll get hot again, and he can use the leverage to make his new album work. Not to mention that the money won't hurt either."

"That's how it was supposed to work for him last time, when he released *Kaleidoscope*. It was critically acclaimed, but it just didn't get the sales he wanted."

"You know, I love hearing you using big words and talk shop. I could sit here all day."

"Go fuck yourself, Debbie."

"I'm trying, but it won't reach."

"Oooh!" Tina squealed. "You're so bad!"

"Anyway, he thinks one of us should step up. Why don't you call Lincoln? He likes you."

"Yeah, right, I'm the leader of the band. Why don't you call him?"

"I'm the bassist. You're Tina Rivera, remember?"

"C'mon, don't start. Besides, you know I'm moving back in with Zeke. If I dropped this in his lap right off the bat he'd have a fit."

"C'mon, where's your tits? Didn't you give him the no strings attached routine?"

"Yeah, with Zeke? Keep dreaming."

"Yeah, he sounds just like Mel Dalton thought he was gonna be."

"Have you heard from Mel?"

"Hell no. He's got too much pride. I'll never hear from him again."

223

"You're the one who broke it off. Maybe you need to make the call."

"Bullshit."

"See, Debbie, that's the problem. You can't keep expecting everyone else to make the call. You've been burning bridges all your life but you never try to build any. Sometimes you have to make the first move. Maybe you need to call Mel. Maybe you need to call Lincoln."

There was a silence.

"I'm sorry. I shouldn't be…"

"Nah, it's okay. You're right. I just thought since you got all the…you know…"

"It's just with all I've got going on with Zeke, and the doctor's appointments…"

"Dammit, Tina, I forgot. I'm sorry. Look, I can come over and give you a hand…"

"No, no, that's okay, I'll be fine. Say, have you spoken to Johnny and Isabel?"

"Nah, not yet. Have you talked to them?"

"Yeah, for a little bit. I think you should call them."

"Why, what's up?"

"They're going through a tough time right now. You should give them a buzz."

"Okay. I'll give you a call this weekend."

Debbie was really starting to have a problem with all the sick talk coming from Tina. She wasn't a hypochondriac. In fact, she was one of the toughest women Debbie knew. Matter of fact, she couldn't think of a time when Tina bitched about anything where her health was concerned. She had taken a few bumps in her time, from roughhousing with David to getting drunk and going face-first on the sidewalk. It was definitely about time to make a visit to Tinaville and find out what was going on.

The next call was to Miami Beach and Carmona headquarters. Johnny and Roth were now major players in this situation. Back in the day, David and Stu had always been the vocalists, while Stu and Duke were the guitar duo. Johnny and Roth had been brought in as window dressing, a quick fix for the David-Stu split. However, with David gone and Stu and Duke as maybes, this might not happen without Johnny and Roth.

"Hey, is this JC Two?"

There was a pause.

"There's only one voice, and one smart-ass, who would give me that. How are you, sweetheart?"

"Just great, John. It's great to hear your voice again."

"You're like the rest of our friggin' crew, allergic to the phone," his voice had gotten raspy from all the yelling over the years. What've you been up to?"

"Same old shit, baby. How's Isabel and Roth?"

"They're great. We're all rolling with the punches like we always do. Running the nut farm, trying to find some crazy kid who wants to be a champion."

"Anything good yet?"

"I got this kid named Jose Marcial. He's a man without fear and his punches got a kick like a mule. Watch for him on the sports page."

"Hey, I'll drop a couple of bucks on him. If he wins, I'll owe you a case of beer."

"That's my Debbie."

"So you talked to Tina?"

"Yeah, I did," he exhaled softly.

"She sounded like you guys had a problem out there. What's going on?"

"You mean she didn't tell you anything? Shit. Look, let me get Isabel on the phone. She's around here somewhere. She handles this stuff better than I do. It's fucked up, you know what I mean? First the thing with Tina, now this. Where does it end?"

"What thing with Tina?"

"That muscular dystrophy bullshit. What, you mean she didn't tell you about that either?"

It hit Debbie like a shot in the stomach.

"Tina's got muscular dystrophy?"

"Oh, geez. Whassa matter with these people? Everybody's gotta get someone else to deliver the bad news. I'm sorry, Deb."

"What do you got, John?"

"Hold on, just a second," she heard him put down the phone. She could hear him cursing and swearing as he yelled for Isabel. She heard commotion, then a female voice before Johnny told her all about it in his Brooklynese.

"Debbie?"

"Hey, girl, how's it going?"

"Oh, same old. How're you? You sound great."

"Well, I've been better."

"Omigosh, Johnny just told me you didn't know about Tina, I'm so sorry."

"Well, don't feel sorry for me. You better feel sorry for Tina after I get hold of her."

"We're praying for her," Isabel managed, feeling a lump in her throat as she heard Debbie's voice crack.

"Dammit, Issy. I'm sorry for losing it."

"That's okay. We know you love her, just like we do. We love you too, we always will."

"I love you guys too," Debbie wept. "So what else is fucked up?"

"It's Frank. Frank has AIDS."

"Oh, Issy," Debbie cried, holding the phone against her breast as the tears spilled down her cheeks. She took the ride out to the Jersey Shore after Frank was born and went back a couple of times when the Carmonas flew up to visit Paco. Frank always knew her as his Aunt Debbie. This was a double blast and it was killing her.

"Debbie, I'm so sorry you have to be hearing all this at once," Isabel waited until she recovered.

"So am I, this is fucking terrible. I am so, so sorry. How's he doing? How are you and Johnny doing?"

"We're hanging in there. The good thing is that it's brought Johnny and Frank closer together. We're all holding on tight, and we've got Roth. You know what they say, it's not over until it's over. They're fighting to find a cure, so we keep praying."

"Dammit. I've been calling everyone about that Internet gossip about Lincoln, and now I get this."

"Yeah, we've been hearing it too. We're just like everybody else, waiting to see if it's true or not."

"I'll find out and I'll get back to you guys. Look, I'll get a break from work and I'll fly down."

"It's not any better or worse right now, so take your time. Of course we'd love to have you, so just let us know."

"I will. I'll call you soon. I gotta go kick Tina's ass."

They shared a tearful laugh.

"I love you, Debbie, you take care."

"Love you too, girl."

She hung up and collapsed in her armchair at the

226

apartment, sobbing piteously as she let it all out. She had never cried the way she cried when David was killed, but this was damn close. These were death sentences passed along to two of the people she loved most in the world, and it had to be coming at a time like this. How was she supposed to deal with this? How was she supposed to keep her eyes on the ball?

She crawled over to her entertainment center and pulled down a bottle of Jack Daniels. She unscrewed the top and tossed it across the room as she sat up against the wall.

Fuck tomorrow.

It was gonna be one helluva night.

Chapter Twenty Six

Debbie remembered opening her eyes and watching the room swirl in the mist before her. With a start, she jerked her head and saw Jerry's naked torso lying alongside her in his king-sized bed. He reached across to her and she bounded out of bed as if it had caught fire.

"Oh, no," he groaned, clapping his forehead. "Please don't do this."

"How in hell," she covered her face with her hands. "Okay, now I remember. You fucked up, Munson."

"Debbie, that was the best night of my life," he raised up on an elbow. "How can you trash it like that?"

"This isn't going to work, Jerry, in any way, shape or form, you can just forget it ever happened."

"How can I forget it ever happened? Tell me, huh?"

"Well, this is the end of the band, for sure," she pulled her jeans on, sitting on a chair by the door.

"What the hell does the band have to do with it? We don't have to put it on the Internet."

"There is no we," she managed to harness her magni-ficent bosom in its bra. "There's you and there's me, got it?"

"Okay," his face dropped dejectedly. "But we're still band mates. You can't kill the band."

"What, you think I'm gonna put up with your hurt puppy shit for the rest of the year?" she pulled on her T-shirt. "I've seen it come and go, and I'm not buying, I'm out."

"You can't do this. We got two more gigs to go, you gave us your word."

"How did you think this was gonna go down?" she stopped, staring malevolently at him. "You thought you were gonna get me drunk and fuck me, and everything was gonna work out perfect for you?"

"Of course I always dreamed of us making love, but that was never the game plan. Look, you were a goddess in that

228

Crusader Concert. I fell in love with you the first time I saw that video. You were my muse, you were my guiding light. You were one of the reasons I got into rock and roll. When I heard about the reunion tour, I hoped beyond hope I'd get my chance to meet you, to get to jam with you. It happened, and it was something beyond my wildest dreams. Of course I wanted to make love with you. Didn't you always dream of making love with Elvis?"

"So what, you wanted to fuck Elvis and you got me?"

"You know what I'm saying. You're my idol."

"Yeah, well, you got your one-night stand," she searched for her purse.

"What is it, my age? Aren't you sick of people discriminating against others because of their age?"

"Don't get smart," she whirled towards him. "You think this is a fucking joke? You know what they call women who sleep with guys half their age? Look, buddy, I don't need this shit."

"Who says anyone will ever know? Look, you wanna keep it a secret, we'll keep it a secret. By the way, I'm not a bad-looking guy. I'm a hard worker and I can make things happen with the band. I've been surfing around, we've got some offers. I know you got your private eye company but you can make some good money on the side with this. But I know it could be more. I've never had mu chance. If I can make this happen, who knows? Maybe we can get some big money. Maybe you don't have to work no more."

"You got it all figured out, don't you?" she squinted at him. "I'll stay home and you can fuck me all day for the rest of my life."

"Why does it have to be something dirty? You act like I pissed on you. I have some self-worth, you know. Girls like me. It's not like you slept with some fucking bum."

"So, good. Go find a girl," she began rummaging through her purse, unsure of what she had stuck in there. She went to work late the morning after she had gotten the double whammy from Johnny and Isabel. She left early, and when she got home she never called Tina. She couldn't have handled it. Instead she went home and started drinking again. She was almost shit-faced when Jerry called and said he got hold of another Hawaiian bud. All of a sudden she wanted to smoke some killer weed, and she told him she'd take a cab to his place. It was all downhill from there.

"What, do you think I stole something from your purse?"

"Don't be an ass. Why don't you put on your fucking clothes?"

"All right already," he rolled out of bed and pulled on his briefs. She couldn't help but notice he was built like David back before Diamond turned into a poster boy for the American Cancer Society. That as probably how it happened. She got fucked up, was feeling depressed over Tina and Frank, and this kid hit her David switch.

"I gotta go," she snapped her purse shut.

"What about practice?"

"What'd I say? That shit is over. You fucked up."

"Don't you do it! Don't!" he exclaimed. "Look, we got something great going with the band. We made magic on that stage. You can't say you didn't notice it. It was all over the Internet. You got to talk to Bull Jack after the gig, and that guy's like a ghost. He don't talk to no one. How can you just walk away from that? At least, Debbie, at *least*---don't walk off from Phil and Jimmy. Give *them* one more chance. Please."

"I'll think about it," she walked towards the door.

"Please," he came around the bed.

"What'd I tell you? Put on your fucking clothes."

"All right," he yanked on a pair of black shorts he had neat the dresser by the wall. "Please."

"I'll think about it," she reached for the doorknob.

"Thank you," he reached out gingerly.

"You put your hands on me and I'll knock you on your ass," she cocked her eyebrow and raised a fist.

"Okay, okay."

She opened the bedroom door and headed across the living room of the apartment to the front door.

"Will I see you at practice?"

"We'll see," she said as she walked out.

She caught a cab and slouched down in her seat against the door, peering out the window as the city cranked up for the morning rush hour. She considered the fact that she had a pattern of getting fucked up after traumatic events in her life, and all it did was make matters worse. She remembered the day the band broke up, the day when Duke met David at Trinity Church and told him he was joining the Army. It was the nail in the coffin, the day the dirty little coward shot Jesse James in the back. David got arrested for trying to get them both arrested for lighting a joint in church. Debbie didn't find out until that afternoon, when David called Tina and tried to arrange bail.

It was the greatest pain in her life at that time, though twenty-one year old Debbie had no idea what real pain was about. Nevertheless, she had a case of beer at the bottom of the fridge for the next band practice that was never going to happen. She also had a pint of Jack Daniels in the bottom drawer of her dresser. Fuck them all, she was going to drink the whole thing without them. She didn't need them. She didn't need anyone.

After she drank the first six-pack, her Dad came down and asked if she heard about David.

"What are you, drinking already?" he growled as he saw the look in her eye as she leaned against the doorway of her apartment. "What's wrong with you? Why don't you come upstairs and have dinner, come see your mother."

"I'm not in a good mood. I'm just gonna stay in tonight."

"Don't get messed up. You got work tomorrow, right?"

She finished half of the pint of JD, and washed it down with the second six-pack after that. By then she was getting shitfaced, and she turned on the stereo to put a soundtrack on it all. There was an alternative station on, and she lifted her bottle to it. *You lousy sons of bitches*, she toasted them. *You made it, we didn't. We're sitting on our ass in our underwear drinking beer on our kitchen floor. You're on the fucking radio.*

At one point she went to the sink for a glass of water and knocked a tumbler over. It broke in the sink and she picked up a big shard. She marveled at it, sitting back down on the kitchen floor and stared at it. Almost as an afterthought, she took a shot at the veins on her left wrist and drew blood. She frowned and took a second shot, and it was a good one. She took a third shot and it began flowing good. It ran down her arm like in a movie, and she took joy in the sight of it dripping onto her naked thigh and running down into the crotch of her panties. She giggled as it looked like she was having her period. Did she bleed like that when she popped her cherry? She was so drunk, she couldn't remember.

She remembered hoping she bled to death, but she was really thirsty and needed a drink of water. That's what she got up for in the first place. She tried to get up but the room was spinning and she slipped and fell back on her ass. She tried again and got to her feet, but her bare heel slipped on the blood and she skidded. She fell hard, her head cracking against the edge of the sink and nearly knocking her out.

She recalled how the radio was still playing, the yuppie bands mocking her as she laid there in her own blood.

Debbie Munson, passed out on the floor
Debbie, don't you love me any more?
Shit.

The second time was after the band arrived at Grand Central Station where the limousines dropped them off after arriving at JFK from Tel Aviv. It was James Lincoln's farewell, the last courtesy after having helped him realize the biggest victory of his career. She had a couple of drinks on the plane and was feeling pretty good, hoping it wasn't going to hit her that hard. The hell it didn't. Stu left first, still devastated as they all were after David's death. He was wearing sunglasses, and he had closed himself down so that he looked as if he was saying goodbye to a bunch of casual acquaintances before he caught a cab. No one overreacted, they all figured they would see him again soon. No one realized they wouldn't see him again for five years.

Next was the Terrible Trio. That son of a bitch Duke stayed behind with his CIA buddies and the rest of the scumbags in Tel Aviv. Johnny, Isabel and Roth were on their way to Paco's, where they were going to stay until they could get situated. Again she had no way of knowing they would decide to move to Miami and open a gym. She didn't hear from them again until they called to tell her Johnny and Isabel tied the knot. She didn't see them again until they brought baby Frank to meet his grandfather Paco.

Baby Frank.
His Aunt Debbie.
Fuck.

Finally there was Tina. Zeke had been calling since he heard about David getting killed, and suddenly they were planning to get back together again. She wanted desperately to get together with her for a drink, but knew it wasn't the time. When Zeke saw Debbie he saw David, and this would have been the worst possible time for them to meet up. Debbie agreed to call Tina, and somehow that didn't happen for a couple of years. Or did it? She couldn't even remember. Where in hell did the time go? Where did the years go?

After that, it was just her and Mel. The last time she saw Mel, it was on the sidewalk in front of Grand Central Station. It was time to go---time to go. He wanted to buy an Amtrak ticket for two so they could unwind on the way to Montreal. He wanted her to stay at his apartment while she got all her affairs sorted out. He wanted her to put all her money from the gig in the bank, close down the office, and start making wedding plans. He had it all figured out.

That's not how it was going to go down as far as she was concerned. She needed time and space. She was going back to her apartment and sort everything out. He wanted to bring her back to Montreal and she decided she was going to call him in a couple of days.

"Debbie, don't do this," she remembered his last words. "Don't walk away from me. If you leave me stranded on this sidewalk, I'm not going to come looking for you."

"I've got to ride, Mel," she remembered her last words. It was like a line out of a spaghetti Western.

They never did say goodbye. She hopped in a cab and watched him through the rear view mirror until they faded from each other's lives for the last time.

She remembered someone writing afterwards that she was like a Mafia don. She kept her enemies close and kept her friends at a distance. Well, this time she was going to prove them wrong. She was going to prove everyone wrong. Debbie Munson was going back to Armageddon one more time. She was going to make this happen by hook or by crook. People weren't going to remember her as a retro act, a hot-looking cougar who had her last hurrah at a Village nightclub. This wasn't going to be another boilermaker party before she rode off into the sunset.

Jerry called the next day before practice, just as he always did.

"Nah, I'm gonna be busy. I'm not gonna make it."

"*What?*"

"Look, you had enough practice and we just played a gig. If you don't have your shit together by now, you never will. I'll meet you at the club Friday night."

"Debbie, don't be bullshitting me."

"Now you're calling me a liar?"

"No, no. Okay, if that's how you want it. I still got your bass."

"Yeah, well, you'd better have an amp there too."

The Bowery Electric was walking distance from where CBGB's used to be. They heard of the impact Demolition made the previous week and were suddenly excited about the unknown band's debut at their place. One of the managers were at the door when Debbie arrived, and she eventually realized he wasn't expecting her to show up. He gave her a drink on the house and escorted her to the rear of the club where her nervous cohorts awaited.

"Hey, that's a cool shirt," Jimmy said as they exchanged high fives and fist bumps. She had 'Queen of Pain' emblazoned in silver over the front of her black T-shirt. Her bosom made it hard to read up close.

"Yeah, well, I had it made for the occasion, just in case we fuck up."

Everybody got a laugh out of that, and they began loosening up with the usual banter. She watched Jerry from the corner of her eye and was very impressed by the fact that he acted as if nothing at all had ever happened. He laughed and joked, and looked at Debbie the same way he looked at the other guys. All of a sudden she started seeing him in a different light, and that disturbed her. She couldn't afford herself to fall into that kind of trap.

She was just as good as playing straight face, and gave it a great shot on stage that night. She really poured it on, almost as heavy as she did at the Crusader Concert. She broke into her martial arts stance when she played her riffs, prancing back and forth as she blasted out her chords. She strutted over to one mic after another, joining the guys in singing the chorus parts. She would walk to the edge of the stage and made faces at the fans, and even tossed some good-natured insults at them which they absolutely adored.

They closed the show with the New York Dolls' "Frankenstein", which brought the house down. Phil played the lead riffs like his life depended on it, and Debbie wielded her bass around the stage like a heavy-caliber automatic weapon. They played it at nearly twice the speed of the original composition, allowing a few slam dancers to start a mosh pit in front of the stage. Debbie played right in front of the slammers, inciting them to madness which left the crowd breathless.

"Hey, Debbie, that was fantastic."

"Fancy seeing you here," Debbie was sipping cold beer after the set as Sapphire Starr came over to the table. "Hey, guys, I'm going over there for a minute."

"Sure," they replied. "We'll be here for a while."

234

"So you're looking to pick up another Pulitzer?"

"No, I just came out of curiosity. It's great seeing you again."

"Bullshit. I know you've been up to see Tina. Planning to get it right this time?"

"I'm a bit past the Crusader era," the black celebrity reporter smiled, dressed meticulously as usual in a $700 dress suit. "I'm planning to do a feature on Tina, then and now. Serious, I just came by to say hi."

"You're a trip, you know that?" Debbie chuckled. "You were just stopping by to do a feature on Lincoln when I first met you. Next thing we knew, you were part of his entourage at Tel Aviv. Then you become our mother confessor, and when we came back you put our laundry out on the street."

"It didn't hurt," Sapphire peered at her. "If it wasn't for the book and the documentary, the whole tour would've faded into history."

"Yeah, we owe you our lives, don't we?" Debbie smirked.

"Maybe up until things started going viral on the Internet. You can't stop progress."

"Whatever. You planning to do it again?"

"It's not gonna happen. Have you talked to James?"

"No, I figured you did."

"No, and you probably never will either. He's locked away worse than Michael Jackson. I don't know if he'll ever leave that mansion again."

"How bad is he?"

"From what I understand, he's worse than David was when he was on that tour. "

"What about the talk that he's gonna bankroll the gig?"

"It costs money to have AIDS. If he leaves anything behind, it won't be much."

It made her think of Frank, and suddenly it crossed her mind that Johnny and Isabel would really need that kind of money. They needed the gig as bad as Debbie wanted it.

"Well, if he makes the gig happen, he'll have more to leave behind. Plus a bigger legacy."

"I wish you the best, Debbie," Sapphire reached across the table and touched her hand. "It was great seeing you again."

Debbie stared her back as she watched the journalist walked

out of the club. The documentary was a stark, no-punches-pulled account of the Crusader Concert Tour. She had portrayed the events leading up to the tour, the whole episode in the Middle East, and the aftermath. She painted Lincoln as a Machiavellian megalomaniac, David as a Shakespearean tragedy, and Debbie as a self-destructive force of nature. The video was heart-wrenching, but the book pulled everything out of the closet. Part of it made her glow with pride, and part of it made her want to gouge Sapphire's eyes out.

She depicted Debbie as jaded and disillusioned, having become a workaholic who drowned herself in her private eye company after watching her Siamese twin murdered before her eyes in Palestine. She made people think there was nothing left, some kind of burned-out shell floating through space.

Debbie was going to prove her wrong. She was going to prove them all wrong.

She got up and walked back over to the band with new resolve. This story was not over yet.

Chapter Twenty Seven

Representatives of the world press had crowded into the conference room hours before the band arrived. The room broke into a tumult as James Lincoln led Hezbollah onto the dais surrounded by TV and video equipment in the smoke-filled room.

"Mr. Lincoln wants to thank you all for coming today," the hulking Toby's voice rumbled through a mic at a podium across the room. "He has taken time from his schedule to accommodate you all with a question and answer session. We ask that you participate in an orderly manner so that the interviewers and interviewees can work together in generating enlightening information for audiences around the globe."

"Mr. Lincoln," a British reporter stood up. "Many R&B enthusiasts around the world feel that this is really a final struggle for the genre in the record industry. They see you as the only hope for a musical form that is fading into music history."

"The same has been said about rock and roll," Lincoln waved a bejeweled hand towards the others on the dais. "I'm sure they would agree that rock and roll will never die. And I say the same about rhythm and blues."

"Mr. Carlucci," a French reporter spoke out. "There are rumors that David Diamond compromised you into playing this event with the release of the *Hezbollah* album, and that your record label was fully aware of the coercion. Do you think this may affect your attitude coming into the event?"

"Like maybe I'd throw the gig?" Stu squinted at him. "Johnny'd be the one to ask about throwing fights." Johnny stood up and threw a wadded napkin at him from across the table to a chorus of laughter from the gathering.

"Mr. Carmona," an Italian reporter asked. "Much is being made of your scheduled exhibitions for Ten Count Promotions. Do you think that one performance may detract from your efforts towards the other?"

"I don't see the difference between the two," Johnny waved a hand. "I stick and move onstage and I dance in the ring."

"Mr. Diamond," an American reporter called out. "There have been reports of death threats against the band, and you in particular, by the revolutionary group Hizbullah for the use of their name and what they call blasphemous writing in your prose and poetry books. Care to comment?"

"My religious beliefs are pretty straightforward. There is only one god," David sneered back. "Me."

"What an asshole," Debbie peered at him through her shades as David flipped her off to another roar of laughter from the crowd.

"Ms. Munson," a Canadian reporter waved at her. She opened her motorcycle jacket wider and threw back her titian tresses to reveal her "MOTHER OF HARLOTS" T-shirt. "Some Arab leaders from neighboring countries have condemned your public image and stated that they would ban you from visiting their states should the entourage plan on doing so."

"You've seen one, you've seen them all," she shot back. "No skin off my ass."

"And a big one at that," David snorted. Debbie reached past Tina and punched him in the shoulder to another outburst from the press.

"Ms. Rivera," a German writer rose from his seat. "You've been sharply criticized by music journalists around the world for participating in this event so close to your scheduled tour with the African National Ensemble this holiday season. One writer compared it to loaning a state-of-the-art scalpel out to a slaughterhouse."

"Wasn't that you who wrote that story?" Tina asked teasingly to a chorus of laughter.

"Actually," she continued as the laughter subsided, "these are my roots, this is where I began, and these are the people responsible for my success. For anyone to deny me the right to renew my spirit while encouraging me to join our African brothers and sisters in reaffirming their international identity and cultural contribution to our world society, I feel, is hypocrisy. I'll be ready to whip the world after I leave here."

"You think I've got tapes on Stu," David leaned into the mic before him. "Wait until they hear what I got on you."

Tina whipped around to face him and accidentally knocked his beer bottle into his lap. David dropped his head onto his arm on the table as Debbie rolled out of her seat onto the floor, kicking her feet as she bellowed with laughter. Her boots struck against the table and began wobbling all the other beverages on the long table.

"Okay," James Lincoln leaped up from the table, protecting his $5,000 silk suit. "Show's over."

"Thank you for coming," Toby rushed to the podium. "Pick up your press kits on the way out. Thank you."

Lincoln returned to his hotel suite and stripped down to his white silk boxer shorts and robe, pouring himself a half glass of Scotch to unwind. He still was not sure as to how this would end. What he did know was that it would be either his greatest victory or final defeat.

He remembered how this all began, nearly a year ago when his heroin contact, Melvin E. Williams, came out to his palatial estate on the Jersey coast with his bi-monthly score. Melvin was a street comedian who hustled dope to make ends meet. Lincoln knew him from the old days and maintained the connection throughout his meteoric rise to fame in the 70's. When Lincoln began paying for high-grade quantities, Melvin's connections opened the spigot so that he was able to invest in an agent and turn his comedy act into a career.

Back in the day, everything Lincoln touched turned to gold. Lincoln rode *Soul Train* into a golden harvest, and his investments blossomed into a golden parachute ensuring his feet would never touch the ground. Only the 80's brought with it the rap music craze, and suddenly black music was no longer the same. He watched Michael Jackson and Prince, his closest competitors, ride off into the sunset, leaving him alone to face the dawn of the new era alone.

Politics was playing a strong part in both American and world history. The Reagan Era had brought on a clash between the Superpowers of unparalleled importance. The focus, as always, had been on the Middle East, and Palestine had emerged along with Lebanon as a major hot spot. Recent developments suggested that negotiations between Israel and the Palestinian Authority were leaning towards the creation of a coalition government in Palestine. The government would be led by representatives of the

Arab, Christian and Jewish communities and, if successful, could lead to an unprecedented withdrawal of Israeli troops from the territory and eventual Palestinian autonomy.

Lincoln and Melvin had fantasized about a Concert for Peace in Africa but realized that the bloodthirsty African warlords could include the entourage in their next bloodbath. The idea of the Palestine tour came as they watched CNN through a heroin daze. Lincoln had his agents contact the coalition government, and their enthusiasm led Lincoln to send a battery of lawyers to Tel Aviv.

The challenge was to hedge his bets to ensure that the event would earn blockbuster status throughout the international media network. He needed to include an opening act that would stir up enough controversy, but not deliver enough of a performance to upstage Lincoln. He contacted one of his connections, Jerry Blackstone, who was a major mover and shaker within the industry. Blackstone came up with a juicy tidbit on the radar over at Arista that Lincoln immediately locked onto.

Stu Carlucci was considered a musical genius, one of the greatest unsung talents since Lionel Richie in his pre-Jackson days. They expected him to usher in a new era of jazz rock, but the winds of change made rap music the next big thing. Market instability made almost every new project a high-risk enterprise, and they needed a boost for Carlucci's profile. All he had in his portfolio was a demo from an unsigned band project. Yet someone at Arista's A&R thought it worth buying and releasing. Problem was, Carlucci's partner would not release it without cutting a side deal, regardless of price.

Whoever had the product was a wide-eyed fanatic who would not relent until they buried him upside down so the world could kiss his ass goodbye, the product in his cross-armed clutch. He sent his agents to dig up dirt on David Diamond, and the deeper they dug, the more intrigued he became. When the Hezbollah reunion gig was announced, Lincoln made sure to reserve a table.

Lincoln's attendance was deliberately leaked to the press, as had been news of his projected Middle East concert. As a result, the show was completely sold out according to plan. Lincoln came backstage to visit with the band and instructed Toby to take Stu's number. The next day, Stu was informed that Lincoln wished to hire Hezbollah as their opening act for the Concert for Peace.

Lincoln wanted to meet Debbie Munson, as much as David

Diamond if not more. He brought them out to his mansion a few days later and interviewed each of them individually. She was dressed to play her part with her black motorcycle jacket, black T-shirt, jeans and biker boots. Unlike David, she had her shades hanging from the front of her shirt so he could see her eyes. At the age of twenty-seven, she was one of the sexiest women he had ever met.

"So you're a private detective. Business seems to be going along pretty good for you, from what my people tell me."

"Yeah, it's okay. I'm finally getting to where I'm breaking even."

"This isn't the way you come across to your clients."

"I'm in a different environment. If I came in here in a power suit and a white blouse, you'd probably scratch me off your tour list."

"So you're playing a role. This isn't really you."

"Look, what the fuck did you bring me in here for?"

"Okay, okay," Lincoln chuckled, holding his hands up. "Listen, I just need to know I'm getting my money's worth here. I'm investing a lot of cash, not to mention putting my career up on the line. You know as well as I do that the parade has gone by for rhythm and blues. I know my name and my music is going to put it back up on the charts, but I need this show---this tour---to live forever. This is going to be my magnum opus. I want to give them an R&B experience they'll never forget, and a show they'll never forget. We were lucky enough for us to be able to put it on a stage that will never be equaled in world history. Only now we got to come up with the goods. Now we got to make it real."

"There's my question. Why hardcore punk? Everybody's gonna wonder why you're not going out with rappers, or New Wave bands, or even Madonna. Is it like you're going out of the way to make sure no one's gonna blow you away?"

"No, I'm thinking *Rocky*, the whole thing," Lincoln leaned over the desk intently. "None of this on paper has a chance of a snowball in hell. It's all a big publicity stunt. The Jews set King Daoud as a fall guy running a puppet state. The Kingdom of Palestine is a ruse designed to placate the PLO and their Arab neighbors. Once the regime folds, Daoud and his Christian Liberation Army becomes major players, and Princess Sabrina becomes an overnight celebrity with her own designer house in Paris. The supporting bands on the tour lay the Punk Revolution to rest, and James Lincoln sings his swan song at the end of a noteworthy career."

"Yeah, well, I call bullshit."

"And so do I, young lady," Lincoln thumped his fist on the desk. "We can't control the political future of Palestine but we can control our own destinies. You can help write a new chapter in the history of punk, and I can do the same for rhythm and blues. But we got to be *real*. We got to let the world see that this is the genuine article. We are in the Valley of Megiddo, fighting our battle of Armageddon, and we got to look the entire world in the eye through them cameras. We got to let them know that we are leaving it all on that stage. If they want to bring what we represent to an end, well, then they gonna have to kill us right there. Right on that stage. This is for all the marbles, Debbie Munson. You step on that plane with me and there's no turning back. I got to know that you're with me, that we're taking this journey together and we're never looking back."

"So you ran this shit by David already. What'd he say?"

"He's already out there. He's in the Valley of Death waiting for us."

And so he was. And they left without him.

She remembered the limousine ride back to Grand Central Station (it was like his responsibility began and ended at the station) where the band went their separate ways for the time being. It reminded her of Hezbollah's first big gig, bigger than the Carnevale street fair they played on Court Street in Cobble Hill. It was after Stu left, when David got to where Lincoln was now in terms of desperation and career choices. Debbie was just as nervous, and she did the same thing she did back when she was counting down the hours before the Memorial Park gig.

She turned to her parents.

Debbie called them after the chauffeur let them out at the Station, and the others went their way as Dick Munson picked up. She told him she was coming to visit, and within a half hour she was at the three-story Munson home, filled with memories and trepidation.

During the cab ride she recalled the day they played Memorial Park. It was David's most outrageous stunt up to that time. He got a permit to play outdoors and scammed a local church to lend him folding chairs. He said they would collect donations for the church, though in reality he hadn't planned to collect a cent. They papered lower Manhattan with flyers, and hardcore punks came by subway and across the Brooklyn Bridge to see what this Punkfest was about.

It was the first time Tina played with her goalie mask, and the last time Stu appeared with the band until the Crusader Tour. They drew a crowd of around two hundred people, most of them wondering what this Brooklyn band was about. David had brought Roth in by then, and his roaring death metal riffs were just what David was looking for. Stu was completely turned off by the new direction, and Duke went with it just to piss Stu off. Roth and Duke came up with five new hardcore tunes that Stu thought was setting the band's progress back a year. Though they got a positive reaction from the Manhattan punks, Stu bailed out the next day.

"It wasn't just that Stu bailed," Debbie said as she stood out in the Munson back yard cooking sausages on the grill with her father. "You bailed out on me."

"What are you, nuts?" Dick growled at her. "Me and your Mom went out there to watch you. We were out there for at least a half hour. It was a nuthouse out there that day. Those kids were a bunch of whackos, worse than David and his friends. There was a guy with his hair done up like the Statue of Liberty. I'll never forget that."

"I was out there playing the biggest show of my life at that time. I kept looking around and I didn't see you. Finally I saw you and Mom all the way at the end of the park. I was getting all set to way for you, and when I caught your eye, you and Mom waved and left."

"So is that what you came out here for, to bitch me out? You're nuts, you know that? How long ago did that happen, five years ago? You're as bad as your mother, bringing that shit up after all this time. Whaddaya want, blood?"

"No, it's just sometimes I feel like I can never please you," her eyes grew misty. "I know I don't always do things you can understand, but I try my best."

"Hey, c'mon, champ, what's this about?" he pinched at her ear. "What's the matter with you? You're my daughter. Of course I support you. Maybe I didn't start a fan club for you and your crazy band, but I never stood in your way. Four years you made all that noise right downstairs from me, and I never complained."

"I'll always appreciate that you did that."

"Yeah, well, you're doing good now. You got your own business, you're doing okay. Of course I'm proud of you, and so is your mother."

"You know I'm gonna do that tour."

"So you already thought it over," he began turning over the sausages.

"Yeah. It's a once in a lifetime opportunity. I gotta see it through."

"That's crazy over there, that Middle East. You can get killed over there."

"You can come. I'll pay your way."

"You know your mother can't make that. Out in the desert, are you kidding?"

"Come by yourself. It'll only be about a month."

"She can't be without me for a month. She's not well, you know that."

"Okay, well, I offered."

"What about that hockey player? Does he know about this?"

"He has no say in the matter. I'm gonna invite him. I was hoping you two could've got to know each other on the tour."

"You aren't gonna be sleeping with him?"

"Daddy!"

"Okay, okay," he waved her off. "C'mon, the sausages are done. Let's go bring them upstairs and we'll have dinner with your mother."

"So are you gonna wish me luck?"

"Of course. Look, you're gonna do fine. Just watch that Lincoln guy. He looks like a con artist to me. Get someone to look over those contracts, and make sure you get every cent he promises you."

"Yeah, okay."

"Who's the champ?" he threw a couple of jabs at her stomach before grabbing her in a headlock and kissing her forehead.

"I am."

They collected their sausages and left the backyard, Debbie holding his arm as he carried the tray. He only wished she knew he was the proudest man in the world.

Chapter Twenty Eight

The Concert For Peace in the Middle East had become a reality.

R&B superstar James "Continental" Lincoln had beaten the odds at last. The Israelis finally consented to allow the fledgling Palestinian government to sponsor the mega-event in hopes of uniting New Palestine and drawing world attention to their cause. The thought of staging the show in the Valley of Megiddo had enraged religious groups around the planet, but eventually they conceded that the legends of the Scripture could be turned into something to benefit mankind.

James Lincoln and the Continentals announced that they would turn the proceeds over to the Palestinian government, content to walk away with the royalties and percentages from recording and film rights. The punk band JC had lined up to open the show reluctantly agreed to do likewise. Lincoln was hedging his bets by performing the songs on his unreleased CD, "Shackled (In The Bonds Of Love)". The recordings would earn billions.

It was a million to one gamble, and Lincoln hit lightning in a bottle. Both soul music and punk rock had seen their days, and the thought of a retro show in war-torn Palestine seemed delirious. Yet Lincoln pulled out all the stops, ransomed his recording empire, bribed and coerced his way over all obstacles. He proved beyond a shadow of a doubt that he was still king. No one, not Michael Jackson, Lionel Richie, Puff Daddy or any of that rap garbage could have done this. James Lincoln would go down in history as the greatest black entertainer of all time.

Yet the task itself lay ahead. Fundamentalist Islamic groups vowed that the blasphemy of such a spectacle would never take place in the Holy Land.

The biggest problem was with the main punk group, Hezbollah. Its lead singer, David Diamond, had issued sacrilegious comments to the press that nearly got them derailed by the American President. The name of the band itself made it a target for the terrorist Shiite group of the same name (despite its English translation 'The Party of God'). Only most of the heat had been brought on by their female bass player. For the life of her, she couldn't figure out what the problem was.

Debbie Munson had spent that Saturday night in downtown Jerusalem along with her boyfriend, ex-New York Ranger Mel Dalton. Escorted by four beefy plainclothes Palestinians, they enjoyed ethnic food at numerous bazaars, stopped for drinks at men-only bistros, and bargained over trinkets that Debbie made the bodyguards carry.

They were a stunning couple. Mel stood six foot at 180 pounds, a handsome man whose black hair was carefully coiffed, his deep suntan offsetting his green shirt and tie and black suit. Debbie, her titian tresses spilling over her shoulders, wore a tight white designer dress and matching heels. Her generous bosom strained within its confines, causing the Arabs to stare in wonderment. Her emerald eyes, upturned nose and bee-stung lips were more than most men could take, all that Mel Dalton could handle. She stood 5'4, 130 pounds of pure heaven, with a tiny waist and chiseled legs that wouldn't quit. At 30 years old, she had a body of a woman half her age. She had nary a wrinkle on her face, and her natural force remained unabated.

They were on the way back to the hotel when an old woman, wrapped in black, hobbled up to Debbie and blasted her in Arabic before a bodyguard shoved the hag aside. Debbie nagged unceasingly until the plainclothesman finally relented.

"She said, madam," the Arab swallowed hard, "that you look like a whore."

Mel and Debbie looked at each other before laughing themselves to tears. The bemused bodyguards followed them as they took the elevator to the sixth floor to David Diamond's suite.

Debbie was extremely concerned about David's health, and had no idea that he had been diagnosed with stomach cancer that gave him about six to twelve months to live. He had dropped from 175 pounds to 140 in the last eight months, and she had chalked it up to his heroin and liquor diet that had seriously compromised the survival of the band long before they made it to Palestine. They were all in their early 30's, having found their stations in life, and this reunion gig was as a dream come true. Only David seemed determined to turn it into a nightmare.

Debbie and David had formed the band in the mid-70's during the last days of the Punk Revolution. David had started a campaign with their unreleased cult classic just months ago, and JC Lincoln happened to be in the right place at the right time. Debbie couldn't believe what was happening, and wasn't really sure she wanted to pick up those pieces again. Yet money talked, and it was enough that she would never have to make another bank loan to keep her private investigations business open for the rest of her life.

When she got the call from David, it was like winning the lottery. When she got to meet James Lincoln, she was absolutely starstruck. Only reality came crashing in when the band reunited at Novarich Studios in the Soho area of downtown Manhattan. She hadn't picked up a bass guitar in over ten years. It was like riding a bicycle, you never really forget but you flop all over the place before it finally comes back to you. Lincoln had freaked out at first and was going to pull the plug on the whole operation. They slithered, they crawled, they dragged themselves to their feet, and finally they were up and running. It was David's fanaticism and Debbie's combativeness that made it happen, just as it had back in the old days.

"Mel," she turned to him in the lobby, "I just want you to know that this has been a real special time for me."

"I know it, Debbie," he smoothed her hair from her face. "You told me how much you and the others sacrificed, all those years of hard work. It's finally happening for you. I'm so proud of you, baby doll. How many women could just kick it into gear after all these years like you have?"

"I don't mean that, Mel," she gazed into his eyes. "I mean having you here with me, being able to share this with you."

"Well, thanks, Debbie," he blushed slightly. She had always been standoffish about their relationship despite the fact he had pursued her relentlessly in NYC for almost a year. She had a longstanding failure to commit that had nearly discouraged him. He had broken an engagement with a top fashion model and put his real estate position on Long Island on hold to take this trip. His friends thought he had gone mad, but Deborah Munson was the kind of woman who could do that to you. "I'm glad you feel that way. This is real special for me too."

"I can be a bitch sometimes," she smiled softly, melting his heart. "It's hard being a single professional woman in Manhattan. You're always worried that one day you can lose it all. Just one bad year can send you right back to Brooklyn. I'm not a young girl anymore, I admit it. I'm not going to go to NYU and take up rocket science. I just can't take chances, you know what I'm saying?"

"I do," his voice grew husky. "I don't want you to have to anymore. I want to take care of you, Debbie. I'm not like anyone else. I'm doing okay out on the Island, I still get my checks from the Rangers. I just want you to give me a chance to prove myself to you. I do everything I can to show you that I care for you. It's just that sometimes you don't want to let me in, Debbie. You've got to let go sometime."

"You're special, Mel Dalton," she clasped her hands behind his neck and pulled him down for a kiss. "You're special to me. I want you to know that."

They rode the elevator to the sixth floor immersed in thought. They knew that, whatever happened, things were going to be much different back in NYC for them.

The white noise hit them as soon as they got off the elevator. Diamond had the entire suite painted black at Lincoln's expense, all the fixtures fitted with black light bulbs. His black-clad creepy crawlers milled about like zombies, and the place reeked of sex, drugs and alcohol. The rugs were strewn with trash and some of the furniture was smashed. Paper plates soiled with scraps of gourmet meals were everywhere. The maids, it was said, were terrified to enter unto such blasphemy.

David Diamond was propped up on the couch by the humongous Aiwa sound system. The Velvet Underground's distortion-driven masterpiece, "Sister Ray", blared at ear-splitting volume. He had cut his platinum hair himself so that he looked like an Auschwitz survivor. His eyes were sunken into their sockets and his cheeks were sallow as a corpse. His wraparound sunglasses hid the parchment yellow of his bloodshot eyes.

"Well, well, well," David croaked. "If it isn't the Bobbsey Twins. Brenda Starr and Basil St. John in person."

"We had a great time out there tonight," Debbie was enthusiastic. "There's so much to see and do in this town. I don't think we'll be here long enough to see everything."

"That's fine," David grinned, reminding Mel of a Jolly Roger. "We're in the middle of the desert. Everything stinks like sweat."

"May have something to do with your friends," Debbie glanced around at the zombies shuffling around the room. "I think

248

you need a change of pace. We're taking you with us to the bazaar tomorrow."

"You and what army?" David began coughing, then hawked and spat green slime onto the carpet before lighting a Camel.

"You look like crap," she said cheerily. "We're taking you out for lunch."

"I don't think it'd hurt you to skip a few meals," David gave her a once-over. "The show's a week from now, y'know."

"Yeah, so?" she patted her tummy. "This dress is size ten. You're the one who needs to get in shape."

"I think you weigh more than I do," David smirked.

"My *mother* weighs more than you do," Debbie retorted.

"The problem, Munson," David peered at her over his shades, "is that you're getting old. There's nothing you can do about that. I can go pig out and get healthy in a week. You can't stop being old."

"What was that?" she asked in disbelief.

"C'mon, Debbie, let's go," Mel pleaded.

"No, wait, I didn't hear what you just said," Debbie put her finger behind her ear. "Would you repeat that?"

"Debbie, please," Mel reached out and held her arm.

"Don't cross me, Mel," she jerked away from him before turning to David. "What'd you just say?"

"Go out and play with your boyfriend," David sighed.

"Hey you!" Debbie yelled over at the scarecrow by the stereo. "Turn that fucking shit off!" The teen stared back uncomprehendingly. David was pouring himself a shot of cognac as Debbie wrenched the bottle from his hand and fired it across the room. It exploded against the Aiwa, and the room became still as the grave.

"Now," she loomed over him. "I can hear you better."

"I said," David sneered up at her, "you look like ten pounds of baloney in a five pound bag."

"*What?*"

"You come waddling in here after eating five pounds of pitas, and expect to tell me how to look?" he chuckled. "Face it, Munson, you're pop rock. I'm punk. You don't have it anymore. You look like Britney Spears on steroids. You and the rest of the band. You all look like you're at an office party on stage. I'm the survivor here. The rest of you are a bunch of sellouts. Posers."

"You're calling me a fucking poser?"

"Look at you, Munson. You got the tits to go around dressed like that? You don't know whether you want to pose for Playboy or Weight Watchers."

Mel cupped his forehead in anticipation of a vicious migraine.

"Hey, you," she said, then reached down and wrenched David's sunglasses off, flinging them across the room. "Look at me. Fuck you!"

"Gee, Debbie Munson, you're my hero," David narrowed his eyes.

"I'll go out and get a gun off one of those ragheads in the hallway, and blow your balls up into your teeth," she screamed in his face.

"I smell alcohol," David replied.

"That's your problem," her lovely features were flushed with anger. "All you do is sit around here with these hopheads and get fucked up all day. Why don't you go out and get something to eat, you son of a bitch? You sick fuck, all you do is talk about people, write your sick fucking songs about everybody else. The reason why you're so miserable is because you're a no good, skinny looking miserable scumbag. Understand?"

"Do you know what a brontosaurus is?" David turned to Mel.

"Leave him out of this," Debbie warned him.

"It was an enormous dinosaur that was so big, it had a brain in its head and a brain in its ass so it could walk," David informed him.

"Okay," a vein stood out in Debbie's temple as she started for the door. "You wait here. You wait right here." The creepy crawlers began making a beeline towards the door as well, blocking her path.

"I think she's going to kill me," David sat up eagerly.

At once the door flew open, and James Lincoln appeared along with six beefy black men and a crowd of reporters from the *Ha'aretz* and other Israeli newspapers. They shrank from the phalanx of the walking dead fleeing the suite, and eventually Lincoln came in to confront the occupants.

"What in hell is this?" he demanded. "This is a pig sty!"

"Not until you showed up," David frowned.

It was at that moment that she realized what was going on here. This was where David lived. Nearly twenty years of cramped motel rooms, sleeping in cars, cheese and crackers. He had done the college circuit as a self-parody, reciting his lyrics with the music sucked out of them. It hit her in her tummy like a bowling ball. He had done purgatory for all this time, and now that Lincoln had brought them here, it wasn't any different. Not for him. He was just hanging on to see if it meant anything.

"Listen to me," Lincoln said quietly, trying to remain calm, his $5,000 powder-gray suit giving him a tentative air of authority. "We need to get a grip on this thing. There are millions at stake here."

"Okay," she held the sides of her head, trying to quell the torrent of blood raging through her temples. "I'm cool, I'll deal with it. Mel?"

She held out her hand, and it seemed as if he had no choice but to follow her out into the light, some misplaced Joan of Arc sacrificing herself on the altar of the world press. He turned to David before coming to her side.

"I won't let you use her like that," he said tersely.

"If I were you, I wouldn't either," David agreed.

Debbie Munson emerged into the hallway as the Jews quietly gathered around. Her face shone as an angel of light. She seemed translucent in the white dress as she fielded their questions effortlessly, casually, as if there were nothing at all unusual or strange about an Irish Catholic woman in her thirties preparing for a punk show in the Valley of Megiddo under threat of death by militant Islamic groups.

"This'll make you rich and it'll make me famous," David rose from the couch, an excruciating pain shooting from his diseased bowels into his cranium. "But it's not about us. This story's about her." Lincoln smirked as David tottered to gain his footing.

"We're so close, brother, so close," Lincoln encouraged him. "Just one more week. Three hours up there, in and out. The dream of a lifetime. I just need you to hold on, brother. Hold on."

"It's out of my hands," David shrugged. "Don't you read the papers? It's Hezbollah, it's the party of God. And the party's already started."

"If only I'd met her - met you people - five years ago," Lincoln stared wistfully at the doorway. "God knows what we might've accomplished."

"Maybe God *does* know what we might've done," David flicked his cigarette butt onto the carpet. "Maybe that's why it's all right here, right now."

The countdown to Armageddon had begun.

Chapter Twenty Nine

Debbie had started to pay attention to the news for a change, and she didn't like what she was hearing. There were new kids on the block, and the PLO and Hizbullah didn't even rate anymore. Hamas now represented a Palestinian majority, and they had ratcheted up attacks against Israel so that the Gaza Strip was in a state of siege. The Islamic State had declared a Caliphate across Syria and Iraq, controlling a large swath of land along both borders. It was now one of the most turbulent areas on the planet, and anyone would agree that a concert in the Valley of Megiddo was a preposterous notion. Calling it a Concert for Peace in the Middle East might be considered an insult to over one million refugees in the region.

It became more obvious than ever that she would have to be the catalyst to get things moving. She could hear the strain in Johnny and Tina's voices, and she never even got to talk to Roth. They might as well have been on another planet out in Miami. The reunion gig must have been the furthest thing from their minds with Frank contracting AIDS. She knew that pushing the issue with them at this time of trouble might have caused an insurmountable rift between them. If they thought for one minute that Debbie was looking past Frank to make the concert happen, they would never feel the same about her again.

This whole situation made her feel as if she was being reintroduced to the 21st century. She started going online more and realized the predicament Stu was in. A three-paragraph story about Stu's production of *Kaleidoscope* resulted in over two hundred comments from posters who seemed to be divided in their opinions. Some contended that Stu was washed up, over the hill and jazz rock didn't matter anymore. Others insisted that his career had been sidetracked after the Crusader Concert and that he was finally getting the individual recognition he deserved. There were numerous remarks about his studio accomplishments, wondering why he hadn't been content to move along in that stage of his career.

The controversy over Tina went far beyond a few undistinguished Internet articles. Many high-profile entertainment magazines and TV shows speculated as to why she was coming out of near-seclusion to participate in something that appeared to be so far beneath her professional level. They were tearing through her closet in pointing to her turbulent relationship with Zeke. They were also theorizing as to whether it was about financial troubles or health issues. Debbie thought it vexing that they had no clue about her battle with muscular dystrophy. Instead they were suggesting that Tina's obsession with privacy was the result of psychological problems.

Debbie was amused by the ripple her shows with Demolition had created. She wasn't getting much more than single-paragraph coverage from *The Daily Beast* and the *Huffington Post*. Most of it was tongue-in-cheek remarks about the female private eye returning to her punk roots in the wake of rumors about a Crusader reunion. Despite the favorable fan reaction to her shows, most observers considered her return to Palestine as less likely than that of Johnny and Roth. They thought MINK was far too successful for her to put it on the back burner.

The articles were eye-opening and gave her consider-able cause for reflection. She had been running the show by herself for the most part. If her face got plastered over the Internet, it would undoubtedly give clients lots of room for doubt. There wouldn't be a whole lot of secrecy if a minor celebrity was spotted tailing private individuals in public. She had the foresight to wear her shades onstage, causing spectators to wonder whether she was hiding the wrinkles one might expect on a fifty-year-old face. Yet most of that was considered questionable in taking into account the shape her body was in. 'Debbie Munson's still built like a brick shithouse', they would say. Still, going back to Palestine might not be the smartest move for someone making a living as a private eye.

The Bitter End seemed apropos as the third and final gig for Demolition and Deborah Munson. They had agreed on three gigs, and none of the band members even mentioned it in their last practice sessions. It was as if they hoped beyond hope that she would stay on. She saw no need to bring it up, especially since she had brought them to a big jump-off point. It was most likely that they could have never landed the gig without her name in the lineup. There was no way they could have said anything other than that she had brought them further than they would have ever gone without her.

This time they were playing in front of a full house, and the opening act asked Debbie to autograph club flyers. She was now more of a public figure, and she lost count of all the selfies she was caught in. Customers took their own photos after pirouetting so that they included Debbie over their shoulders. She singled out a couple of cute guys, calling them over and teasing them before having someone else snap their pics with their arm around her. They thanked her profusely before she went back to have beer with the band.

They played their first set and it showed that Demolition was in their full glory. Jimmy flailed away, the reverberations of his cannonade being felt by spectators in the front tables around the stage. Debbie had also been turned up, and her bass notes and chords blasted their way through the club.

Phil was trying out licks had hadn't played before and each of them sizzled as he wielded his lead riffs like a steel whip. Jerry hammered his rhythm chords home, building a concrete platform for each song that allowed the band to lift off into the stratosphere.

Debbie was patting her brow with a dinner napkin and was caught off-guard by the sight of a figure looming from the audience. Stu Carlucci came over and gave her a big hug, resulting in an explosion of camera flashes behind them. She introduced him to the band before he took her off to the side for a quick chat.

"Feel like coming up and doing a song with us?"

"Nah, I'd just slow you down," Stu chuckled. "You look fantastic up there. If you were trying to get tuned up for that reunion gig, I think you're in the zone."

"What about you? You been doing any punk rocking lately?"

"I've been having some problems with the marketing people," he frowned. "Their research is creating doubts, and they're rethinking the advance promos and the whole tour campaign. It's not a question of breaking even, it's about them staying ahead of the competition."

"They have jazz concerts and festivals all over the country. Anybody who says it doesn't sell anymore is a lazy bastard who doesn't know where to look."

"Well, I'm not giving up. It's not over until it's over."

"You know, maybe history's repeating itself, Maybe the Reunion Tour can act as a springboard to boost your album sales."

"They need to make a decision in the next couple of weeks.

There won't be time to wait and see if the reunion's gonna happen."

"Shit."

"Hey, girl, this is your night. Get back over there with the guys. I'm out there cheering for you. You're kicking ass up there, go on up and finish what you started. No prisoners."

"Okay," she exchanged hugs with him. "Let's grab a beer after the show."

"Yeah. Now I may have to take off, but you give me a call during the week."

"Don't walk out on us, there's be a question and answer session."

He grabbed her again and gave her a kiss on the cheek. After that , they returned to their separate realities.

She was beginning to realize they were drifting farther and farther apart than ever.

The next day she got a call from Jean-Luc Renaud, who invited her for dinner at Keens Steakhouse at West 36th Street. She greatly enjoyed visiting the historic dining place, whose 20th century ambiance and collector's item photos covering the walls never failed to impress. Only she had to keep her priorities in perspective. Getting caught up in a whirlwind romance with a dashing Canadian millionaire would be a certain distraction from her goals.

She knew there was no way in hell she could ask anyone for advice. Her biological clock was ticking, and she had no idea whether or not she could've had kids. She always subscribed to the theory that family was hostage to fame and fortune, and saw how the band had been affected by the concept. Johnny and Isabel had a kid, and they paid dearly for continuing to pursue Johnny's dream in the process. Duke and Lucy had a son and a daughter. Only that dumb bastard thought he was going to continue double dipping for the rest of his life. He had no idea that the military was going to come to collect. Now he was overseas for life, his family three people in pictures in his wallet.

She seriously doubted she could be someone's mother, and not because she couldn't be knocked up (although she wondered if thirty years of birth control left anything in her plumbing). She wondered if Debbie Munson the punk rocker could ever be quenched. Would she be like a mother wolf protecting her cub? Would she be ready to rip the head off the butcher, the baker and the candlestick maker for looking crooked at her child? Would she leave her child an orphan if her spouse ever got abusive? Big questions.

Jean-Luc was a handsome mofo who reminded her of Mel Dalton though he was twenty years older than Mel had been way back when. He had also played hockey but never made it to the NHL. He bounced around the AHL for a while before making some brilliant business investments that made him independently wealthy. Despite herself, she did some snooping. She found out that even if he lost everything overnight, there was enough socked away for him to die a rich man. He was captivating, well-mannered, educated, and sexy as a fifty-something could get. This was going to be another boneheaded Munson play.

"Well, Deborah, have you considered my proposal?" he asked with his pantie-moistening Quebecois accent, peering into her eyes through the candlelight flickering over the table. They didn't normally have candles at the tables at Keens, but Luc usually got what he asked for.

"You know, ever since I was a kid, people always called me Deborah when they were serious as a heartbeat," she smiled. She wore a black dress and her thick red mane spilling over her shoulders. Half the men in the restaurant would have proposed marriage to her on the spot if they thought they had a chance.

"Perhaps I am that serious. We are leaving for Europe next week. I would love nothing more than to have you with me."

"I've just got too much on my plate right now. They're still taking about that reunion gig in Palestine. I've got some important calls I need to make."

"Make them from Europe. If anything develops, I will have you flown back."

"There's a couple of bids coming in."

"I will pay double."

"You really are something," her laugh tinkled in a way that stole his soul. "Look, we both know where this is going. I'm just not ready yet. You're the most wonderful man I've been with since Mel. If I go to Europe with you, it's all over. I need time to decide if this is my time. If you can't wait me out, I understand."

"Who would not wait for Debbie Munson?" he sipped his

wine. He sure was something.

"Thank you, Luc. You don't know how much I appreciate that."

If anything killed any chance of her going to Europe at the last minute, it was the call that came from Miami that week. That damned, damned call.

For all intents and purposes, it was the last roundup. Frank Carmona had died of AIDS, just like that. He slipped past everyone in death just as he had in life. He was the anxious little kid who was out the door after enduring the hugs and kisses of everyone at the family reunions. He was the enigmatic teenager who charmed everyone as he worked the room and made sure they had their Frank time before he disappeared. He became the intelligent young man who wasn't quite what one expected Johnny's son and Paco's grandson to be. Everyone was in denial, and learning that Frank was gay and had AIDS was just like hearing he had died. No fucking way.

She called Tina but the poor bitch was stretched out big time. There was the ongoing thing with Zeke, who was undoubtedly trying to direct traffic upon hearing of the tragedy. Tina would have gone ballistic, and upon calling her sister Carmen it would've gotten worse. She now had to wedge all this shit in between her doctor's appointments. Debbie could appreciate what was going on, putting herself in Tina's shoes for the first time. She wasn't going to throw a hissy fit and insist that it was Tina's turn to call back. She would leave a message and tell her they could meet in Florida if they couldn't fly down together.

Suddenly she started thinking it was all catching up to her, and maybe she was coming to terms with her age at long last. Things were forcing her to become more understanding, more sympathetic. In the old days it was David and Debbie telling everybody to man up. Now that Debbie was older and alone, she was able to appreciate how everyone else was getting older. Plus, unlike her, they had people who were depending on them. She was going to have to encourage them to take care of their responsibilities, putting her agenda on the back burner.

The times they were a changin'.

"Debbie?"

"Tina. You actually check your messages these days?"

"More like you're actually leaving messages. I've been so busy, it's ridiculous. What're you up to?"

"I was making plans to go to the funeral. You going?"

"Of course. Zeke already made reservations.

"Well, that's that. I was gonna see if we could've flown together. No problem, I'll see you down there."

"That's great. Geez, this is so terrible."

"Yeah, I know. Poor kid."

"They said something about meeting at the Olive Garden near the airport. That'll make it easier on everyone to get a room and get situated. It's on West Flagler Street. I'll send you a text with the directions."

"When are you gonna be there, tomorrow night?"

"You betcha. I can't wait to see you again."

"Yeah, it'll be good. I'll see you then."

Debbie called Jerry late Friday afternoon and asked him if he wanted to take the ride with her to the airport. She figured it would be the best way to let him down. She didn't see any reason why they couldn't stay friends. It wouldn't even be a bad idea for them to get together and jam once in a while. He was a good kid, and it wasn't right for her to penalize him for her getting drunk and giving him some pussy. Besides, he had held true to his word and not mentioned it once. No calls, no remarks, nothing. He had been a perfect gentleman and deserved her thanks.

Damn, she really was changing.

He looked like he was changing too. He had on a classy blue silk shirt and black slacks along with his biker boots, their Western cut matching up well with his semi-formal look. She was wearing her black business skirt suit with her white silk blouse. It killed her to think they looked like an aunt taking her nephew to dinner.

"Well, don't you look cool," she greeted him out in front of her apartment building. He arrived in a cab and put her travel bag in the trunk.

"You look Debbie-licious," he grinned.

"Yeah, right," she chuckled as he held the cab door open for her.

"I'm real sorry to hear about your friends," he said as the

259

cabbie headed for the highway en route to the airport. "That was Johnny Carmona and Isabel Cabales' son, huh?"

"Yeah. Life sucks, and then you die."

"Speaking of which, you think you'll be able to come down and jam sometime?"

She couldn't help but be impressed. Any other guy who had all that weight behind him would've been leveraging the shit out of her by now. He was so cool, so damn mature. If he was trying to show her something, he sure as hell did.

"Yeah, well, let's see. Maybe we can keep it to once or twice a month for now. I don't want to make any commitments. I told you about the conflict thing, getting my face too recognizable. And I'm not about to do the Tina thing and wear a mask onstage."

"She doesn't still do that, does she?"

"No," she looked at him.

"Just asking. Hey, sounds cool to me. Whatever's good for you. The guys love playing with you."

"Yeah? How about you?"

"I don't think you even need to ask," he tapped his knuckles against her shoulder.

"I gotta admit, you guys are pretty damn hot. Those shows reminded me of the old days with David, back when we first got started. You guys have a lot of energy, you can go places. Just don't take your eyes off the ball and keep that team spirit. If you ever start moving up, I can damn sure guarantee you're gonna need it."

"I read the book and the novel. They're like my User's Manual. I know where you're coming from."

They finally reached the airport, and he pulled her bag out of the trunk before she headed inside. She turned to face him, a big smile on her face.

"Hey, thanks for giving me a ride. And thanks for everything. The band and all."

"I'm expecting there'll be more ahead," he got serious.

"Yeah," she smiled into his eyes. "We'll see."

As an afterthought, she cradled his face in her hands and kissed him softly on the lips before disappearing into the airport.

Chapter Thirty

Isabel took a sip of her Chianti as she stared vacantly out the window at Olive Garden that evening. She kept on fighting a wave of hysteria that threatened to consume her all evening long. If the horrors of menopause were just down the road, this was certain to become a suitable training ground.

Stu Carlucci had come and gone, sitting with Johnny and Isabel until the parlor closed, then buying them a drink at the reception at Olive Garden before departing. His dirty blond hair was streaked with white, deep frown lines and furrows on his brow compromising his boyish features. He was still as effervescent as ever, but it seemed as if he was tired and the effort of being Stu was gaining on him.

Stu had watched his own world collapse before his eyes just forty eight hours earlier. His manager, Danny Spivey, had visited him at the loft on John Street and was the bearer of grievous news.

"Stu," Danny dropped into a sofa chair across from him in the darkened living room. "Bad news. *Ether* just dropped to 120 on the charts. We're not gonna make it."

"So they won't renew my contract," Stu brought his fingertips together before him as he leaned forward on his recliner. "It's over."

"NFW," Danny growled. "No fuckin' way. You're the greatest jazz rock performer I've ever heard, and I've been in this business for over twenty years. There is no way your music will not be heard."

"Music's like children used to be," Stu managed a grin. "Seen and not heard. It's all videos, hip hop, MTV. I'm a dinosaur, Danny."

"Look, I got Blue Velvet and Supersonic both looking for new artists," Danny was adamant. "It's not like it used to be. With any kind of weight behind us we got the Internet. There's You Tube, My Space, Amazon, EBay, all that shit. We can market our own stuff, I can hire a team of marketers to work the Web to sell our stuff."

"I've had it, I'm hanging up my gloves. I can't fight anymore. I'm not a kid, I'm forty-five. I can't deal with the bullshit. I can get studio work. I can rest on my laurels. What I can't do is handle any more pressure."

"*I* handle the pressure. You just do what you were born to do, create great music."

"When you cut a record with a small label, you have to tour to promote the record. I can't do that anymore. I took the deal with Arista because they promised no touring. I can't go back to the minor leagues, Danny, I'm done."

"Don't you want to hear the applause one more time? It's more than just making music, you were born to perform. We can make it a pleasant ride. None of that wild road shit. We'll book the best hotels, have the best food, I'll have an event director find cultural things to do at each stop. We'll go out in style."

"The last time I went out," Stu gazed over the fist under his lip, "somebody grabbed me in a hallway in a heavily guarded hotel at gunpoint. They took me out to the desert and told me that they were trading me for drugs, and if they didn't get what they wanted I would die. My friends came out to save me, and one of them had his lungs blown out right in my face. I still have dreams about that night. I don't want anything to bring that back to me."

Danny rose and walked over to Stu, putting his arm around his protégé as Stu wept quietly.

"Okay, Stu, it's over. It's been good. It's been real good."

Isabel might have agreed with that statement. Though she was nearly crippled by her loss, there was something about funerals that renewed the spirits of the survivors, made them appreciate what they had left amongst each other. Lucy was there with her two kids, helping Isabel play hostess, having flown down from North Carolina to be with her at this time of need. She was beside herself with regret for Duke not having been there, but the pullout from Iraq was imminent and Duke could not be spared from the effort. Isabel's heart was further torn by the memories of how close she and Lucy had, been, and how life had allowed them to drift apart via time and distance.

"Hey, girl, who pushed you into the Fountain of Youth?"

Debbie Munson whirled as she recognized the voice of

Isabel behind her just as she entered the restaurant. Debbie whipped off her sunglasses and grabbed Isabel in a tight squeeze.

"Oh, Issy, how great to see you!" Debbie squealed. The girls released each other and they looked joyously into each others' faces. Outside of a couple of barely perceptible wrinkles near her eyes and mouth and a few pounds, Debbie appeared not to have changed one bit.

"Let me buy you a drink," Issy grabbed her arm.

"You can buy the next round," Debbie smiled.

The women walked arm-in-arm to the bar where they ordered margaritas. They exchanged pleasantries about daily life in their respective areas, Debbie trying hard to remember what she could about long-past trips to Florida while filling Isabel in on the myriad differences in NYC then and now. She couldn't bring herself to tell Issy about her new band, it might have opened up a wound. She downplayed her business successes, again not wanting to make herself appear to be the one who fell into clover at a time like this.

Yet, as Issy excused herself at length and melted back into the group, she felt more alone and isolated than ever in her life. At least they had each other, they had their friends and family, their homes, their lives. She wasn't sure what she had, not anymore.

At once she thought of Duke, and realized that this was the best time to call. Every time she had tried to get patched through recently she was told the same thing, and her PI business was busiest after dark. She punched the speed dial on her cell phone and waited through the now-familiar beeps and pauses before she reached the base in Baghdad.

"How may I help you?" the authoritative voice on the other end inquired.

"I'm trying to reach Major Marduqueo Gallegos," she said crisply. "I've called a couple of times earlier this week. I'm calling from the USA."

"May I ask who's calling?"

"Tell him it's an old friend."

Major Gallegos waved his aide away impatiently as he took the call in his plush hotel suite overlooking the streets of downtown Baghdad.

"Debbie Munson," he couldn't believe his ears. "How in hell are you, girl?"

"Great, Dukie," she gushed. "What's up with you?"

He closed his eyes and tried to imagine what she looked like now. The thirty-something Debbie in Palestine was a ripened fruit, beautiful beyond expectation, the perfection of that incredibly gorgeous teenager back in Brooklyn. A fifty-something Debbie would have broken something deep inside him. A line, a wrinkle, a gray hair would have shattered whatever illusions he still treasured at this stage of his life. Iraq had destroyed every good and noble thing he could ever remember. This would be the straw that would break his back.

"Well, the President's moving us over to Kabul," Duke peered out sightlessly at the bustling streets below. "Hopefully the weather'll be better."

"Have you heard anything about the USO concert? There's stuff all over the Internet about the Iraqis sponsoring a reunion show in honor of the withdrawal."

His aide reappeared and laid a folder on his desk before departing. He knew what it was. Four more kids this morning. Another car bombing. A swift kick in the rear on the way out. It made his stomach churn. He hated this fucking place more than he ever hated anything in his life.

"Yeah, that old rumor mill," Duke managed a smile.

"Well, what's it looking like? Have you heard anything from Stu or Johnny? I've been leaving messages with Tina, she'll probably be calling anytime now."

"I don't know, Debbie," he looked out at the truckloads of soldiers being driven out for their morning patrols. Al-Qaida was getting braver, they knew that response time was decreasing and that public clamor might speed up the process. He winced at the thought of any more of his kids getting hit. "They don't like us very much out here anymore."

His kids.

"Well, what's up with USO? I thought they operate for the troops, not the pols. I'd come out, and I'm sure the others would. Have you decided if you'd play?"

Duke remembered the other day at the PX when a PFC came up while he was waiting on his daily bottle of Jack Daniels.

"Major Gallegos, Sir," the man saluted. "It's an honor, sir."

"At ease, Soldier. Do I know you from somewhere?"

"No Sir. It is my privilege to report that I recognize the Major from here on base, and that I have seen his accomplishments as a musician in civilian life, sir."

"This isn't civilian life, Soldier, and I don't give a damn what you know about civilian life. My ass and the ass of your fellow soldiers depend on what you know about killing. Is that clear?"

"Yes Sir!" the young man boomed. "The private respectfully asks whether the Major will participate in the Crusader reunion, Sir!"

"Son, I need to know the source of that information. If I find out about any discrepancies in what you tell me, you will stand tall before the Man."

"I got the information from the Internet, Sir!"

"People with shit for brains get information from the Internet. Do you have shit for brains?"

"No Sir!"

"Do you believe our country can be properly defended by people with shit for brains?"

"No Sir!"

"On which website did you come across this falsified information?"

"Www.punkamania.com, Sir!"

"Are you calling me a punk?"

"No Sir!"

"Did this website make you assume that I was playing in a punk band?"

"Yes Sir!"

"When you assume, you make an ass of you and me. Did you ever hear that saying before?"

"Yes Sir!"

"Do you think I'm an ass, Soldier?"

"No Sir!"

"Well, then, you will not rely on information you have not confirmed to be true!"

"Yes Sir!"

"Get out of my sight!"

"Yes Sir!"

"Why are you still standing here!"

"The private respectfully asks whether the Major will participate in the Crusader reunion, Sir!"

"I don't know, Debbie," Duke walked over to the window, watching the roads fill with clouds of dust as the children ran along the sidewalk cheering and yelling. "It's real crazy here these days."

"Do you want to play?" she asked plaintively.

"Yeah," he managed. "I want to play."

"Gee, that's great," she could hear the hesitancy in his voice. "I'm really looking forward to this. I can't wait to see you again, everybody else, too. It'll be like old times."

"Yeah, sure. Hey, uh, Deb…"

"I know, I know, I gotta go too. Give my best to Lucy and the kids. Talk at you soon. Love you, Dukie."

"Love you, Deb."

He watched sightlessly as the trucks full of young people with dreams of glory continued along the path to reality.

Table of Contents